RENAISSANCE

By

Larry Mason

International Standard Book Number 13: 978-0-9727707-9-8
International Standard Book Number 10: 0-9727707-9-8

Library of Congress Control Number: 2007930993

BluewaterPress LLC
2220 CR 210 W Ste 108 #132
Jacksonville, FL 32559
http://bluewaterpress.com

This book may be purchased online at http://bluewaterpress.com

Book I

Chapter I

In my youth, I saw the world wake up from a thousand-year-old sleep, then in my years of ripe manhood, I saw it, once again, crawl back into bed; but in my wishful heart of melancholy old age I believe that it is only napping, and soon, once again, the world will rise up into the light of reason, beauty, and possibility. I am old and tired. I pay the price for the gift of so many years of life; my senses fail me, I can barely move about for the aching in my joints, and I have seen the passing of all who I have known and loved. The last of my old friends, the enigmatic genius, Michelangelo Di Lodovico Buonarroti Simoni died just this past year. It feels rude of me to have lived for so long, while all the others have left; it's like we were all together at some celebration and they have all left, but I didn't know when to leave. So I am still here. But alas, I feel that my time is nearing an end, so I thought I would, in one last backward glance, put down for history this account of my life; the life of Lorenzo Demarco from Florence, sometime painter, monastic student, soldier, officer, statesman, interpreter, writer, son, brother, uncle, father, lover, husband, and friend.

My world began in late May in the year of our Lord 1482, in the town of Florence, though it was several years until I would become aware of this. My papa, Sabastiano Demarco, named me after Lorenzo de' Medici, known affectionately as Lorenzo the Magnificent. My father had three true passions – aside from being passionately in love with my mother, Katarina – one was his belief in the one true faith, the second was his love for art, and the last was his devotion to Lorenzo de' Medici. Papa believed in the strong, benevolent hand of a single, all-powerful ruler, the kind of leader that Machiavelli would later define in detail in his masterpiece, "The Prince." He would always say, "We must respect, and obey our earthly authorities, for they would not be our earthly authorities if God had not ordained them to be." I wonder if after all that has happened, in the end, before he died, if he still believed this?

I have my own opinions of the magnificence of Lorenzo de' Medici, but I will invoke writer's privilege and keep them to myself. He was firm and sometimes generous. He laughed easily and participated in the traditional festivals, as well as organized many of his own; some would say he organized too many frivolous celebrations that were excessive and wasteful. Most of all, he helped to bring beauty to Florence, or I should say, more beauty to Florence; my city was always graced with great loveliness. Nestled in a valley of farms and grazing lands, among gentle rolling hills along the Arno River, the majestic walls of Florence surround the houses and magnificent buildings as they rise up to the heavens. Everywhere you look it can be seen, the great skill of her artisans and craftsmen in the inlaid work of her architecture, and the extraordinary skill of her artists in the numerous sculptures, gardens and fountains. Inside the best homes and public buildings, beautiful tapestries, furniture and paintings can be seen and admired – many have come from abroad, but so much of the great pieces of art were created within her great walls. It is these great pieces of art where some credit must go to the magnificent Lorenzo; he paid the highest for the best artists in the area and brought them to his court in Florence. I don't know if he was truly a patron of the arts, or even understood art at all, but he certainly enjoyed being around artistic people. It was he who took the young Michelangelo under his roof and helped him become a brilliant artist – mainly by exposing him to the wealthy people who would become his patrons. I've often wondered if I had been a little older, or Lorenzo the Magnificent had lived a little longer, then maybe I could have been a part of his court, and perhaps my skills as an artist would have advanced to the level of some of my contemporaries. I too could have been a great artist instead of a moderately skilled portrait painter. It would also have helped if the Lord had given me a little more talent.

My mother never wanted me to be an artist – in a real sense she got her wish. Mama wanted me to be a priest. From my earliest years I was under the tutelage of Fra Domenico Salviati, a Dominican priest. It was under his patient teaching that I discovered my true gift was for language; he taught me Greek and Latin in which I excelled. Fra Domenico would assign me a passage in the Bible and then have me translate it into Italian, and then he would have me do it again and again. "Repetition is the key to recognition," he would say. I can still hear his voice, "Good Lorenzo, now, again please, could we do it again please." Mama taught me her native language of German, which I also picked up quite rapidly. Mama said that this gift of language was a sign from God that I was to do his work saving souls. In my early world, the priest was still the only way to salvation; he was the emissary of God through which the road to heaven traveled, and the communicator of the word as interpreted by the church. It would be almost thirty years before this belief would be challenged. Actually, the one true faith was being challenged in Florence during my early years. Perhaps that explains the brief popularity of the reactionary, Savonarola.

One of my earliest memories is of hearing the fiery voice of Savonarola. Michelangelo once said that, even in his later years, he could still hear the voice of Savonarola in his head; I still hear it too. He would begin softly, so everyone would have to be quiet and still to hear his words. Even in a crowd of thousands and from many yards away, his deep resonating voice could be heard as it would slowly build, stronger, becoming louder and louder, then it would explode, like thunder and his words would echo in my head; even now they echo in my head.

"The people are oppressed by taxes, and when they come to pay unbearable sums, the rich cry, 'Give me the rest!' When widows come weeping, they are told, 'Go to sleep.' When the poor complain, they are told, 'Pay, pay.' And what is it they need with our last small piece of silver? Vanities! Vanities!"

Though it was a hot day, I felt a chill, and instinctively, I buried my small frame into Fra Domenico's thick, black robe.

Fra Domenico gently patted me on my head and quietly said, "All right, Lorenzo, I think we have heard enough for today. Let's get you home."

We pushed our way through the dense crowd – Fra Domenico pushed while I clung tightly to his robe – and came out onto the winding road, paved in cobblestones, that led back into the Santo Spirito Quarter of the city. Florence is divided into four quarters: the Santo Spirito, on the left bank of the Arno River, and Santa Croce, San Giovanni, and Santa Maria Novella all on the right bank. We were nearly to my papa's shop, just inside the Porta a San Pier Gatolini – the main gate entering the city on the south side of Florence – before the ringing of Savonarola's voice had died down in my head.

Being a gunmaker, and one that specialized in making cannon, meant that Papa's shop was quite different than the average trade shop in the city. From outside, the shop looked much like most of the other shops on the street – via dei Serragli – except it was larger than most; gunmaking was very profitable. Papa seldom used the front door, which led to his showroom; he had little need for a showroom because most of his business was done outside of his shop. Most of his work was performed in the field or in nearby towns, as the need for good cannon arose. Papa would bring with him his preferred tools and the patron would usually supply the rest. The bulk of the shop was a warehouse used to store scrap metal to be melted down for small arms and armor, and to store wood for the stocks and the shafts of pikes, and various other weapons. There was also a work area with plenty of tools, a forge, cooling vats and various other large pieces of equipment. The warehouse had no direct access to the outside – you had to go through the showroom in front or though the living area in back. The living area consisted of three rooms. There was a large room that served as a kitchen, living and dining area; the room opened up on a back street that ran parallel to the main road out front. The only furniture in the large room was a small wooden dinner table with two benches – one on either side – and a single x-chair that always sat in the corner except when company was over. Mama and Papa had one of the other rooms and I had the other to myself. I sometimes wonder what it would have been like to share that little room with brothers or sisters. As it was, having so much privacy spoiled me and made me less suited for the often-tight shared quarters I would experience in my travels. We had a cellar; the door was under the dining table. Down there we stored our most treasured possessions, food, and wine.

In his shop, Papa didn't make the fancy suits of armor and expensive guns; he made the simple, but reliable, weapons and armor for the common foot soldier. It was these common soldiers and militiamen that most frequented his shop. I believe Papa would have preferred to have just made these simple weapons and dealt with the common folk; this would have meant he could spend more time at home with Mama and not have to take such long trips, lasting for months or even a year, depending upon the campaign. But it was the army's need for cannon that paid the bills. Papa did not and would not make a decent profit from making small arms; he never charged a man more than he could afford and often worked for cost. Papa would say, "It's a sin to send a man into a battle ill equipped and defenseless." When forging cannon on a major campaign, he would often see the numerous pikemen and regulars go into a fight with antiquated arms and armor; sometime with no armor at all. If you survived the first assault you could possibly scavenge equipment from the dead. It was not uncommon for Papa to use his scrap metal or pieces of used armor and weapons to equip one or more of these unfortunate men, at the expense of his profits.

As we made our way through the moderately populated, morning crowd, I saw Papa coming toward us; he saw us first. There was a hard look in his big brown eyes. He shook his head and asked, "Are you sure, Fra Domenico, that the boy should be listening to that mad monk?" I let go of Fra Domenico and ran into Papa's open arms; he lifted me up and kissed me on both cheeks; his eyes softened and he smiled at me. Then he put me down, patted the back of my head and said, "Oh, Lorenzo, you are getting to be much too heavy for me." He had lifted me up and put me down with such ease, I knew he was just teasing. Papa was not a large man, but he had powerful arms and a broad upper body from his work with metals.

"We agreed that Lorenzo's teaching would be my responsibility," Fra Domenico said sternly. "I do not want to be second guessed."

Papa smiled, and said, "But surely, Fra Domenico, don't you think that a boy so young should experience more of the joys of life before he has to take on its' burdens. He should be allowed at least an hour or two a day to do as he pleases. After all, his time will come soon enough when he will have to work..." Papa was about to say work for a living, but caught himself before the words came out. Papa was not convinced that I should or would go into the monastery. He did not regard the priesthood as proper work for a man, and Fra Domenico knew this. So if Papa made a reference to me working some day, then his message was clear; I might not be a priest.

Fra Domenico understood Papa's incomplete thought. He frowned, shook his round head and said, "It is never too early to learn that the world is an evil place filled with sinners, and that it is only from the church that we find salvation through the word of God." He made the sign of the cross in the air and whispered a small prayer and continued, "These are even more essential lessons for a priest, and so they must be ingrained in his very soul. But if you have changed your mind about Lorenzo's education, I'm certain that I can find better uses for my time. And I trust that you will explain to Katarina ..."

"You are right, you are right," Papa interrupted. Let us not argue about it, Fra Domenico," he added with a smile. "Now, why don't we go inside and find out what Katarina has fixed for us. All of Savonarola's talk of evil and eternal damnation is bound to build up your appetite. And, if we are to be condemned, should we not be allowed, as was our Lord, to have our last supper?"

Fra Domenico tried to remain grim, but soon a smile crossed his face, then his round belly shook with a chuckle. He said, "Sabastiano Demarco, you are a good man, but sometimes I think your humor is inspired by the devil."

We sat at our usual places around the small wooden table – me on one side and Mama and Papa on the other. Fra Domenico sat in the x-chair; the little chair creaked under his massive frame. Mama served cinestrata soup with bread and wine; it was delicious, as usual. Mama always made her cinestrata with extra cinnamon and nutmeg, just the way I like it.

Mama was a beautiful woman. I know that every young man thinks that his mama is beautiful, but even objective eyes would agree – Mama was special. She was tall, for a woman – slightly taller than Papa – but not too tall. She had straight shoulders, long legs, and was well proportioned – round where a woman should be. She carried herself with elegance, like a woman of much higher rank than the wife of a simple artisan. She had classic German features: sandy, blonde hair; pale, almost-white skin; small, gray-blue eyes; a tiny sharp nose, slightly turned up; and thin pink lips. There was always a pleasant expression on her face and a stoic smile – a slight grin that squinted her eyes slightly, but exposed no teeth. Her look fit her demeanor – quiet, thoughtful, pious, and at peace. At least that was the way she always seemed to me. As I said, a child's view of his mother is not always the same view as the world's. She rarely raised her voice, but always made her opinion known – usually with few words – even when she disagreed with Papa. Her premature passing left her forever young and beautiful; the price you pay for so few years of life.

I painted her picture, but my limited skills did not capture her true essence. If only she had still been around when Raphael was in Florence. Though I did not know him that well, I'm sure he would have painted her for me, or at least helped me fill in what was missing; he found it hard to say no to anyone. I knew Michelangelo well enough to ask him, but I'm certain he would have turned me down; he found it easy to say no to everyone. But this is all irrelevant because while Michelangelo was in Florence when Mama was still alive, I didn't meet the man until after Mama's passing.

"Sabastiano Demarco, I will not have you speak so about a man of God," Mama said quietly, but firmly. "Savonarola has a good heart. He speaks for those who cannot, the poor, as well as all the hard working people of Florence. De' Medici is too busy decorating his court and entertaining the rich to care for the rest of us, which is most of us. We need a voice to say what we do not dare for fear of his harsh reprisal."

"Here, here," echoed Fra Domenico.

"Look Lorenzo, see how they gang up on me in my own house," Papa said to me with false anger. I smiled at Papa, but knew I was not to speak.

"Is that it, my friend?" asked Fra Domenico. "You disapprove of Savonarola because he openly attacks the Medici?"

Papa furled his brow and shook his head. He said, "My faith in Lorenzo de' Medici is independent of my contempt for Savonarola." Papa took a sip of his wine then continued, "Savonarola would have us fall back into ignorance and give up the light of beauty and reason that shines on Florence. He would have us go back into the darkness of the 13th century. The good old days..."

"No, Sabastiano," interrupted Fra Domenico, "he just wants to bring back God and the republic to Florence..."

"Bring back God?!" Papa interrupted. "If God was ever in Florence he is surely here now. Where do you think that the light is coming from? And we have a republic, but a republic needs a single voice to get things done, or else all the guilds and the Signory would be too busy arguing among themselves, in their own self-interest, to accomplish anything. Now if Savonarola had his way, he would be that single voice himself." Papa paused when he caught a glance from Mama; it was subtle, but the look meant that Papa should change the subject. Mama didn't like arguing, particularly at the dinner table.

Before Fra Domenico could respond, Mama offered him some more wine and gave him some more bread; he accepted both eagerly. Fra Domenico's veracious appetite gave Papa time to steer the course of the conversation to common ground. Just as Fra Domenico opened his mouth to speak, Papa started in on the Turks. It was Papa's complete devotion to the one true faith that made him hate the Turks. They were the enemy, because by their existence they cast a shadow of a doubt over our own beliefs; there can't be two distinctly different answers to the same question. At least that's the way I saw it. Though we knew little about Islam, we knew that it was not our faith; therefore, it must be wrong. They did not accept any of our truths such as the existence of the saints or the divinity of Christ. Without these basic truths how could they possibly expect to get into heaven? What else could they possibly believe in? That's what I used to wonder. Papa was convinced that the Turks were put here just to test our faith; that meant that there were an awful lot of souls being sacrificed by following a false God, just to get us to believe what we already were devoted to. But then I was just a young boy; what did I know. I believed everything that Papa said.

"The infidel is creeping ever closer in the East," Papa began. "Only the Hungarians stand in the way of them and us."

"God bless them," said Fra Domenico, as he made the sign of the cross in the air and whispered a small prayer.

"Amen," said Papa. "I hear that the Venetians are planning another campaign against them soon, to gain back some of what has been lost."

Still in a combative mood, Fra Domenico frowned; he shook his head in contempt. He said, "Those Venetians, Sabastiano," accenting Venetians, "they do not fight for God. Sure, they will fight, but only for their own self-interest, to gain more territory for Venice. Remember that it was Venice who refused to join the Holy Alliance during the great siege at Otranto, and if Otranto had fallen, all of Naples would have been threatened, and then perhaps Rome itself would have been taken. Who knows what would have become of us if that had happened."

Papa nodded in agreement, smiled slightly and said, "You're right, Father. They would not fight with us then, but they fight now. Shall we refuse to fight with them just because they did not join us then? Aren't the infidels still our true enemy? And, is not the enemy of my enemy my friend? I tell you, if I were a single man, without responsibility, I would sail with the Venetian fleet. And I tell you something else, if we don't stop all of our petty bickering, they will take us down one by one. Just the way they have taken down so many others. If Hungary falls, then Venice, it will be our turn soon, and who will stand with us, if we do not stand with them now? We can't fight them alone and win. So now, we can't expect them to fight alone and win. If we could just stop fighting amongst ourselves, we could crush the infidel. We are so divided now, but still we manage to hold them back. Imagine what we could do if we were united and fought, side-by-side, as one."

Again, Fra Domenico made the sign of the cross in the air and whispered a small prayer, and said, "Amen. The French and the Spanish have to stop fighting over control of our lands, and join with us under God, together with the Hungarians we could easily drive the Turks back into the hellish womb from which they have spawned."

"And what of the Empire?" Papa interjected. Their lack of leadership has made them useless in our cause, except as mercenaries. But Frederick is old and Maximillian will surely succeed him soon. The Germans are the best soldiers in the world. By themselves, a united German army could push the infidel off the continent, and maybe even recapture Constantinople."

As Papa and Fra Domenico went on, happily unified in their hatred for the Turks, Mama was reminding me of my table manners.

"Sit back, Lorenzo," she said quietly. "Don't crouch over your food, and eat slowly."

Mama had adapted the Florentine propensity for good table manners, and passed this trait on to me. To my disgust, I would find in my travels that we might have been the only ones in the world who did not graze like common field animals. Mama's own people, the Germans, were the worst; for a long time, I could hardly eat in their company without feeling revolted.

Papa and Fra Domenico continued to eat and talk long after I was through. Mama reminded me not to clean my teeth with my napkin; I put my napkin on my plate. I no longer listened to what was being said. Instead, I found myself watching Fra Domenico; his massive frame dwarfed the little x-chair. I watched and wondered how long it could continue to hold his weight. He must have weighted well over two hundred pounds, and a good portion of that bulk was in his massive balding head. The bags under his large, brown eyes, his puffy cheeks and jowls, his fat lips, and even his thick ear lobes all hung down – overcome by their weight. Only his broad nose, standing straight out, defied the trend to slide downward. The little x-chair creaked, but held its own.

Fra Domenico was my best friend in my youth. I spent so much time with him buried in my studies; I had no friends my own age. I loved this man who was my teacher, and I owe him so much. He was a stern teacher, as good teachers must be, but he had a kind heart and a gentle soul. My ability to learn so quickly impressed him, but he knew that my attention and passion was not always directed toward the faith and that concerned him. "Someday you will have to choose," he would say, "between the ways of God and the ways of men." I wanted both, I found both, but in the end, I don't understand either; the Lord moves in mysterious ways and men move in ways totally incomprehensible.

I was helping Mama clear the table when the, now post-meal, conversation turned to the topic of my studies.

"Lorenzo is exceptional in his abilities," said Fra Domenico. "There's no question that he has great potential, and will undoubtedly go far. I dare say that he will someday, and someday soon, surpass my meager abilities to teach him. The only thing that will keep Lorenzo out of the monastery is contaminated thought. Sometimes Lorenzo suffers from a lack of concentration. Lorenzo is all too often distracted by corrupt humanistic ideas, which some seem to believe are somehow enlightening and thought provoking, and these are good things. I do not see it that way. How can any new thoughts coming from the whims of common men possibly compare to the time tested truth contained in the mind of God? How can any God-loving man condone this pestilence of the mind, knowing how easily it is spread, particularly, to the young? For the young do not have the resources of time tested faith to fight simple-minded rhetoric. Should we not be protecting our children from these very ideas and thoughts, instead of turning... "

Papa knew it was he who was being criticized – possibly attacked – and defended himself. "I understand, Fra Domenico," Papa interrupted. "But Lorenzo is just a boy, and he should be allowed some time to pursue childish things. When he is a man, he will ..."

It was Fra Domenico's turn to interrupt. "Ah, but these are not childish things, as you call them," he said sternly. "Lorenzo is being corrupted by the times, this place, this town, and from this house. This art thing, for example, is not a common childish pursuit, and it promotes secular ideas. I have often found him daydreaming and doodling in the margins of his studies."

"What is wrong with that?" Papa asked, with a smile.

"Ah ha, then you are encouraging this art thing," snapped Fra Domenico. "It is as I suspected."

Papa ignored his comments and repeated his question, "What's wrong with a little drawing?"

"It's a waste of good ink and paper," barked Fra Domenico.

"But these doodles, they are good aren't they?" Papa asked, still smiling.

"That's hardly the point," Fra Domenico shrugged.

"Sure it is," Papa said sardonically. "If these doodles are good then you can hardly call it a waste of good ink and paper. Perhaps the boy has talent."

Mama joined in on the side of Fra Domenico. Mama and Papa often argued over my interest in drawing and painting. It was one of the few things that they ever really disagreed about, and to be the cause of that – although mild – conflict, still pains me.

"It's disrespectful to the Father," Mama said, "and you should not be encouraging it, Sabastiano. Fra Domenico gives so much of his time, and Lorenzo should not be allowed to waste that time on such nonsense."

Papa sighed deeply and said, "God created so much beauty in this world, and art is just man's attempt to capture some of that beauty, out of love and admiration of God's work. And that is not nonsense. But..." He paused to make sure that his next words were heard. He said, "I do agree that Lorenzo should not be wasting the good Father's time. All teachers have is time and knowledge, and neither should be wasted on inattentive or ungrateful students." Papa turned to me, and in his best stern voice he said, "Lorenzo, you know you should not be wasting the good Father's time. You know he has given so much of himself, just to help prepare you for the calling of the Lord. It is not right for you to be doodling during your lessons. Save your drawing for your own time. You understand?"

I nodded my head that I did, and was about to say so, when Mama spoke up. "And you had better keep on him about it this time, Sabastiano. You know how you let Lorenzo get away with so much. I don't know why you don't just forbid him from drawing altogether. It's just a waste of time. What does a priest need with paintings and sketches? But if he must draw, do it on his own time, not on the good Father's. And you had better punish Lorenzo if he disobeys you." Then Mama turned to me, gave me that angelic stoic smile and said, "I'm sorry, Lorenzo, but it is for your own good. Some day you will understand."

Mama was right about Papa and discipline; he wasn't very good at it. He was too kind hearted and gentle a man – an odd combination for a gunmaker – to punish me. Though I must say, I didn't really need much external discipline; with the exception of things that pertained to my art, I always did what I was told. In defense of this exception, I could not help my passion of drawing and painting. Sometimes I just found myself sketching without even thinking about it. Whenever I had a pen in my hand, it just seemed to come out of me. Sometimes it was in the form of illustration of text, and other times it was an unconscious attempt to capture something I saw around me. I never thought of it as a distraction, and believed that my sketches actually helped me retain what I was learning. Mama was also right about me, someday, understanding her objections to my art. I know now that if I had focused on my studies, and not had the distraction of my drawing, I would have become a priest; thank God for the distraction.

Mama, Papa, and Fra Domenico continued the familiar discussion about my studies, my future, and my enthusiasm for art; nothing was resolved and never would be. I know now that Mama and Fra Domenico only wanted what, they thought, was best for me, but I have always been grateful for my papa's steadfast, stubborn resistance to their demands. I didn't mind my studies; as I have said, I actually enjoyed learning. At the time, I thought I really wanted to be a priest – what does a boy know about what he will want when he is older – but I loved art and always have, all of my life. Sometimes a boy does know what he will want when he is older.

Everyday, after the morning meal, I spent hours studying, on my own, in my room. My most frequent, and favorite activity – because I was so good at it – was translating the Bible from the Latin, to Greek, Italian and German. German was the one I had the most trouble with because I had no other written sources to accumulate diction, so I had to constantly ask Mama for the words. But as my German vocabulary grew, it too became an easy translation. If I had kept my notes, I wonder how my work would have compared to Luther's translation.

On a piece of paper I would write, three columns across, first the Greek, then the Italian and finally the German. I found that through the repetition and the thoughtful study of the words – necessary in translation to not just one, but three languages – I came to know that holy book that had ruled the continent for a thousand years. Though I must admit, I did not always understand its' meaning; I still don't. There are so many contradictions, and stories whose meanings had to be explained to me by Fra Domenico or Mama, but if they hadn't told me, I would have never understood them. It seemed to me that the true measure of faith wasn't in God or the Bible, but in those who told you what the book meant; they were the ones telling you what to believe. I guess that's why there would be so many objections to translating the Bible into common language; then the book would be open to anyone's interpretation – anyone who could read. But I am getting ahead of myself.

After several hours of writing and translating, the words began to stagnate in my mind; I found myself reading the same passage over and over. I knew it was time to put the work away until next time. I closed up the ink to keep it from drying out, and then folded up my papers, and put them in the little wooden box that Papa had made for my studies. The Bible stayed out because Mama and I often read together in the evening. I got off my stool and put the box in the small cassone at the foot of my bed, where I kept most of my meager possessions. I left my pen on the writing table in case I had time later to do some drawing.

As I came out of my room, Mama was sweeping the floor when she saw me. She gave me a smile – her eyes squinted – she stopped sweeping and asked in German, "Have you finished your studies for the day?"

I answered, also in her native tongue, for we often spoke in German when we were alone. I said, "Yes, Mama. May I go and watch Papa work for a while?"

"Of course, Lorenzo," Mama said.

I didn't really have to ask; Mama always said yes when I asked to go watch Papa work, but it was part of my upbringing that required me to ask. I started to leave when Mama spoke.

"I've begun to notice that you no longer want to spend any time with your mother," she said with a hint of false hurt in her voice. "I suppose it is because you are growing up, and you no longer need so much. At least not anything that your mother can provide."

I knew she was only teasing, so I played along. I said, "Of course I still need you, Mama. I don't know how to cook, so who would feed me?" Then I laughed.

Mama's smile broadened slightly and she said, "You little weasel. You think you are funny. Well, perhaps you are. But you are not too big to give your mama a kiss. So come here and kiss me before you run off."

Mama bent down and I kissed her; she patted me on the back tenderly, then I was off.

It always seemed odd to me that a peaceful, softhearted man like Papa would be a gunmaker. Papa was not an ambitious man and he did not seek fortune or much of anything. I do not mean this in a bad or disrespectful way – I loved my papa – but he was what most people would call lazy. He only worked because he had to and would have much preferred a life of leisure. Papa did not choose his profession; it was more like it chose him.

Like many young unambitious men, Papa was forced to take a military career; it was join the army or starve. Early in his military experience, he was sent to Wittenberg Germany with a small detachment to purchase guns from a certain well-known gunmaker, Philipp Melchoir. On the first day he was in the craftsmen's gun shop, as Papa told me, while watching Philipp Melchoir work he became totally and completely captivated by what he saw; what he saw was Philipp Melchoir's daughter, Katarina. Now for all the ambition Papa lacked for a trade or a career, he had an abundance of ambition when it came to love. Papa was able to convince my grandpa that he was very interested in learning the gunmaking trade, and because of Melchoir's reputation, grandpa was able to convince the army to let my papa stay with him as an apprentice; the army could hardly refuse the chance to gain an apprentice of Melchoir's as their gunmaker. Papa says that he practiced the art of gunmaking by day and the art of love by night. So that's how my unambitious papa became a gunmaker, and in another sense, how I came to be.

I went into the shop and saw Papa slightly bent over his anvil and pounding a white-hot piece of metal with a hammer; his powerful arms flexed. He squinted his big brown eyes as a small stream of sweat ran down between them and dripped off of the tip of his big, hawk-like nose. He pounded again, and again, sparks flew, until finally, he was satisfied, stopped pounding and examined his work.

I know I wasn't thinking about it at the time – it wouldn't have occurred to me then – but, looking back, I was beginning to look a lot like my papa. I would grow up to look a lot more like him. Neither of us were big men, but we were well-proportioned and very fit. I also had Papa's olive skin and black, curly hair, and mine would also turn gray early in my thirties. I didn't inherit Papa's hawk-like nose or other large facial features; I had my mother's small nose, thin lips and gray-blue eyes.

I watched for what seemed like a long time, and when Papa finally saw me standing there, he put down his tools, wiped the sweat from his face with the back of his hand, and waved for me to come to him. As always, Papa lifted me up, hugged me, kissed me on both cheeks, and reminded me of how big I was getting.

"Oh Lorenzo, you are getting to be so big," Papa said, as he lowered me down.

"I'll be too big for you to pick up soon," I said proudly.

"Never," Papa playfully barked back at me. "The day you get too big for me to lift in my arms, or I become too weak to pick you up, is the day I die."

Papa was true to his word; he never stopped picking me up, hugging me, and kissing me on both cheeks until the day he died.

We talked for a while about nothing important, and then I remembered something he told me. It didn't make much sense to me at the time. I only remember it because it was very important to him and he wanted me to understand.

"This is something very important to me, and I want you to understand," he said. "It might not make much sense to you, but maybe it will later, so I'm going to tell you anyway. Now you know that I am committed to the one true faith and I am a peace loving man, except, maybe, when it comes to the Turks, but being infidels, they don't count. I also support, though not as enthusiastically as your mama, you're studying for the priesthood. And despite his foolish support for that crazy monk, I have the greatest respect and love for Fra Domenico. I might have even become a priest myself if it wasn't for... that is you have to... what I'm trying to say is that you are not allowed... you have to take a vow of celibacy."

"Celibacy?" I questioned.

Papa looked away to hide his face – a little amused and a little embarrassed – then he looked back at me and said, "You'll understand that later too." As Papa predicted, what he was saying wasn't making much sense to me. Papa read the confused expression on my face and said, "I didn't mean to confuse you, Lorenzo. I got a little sidetracked. Now this is the important part. I consider myself a good, God-fearing, pious man who believes in peace and the preservation of life." He paused, then said, "I make guns, cannons that are used to kill people, and the Lord is pretty clear about how he feels about killing, 'Thou shall not kill.'"

When Papa hesitated, I tried to be helpful and said, "But Papa, you never killed anyone, have you?"

Papa smiled and said, "No, no, I haven't actually killed anyone, that's true, but don't you see? I have certainly made it easier for others to kill. And sometimes I think that, that... making it easier may also be a sin."

Papa looked troubled; he obviously had spent much time contemplating this conflict between his faith and his trade in his mind. The reason why it didn't make much sense to me at the time is because I didn't see a conflict; a child's faith in his father and in his God means that whatever his father does must be what God wants.

I said to Papa, "Papa, if God had not wanted you to be a gunmaker, then he would not have made you one. And if God did not make you a gunmaker, then you would not be one, because you would not do anything that God did not want you too."

Papa smiled at my simple faith and circular logic, and I believe that my words might have comforted him, in a small way, but he still felt the need to explain – try and explain – his position to me. Well into my early manhood, this would be a reoccurring theme in our conversations. Part of it might have been for me – he wanted me to see him in a positive way and not condemn him for any apparent contradictions in his behavior – but most of it was his own personal, internal conflict, and guilt over what he was doing and his faith. Papa went on to explain the need for guns in a violent, unsafe world; the good and the pious have the right to protect themselves from the evil and the sinful. When he finished, he invited me, as he often did, to go with him to the Piazza della Signoria on business. He was going to meet with a condottiere – the condottieri were the professional soldiers who roamed the Italian countryside selling their services to the highest bidder. Ironically, they seldom fought major battles; they preferred sieges and bombardments – thus the need for cannons.

"Before you tell Mama you're going with me," Papa said, "you can sneak these into your room." He pulled from his pocket and handed me two new brushes and several small jars of paint. "Slip these into your pants," he said as he squatted down and helped me tuck them in front. "Hold on to these, you don't want them to fall out in front of your mama," he said. Then, with a sheepish grin, he looked over my shoulder to make sure we were still alone. "Follow a few steps behind me," he said. Then he winked at me and added, "I'll distract your mama, while you put these things away."

When I came out of my room, Papa was standing, with his arm around Mama, next to the open door; a warm breeze blew in. Papa was dressed in his best doublet – he only had three – with his belt pouch tied around his waist. Mama motioned for me to come to her. She said, "Come Lorenzo, give your mama a kiss before you go." I obeyed, then, Papa and I were out in the sunshine walking – heals clicking on the flagstones – toward the great square; it was only about a mile and a quarter to the square – the Piazza della Signoria.

We crossed the Arno at the Ponte alla Carraia – one of only four bridges that connected the two sides of the city across the great river. On the bridge, we stopped to watch the fishermen, downriver, throw their nets. One of the men, standing on a scaffold at the edge of the city walls, lost his straw hat to a gust of wind; it fell into the water. He scurried down the ladder and as he reached out for his floating hat, he fell in making a big splash. Papa and I laughed as the other fishermen cursed him for scaring away the fish, then we went on our way.

As we approached the Piazza, I could see the tower of the Palazzo Vecchio – the town hall – and the great dome of the magnificent Cathedral of Florence, also known as the Duomo. Papa told me that the great dome was the first of its kind in all of Italy, perhaps the world. Papa was very proud of this fact and always reminded me of the dome's history whenever we went to the Piazza – he referred to it as a symbol of Florence's greatness.

"See the great dome, Lorenzo," Papa said. "It is a symbol of Florence's greatness. It was the first of its kind and now they copy it all over the continent. It was designed by Filippo Brunelleschi." Then he asked me, as he always did, "Do you know why it is so unique?" Of course I knew, but I just smiled up at him and let him go on. "It's size, that is why it is unique. Nobody ever made a dome that big, that grand. The designer who built the rest of the cathedral couldn't figure out how to bridge the gap – his concept outreached his abilities as an architect. So the Cathedral of Florence sat unfinished for almost twenty years until Brunelleschi came along and finished the job."

Once in the Piazza, we crossed over to the Palazzo Vecchio where Papa, almost immediately spotted the condottieri he came to meet; after a brief introduction they began to talk business. I tried to follow their conversation, but was soon lost, and then I became distracted by something I saw in the square. On the far corner of the Palazzo Vecchio – pointing out toward the Piazza – stood a temporary wooden gallows. Hangings were a regular occurrence in Florence, but the location of the executions often varied depending in what quarter the offense was committed. Most executions, and the most important ones, occurred here in the Piazza. From the gallows hung two men, with their hands bound behind their backs. From their appearance, it was obvious that they had been there for several days; the warm weather had taken its toll on their bodies. Knowing Papa would be busy for a while, I decided to move a little closer to get a better view. I was still a ways away when the wind shifted and a nauseating odor confirmed that they had been up there for a while. I was used to seeing corpses – you never get used to smelling them – but these two intrigued me. Who were these poor fools? What did they do that earned them the dubious honor of an execution in the Piazza della Signoria, right in front of the town hall?

It seemed to me that hanging, as well as with many other forms of public execution, must be a very humiliating way to leave this world. One of the poor soul's breeches had fallen down to his knees exposing his bare backside, now burnt and blistered by the sun. Papa had explained to me the difference in hanging by breaking a man's neck, or by strangulation; breaking the neck was more merciful, and strangulation was meant to make the victim suffer. It was clear that these men had strangled to death: their tongues were extended and black, their faces were bloated, and their eyes were bulging out of their sockets.

Most people passed by with hardly a glance in their direction, but there were several men in black robes standing in front of the gallows, praying. One of the men was Fra Domenico; quietly, I walked over to him. Up close, the smell of rotting flesh was overpowering. I now recognized the other men as followers of Savanarola – young zealots that referred to themselves as, "bands of hope."

When Fra Domenico realized I was there, he stopped praying with the others, made the sign of the cross in the air and whispered a small prayer, and told me to take a good look and remember it well.

"Take a good long look, Lorenzo, and remember it well," said Fra Domenico. He reached out to me and put a hand on my shoulder, and continued, "I know that your papa supports the Medici, and I do not wish to come between a father and his boy, but this is ..."

"You need not worry about coming between me and the boy," Papa interrupted. "Unlike you, and those you so admire, I am not afraid of the free exchange of ideas. I want Lorenzo to learn to be his own man."

Fra Domenico frowned – his thick lips curved downward at the ends. He said, "Sabastiano, don't you stand there and play the superior. I sat at your table this very morning and listened to you praise the Medici, and put down the great and pious voice of Girolamo Savonarola. Do not pretend not to take sides."

"I'm not pretending not to take sides," Papa said confidently. "I have a side. I just mean that, while I will tell the boy what I believe to be correct, I am willing to let him hear other views, no matter how wrong or foolish I believe them to be. Ultimately I am willing to let Lorenzo make up his own mind." Then Papa smiled and said, "Now come on, Father, let's not start up again. Why don't you tell us why you are here lending your valuable time to these two unfortunates? And why is the band of fools here..."

"They are here to pray for their souls, as am I," Fra Domenico interrupted with contempt in his voice. He made the sign of the cross in the air and whispered a small prayer, and then continued, "They have vowed to stay here and pray until the bodies come down. I, as have many of my brothers, come down regularly to offer our support and prayer."

"Well that's very good and thoughtful of you," Papa said, trying hard to sound sincere. "But I understand that these boys may be up here for a while. They are to be made an example of."

Fra Domenico shook his head and said, "We have seen far too many rotting corpses under the name of, example for the people. When the last of us is up there, whom will the example be for?"

Papa laughed and said, "Your rhetoric is getting sharp, and quite clever. Savonarola is rubbing off on you. But like him your passions are misplaced, or at least exaggerated. We live in violent times, Father, but justice and order still prevail." Papa gave a gesture with his hand toward the hanging men and continued, "Thieves and vandals do not fare well in Florence and can expect a short life. I see this as a good thing. It tells other would-be offenders that they should choose another profession, or pick another town to apply their trade."

"Sabastiano Demarco, I am shocked," barked Fra Domenico. "How can you put these two fine souls in the same category as common thieves?"

"Where else should I put them," answered Papa. "They stole property, defaced and attempted to destroy an artistic masterpiece."

"Where have you been getting your information?" questioned Fra Domenico. Without waiting for an answer, he continued, "You have been misinformed, my friend. All these boys did was to dump a little excrement in protest of tyranny on the statue of Judith and Holofernes and on the fountain next to it ..."

"I heard that they also stole a silver chalice," Papa interrupted. "Which they used to drink the rest of the wine that they had been consuming heavily."

"Yes, yes," said Fra Domenico. "A stupid little chalice. It was lying outside by the fountain, so they picked it up and took it with them, just to use to drink the rest of their wine. They had been using a leather pouch to drink from, and then they stumbled, by chance, upon a chalice, so they decided to borrow it – a civilized gesture, to drink from a cup. This is hardly a crime worthy of forfeiting one's life." Fra Domenico was becoming frustrated and it showed in his voice. He barked, "Not worthy unless, of course, the statue, the fountain, and the chalice happened to belong to the great Lorenzo de' Medici."

"Come on, Fra Domenico," Papa replied with contempt. "They were common thieves, well known for their unlawful deeds. But you, and your friends here, have made them out to be martyrs. Not only that, they were stupid common thieves. They stole a chalice from the most famous man in Florence, and then tried to sell it here in town. And then there's the statue. Donatello's, Judith and Holofernes, was created as a statement against tyranny. For Lorenzo to admire it so, just shows his compassion and understanding for the people. For them to pick this statue to deface further shows their stupidity – assuming their attack was actually intended as a protest. But I don't believe – and most people, including the men on the Signory, agree with me – that this was not a protest against tyranny, but the final drunken deed of a couple of professional criminals."

"So they were ignorant of the statues significance," snapped Fra Domenico. "They were common, uneducated men, simple and poor. Perhaps they had a history of some past indiscretions, but what they did here, was it really worthy of their punishment? Did the Medici have the right to have them killed? For this misdemeanor?"

"Wait a minute," Papa interjected. "This was not Lorenzo's doing. It was the Signory that handed down their punishment. It is the counsel, not Lorenzo, that has decided to come down so hard on crime."

"And whom do you suppose controls the Signory?" snapped Fra Domenico sarcastically.

Papa sighed deeply, and said, "I do not wish to continue arguing with you over these two." Then Papa made a gesture of fanning his nose, and added. "And I do not wish to continue smelling them either."

Fra Domenico hesitated. I believe he had more to say, but he let it pass, and chose to comment on what they both agreed on. "The odor is overwhelming. I don't know how the, Band of Hope, can stand it. I guess I just have a weaker constitution and a lower level of commitment."

"Or just a keener sense of smell," Papa added.

"Perhaps," Fra Domenico agreed, as he made the sign of the cross in the air and whispered a small prayer one more time.

We moved away from the gallows toward the opposite end of the square. We were following the lead of Fra Domenico who was heading toward the Duomo, where a small crowd of people was gathering.

On seeing the crowd, Papa said, "I'm afraid to ask, or do I even need to?"

"Yes, it's Savonarola, they are coming to hear," said Fra Domenico. "He will be delivering a sermon in a few hours."

"Twice in one day, Father?" Papa questioned without really asking. "Well I'll say this for you, you're loyal." Then under his breath, barely loud enough for me to hear he added, "or crazy."

We parted with Fra Domenico in front of the Cathedral of Florence. Kind words were exchanged between them, along with a reminder to me about being prepared for my morning lesson. Then Papa and I headed home; we passed Savonarola's long procession on the way. A cool breeze swept over the city.

Mama and I read from the book of Job – from Latin to Italian, then German. We hadn't gotten very far when I began to feel a little tickle in my throat; I complained to Mama.

"Mama, I feel a little tickle in my throat," I said.

Mama looked concerned. She said, "Open your mouth." She looked inside, but didn't see anything unusual. She said, "I don't see anything unusual, but we better not read anymore tonight. Let's give your throat a rest. And just in case, I think you should say a prayer to Saint Blaise to cure you of that tickle. Now give me a kiss." I obeyed. "Now get into bed." Again, I obeyed. She blew out the lamp. The room was totally dark, but Mama had no trouble finding her way to the door. When she opened it, a shaft of yellow, flickering light streaked across her body and onto my bed. Mama turned back toward me, smiled with her thin lips and squinting gray-blue eyes. In that light, her beautiful sandy, blonde hair and white satin skin made her look like an angel. Then she said, "Goodnight, Lorenzo, Mama loves you," and closed the door.

I waited several minutes – staring and listening in the dark – then I got up, felt my way to the foot of the bed, opened the cassone, pulled out my little wooden box, stumbled to my writing table, opened the box, removed a small candle, and lit it. As my eyes adjusted to the dim light, I laid out a piece of paper and opened the ink, then I picked up my pen – left on the table from the morning – and began to draw. My subjects were the two hanging men I had seen that afternoon outside the Palazzo Vecchio. I was able to do a pretty good job – at least I thought so – considering I was relying only on memory. The thing I remembered the most about the victims – besides the awful smell – was the indignity of their appearance. Their lifeless bodies hung there, for all to see, two rotting corpses, bare flesh exposed, faces swollen and unrecognizable – a pathetic and humiliating way to die. I had finished my sketch when I heard Mama and Papa in the other room. Almost as a reflex triggered by the sound of their voices, I blew out my candle, but there was no need; Mama and Papa were not coming to check on me. They were just talking.

I waited in the darkness until my eyes adjusted just enough so I would not stumble; a thin strip of light was coming in from under my door. I walked toward it. I thought I heard my name; curious, I opened the door ever so slightly and peered out the crack.

I could not see them – they were behind the table on the ground by the fireplace – but I could hear them. To my delight, Papa asked Mama to let me pursue my passion for drawing and she agreed – as long as it didn't get in the way of my studies.

"We will let him do his drawings, as long as it doesn't get in the way of his studies," Mama said.

"Then I think I should look into finding someone to look at his work," Papa said. "To see if he has any real talent. Of course, I think he does, but who am I? Just a poor gunmaker."

Mama didn't say anything. I always wondered if Mama agreed to let me draw because she knew I had no special gift, and would give it up once someone who knew better had confirmed this fact to me.

Then it got quiet. I waited several minutes and heard nothing but the crackling of the fire and a few soft muffled moans. I was just about to close the door and go to bed, when I saw my mother stand up from behind the table; she was naked. Her ivory skin glowed, yellow, in the firelight. She stood there alone, not moving, for several seconds, then my papa stood up; he was also naked. Papa moved up close to Mama until their bodies touched – they kissed softly – then Papa lifted Mama up by her bottom; she wrapped her legs around him. It looked really funny to me, at the time, and I almost burst out laughing. Good taste prevents me from saying anymore of what happened. I didn't really understand what I saw that night until many years later, but suffice it to say, my lack of siblings was not due to a lack of trying.

Chapter II

The year 1492 was an important year in Florence and the world: Columbus landed in the New World; Lorenzo de' Medici died; Lorenzo's son Piero began a brief two-year reign; the Spanish kicked the Moors off of the continent in the west; Charles VIII became king of France; Alexander VI became pope; and I turned ten years old. We didn't learn about Columbus' discovery until after this pivotal year, but when we did, Papa practically burst at the seams with Italian pride. He liked to remind anyone who would listen that Columbus was Italian, and would even insist that the great explorer was from Florence. Whenever Papa was corrected with the truth – Columbus was from Genoa – Papa would dismiss the fact with his own brand of logic. "No man from Genoa could possibly have performed such a feat. Like most fools outside of Florence, the people of Genoa think the world is flat and surrounded by ocean like in one of those primitive circle and cross maps," he would say. Therefore, "He must have been from Florence." I think Papa knew the truth, but he preferred to tell it his way.

Papa took Lorenzo de' Medici's death pretty hard. He predicted that it would mean hard times for our city; Papa was right, of course. They say Savonarola predicted Lorenzo's death, but I believe that this was just religious propaganda for his followers – the story seemed to confirm Savonarola's heavenly connections. Piero de' Medici took over briefly but he was not his father; he lacked Lorenzo's strength, leadership, charm, and good luck. Lorenzo was known as "The magnificent." Piero was known as "The Fool," Piero the Fool. Piero was forced to flee the city and, once again, Florence became a republic. Unfortunately this would not be a good thing. Savonarola's pious influence would soon gain control over the council, the Signory, and his views would become the law in the city – this would lead to disaster for Florence and him. For some reason, Savonarola was not able to predict his disastrous reign or his own downfall; perhaps his heavenly connections had been severed.

When Ferdinand of Spain announced that the Moors had been defeated and pushed out of Spain – effectively removing them from the western part of the continent – Papa was thrilled. His joy was slightly offset by the news from Hungary; the Turks defeated the Hungarians at the Save River, strengthening their hold in the region. So while we had won ground in the west, we had lost ground in the east. The reign of the new French king, Charles VIII, would mean trouble for Florence and the rest of Italy. The new pope, Alexander VI would also bring problems for our city, but that would be due to Savanarola and his apparent alliance with the new French king. So removing Savanarola improved our relationship with the new pope, but led to our problems with Charles VIII. But alas, I am getting ahead of my story – back to 1492.

My tenth year of life would be my last good year. It would be my last year as a boy, and the last good year for my little family. It didn't all go bad at once; it seemed to change slowly and imperceptibly. And it wasn't really a change from good to bad, but more of one from innocence and contentment, to responsibility and turmoil. I would soon begin to learn about normal human suffering due to love and death, as well as the abnormal suffering caused by what we often perceive as evil in the world. But I was still unscathed and unscarred in 1492.

My city seemed to know that this was to be my last good year and gave me a grand send off by putting on the grandest festivals – the best that I remember. Carnival was magnificent, and the May Day Festival was really beautiful, but the Feast Day of Saint John, in June, was the best. Saint John is Florence's patron saint, so unlike the other festivals that are often shared in celebration in other cities, this one was our own and therefore special to Florentines. The whole city participates in Feast Day, with every quarter decorating in their own unique way using banners of cloth and colorful ornaments. All of Tuscany joins in and comes to the city baring symbolic tribute in the form of small trinkets, baskets of food, and barrels of wine. There's lots of drinking and feasting all over the city. There's also music, plays, parades, horse races, and lots more.

I remember getting ready on the day of the feast and being very excited about going out and seeing everything. Adding to my excitement was an announcement by my papa that he had found me an art teacher – Maestro Tommaso Bramante. Bramante was a minor artist, who once worked, briefly, for the Medici. It turned out that Bramante had done little work of his own, since his early promise, and mainly lived off of teaching others. Teaching for him meant touching up his talented student's work and adding minor changes, then passing it off as his own work, and patronizing those of us with lesser ability just to collect a fee. Papa said that he had shown Bramante some of my drawings and that he thought that I showed some hints of talent.

"Bramante says that Lorenzo shows some hints of talent," Papa said.

Mama frowned and said, "Some hints? Not very encouraging."

"Don't mind that, Katarina," Papa said, "All art teachers talk like that. That's just their way. They like to play down a person's talent at first until they become their student. Then they work with them for a while, add their personal touch and wisdom to the student's work, then suddenly the student is a genius. All because of the teacher's patient tutelage."

Mama smirked again, and said, "If that's all he's going to do and you know it, then what's the point of sending him to this, Bramante?"

"A good teacher's approval adds legitimacy to the artists work," Papa said. "It's not like you or I saying Lorenzo is good, that means nothing to patrons, but if Bramante says it, ah, then it will mean something. Besides, he can make contacts for Lorenzo, open doors for him, get him name recognition for his work. Then if the boy moves in the right circles, who knows."

"I think Lorenzo should have to paint something first," Mama said. "Before we start talking about talent. What has he done, but a few drawings, and sketches?"

"Oh, he'll paint," Papa said. "Everyday, he will paint, and paint, and paint."

"Everyday?" Mama questioned. "What about his studies? You promised me that his drawing and painting would not interfere with his monastic training. And what about Fra Domenico?"

"The boy will keep up with his studies," Papa said. "And as long as his studies aren't affected, Fra Domenico will have nothing to complain about. You'll keep up with your studies, won't you, Lorenzo?"

I smiled at Papa, but knew better than to get involved in their discussion; Papa understood and didn't expect me to answer. We all finished getting ourselves ready in silence.

Papa was dressed in his best doublet and breeches; his belt pouch hung on his hip. Mama wore a soft, red, tight-fitting, square-necked, sleeveless bodice, and a matching skirt with golden, lace trim. Mama hated wearing hats, but it was the style; every woman over the age of thirteen was expected to wear some sort of headgear. So Mama wore a modest, embroidered, golden, muffin cap that matched the lace on her skirt, and her golden, laced, belt pouch. When it came time to leave, Mama looked me over and found me presentable, except for a lock of errant hair that refused to stay down with the rest. Mama tried several times to force it down by dampening it and pushing it down with her fingers, but it continued to defy her and nature by forcing itself skyward. Mama frowned, shook her head, sighed deeply, and decided to just let it be. I can't remember what I was wearing; I can't remember what I was wearing yesterday. I'm sure I was dressed as a person of my age and stature should have been – then not yesterday – Mama would have made sure of that. I'm not as confident about the appropriateness of what I was wearing yesterday.

When we first stepped out on the street it was hazy, overcast, but as we passed our neighbor's shop along the Via dei Serragli – decorated in bright red silk cloth – the sun shed its' veil, filling the day with light and warmth. Decorating shops in brilliantly colored banners of cloth is part of the Feast Day celebration, but we didn't have a real storefront to decorate so we didn't observe that part of the festivities. We wandered, seemingly without direction, through the Santo Spirito Quarter taking in all the sights and sounds. We had to stop for a moment to allow a procession of monks, carrying holy relics, to pass. They were followed, close behind, by a parade of citizens that filled the entire street. Mama and Papa were each given a candle by a man with an unnatural smile; Papa said he had probably had too much wine. We saw Fra Domenico in the procession – at the back of the group of monks and just in front of the trailing crowd – and he too wore an unnatural smile; Papa said he had probably had too much Savonarola.

I remember that Papa looked so proud – his chin was up and his chest was out – as he strolled along next to Mama. Mama seemed to glide along, as if she were floating just above the pavement; she gently held onto Papa's arm. Mama had that look of contentment that she always had, but I believe that she was also proud – proud to be seen with Papa. Occasionally, their eyes would meet and I knew – anyone who saw them also knew – why these two people were together. If souls of infants come from heaven, then their souls were picked by angels to be together long before they were born.

As they walked together, I ran out in front to see everything first, and take it all in; everything was so beautiful. Of course, there was the usual number of pickpockets, beggars, and prostitutes applying their skills – as was expected with any public event in Florence – but I could easily overlook them, for they overlooked me; I was not a viable target for their vocations. The majority of the people enjoying the festivities were commoners like peasants, small business owners, and farmers – most people are peasants, small business owners, or farmers – but there were also soldiers, public officials, and nobility in the streets. Festivals are the great societal equalizer; rich and poor mingle in the crowd, laugh at the same plays, dance to the same music, eat the same foods, and drink the same wines.

By afternoon it was seasonally hot, and on a typical June day the air would be filled with a variety of unpleasant odors such as: steam from cooling metal, kilns burning fuel, garbage, human waste, animal waste, raw fish and decaying flesh. But everything is cleaned up for festival days, and tradesmen take the day off averting the natural odors of the application of their vocations. Florence breathed pleasant aromas from flowers, sweet perfumes, and all the different foods being prepared on the streets. The sound of Florence was also much different on festival days; everywhere pleasant voices, laughter, and music – lots of music – could be heard.

Many of Florence's small business owners relied on festivals to make their biggest profits of the year. Stalls were set up to sell everything from linens and cloth, to engravings and cabinets. There were also a number of artists selling paintings and drawing portraits. Grotesque caricatures were very popular with the commoners, particularly ones of famous people like the pope, the Medicis, or even Savonarola.

The plays or satires being performed in the various corners of the city, like the caricatures, were often used to make fun of the elite. This was usually seen as fun and harmless venting, but sometimes this was not the case; in conservative times such mocking of authority was not allowed and open ridicule of certain people could bring harsh reprisal.

We stopped to watch one short play. It was a hilarious little sketch that revolved around the beheading of a farmer for public perversion. There were caricatures of Savonarola and the members of the Signory, who pranced about on stage and shouted condemnations and demanded the punishment for the accused. The actor playing the accused, the farmer, was quite funny; he hopped about, with his hands tied behind his back, proclaiming his innocence in a silly voice. He was dressed only in breeches – no shirt – and just below his belt there was this exaggerated bulge of his manhood. At the climax of the performance, the farmer was bent over by two men, his eyes were closed, he braced for his execution, and then the mighty axe was wielded, but instead of chopping off his head, at the last possible moment, he was stood up, and the executioner castrated him.

The audience squealed with delight. I still laugh when I see that silly man, in my head, jumping in joyous relief that his life had been spared, then suddenly realizing what he had lost. I remember Papa saying that he may have been better off losing his head.

"Oh, that hurts, just to watch," Papa said, still laughing. "You know, that poor fool may have been better off losing his head." I giggled, and Mama smiled as she shook her head. The crowd was still laughing as they began to move away from the stage.

"What's next?" Papa asked. "Unless, you would like to stay for the next performance."

Mama smiled and shook her head again, and said, "Oh no, once was enough for me, thank you."

"Oh, Katarina, you were laughing pretty hard," Papa said – he exaggerated – as we slowly began to reenter the moving crowd on the street.

"Yes, I was amused," said Mama as she giggled and smiled broadly – showing a rare glimpse of teeth. "It was funny, but I don't wish to see it again. Besides, we have so much to see, and we are boring Lorenzo just standing around watching a silly play."

"I'm not bored, Mama," I chimed in. "I could stay and see it again."

"Don't contradict you mother, Lorenzo," Papa said with false sternness. "You're bored." Then he laughed, and said, "Mama's right, there is so much more to see. So back to my question, what shall we do next?" Shall we go to the parade? I heard that there are going to be even more floats than last year, with lots of color and banners. Or how about the horse races? No, they don't start until later this evening." Papa thought for a moment, as we slowly walked on – Mama was still holding his arm. I was a few steps in front of them – walking backwards – waiting to hear Papa's next suggestion. Then Papa suggested, "We could go over to the Palazzo Vecchio and watch the prisoner release."

Mama looked hard at Papa to judge his sincerity, and could tell right away that he was kidding, but I could not. I protested, "No, Papa, that's not any fun."

"Sure it is, Lorenzo," Papa said. "We can cheer on the prisoners as they are paraded before us, then we can offer our forgiveness, and call for their release. It really would be a good lesson for you in mercy and forgiveness."

I still didn't know Papa was kidding, so I began to plead. "No Papa," I said. "Let's do something else. Something fun."

Papa laughed and mercifully told me what he knew I wanted to hear, "All right, Lorenzo," he said, "let's find those floats instead." Then he couldn't resist playing with me just a little more. "You know," he began, "the floats are going to be ending up parading around the

Piazza della Signoria. So if we following them there we will be right there at the Palazzo Vecchio…"

"Papa!" I whined. He just laughed and Mama smiled.

We were almost to the Ponte alla Carraia, when we first saw the bright banners and streamers from atop the floats; they were across from us on the north bank of the Arno, just preparing to head up the road to the Piazza della Signoria.

As we stepped onto the bridge, our attention was drawn away from the glorious spectacle of the floats to another, subtle, and more ominous spectacle. The bridge was lined with men in black robes, praying out loud. Their prayers condemned the vanities and excesses of the festival – everything from the fancy dress to the overindulgence of food and drink. Papa tried to dismiss them by, once again, calling them the "band of fools," but I could tell that he was worried. With Lorenzo gone, who knew how much the influence of Savonarola and his followers would grow. My city was vulnerable; Peiro de' Medici was no leader and fear from foreign invasion and economic collapse ran high. Anything could happen, and anything might not be a good thing, but it wasn't going to happen today. Today my city lived as if there was no tomorrow, but alas, there is always a tomorrow.

I had my first art lesson with Maestro Tommaso Bramante a week after the Feast of St. John, and they continued, at least, once a week throughout the summer. In the fall, Papa surprised me by clearing out his, rarely used, showroom and converting it into an art studio; he insisted that he didn't need it. I suppose I didn't need it either, but at the time, it was great; it made me feel like a real artist. I had an easel, canvases, a chair, and a large wooden box for all my supplies; I no longer needed to keep my paints and brushes in my room. I had everything a young artist needed – except talent.

I remember the day Maestro Bramante first came to my studio; I wouldn't call him maestro now, but I did what I was told then. I had been going to Maestro Bramante's studio for instruction all summer, but when he learned that I had my own studio, in Papa's workshop, he insisted on coming to me. Tommaso Bramante was drawn to money like crows to carrion. He used coming to my studio as a means to get closer to Papa. It was also at this time that I realized that gunmaking was actually a very profitable business; Papa had always played the pauper. It's not surprising that I should think of crows when I think of Bramante; he had a nose, which in profile formed a bent triangle resembling the beak of some massive bird-of-prey. His other features were small and his face was thin, as was his tall frame, this made that nose of his even more prominent and overbearing.

I was working on my masterpiece – a portrait of Mama – while Bramante was looking over my shoulder giving me instruction and insincere encouragement. I was concentrating on my work, but I couldn't help but notice Bramante was distracted; he kept looking back through the doorway into Papa's work area. He even asked me if Papa was back there working. It was obvious that he was, because we could hear the sound of a hammer striking metal. When the sound suddenly stopped, Bramante became very excited; I could hear him pacing behind me. His anticipation was rewarded when Papa came through the door wiping his hands on a towel.

Maestro Bramante immediately scurried over to greet Papa in such a way that you would have thought Bramante was at home and Papa was the visitor – he even spoke first calling Papa, Signore Demarco. When Papa responded addressing Bramante as, Maestro Bramante, he insisted that Papa call him Tommaso, and that maestro was only for students.

"I insist that you call me Tommaso," Bramante said. "Maestro is only for my students. It gives them a sense of their place. Don't you agree? Huh?" Papa just smiled, so Bramante continued. He said, "Besides, you are the one who is paying me to teach your son. I am, in fact, your employee. I work for you. Perhaps I should call you maestro, huh?" Again Papa just smiled. Bramante was working desperately to get on Papa's good side. "Even if I wasn't working for you," he continued, "I can tell that you are a man of means, who demands respect, with this shop, one of the largest in the quarter. Your reputation as a gunmaker is known all over Florence. Surely you should have some title, just as ..."

"As I've told you before, Signore Bramante," Papa interrupted, "you have been misinformed about my means, I am just a modest gunmaker who earns just enough to care for his family. So you may call me Sabastiano, or Signore Demarco, which ever you feel the most comfortable with."

"In that case, let us speak as friends," said Bramante with a broad smile glued on his face. "I shall call you Sabastiano, and please, call me Tommaso."

Papa agreed and they began to converse about everything from the weather to politics; Bramante was careful to let Papa do most of the talking, and was cunning enough to agree with everything he said. Even on the sensitive issue of Savonarola, Bramante carefully mirrored Papa's opinion completely. Then when Papa spoke of his sadness over the death of Lorenzo de' Medici, Bramante even managed to bring a tear to his eye and a lump in his throat. In fairness, Bramante may have honestly felt as Papa did about my city's late benefactor, but I doubt it.

The Bramante I would come to know only felt passion for three things – wealth, art, and more wealth.

As their conversation waned – Bramante was now doing most of the talking – Papa worked his way around to see what I was painting. I believe I captured only about one tenth of the beauty that was my mama. I actually had captured more in the sketch, under the layers of paint; from the beginning I was quite good at drawing. That's probably why Papa was so sure I was meant to be an artist. My painting skills were still years away from rising to the level of mediocrity. But even with my limited abilities – capturing only a tenth of her loveliness – the painting was something special. I only painted her from the waist up so I could concentrate on her face. I had her German features basically right, and had the correct hue for her ivory skin, but those squinting gray-blue eyes and that thin-lipped smile just weren't correct. I think the only thing I really did superbly was the hair; I painted every sandy blonde strand one at a time, with a thin brush.

Seeing Papa's eyes widen, Bramante stopped in mid-sentence and turned to see what had captured his attention. He immediately turned my painting and Papa's reaction into a benefit for him. "Oh, I see you've noticed what we have been working on, huh?" he said with a sardonic smile. And yes, he did say we; he saw Papa's reaction, immediately assessed that it was positive, and Bramante knew he could exploit it. "Lorenzo's skills are coming along, wouldn't you say? Huh?" he said, still smiling. "We still need to do some work on those brush strokes, but we haven't been at it that long. These things take time."

Papa glowed with fatherly pride, and he mumbled, "Jesus, Mary, and Joseph, it's beautiful." He stared at the painting a little longer then he looked at me and said, "Come here boy." I obeyed, and he lifted me up with his big hands, hugged me, and then kissed both cheeks. Then he put me down and went back to staring at the painting. Several more seconds passed, then he abruptly said, "I have to get your mama. When she sees this she will know, as I do, what God has put you in this world to do."

Papa disappeared into the shop, but he quickly returned leading Mama by the hand. To my surprise, even Mama seemed to be impressed by my effort – perhaps moved or touched would be a more accurate description of her reaction.

Her eyes squinted; she smiled and said, "Lorenzo, it's wonderful." Then Mama kissed me.

Bramante, who could never read Mama like he could Papa, misinterpreted Mama's reaction and tried to capitalize, on what he thought, was her apparent appreciation of my skill. "The Lady has an eye for quality," he said. "But with such a lovely subject, we should expect nothing less. Huh? The boy is coming along quite splendidly, don't you agree?"

Mama ignored him, but Bramante continued to praise my work, careful to point out his contributions and my vast potential – provided I remain under his tutelage. This would be a theme from Bramante for the next couple of years – my potential, channeled by his expert guidance, equals brilliance. But I didn't care what he said that day, or how much credit he tried to take, for I had succeeded as an artist; my painting had brought happiness and admiration from the only audience that mattered. Little did I know that at the age of ten, I had already reached the peak of my artistic achievement.

Of course Fra Domenico didn't want to see me wasting my time studying art; he knew my talents as a linguist and was training me to be a priest. One day, while we were working he told me his thoughts on the subject of art. I was having trouble concentrating that particular day and apologized to him and told him that it was hard, and that I wasn't feeling well.

"I'm sorry, Fra Domenico," I said. "It just seems hard today." Then I offered a weak excuse. "I'm not feeling well," I said, but it was a lie.

Fra Domenico frowned; he knew I wasn't ill. He said, "You seem to be having trouble concentrating all the time, lately." He paused; I didn't try to speak, so he continued, "Is it this painting thing? I hear you've been taking lessons from Tommaso Bramante." It wasn't a secret, but I knew Papa hadn't told Fra Domenico about Bramante; Papa was putting it off to delay the inevitable argument. So now he knew, somehow, and it, as well as lying to him about being ill, was making me feel ashamed and guilty; I said nothing. "You know, I know of this Bramante," said Fra Domenico. "He is not an honorable man. I have heard several stories of his business dealings. I don't think he can be trusted. I don't know about his skill, as an artist, I am not familiar with his work, and I don't know what kind of teacher he is, but have your papa keep an eye on this one. You keep an eye on him too, Lorenzo."

"I will, Fra Domenico," I said sheepishly.

Fra Domenico was being surprisingly calm and understanding about the news of my art lessons, so I tried to repay his understanding by reassuring him that I would work hard on my studies and was looking forward to dedicating my life to God. I don't remember my exact words, and I probably didn't say it this well, but I said something like, "There are many ways to dedicate your life to God, and I will be able to do it by teaching his word and by painting. You have said that God is beauty and perfection. In art, the painter strives to find beauty and perfection in his work. So as a painter I will look for God in my work." Unfortunately, he wasn't there.

Even as I clumsily tried to defend my artistic aspirations, Fra Domenico did not get angry, as he had in the past, or try to argue against me. Instead he just reminded me that when God gives you a talent, you should use it to do his work.

"When God gives you a talent, you should use it to do his work," said Fra Domenico. He made the sign of the cross in the air and whispered a small prayer and continued, "You should not squander it away for earthly gains, such as wealth. I don't know about your ability as an artist, but I do know that you have another gift, the gift of language. I struggled to learn Latin, and in different degrees, so did most of my brethren, but to you it comes like it was all born there in your head, and you just needed someone like me to pick it out for you. I believed, perhaps mistakenly, that this was a sign from God that you were chosen to do his work, simply because you can speak his language so well, better than most. But I have also observed that you can write and speak in German. And your papa told me that he had a Spaniard in his shop, and by the end of the afternoon, you were having a conversation with him. So your gift, from God, is not simply Latin, but all language. You probably could even learn Hebrew and read the words of God in their original form. " He paused then added, "Whatever you do, you must use this gift of language. Now, again please, could we do it again please?"

We went back to work and nothing more was said on the subject. Now both of us knew we were just going through the motions. I believe that Fra Domenico knew, even before I was completely sure myself, that I would never be a priest.

Chapter III

Pope Alexander VI would do a lot in his short term to affect my life and my city. One of the first things he did was to divide the world between Spain and Portugal – as if he had the right. This was meant to end a dispute between these two powers over the newly discovered territories, and was generally effective as long as the two powers, primarily Spain, could enforce it. The Spanish took the Pope's order more aggressively than the Portuguese. The word of the pope was as good as the word of God, therefore God had ordained the conquest of the New World, which turned out to be a vast new continent filled with millions of people. When it was discovered that these people worshiped pagan idols, the conquest became a spiritual quest; it was our Christian duty to convert these people and save them, even if they didn't want to be saved. Since we were giving them salvation and eternal life, the least that they could do in return was to be our slaves and give us all their gold and silver. But once again, I am getting ahead of my story.

The first thing that Pope Alexander VI did that affected my city was nothing. Charles VIII of France invaded Italy with the support of the Duke of Milan. So after passing through the Po Valley without resistance, the French moved on my city. Savonarola used this disaster to affirm his power and confirm his special relationship with God; Savonarola had predicted that the sword of the Lord would fall upon Florence. The French were providing the sword; the question was how hard it was going to fall. Piero de' Medici appealed to the Pope for help – as well as to the empire and our neighboring cities – but Alexander did nothing. In his defense, there wasn't much he could do; there wasn't enough time to raise an army to defend Florence. With no help in site, Piero fled the city through the Porta San Gallo under the cover of night, and hid in exile in Venice.

King Charles VIII entered my city through the Porta San Freliano, less than a mile from Papa's shop. He rode atop a massive black horse, and was flanked by four knights carrying a canopy over his head to shelter him from the sun; his generals were at his side. The procession was grand, consisting of: the royal body guards; more than a hundred knights on foot; the Swiss guard; ten thousand infantry men; three thousand cavalry; six thousand archers and crossbowmen; and a dozen artillery pieces drawn by horses. It was an amazing site, I'm told, but I saw none of it. Papa chose to stay home, and there we stayed for the eleven days the French occupied my city. It was a relatively peaceful occupation, and then Charles took his army on to Rome, and then Naples.

With the French gone, and the Medici in exile, a void was left in the government, so a republic was once again established in Florence. The Signory employed my future friend, Machiavelli. But the true power in Florence was still being wielded by one man – Savonarola. He and his supporters made it clear that they were in charge, and thusly began a dark period in my city.

Life under Savonarola was mercifully brief. I was fortunate to be too distracted and too young to be too effected by the new reign. I spent much of the time in Milan with Papa – Papa and I made three trips to Milan in five years. I was also too preoccupied with my art to care much about local politics. But even if you didn't care about politics, it was impossible not to notice the changes in my city. A mob of Savonarola supporters looted the Medici palace. They stole or destroyed valuables including works of art. Then they took the Statue of Judith and Holofernes and put it in the public square, as a warning to future, would be tyrants – namely the Medici if they ever tried to return. New morality laws were passed against things like gambling, swearing, dirty songs, fancy clothes, and horseracing. The Bands of Hope went through the city collecting money for the poor, and personal items that were considered immoral. These things, labeled vanities, included: jewelry, some books, wigs, some works of art, mirrors, perfumes, masks, beads, fans, and all types of clothing. People were expected to dress plainly and anyone violating this rule may have the clothes ripped from their backs as they walked in the street. Our festive carnivals became strict religious pageants where these vanities were collected and then publicly destroyed in a massive, "bonfire of the vanities." Once a merchant from Venice offered to buy these vanities – instead of seeing them destroyed – to sell abroad, but he was turned down, and then they burnt him too, in effigy.

A lot of citizens saw good, at least at first, in what was happening – Fra Domenico, for one, saw these changes as the saving of Florence, and believed that they were creating a holy city. Many believe that my city had become too decadent with art and humanist ideas, and was now being purged of these sins. Some prominent citizens joined in the purging by destroying their own vanities. Artists like Fra Bartolommeo, Lorenzo di Credi and even Alessandro Botticelli joined the movement and went as far as destroying some of their own work.

The French invasion gave Savonarola the power, but it also led to his downfall – if not the invasion itself, but the alliance with the invader. The French marched down the peninsula relatively untouched. This was not surprising because most campaigns, familiar to Italians, were led by the condottieri and were more political than violent. An army threatens a city, money is paid, power often changes hands, and then it's all over. But a year after Charles VIII's invasion, on his way back to France, a real battle was fought. The Pope organized a Holy League that raised money and an army to fight the French. Venice and Spain joined the Pope, as did the Emperor Maximilian and Lodovico Sforza, the Duke of Milan. It was true that the Duke had invited the French into Italy in the first place, but now he feared that he might lose his kingdom to the invaders – so he joined the league. Savonarola kept Florence out of the alliance; a decision that the Pope would not forget, when the conflict was over.

The Holy League and the French armies met at the foot of the Apennine Mountains, in northern Italy, along the banks of the Taro River, in the battle of Fornovo. It was the bloodiest and most savage battle fought in Italy in a hundred years. The league army took the heaviest casualties, being outmatched by French experience and artillery, but the French were badly outnumbered and were forced to give up the field. Both sides claimed a kind of victory: the French escaped a superior force and made it back to France, wounded but intact; the Holy League won the field and forced out the invaders. They also captured the French baggage train which included such treasures as: a helmet and sword that had belonged to Charlemagne; jewels; a piece of the true cross; the royal seals; and the king's pornography collection which consisted of a book of naked women and sketches of various acts of lewdness. Fornovo proved to be just the beginning; the beginning of more than 60 years of Italian wars.

Papa foresaw the inevitability of the bloody conflicts to come. It was the day we left on our first trip to Milan, and after the French had left Florence. Papa told me that in order to maintain independence from each other – Florence, Venice, Milan, Rome, Naples, and the various smaller states – one state would often invite in outsiders to fight their battles to shift the balance of power in their favor, always careful to control and manipulate the outsiders like pieces on a chess board. Spain, France, and the Empire had grown in wealth, strength, numbers and power and would soon begin to come to Italy uninvited, using our lack of alliance and mutual mistrust to reduce us to pawns in their chess game. Papa compared beating the French invaders out of our country to killing rats in our house.

"Beating the French invaders out of our country is a lot like killing rats in our house," Papa said. "You may get rid of them for a time, but as long as you have something they want, they will come back."

"Well at least the Duke has come to his senses," Mama said. "If they can be stopped in Milan, all's the better for us. Then it won't matter what Savonarola wants or does. He can invite them back, but it won't mean a thing if they can't get here."

"I'll do my part," Papa said. "I'll make Sforza the best cannon on the continent, the rest will be up to him and his generals."

Mama smiled at Papa with narrow moist eyes; there was concern in her face. Softly, she spoke, "You come back to me, Sabastiano." She leaned in and kissed Papa, tenderly. Mama added, "And look after my boy." Then she turned to me, kissed me and said, "And you look after your papa." I couldn't think of anything to say – I was excited to be going, but sad to be leaving Mama – so I just nodded my head.

We climbed atop two horses, courtesy of the Duke of Milan – mine was black, and Papa's was gray. Our escorts – four mounted Swiss Guardsmen – were anxious to get moving, so there wasn't any time to drag out the goodbyes. I looked back at Mama as we slowly moved down the street; she forced a thin-lipped smile and waved at me.

We passed Fra Domenico on his way to the shop. He called out, "I will watch over Katarina, don't worry. Have a safe trip." He whispered a short, little prayer to himself, made the sign of the cross in the air and waved to us, and then he hurried to Mama's side.

Leaving Mama was really hard, but the lure of the adventure kept my thoughts from laboring over missing her. This was my first trip away from my city, so everything was fresh and exciting. The first part of the journey was filled with familiar surroundings – lush gardens, farm fields, forests, and green rolling hills – but when we reached Mantua and turned west down the Po River valley, the land opened up into a vast level plain. The Plain of Lombardy was filled with color, fertile lands, and life. We stayed in inns along the way, but one night – the last night before we reached our destination – we slept out under the moonlight beside the river. I never saw so many stars. Papa showed me the constellations and the mysterious wanderers called Mars and Jupiter. I awoke in the morning to the sound of birds, lots and lots of birds. Their songs reminded me of our festivals, where so much music is played at the same time, one melody on top of another, coming at you from every direction, so chaotic yet beautiful; I lay there on the ground, quietly listening, until their music was broken off by the noise of hacking coughs from one, then all of the guardsmen. Our escorts were crude men, hard-bitten, intimidating, experienced, Swiss Guard. They spoke a dialect of German that I was barely able to understand, but it didn't matter because they directed little conversation toward us. I had never met men like them before, cold, hard and crude; they made me uncomfortable. Papa said that we were being honored to have such an escort, and that it showed that the Duke was serious about fortifying his borders. One of the men, Philipp, when he realized that I spoke German, talked to me a little. I learned several new German words from Philipp, but I don't think Mama would have been impressed with any of my new vocabulary.

We were only miles from the city – I could tell because the road was getting wider and was finely paved – when Papa began to talk to me in earnest about what to expect when we arrived in Milan, why he decided to bring me along, and the art of forging cannon. This was the first time I remember Papa talking to me about his work. He didn't explain the process in any detail; I probably wouldn't have understood if he had. He told me that I didn't need to know the particulars because he didn't want or expect me to follow in his footsteps.

"I do not want or expect you to follow in my footsteps," Papa said, as we rode side-by-side; our escorts flanked us to the front and rear. "But a father wants his son to understand what he does and to take pride in his work."

"I am proud of you Papa," I chimed in. "And you must really be good at it for the Duke of Milan to send for you."

"Well," Papa said with a proud smile, "I do all right. I'm good at what I do, but I think that the Duke just needs all the help he can get. He expects war, and needs to build up his defenses fast. There are foundries that make cannon in Milan, and some of the finest armourers are within her walls. But armourers primarily make armor and small weapons. I'm sure cannons are being forged in the foundries, but they need to be sure that what they are producing is quality or else they can blow up on the field, and there are other considerations. I'm sure they can make cannon without me, but the Duke is pressed for time, and lack of time means haste, and haste makes waste; and waste means wasted materials and faulty cannon."

"So you are the best," I exclaimed, "and that's why they need you."

Papa laughed, "Well, I don't know, but I do make them so they don't explode."

Papa went on to explain the various types of artillery such as: double cannon, with 100 pound shot; cannon, with 50 pound shot; culverins of various sizes; sakers; falcons; and falconets. The Duke would have to decide on size and range, as well as between quality and quantity. Iron cannon are cheaper to make. For example, an iron 50-pound cannon may cost as much as 450 ducats, while the same size brass culverin would cost 750 ducats. But iron cannon are less reliable on the field and are more prone to blowing up, this is due to the heat and pressure, and also the fact that the cannon is forged in two halves and then are bound together with iron rings. Brass can be forged in one solid piece, and made thick in the breach. This reduces the risk of explosion, allows for more shots per hour, and gives the weapon a longer range, because more powder can be packed in safely. Some cannon is better for infantry support, like the smaller falcons and sakers, while others, with the larger, more powerful shot, are good for siege or bombardment of a stationary position. But not only are larger cannon more expensive, they are also less maneuverable. This may be a consideration on the field when speed may be a critical part of the battle. It was also important that all the foundries were in agreement on the size and type of weapons to be produced. There was no real standard, so Papa wanted to make sure that such things as weapon makers and shot producers knew what they were supposed to be making; it would be of little use and a great waste of time if one foundry produced 14 pound culverins and 10 pound cannon, while the other produced only 12 pound shot. These are the kinds of things that Papa expected to work out on this first trip to Milan. He told me that he did not expect to do any actual work – preparations such as the gathering of materials and deciding on the types of weapons would take time and Papa was not going to wait around if he didn't have to. We would return for the casting of the die and the actual making of the cannons on a later date. Papa did not plan on staying in Milan for more than just a few days; the trip there and back should take longer than the stay. So why did Papa want me along? I wondered.

"Why did you want me along, Papa?" I asked.

Papa hesitated, then said, "I thought it was time you got out and saw a little of the world. Most people never leave the town that they are born in. Who knows, this may be your only chance to go somewhere. You are enjoying yourself so far, aren't you?" I nodded that I was, and he continued, "I think you'll find Milan interesting, it's not home, but at least now you'll have someplace to compare it to." He hesitated again, long enough that I thought he was through, and then he said, "You know I wish for you every opportunity as an artist. And, well, I don't know him really, I never really did. It's more like I knew of him, but everybody knew of him. I did meet him. We used to say hello to each other when we passed on the street. Sometimes we would talk a little, but that was years ago, back when he was living in Florence. I don't know if he will remember me. The Duke has employed him for years, and now he is working on fortifications for the city. He is a brilliant military strategist, as well as being a magnificent architect, sculptor and painter. I thought if you tagged along with me, that you might get the chance to meet him. Then, who knows. You could show him your drawings in your notebook, or better yet, I could give them to him. He takes on apprentices. It really could be a great opportunity for you. At least that was my thinking."

So then I knew why Papa had me bring along my art supplies and had been encouraging me to sketch the scenery in a notebook he had bought for me, but whom was he talking about? He was rambling like a man with his mind opened – lots of running thoughts that were not necessarily well connected. Finally I had to ask.

"Who, Papa," I said, interrupting his oral thoughts. "Who might we meet?"

He paused, and then said, "Maestro Leonardo, Leonardo da Vinci."

Nestled in a scenic valley in the Po basin, it was easy to see why Milan had grown into a large and prosperous city. The land around the city is very fertile and capable of supporting a large population. The climate was much like ours – hot in the summer and not too cold in the winter – but it's much wetter than in my city. The Alps in the north and the Apennine Mountains to the south surround the valley. There are just a few well-traveled passes connecting the Empire and France in the north to the Mediterranean, and the rest of Italy; Milan is at the focal point of these passes. Because of this strategic location, the city became an important commercial trade center; a fact not overlooked by France or the Empire who both did and would continue to make claims to the region, and even fight for it.

It was hot and humid on the morning that we approached the city, and a mist rose over the marshland filling the valley with fog and made it difficult to see more than a few hundred feet; I heard Milan before I saw it. It sounded like my city – people shouting, voices laughing, dogs barking, horses neighing, hooves hitting cobblestone, cartwheels turning, and church bells ringing. Through the mist, I began to see outlines of great spires and the towers from the city's massive walls. As we got closer, the mist cleared – it was burning off as the sun rose – and I could see that Milan looked nothing like my city; it was far more rigid and hard looking, less elegant than Florence. Milan appeared a lot more industrious than my city, and less interested in esthetics. There were lots of cannels, and though some were scenic, their linear perfection implied that their function came before their form. Everywhere I looked there were walls and towers, and walls and towers inside the walls and towers. Walls and towers surrounded my city, but they were not like these. In Florence, the walls were like a beautiful frame around a magnificent painting, and they invite you to come and look inside. In Milan, the walls were a barrier around a frightened city, and they warned you to keep out. Then, on the edge of Milan, there was the massive Castello Sforzesco – a castle large enough to be a small city. At the time, I thought that Milan must have been the most fortified city on earth.

Papa was right, the trip took longer than the visit; we had only been there for a few days, when Papa told me that we were already leaving. I didn't get much time to see the city, or meet the great Leonardo, but I was still glad to be heading home; I missed Mama. For most of the stay, Papa was irritable and constantly shaking his head in disgust – very unlike himself, though I had never been with him away on a job or separated from Mama before. Perhaps work, or being away from Mama, or the combination of both, always made Papa act like this. He was particularly distressed when he returned to our room, at night, after a long advising session with the Duke's generals. He would pace the room and mumble to himself, and I knew it was not my place to ask him what was wrong; he said nothing to me about his troubles while we were in Milan. On the trip home, all the frustration began to come out. After a quiet first day, Papa began talking and didn't stop until we saw the spires and gables of Florence. He told me everything, some things more than once, and as he spoke, and we got closer to home, his frustration eased, his demeanor lightened, and his tone softened. By the time we reached my city, he was the old lighthearted, good-natured Papa I knew.

From all that he had said – some things I didn't understand – it seemed to be the lack of organization and coordination that seemed to irritate

Papa the most. As he had feared, too much was going on without communication. During times of crisis, some businesses really profit from the panic. Production of weapons and armor was high, but the quality was low; speed was replacing efficiency. Quick profits were being made, at the cost of shoddy goods. One of the worst things being done, according to Papa, was the production of unnecessary items, like shot for cannon that didn't, and wouldn't, exist. I guess this bothered Papa the most because it affected him the most. All this wasteful production was causing a shortage of materials, particularly copper for making brass cannons. When we left, they were just beginning to gather up – and by gather I mean confiscate or even steal – all the copper in the city and outlying area; anything copper was being taken to be melted down. The confiscation of copper also bothered Papa because they were destroying works of art, and Papa loved art. Papa believed that art was timeless, and great societies are measured by their artists and their works, like ancient Rome and Greece. Through the works of men like Botticelli, Donatello, Leonardo da Vinci and Michelangelo, Papa saw the mark of greatness for Italy and Florence. I knew he wished that, some day, I would add to that mark.

Among the copper being collected was some that was to be used for a great work of art that would have been, but now would not be. This effected Papa deeply as he told me.

"Alas Lorenzo," he said. "A great work of art that would have been, is now not to be. For twelve years Leonardo has worked on a project of epic proportion – a great statue of the first Sforza, Francesco, atop his horse. The equestrian was to be an amazing sixteen feet high, cast in bronze. But, now, because of the shortage of copper, the metal for the statue is being diverted away from what would have been a timeless masterpiece, and given to me, to make cannon." Papa paused, and then waxed philosophical, "We are living in a strange time, Lorenzo, one where we are capable of creating much beauty and grace, and at the same time, much death and devastation. And the only difference between them is in the dye we cast."

It was more than a year before we made our second trip to Milan, and in those months at home, I spent many days working with Bramante, and very few hours working with Fra Domenico. It was during those many days that I began to realize that Bramante was not a sincere man. He continued to court Papa's affections – Mama would usually avoid him – and he continued to praise my work, and tell me that I had potential. He was right about one thing, I did find that I had one exceptional artistic ability – I could paint hands. Many young and even experienced artists have at least one weakness in their work, and painting hands is one of the more common weak areas. When an experienced artist has a problem area, for a fee, he often pays a specialist to do what he cannot do that well. Bramante noticed my prowess for creating natural, well proportioned hands, so he began to bring me other artist's works and had me paint the hands for them. Of course Bramante collected the fee for the work I did. I must have worked on a dozen paintings that year – besides my own work – just painting hands. I guess I could have been a career artist after all, if I would have devoted myself to just hands work, but that's not the path I chose, and I'm glad it wasn't; I didn't find much satisfaction in the work. I didn't feel like a real artist.

Bramante used to say, "Many of the things that men create are made up of contributions by many individuals. Even in art this is true. Consider the Duomo. It took many men and more than one architect to finish the work." Perhaps Bramante was actually trying to tell me the truth, for once. Maybe this was his way of telling me that I was not good enough to be an artist on my own. Of course, "his way" including continuing to collect a fee from Papa for lessons when he knew they were a waste of time, and to use me to paint hands for other artists. These things alone wouldn't necessarily make a man dishonest or insincere – they could be considered as just good business practices – but Bramante's character, or lack of it, was beginning to become clear to me.

The summer before we returned to Milan was a hard one for my city. Savonarola's leadership had weakened the economy. Trade was down due to: a decrease in demand for "vanities;" fear by outside investors and merchants of persecution, or loss of income from attacks from the "Bands of Hope;" fear by all investors to invest in an unstable economy; and the expulsion of the Jews. There was also a poor harvest that summer throughout the countryside, and people without means were dying in the streets from starvation. Then there was an outbreak of the plague.

The Pope called upon Florence – the people – to lock up Savonarola, or send him to Rome. Pope Alexander VI was still bitter over Florence's or Savonarola's alliance with France during the invasion, and the rejection to support his Holy League. There were constant threats from the Vatican, that summer, ordering Savonarola to stop his preaching, and if Florence didn't stop him, the pope would lay the city under an interdict. There was even talk of military intervention, perhaps an invasion. Again, Pope Alexander VI's actions were to affect my city.

So it was no surprise, on the day that we rode out of the city – once again with an armed escort – that there was shouting and unrest in the streets, and through the noise I heard a voice say, "The Pope has excommunicated Savonarola." I know with such uncertainty, Papa was concerned about leaving Mama alone, but he had made a commitment to the Duke; we rode on.

The second trip – the road to Milan – was far less exciting than the first; it was no longer a new experience, plus it rained almost every day. When it didn't actually rain, the days were still cloudy, and the nights were distinctively chilly. Thinking back, it probably had a lot to do with the weather, but I remember wishing that I had stayed home; I felt miserable and I was missing Mama before we even got half way there. Philipp was among the guard again, and we talked a little. He told me he had a wife and two young children in Milan, and shared with me a few more off-colored stories, but he had little time for me; I think he didn't want to appear too soft or jovial, spending time with a boy, in front of his companions, though I don't believe that he could have been more than a few years older than me; I was fifteen or sixteen at the time. Now once we got to Milan, there was plenty of excitement. This time, Papa worked constantly, and I spent most of my time on my own – that is, away from Papa, but not necessarily by myself. I was old enough to take care of myself, but still too young to be mistaken for a man; I was almost as tall as Papa, but I was not muscular like him. I was thin, almost too thin, and it would be about a year before I could grow my facial hair, though it was not the style to do so until a man had reached a more mature age. After our second day in Milan, I didn't spend much time exploring on my own. That evening Papa came back to our room with some extraordinary news. But before he said anything he picked me up – which now meant only a few inches off of the floor – and kissed me on both cheeks, and reminded me of how big I was getting. His news was that he had met with Maestro Leonardo da Vinci at the court of the Duke, and to his surprise and delight, Leonardo remembered him well. Papa spoke so fast and with such excitement, that his words ran into each other, and his sentences often went off into dead ends, only to be picked up at some other point of thought and taken in another direction. The first thing I got out of what he was trying to say was that, to Papa's amazement and delight, Leonardo not only agreed to look at my work, but also invited me to come along with him on a project he was working on. After that, Papa proceeded to tell me everything, that is every little story and antidote he had known or heard about the great man. Papa called Leonardo a great man because, according to Papa, art was in the left hand of God. Therefore, anyone so gifted in art must be a great person, because they were blessed with the left hand of God.

Leonardo was older than Papa, but not by much. By the time Papa and

Mama had settled into his shop in Florence, Leonardo had already gained a substantial reputation as an exceptional artist. This reputation first emerged when Leonardo was working as an apprentice for the distinguished Florentine artist Andrea del Verrocchio. Over a period of ten years, Verrocchio taught Leonardo everything he knew about art from mixing paints and making brushes, to sculpting in various mediums, and painting. Leonardo taught Verrocchio – art. There was a story going around Florence that when Leonardo was first allowed to contribute to an important painting of Verrocchio's – the Baptism of Christ – Verrocchio was so impressed by Leonardo's skill – he created the kneeling angel at the left of the painting – that he vowed to never touch color again. This was not said out of anger or self-condemnation, but simply because Verrocchio recognized the ability in Leonardo – the perfection – and knew he could never, no matter how hard he tried, reach that level, so for a moment Verrocchio wondered if he should even bother to try.

Of course, Lorenzo de' Medici wanted Leonardo to work for him, and when approached, Leonardo agreed to work for the great patron. His first project was to be a large painting of the Adoration of the Magi for the monastery of San Donato a Scopeto. Then he was commissioned to do a portrait of St. Jerome, but he never finished either one. Another commitment, an alter painting for St. Bernard, the chapel of the Palazzo Vecchio, was never even started. Instead, Leonardo entered the service of Ludovico Sforza as "painter and engineer of the Duke," a position that he openly applied for. It would seem that Leonardo wanted to leave Florence despite the commitments he had undertaken.

Papa first met Leonardo after the artist's apprenticeship with Verrocchio. They met in a street Market, near the Ponte Vecchio, just off of the Piazza della Signoria, when Papa physically ran into Leonardo – knocking him to the ground. Of course, Papa helped him up – not recognizing him at first – and apologized, and then Papa realized whom he had just run over. Papa couldn't remember exactly what he said – he was so excited – but whatever it was, it amused Leonardo. Leonardo wasn't injured and insisted on taking a portion of responsibility for the collision, and he even said that it was all right, that it was his fault.

"It's all right, it was my fault. I should have been watching where you were going," Leonardo said to me, with a sly grin. "At least that's what I think I said. Your papa must have said that he was sorry at least twenty times. I told him to forget it."

We walked through the cool Milan morning. The streets were busy compared to my city. I thought it might have been because of the possible coming crisis, but Leonardo said that it was always this busy.

"The next time I saw Sabastiano, your papa, he was still apologizing," Leonardo continued. "But eventually, by our third or forth encounter, we got past that first abrupt meeting and onto polite conversation. We eventually found out that we had one thing in common – besides a passion for art – metal casting. Your papa is such a devotee of fine art that he was delighted to share with me all that he knew about dye casting. Actually there was not a lot he could teach me that I didn't already know, but it was one thing we had in common besides the weather that we could talk about."

At first, like Papa, I was in awe of Maestro Leonardo – so much so that when I was with him, I completely forgot how much I missed Mama – but soon I began to see him as an ordinary man. An ordinary man who just happened to be a great artist and engineer, and about ten times smarter than anyone else. Despite his genius, Leonardo was very personable and easy to talk to, though I was often aware that he was talking down to me. He had a quiet confidence and didn't need to impress anyone, but I think he enjoyed pleasing people with his gifts. It was funny, but I actually think Leonardo enjoyed trite conversation about things like the weather, prices at the market, and political or social gossip. Perhaps it was because it made for an escape from the complex thoughts and ideas that occupied most of his conscious hours. Almost anyone – perfect strangers – would come up to Leonardo to talk to him about nothing important, or sometimes just to ask a question about art or science; Leonardo was always friendly and relaxed. Yet despite Leonardo's apparent enjoyment of companionship, he preferred to be alone with his private thoughts and observations. He once said to me, "When you're alone everything belongs to you, but when you're with a companion only half belongs to you."

Leonardo smiled a lot, but laughed little; he often seemed to be mildly amused by almost everything, as if life were a joke and he was the only one who got it. For a man in his mid-forties, he was in pretty good shape, and he was a fairly good-looking man, who was probably once quite handsome. Despite his exceptional looks, I don't recall hearing many stories about Leonardo and women. Perhaps he had many lovers, but was just very discreet in his affairs.

While recollecting his many conversations with Papa, Leonardo spoke fondly of his days in my city – so warmly that it made me wonder, why did he leave Florence?

"Maestro, why did you leave Florence?" I asked, as we approached the monastery at Santa Maria della Grazie.

He paused before he answered, and smiled like he had been asked this question before, or at least had thought about the answer, many times. "I love Florence," he finally said. "But Florence, the Florence of Lorenzo de' Medici, was a little too aloof for my taste. To be in his court, was to be around people who believed that the world would be a much better place if more people just sat around and thought about the ideal world and then lived by these thoughts – applied their presumed genius. It seemed that thoughtful opinion was far more valued than keen observation and experience. Milan is more practical and realistic and open to learning through sensible, experience-orientated study. I wrote the Duke and offered my services and Ludovico Sforza was so impressed with my ideas that he offered me dozens of interesting projects right up front, and has kept me busy ever since." Leonardo looked at me and smiled again; he knew he was confusing me. Then he said, "Here in Milan, we do things. In Florence, they prefer to just think about things. That's not quite it, but it's the general idea."

I was still confused. I asked, "Didn't you have several commissions in Florence, to do things, when you left? Some work you even started."

"Yes I did, and I have some regrets about not finishing what I had promised to do," said Leonardo. "I believe a man should keep his commitments, but there are more important things in life than painting."

I was still a little confused; I thought he meant that there are more important things in "art" than paintings. So I said, "Papa told me about the equestrian statue of Francesco Sforza. He said it was to be sixteen feet high, twice the size of Verrocchio's great equestrian of Bartolomeo Colleoni. Surely, it would have been the grandest of monuments. Papa was very disappointed to hear that cannon, that his cannon, were to be made with the metal that was to be this great work of art. I was sorry too, but perhaps there will be another time, when this threat of war has passed…"

"Oh don't worry about that," Leonardo interrupted. "I've gotten over that," he said, but his tone seemed to say otherwise; I detected at least a hint of regret. He shook it off and continued, "Besides, I have so much to do here, painting and sculpture are just a small part of my duties here. I also consult on architectural projects, design weaponry and fortifications, and do various engineering tasks. On top of all of this, I have apprentices in painting, and I am working on putting my thoughts and ideas down on paper." Then he handed me a notebook and said, "Here have a look."

Quickly I opened the notebook, and then slowly turned through the pages. The notebook was filled with superb sketches and drawings designed to illustrate the various principles of painting. I was so struck by the brilliance of technique and elaborate detail that it took me several minutes, and many pages, to realize that the writing was, that is the words, were backwards. I had little trouble getting the meaning of each point Leonardo was making with his illustrations without the benefit of words, but of course I was curious as to why anyone would write backwards. So I asked, "Why are the sentences backwards?"

Leonardo smiled and said sardonically, "You noticed." Then he asked, "Now tell me, when did you notice that the sentences were backwards?" I was puzzled by his question, so he clarified it by asking, "Was it right away? Or did it take you a few seconds?"

I think he knew my answer before I said it, but I gave it anyway. "It took me a few seconds... well actually, it took a few pages for me to realize what you had done," I said.

"Well that's why," he said, and then he paused knowing full well that he had not answered my question. This was done for effect. He continued, "I want the images to speak for themselves. The drawings are the important part of the message. Your observations should tell you, as you have attested to, the meaning of each page. Once you have the meaning, then you hold the book next to a mirror, and read the supplemental words. The illustrations are the important things, and the text is just meant to be a complement."

I handed him back his notebook, as we entered the monastery, and then made our way into the refectory. The room was quiet, empty, and a little dark. Leonardo's notorious slow progress forced the monks to eat in another area while the work was being done. Often Leonardo had apprentices mixing paint for him, but his erratic schedule often made it hard to arrange help in advance, so when I was with him, I acted as an assistant and performed many helpful little tasks. Leonardo lit a lamp. As the soft flickering glow filled the room, my eyes were drawn to the wall overlooking a long, heavy, wooden dining table. It wasn't quite finished, but enough was completed to see that Leonardo was on the verge of completing a masterpiece. Such color I have never dreamed, such detail I have never seen, and such perception of depth and dimension I never knew was possible. Standing there, in that instant, before such a display of Leonardo's brilliance, I understood what Verrocchio meant when he vowed to never touch color again; it was magnificent. The mural was of the Lord's Supper and was not only excellent in every aspect of art, but also clever in being thematically appropriate for a refectory.

I don't know how long I stood there, absorbing that superb manifestation of the left hand of God. Time passed without me. I realized this when I suddenly noticed that Leonardo was up on the scaffold – painting. He had prepared his paints and began working without me noticing. Then I mumbled – I didn't even realize that I had said it out loud – something like, my God it's beautiful.

"My God, it's beautiful," I said.

Leonardo smiled at me over his shoulder, and then went back to his work. He said, "Nice to have you back, Lorenzo." He paused, and then added sardonically, "So you approve, unless, of course, you were referring to the refectory's fine dining table. I believe it's oak, quite nice, actually. They haven't been able to get much use out of it lately, but I will be finished in here soon."

"Yes," I stammered. "I mean, yes, it's a fine table, but Maestro your mural is... magnificent." I struggled to regain my composure so as not to sound so much like an over-zealous art enthusiast, but more like a well-informed admirer; I was not successful. "I bet the monks who eat in here, must feel privileged and eternally grateful to dine with this... view, as well as have the chance to watch you work."

"You might think so," quipped Leonardo. "But you know, those monks, they hardly give me a second look, or say anything about my work. They just come in and eat, and then go about their business. I guess they are not art admirers like us. I suppose that they have their calling and we have ours."

"Ours," he really said "ours," and being included by Leonardo in the world of esthetic creation was a tremendous honor, and it gave me confidence to ask the question that had been in the back of my mind since we met, what did he think of my artistic abilities; Papa had given Leonardo my notebook of sketches prior to my introduction to the great artist. I recall that when I finally got the question out of my mouth it came out very blunt and abrupt. "What did you think of my sketches?" I asked.

"Yes, your notebook, I've looked over your sketches and they're really quite nice," Leonardo said without missing a stroke. "Your papa was quite anxious about giving it to me so I thought I'd better give it a quick look. You can take it back, I'm through with it. It's on the table over there, under one of my notebooks. Your papa's really very proud of your talent and somewhat justifiably so."

Glowing with pride from the apparent praise from the great artist, I went to retrieve my sketches. The notebook wasn't actually under Leonardo's, but wedged inside his, and mine was open; it was open to a sketch I did of the Po Valley just east of Milan.

"Some think that artistic talent comes from the heart, others think it comes from the soul," Leonardo said, still working. "Some even believe it's as simple as coming from the hands. Then there are those who don't bother to question where it comes from, but just accept it as a gift from God." He paused then added, "I believe that it is a gift, perhaps it comes from God, but the gift is scrupulous observation."

As Leonardo spoke, I opened his notebook to the page that had been wedged open by my notebook. It was not wedged in by accident, but to where he had sketched his own version of the Po Valley, east of Milan; his point was made and my heart sunk. I didn't expect to be anywhere near his level of ability, but somehow I thought that maybe I had the potential to get near that level; compared to his sketch, my drawing looked like a child's scribbles. He never said anything directly criticizing the quality of my work, instead he went on talking about the difference between looking at a thing and seeing a thing, and he said that I, like most people, look, while he sees.

"You Lorenzo, like most people, look, while I see," Leonardo said. "Now technique, anatomy, perspective, even drawing and painting can be taught, but seeing? I don't know for certain, but I believe that seeing can only come from God, or at least it is something that comes with you when you are born into this world."

At that moment I noticed that Leonardo was painting on dry plaster. Perhaps in response to being told that I didn't have the perception of an artist, I found the courage to criticize the great Leonardo. Bramante had taught me that you never use oil on dry plaster, particularly when the surface is prone to dampness. I said, "I was taught never to use oil on dry plaster, particularly when the surface is prone to dampness. The paint will crack or flake off when it dries. It may even run before it dries."

Leonardo stopped painting and smiled at me, he said, "Don't worry, Lorenzo, I'm using a mixture of tempera and oil paints. It's a special blend of mine designed just for this type of surface. It will be all right."

This was one thing that Leonardo was wrong about, for this brilliant masterpiece, The Last Supper – ironically one of the few paintings Leonardo bothered to finish – began to chip away soon after he finished his last stroke.

We had been gone so long that it felt great to be heading back to Florence; I was anxious to see Mama. I saw Leonardo many more times before we left Milan – almost every day for two weeks – but we never talked about painting or art again. He truly was a most remarkable man. He had so many intellectual interests in a variety of areas, and Leonardo excelled in all of them. I had trouble keeping up with him most of the time, but he always made an effort to try and explain things in language I would understand; there was a bit of a teacher in him.

The Duke kept Papa busy – I hardly saw him that last month – but Papa said he did get things up and running; his cannons were being produced. The Swiss Guard, including Philipp, once again escorted us on the trip home, but turned back to Milan and left us alone, just miles from my city.

We entered my city from the north through the Porta S. Gallo. The streets were surprisingly quiet – I thought it might have been because it was Palm Sunday – until we neared the Piazza della Signoria. At first it seemed to be just some normal random bits of excitement – loud voices, shouting, a few people running through the streets – but as we moved on past the square the shouting became more regular and there were lots of people running, and many were heading out of the Piazza; I also thought I saw smoke in the distance. I was curious and I think Papa was too, but we were tired and I think we would have gone straight home if we hadn't seen Fra Domenico; he looked exhausted like he had been running, and his face was bright red and wet with perspiration. He was wandering about a little dazed, he seemed confused, and he was having a little trouble catching his breath. Quickly Papa ran over to him, but Fra Domenico was so disorientated that, at first glance, he didn't seem to recognize Papa. Papa helped him to the ground and propped him up against a building, removed his flask from his belt and offered Fra Domenico some wine; he drank like a man dying of thirst. It took him several minutes to orientate himself and to catch his wind, and when he did Fra Domenico told us a story that we could hardly believe had happened in Florence.

"You will hardly believe what has happened in Florence," said Fra Domenico, still panting. He took another long drink and continued, "Savonarola, you will be happy to know, is in great peril. As we speak, he may already be dead." Fra Domenico made the sign of the cross in the air and whispered a small prayer, and then, with Papa's help, he struggled to his feet. He said, "Please, Sabastiano, I beg of you, help me get to San Marco, that is where Savonarola is and where the people are retreating to, to escape from the mob. At least come with me part way, while I regain my strength."

"Of course," Papa agreed, and the three of us started for the monastery of San Marco. As we walked, Fra Domenico related the events that led up to Savonarola's great peril, and us finding the good Father red-faced and out of breath. It began after one of Savonarola's sermons.

"It began after one of Savonarola's sermons," said Fra Domenico. "In the sermon, Savonarola said he felt himself burning and was inflamed with the spirit of the Lord. This gave Fra Francesco da Puglia the chance he had been looking for to confront Savonarola. Francesco is a Franciscan and you know they have been looking for a way to get back at us Dominicans and our leader. This Fra Francesco, decided to use Savonarola's words against him, and so he came up with the audacious challenge of a trial by fire."

"Trial by fire," Papa said, shaking his head. "I thought such foolishness had passed into ancient history."

"It has," replied Fra Domenico. "I mean it had, until Fra Francesco suggested that he and Savonarola walk through flames together. Savonarola declined the offer, saying that he was reserved for more important work. Of course, Fra Domenico da Pescia, dying for a chance to show his loyalty, offered to take Savonarola's place. Now Fra Francesco refused to take the challenge with anyone else but Savonarola. So another Franciscan, Fra Giuliano Rondinelli said he would take Francesco's place.

"After much debate, both sides agreed to the substitutions and the trial by fire was set to take place yesterday, in the Piazza della Signoria. It was also agreed that if Fra Domenico da Pescia died in the trial, then Savonarola would be banished from Florence. If Fra Giuliano died, then Fra Francesco would be banished. A thirty-yard path, in front of the Loggia dei Lanzi was set up lined with piles of sticks soaked in oil on either side. The sticks were to be lit, and then the two monks were to walk the thirty-yards.

"For the trial, the city was shut down, and all strangers were ordered to leave the city. As you might expect, a large crowd gathered to watch expecting to see this spectacle, but what they got was another kind of spectacle, one they didn't want to see. Then all roads to the Piazza della Signoria were barricaded, allowing no one to enter or leave after ten o'clock in the morning – the time the event was scheduled to begin. The crowd grew restless as the two sides argued for hours over how things were to proceed. For instance, Fra Domenico da Pescia entered the arena wearing a bright red cape, and this was thought to be enchanted by Savonarola to protect the monk from the flames, so he was forced to change his robe. Then Fra Domenico da Pescia wanted to take a crucifix into the flames. This horrified the Franciscans. Other arguments broke out until finally, God spoke bringing a storm over Florence. It thundered and there were huge bolts of lightning, then the sky opened up and the rain fell on the square. I swear, Sabastiano, it seemed to have only been raining in the Piazza della Signoria. Then it was announced that the trial by fire was to be called off."

As the three of us approached San Marco, I could tell that the smoke that I had seen earlier was coming from the monastery, but it was now subsiding.

Fra Domenico continued, "So that was yesterday's fiasco. Today, I guess yesterday's crowd wasn't so forgiving or forgetting. They weren't too happy about the cancellation of the trial. They were promised blood and they were going to get it. I was at mass in the Duomo when a mob stormed in the Cathedral. Can you believe it, Sabastiano, a mob desecrating the great Cathedral of Florence, at a mass, on Palm Sunday?" Papa could believe it. I could believe it; even at fifteen I knew that when the people of my city were angered, very few places, things, or days were considered truly sacred. He went on, "They were looking for Savonarola but he wasn't there, but they were willing to attack any Dominican or even Franciscan, for that matter. Someone threw a stone and a monk was struck dead. More stones were thrown and large sticks were wielded at the parishioners as the mob rushed the altar. We broke and ran for our lives. Unfortunately for me, I am not so well-equipped for the task." Fra Domenico patted his stomach, then added, "But fortunately, in the confusion, I was able to slip away, unseen, except, again fortunately, by you and Lorenzo." Then once again, he made the sign of the cross in the air and whispered a small prayer.

On the way to San Marco we saw bands of rioters cursing Savonarola, and committing various acts of vandalism; Fra Domenico got several long looks from angry faces, but we walked on untouched. When we arrived the walls of the monastery were besieged by a mob armed with sticks, stones and torches. Wisely, Papa stopped our advance while we were still a moderately safe distance away. Fra Domenico protested – he wanted to go on and get closer – but Papa insisted that we keep our distance.

"Keep your distance, Fra Domenico," Papa said. "There's nothing we can do right now. Your friends and brothers are inside, presumably safe, for now. Anyway, I don't think that mob is going to let us just walk past and go in. Even if we could get through them, how would your brothers know it was you trying to get in, and even if they did know it was you, do you think that they could chance opening the doors?"

Fra Domenico was forced to agree, so for the moment, we stood and watched. Dozens of angry men were banging on the walls and shouting for Savonarola to come out, but there was no response from the inside; this only intensified their rage to the point that several of the men with torches tried to set fire to the monastery wall. It was then I saw the first man killed; several lances came thrusting out from over the wall and one of the, would-be arsonists was impaled down through the chest. He dropped his torch and his whole body quivered for several seconds – he looked like a marionette – and then he dropped dead. Next, we heard several shots of gunfire coming from San Marco, as another rioter fell.

"Dear God," mumbled Fra Domenico, "the fools. Some of the monks must have hidden a stockpile of weapons in San Marco." Then he shook his round head and said, "An armed monastery. I know Savonarola did not approve of this. He always said to seek protection from our enemies only through prayer."

The crowd began to retreat in panic – pushing in all directions and trampling several men underfoot – and then, before the mob had moved substantially back from the wall, a pinnacle from the top of the monastery came crashing down on their heads, crushing several and injuring others; several monks had pushed the spire off the roof of San Marco. Despite some panic and confusion, the rioters made a counter-attack. With their blood being shed, they became more aggressive and savage; two monks were pulled over the wall, beaten and torn apart – their limbs were removed. Then the attackers breached the wall; another monk was tossed over the top and promptly stomped to death by a cheering mob. Suddenly, the doors of the monastery were flung open and the crowd surged forward through the opening. With Fra Domenico leading the way, we followed. Inside we saw blood on the walls and the cobblestones of the walkway, and several bodies of wounded and dying men – monks and rioters. One of the wounded was crying for help and another was calling for water. Fra Domenico whispered a prayer and made the sign of the cross for each one of the fallen, regardless of which side they had been on. Surprisingly, I didn't fear for our safety until we came under the attention of a couple of the rioters; I saw them staring in our direction from across the courtyard. One of the men pointed and called out something I couldn't understand; there was lots of noise, so it was difficult to hear.

Papa saw them too and said, "Fra Domenico, your robe. Those men think that we are from the monastery."

"I am," replied Fra Domenico.

"This is not the time or place to profess your loyalty to your order," Papa barked. The men began to cross the courtyard toward us. Papa added, "We've got to get out of here, and now!"

"I am inclined to agree with you, Sabastiano," said Fra Domenico with a hint of fear in his voice.

We started to move away from the approaching men, but as luck would have it, at that moment someone shouted, "The guard from the Signory is taking Savonarola! The coward was hiding in the library the whole time!" The mob, including the men who were stalking us, rushed out of the monastery and back onto the street to catch a glimpse of the fallen idol; we followed. I had seen Savonarola in many faces – fiery, passionate, divine – but this was the first time I saw him humble. He walked slowly with his head bowed and his shoulders slumped, as a crowd gathered along his path to jeer him and shout obscenities. I almost felt sorry for him. No, I take that back, I didn't feel sorry for him. We followed the crowd part way – Savonarola was taken to the Alberghettino in the tower of the Palazzo della Signoria – before Papa decided that we should be heading home.

"We should be heading home. I know the boy is anxious to see his mama," Papa said. "There's nothing else to see or do here."

Fra Domenico reluctantly agreed; not anxious to get back to San Marco, he also agreed to walk us part of the way home. This gave him time to tell us the hardships that had fallen upon my city. Though Fra Domenico wouldn't admit it, many of these hardships were the direct result of Savonarola's preaching and practices. Things, like business and public health, were not so good when we left, but in the months of our absence much had gotten worse.

"Things were not so good when you left, Sabastiano," said Fra Domenico, shaking his big round head. "But in the months of your absence much has gotten worse. At first, the famine had mainly affected the poor, because prices rose to compensate for the short supply of food. It cost more, but people with a little means were at least eating. This brought on a lot of resentment, from those who could not afford to feed themselves, so crime has been running rampant. In more places than I like to admit, it isn't always safe to walk the streets. The outbreaks of the plague have been more frequent, though I believe things may be getting a little better. The last few weeks have seen fewer deaths than the last few months."

Fra Domenico talked most of the way until we reached the Ponte alla Carraia, and then he bid his farewell and halfheartedly headed back to San Marco; Papa and I crossed the Arno on the Via dei Serragli and entered the Santo Spirito Quarter.

In the aftermath of the riot we witnessed on Palm Sunday, Savonarola was tortured by strappado – his hands were tied behind his back and attached to a pulley, by which he was raised off of the ground, then dropped halfway back down with a snap. This variety of torture was very popular with the church, particularly with the inquisition, and it required the victim to make a variety of confessions. Savonarola made all of the confessions, but then retracted them once he was let down; the process was repeated until they got a confession that stuck. Together with Fra Domenico da Pescia and another avid disciple, Fra Silvestro, Savonarola was found guilty of schism and heresy – of course he was found guilty, he confessed – and condemned to death; the three were to be hung in the Piazza della Signoria. This led to another public spectacle – the last in a long line involving Savonarola. We did not attend the spectacle, but Fra Domenico was in the crowd that day and told us what happened. Before he was executed the crowd mocked Savonarola with curses and cries like, "Prophet, now is the time for a miracle!" and "Save Thyself!" Savonarola was calm and prepared for death. He answered the crowd with, "The Lord has suffered as much for me." Without much delay, Savonarola and his two faithful companions were hung. While the bodies were still swinging, a fire was lit under them. The flames rose up and consumed most of their earthly remains, but not all – their limbs fell off, but the trunk of their bodies remained hanging. Stones were used to knock down their remaining parts, and the fire was stoked with more wood and oil to finish the job. Once they and the scaffolding were completely consumed, their ashes were thrown into the Arno.

It was good to be home and we immediately settled back into the old routine – Papa went back to work in his shop, and I painted with Bramante, studied with Fra Domenico, and practiced my language skills with Mama. The months passed. If I knew that the sand in the glass of our time together was almost out, I would have spent more time with Mama, but as it was, I found myself avoiding her whenever possible; Mama still believed I was going to be a Dominican like Fra Domenico and I could not find the courage or heart to tell her otherwise. When we were together, Mama noted that her son was growing up and becoming a man.

"My son is growing up and becoming a man," Mama said in a melancholy voice; the firelight danced in her moist gray-blue eyes. She took a long look at me, smiled and said, "I haven't really had the chance to tell you, I haven't seen you that much lately, but you're really looking more and more like your papa – maybe you're even a little taller. Of course you don't have Papa's big hawk-like nose, or his brown eyes, but even without them you look a lot like him. You're still a little thin, you should eat more, and you don't have his arms, and probably never will – all that pounding. For the same reason, my papa had those big arms too. But you are so..." She was talking herself into crying, tears formed in the corners of her squinting eyes as she forced a weak, soft, thin-lipped smile. "You've been away from me for such a long time these past few years," Mama said, choking back more tears. "Soon you'll be leaving me for good. I left my family in Wittenberg to come here, and never saw my mama and papa again. I think that my brothers are still in Wittenberg, at least the last time I heard anything from them they were, but I know that I will never be going back to see them. So I can hardly blame you if you want to leave, and never..."

She couldn't finish her thought, or perhaps she was finished. I knew that I would be getting out on my own soon – if Fra Domenico had still believed in my commitment to the monastery, he would have already insisted on me coming to San Marco – but I couldn't stand to see my mama cry so I promised her that I would be around for the rest of her days.

"Oh Mama, I will be around for the rest of your days," I said. Then I reassured her by adding. "I don't want or need to go anywhere. I have been to Milan twice and it's a great city for sure, but it is no Florence. So what could the world possibly offer me that I could not get right here? Surely there is no place anywhere like our city. I love it here, I think it is the most beautiful place on Earth, and I will always want to be close by you and Papa."

"I never thought you would leave Florence, Lorenzo," Mama said as she wiped the single tear that escaped her eyes. "Maybe it's because you're the only child I was blessed with, but I'm finding it hard to accept you growing up and leaving, even if it's just ..."

"Who said anything about the boy leaving?" Papa said as he emerged through the floor from the cellar. He closed the door and slid the large, wooden dining table back on top, and then he said to me, "You planning on going somewhere? Lorenzo?" I shook my head awkwardly as if I had been caught in a lie, and searched for something to say, but nothing came out. Papa winked at me to let me know he was kidding, but he made sure Mama didn't see his gesture. "Well I say it's about time the boy gets out," he said.

Mama knew Papa too well; she knew he was teasing her even without the benefit of seeing Papa's wink. "I guess so," she said dryly, playing along. Then, as if I wasn't in the room she added, "I guess no matter what you do, how much you care for them, feed them, clothe them, they all leave someday."

"That's right, Katarina, and with the boy gone, there will be more space for us," Papa chimed in. "And I know exactly how we can get rid of him. We can sign him up on Columbus' next voyage to the New World."

"I don't know, Sabastiano, we may not get him back," said Mama, dryly. "And it would be nice to see him every once in a while."

"Oh, I forgot, you are afraid that the boy would sail off the edge of the world," Papa said in a mocking voice. "You see, Lorenzo, your mama's people, trapped up there in the center of the continent still use those old circle and cross maps, with Asia at the top of the world, us on the left and Africa on the right. Then they believe that a great ocean surrounds these three land masses, so we are like on a big island in the middle. But we know better, down here."

"Now, now, Sabastiano, it wasn't so long ago that your people believed the same thing, and followed the same maps," Mama said.

"True enough, I suppose," Papa conceded. "But you don't have to worry about any of that stuff. The boy didn't seem to like traveling all that much. He didn't seem to take to the outdoor life, or the long days of riding or walking. I think he will be living out his days right here in Florence."

"Yes, I agree and I have said as much, and Lorenzo has recently admitted as much to me," Mama said. "There is no reason why he shouldn't take his vows right here. I will get used to him not living here, and San Marco isn't that far."

The sudden reference to my monastery commitment made the playful moment suddenly awkward for me, and I believe for Papa also. There was an uncomfortable silence between us, but it was broken by a loud, unexpected knock at the door; few people besides Fra Domenico ever came to our back door, plus it was a little late for visitors. We looked around at each other, thinking the same obvious thought, who and why is someone at our door? The mystery was soon solved when Papa opened the door. A rush of cold air filled the room. You know, I don't remember the man's name. You think I would considering the chain of events that followed. I do remember his wife's name, Donna. They attended mass, as we did, at Santa Spirito, and Mama and Papa knew them just well enough to smile and say hello on Sundays. Mama and Papa didn't know anyone well, besides Fra Domenico, and I believe that they preferred it that way. Papa was away a lot, and so when they were together they only had time for each other. Things may have changed if they had grown old together – love often changes in advanced years – but I like to think that they would have stayed the same adoring pair I remember.

The man at our door was in distress, he looked tired and his eyes were red and swollen from crying; Papa invited him in. He looked at Papa but he was talking to Mama. He told us that his wife was dying, and that he had four young children, and he was in desperate need of help to care for his wife.

"My wife is dying," he said, "and I have four young children. I am in desperate need of help to care for my poor wife."

Papa looked puzzled. "I understand, but why come here?" he asked. "It's true that my wife has some experience in caring for the sick, but how did you know that? Surely you must know someone more experienced and more familiar with you and your wife's situation. I don't..."

"She has the plague," he interrupted. Papa nodded his understanding, even those of means found it difficult getting care for plague victims. He continued, "Many people, many from our own neighborhood, sad to say, have died alone and unkempt, for nobody wants to come near them. Even in death the Sextons are the only ones who will deliver the body to sacred ground, and they can't be trusted to perform the task the way God intended unless they are well paid. It is well known in the Quarter that your wife, God bless her," he made the sign of the cross in the air, "is one of the few who is not afraid to go into a house where there is plague, and every time God has blessed her and protected her from getting the sickness. She has brought dignity and comfort to so many whom would have had neither. To many she has been a saint, you must be very proud."

Papa was visibly confused – it was apparent that Mama had not told Papa about her nursing plague victims – but he managed an awkward smile and a nod in acknowledgement of the man's praise of Mama. The man continued, "I cannot properly care for my beloved Donna. I have sent the children away for fear that they will get the sickness, but still I do not know how, and it is so ... hard ... Please Signora Demarco. She doesn't have long. She has the gavaccioli. She can't have more than a few days left..." His voice cracked and he fought back tears. Most people died within two or three days after the appearance of the gavaccioli – the swelling in the armpits and groin.

Mama grabbed her shawl, for it was a chilly night. Papa looked at her, a question in his eyes, Mama answered, "The plague got really bad for a few months while you were in Milan. It has gotten much better lately. There was nobody to care for the dying. What could I do? I had to help. I knew God would protect me. So many died alone, while others suffer indignities such as men caring for women when they aren't even married. I had to do something. I couldn't help everyone, but I had to do what I could. I have some training as a nurse, was I to just pretend I didn't when so many needed my help? Everyone is afraid to go near the stricken."

"And you are not afraid?" Papa asked softly.

"Yes, Sabastiano, I am afraid," Mama said, as she looked into Papa's big, brown eyes; he grabbed Mama and pulled her to his chest. I heard her whisper, "I love you," and then she said out loud, "Nobody should die alone, nobody. God will look after me. He always has. Now kiss me so I can go tend to poor Donna."

Papa obeyed, and then Mama gently pulled away from him. She said, "I'll be back in a few days."

Papa didn't want to let Mama go, but he had little choice. In desperation, he offered to go along, but Mama told him there was nothing for him to do; he knew she was right. I asked Mama if there was anything I could do. She told me to take care of Papa and to pray to Saint Sabastine to ward off the plague; I promised to do both. Then I kissed Mama goodbye – it was the last time I saw her standing – then she was off into the night with the man whose name I cannot remember.

The night after the man came for Mama, there came another knock at the door. This time it was the Duke's Swiss Guard, and once again Philipp was along. Philipp told us that the Duke believed that French invasion was imminent. The new French King, Louis XII, was outraged that Milan was never taken and was threatening to correct that oversight. Papa wasn't convinced that the threat was genuine, but agreed to go anyway. He sent me to San Marco to get word to Fra Domenico. In turn, Fra Domenico would contact Mama, and then look after her again while we were gone. Papa just assumed that I would want to go along again for the chance to learn more from Leonardo. I never told Papa what Leonardo really thought of my abilities; I didn't have the heart to disappoint him. So I went along to Milan. Thinking back, of course, I wish I had stayed home.

You know I think that Philipp might have been fond of me – in the small way a young man like that could be – because he shared some of his time with me and he was the only guard to accompany us on all three of our trips. He was a little more talkative than he had been on our previous trips. Perhaps it was because I was a little older and he related better to men than to boys, or maybe it was that battle was in the air and he was excited. I learned that he had a son – since I had seen him last – to go with his two daughters. I believe that it was when I was listening to Philipp talk about his children that I first looked forward to the thought of having my own. I still think about having more children, but now it is a backward thought.

The Duke was right about Louis XII; by the time we arrived in Milan, the French had already taken the city. The reason for their quick success was that Ludovico Sforza was in Innsbruck trying to enlist the aid of the Emperor of the Holy Roman Empire, Maximilian, and during the Duke's absence his trusted generals gave up the city without a fight. The French soon found themselves in trouble from the masses when they tried to extort taxes from them; the people along with some military support forced the French to retreat to the heavily fortified Castello, but not before they commandeered most of the city's armaments including Papa's cannon. With the Duke gone, the city gone, and his cannon gone, Papa saw little reason to stay in Milan. Then we found out that Leonardo had already fled the city for Venice – more reason not to stay. Finally, we heard a rumor that the French planned to march on Florence; now we knew we had to go home. We planned to rest up for a day and then head back to my city alone. Disappointed that they missed the invasion and the little fighting that there was, Philipp and the guardsmen were anxious to join the siege of the Castello with the hope that when the Duke returned there might still be a fight; the guardsmen would not be returning to Florence with us. They met up with the rest of their unit – which meant that they were now twelve in number – and we set up camp for the night. I remember thinking that I hoped they met up with the rest of the besiegers before the besieged found them; there weren't many in number but they were brave. Philipp told us that we could take the horses back to Florence.

From the reaction of the other guardsmen, I don't think Philipp had the authority to give us the animals, but he did so anyway. We were grateful for the favor; it would have been a long walk home.

Stories were going around that the Duke would soon be back in Milan and that he would rally the army and drive the French out of the Castello and the city. Unfortunately for Ludovico there was also the story that the French had not only raided the Duke's armaments, but also stolen most of his, and the city's, wealth. This meant that there was nothing to pay the army. So there was yet another story going around that said that the army – being made up of mostly condottieri and other mercenaries – would desert before fight if funds were not available. None of these rumors detracted Philipp or his fellow Swiss Guardsmen. Though their numbers were small, they were determined to fight. Philipp told me that there were other Swiss Guard units and the Duke's elite soldiers scattered around the city who were preparing to fight, regardless of payment or lack of leadership, and that he and his fellow guardsmen planned to meet up with them. I think that this might have just been Philipp's idealism getting the better of him. I had always heard that while the Swiss Guard were good, they generally followed the motto, "no gold, no Guard."

A few regular soldiers wandered into the Swiss camp, and since we were there, and these brave men were preparing for battle, Papa did what he always did; he helped anyone who needed armor or weapon repairs. Papa sharpened swords and halberds for the Swiss Guardsmen; their armor was in no need of repair. However, many of the regular soldiers who wandered into camp were ill-equipped. Papa worked for the rest of that day and most of the night, getting little sleep, doing what he could do – mending armor – to prepare men for battle. But the army never materialized; not enough soldiers had returned to mount a serious attack. The Swiss Guardsmen, true to the tradition of a soldier's discipline and bravery in the face of overwhelming odds, and despite the tradition of "no gold, no Guard," planned to engage the enemy, with the belief that they would meet up with the other units, and that the Duke would arrive with the main force of his army.

I slept a little that night, then just after dawn, we were riding out of the city not far from the Castello. Philipp and the Swiss Guardsmen set out an hour ahead of us. As we passed the great fortress – from a safe distance – Papa said that he was glad we were leaving, and that the French would not be held up in the Castello for long and that he feared that Florence may be next.

"I'm glad we are leaving, Lorenzo," Papa said. "The French won't be held up in the Castello for long, and Florence may be next. They may be angry at the loss of their ally, Savonarola and seek revenge on us. And with what Savonarola did to the city, I don't think we have physically recovered enough to mount a sufficient defense against an invasion, and we haven't recovered enough economically to raise the money to pay the condottieri." He paused then added, "I'm sorry I dragged you along this time. There was no need to put you in danger, and now that you are a man you could have looked after Mama."

"That's all right, Papa," I said, "You didn't know that Leonardo had fled the city, or that the French would be here."

"Yes, I know," Papa said, "But Philipp told us that war was coming to Milan, and I didn't take his word on the French threat seriously. I should have at least accepted that there was a good chance that they were right before I let you come along. There was really no need for…"

Papa stopped in mid-sentence, and pulled up his horse; he was looking off in the distance toward a clearing just up another fifty paces and off to the side of the road. I stopped and backed my horse next to Papa's and looked to see what had stolen his attention. About twenty French knights, surrounded less than half as many Swiss Guardsmen. The fighting was fierce; two guardsmen were already down, along with about a half-a-dozen French knights. The French were men-at-arms, and the Swiss Guardsmen were dismounted cavalry; their horses could be seen off to one side by a small pond. Perhaps the French, on patrol around the Castello had surprised the Swiss as they watered their horses. Papa motioned for us to get off of the road – on the opposite side as the conflict – and into the high brush and trees. We crept along slowly, out-of-sight, and as we neared the fight, sounds of battle could be heard – metal clashing against metal, voices shouting, cries of pain, along with various grunts and moans. As the sounds got louder we knew we were getting closer – dangerously close. We could have easily passed by unseen and been on our way, but curiosity drew us back to the road; we had to see what was happening. We dismounted and cautiously led the horses to a place where we could see across to the clearing, but still had some measure of cover from the brush. The action was in clear view. More men had fallen on both sides, but the French were taking the worst of it; the Swiss had fought to almost even numbers. All the combatants looked exhausted; their attacks were fierce, but their movements would slow after a strike, stealing valuable rest, and then they would hit again. Then suddenly, from the direction of the Castello came a dozen French cavalry; they crashed into battle overwhelming the odds. The valiant Swiss Guardsmen fell, one by one. We were about to move on when a slashing blow from a mounted attacker tore off the helmet of one of the final Swiss defenders, knocking him to the ground. The ferocity of the strike was what brought a pause to our retreat. At first we thought he had been decapitated, but he got up, obviously dazed and unable to continue to fight. He was weak and disorientated. He was defenseless. He was Philipp. I felt a strange pain in my gut, one like I had never experienced before. The cavalryman, who had struck down Philip, dismounted and wielded his sword, this time across my friend's chest, once again knocking him to the ground. Philip crawled a few feet to retrieve his sword, and then managed to use the weapon as a crutch to pull himself upright; he tried to fight, but he could hardly raise his sword. I wanted to look away, I wanted to leave, but I stayed and I watched.

The next strike from the Frenchman was cruel and deliberate, designed to torture and horrify, before bringing death. He cut Philipp just below the breastplate, not too deep, from one side to the other. Philipp fell to his knees just as much of his lower insides spilled onto the trampled grass and mud. If it wasn't real, if it wasn't Philipp, it might have been comical – like in a festival comedy – watching the pathetic desperation on someone's face as they tried, in vain, to gather up their insides and return them to the body. Philipp managed to get some pieces back in, but most of him was still hanging out or on the ground; he tried to hold his wound shut with one bloody hand and retrieve his parts with the other. The comic horror ended with a swift slashing blow from the Frenchmen's sword that mercifully lopped off Philipp's head.

I was angry, but I felt helpless, then suddenly I became violently ill; my knees buckled. Quickly, Papa hooked me around the waist with one arm, led the horses with his free hand, and took us back away from the road and further out-of-sight. It was there, in the relative safety of the brush that I violently heaved up everything that was in my stomach. Papa gently patted me on the back, and asked me if I was all right.

"Are you all right, Lorenzo?" Papa asked.

I nodded I was, and when I was able to clear my throat and speak, I cursed God for having to witness such a horrible act, then I asked, "Why did that make me so sick. It's not like I haven't seen death before. Maybe not worse, but surely I have seen things equally as repulsive...sickening..." Again I was sick, but this time nothing came out – I was empty. I felt like I too was going to lose my insides, but unlike Philipp, mine were going to come out my mouth. Finally the reflexive heaving subsided, leaving my throat and stomach, raw and sore.

"He was your friend," Papa said. "It's different when you know someone. This was the first time you have experienced death so personally. Plus it was a very unpleasant way to die."

I nodded, wiped my mouth, and said, "I guess we were friends, but I didn't know him that well. What's it going to be like to lose someone I really love?"

"Well, Lorenzo," Papa said, "since right now, I love everyone you love, I hope you don't find out too soon."

An honorable soldier's death is one that comes at the end of a great fight, defending or attacking the enemy for a glorious cause or personal honor. Perhaps in a small way, Philipp achieved that mortal distinction; he was fighting against great odds and died bravely. But in the greater sense, Philipp's death was unnecessary and meaningless. The majority of the Duke's army, fearing that there would not be enough funds to compensate them adequately, and knowing that they could not, or would not be allowed to rape and pillage Milan, never joined Ludovico Sforza, and many of those who had already rejoined him deserted him. There was no great battle for the city. The French simply came out of the Castello and captured the Duke. Watching my friend disemboweled then decapitated, was my first real taste of death, and it was just the beginning. I would lose a lot of people in my life.

We returned to my city on a warm spring evening. Exhausted and anxious to get home, we took the straightest course to the Santo Spirito Quarter, and headed down the Via dei Serragli. When we got home, Papa went right inside; I took the horses to the stables around the corner from the shop. When I got back and went inside, to no surprise, Fra Domenico was sitting at the table. What was a surprise was that Papa was sitting with his head in his hands, staring down at the floor. I didn't have to ask or wait long to find out what was going on. Fra Domenico told me my mama was dying; she had been stricken with the plague after attending to Donna.

"Your mama's dying, Lorenzo," Fra Domenico said gravely. "She was stricken with the plague after attending to Donna. I'm afraid she doesn't have much longer. She has the fever and the gavaccioli under both arms and, God forgive me, I had to attend to her personal needs, there are not many women like Katarina who will dare to care for other women who are stricken with the plague, so I know that your mama also has the gavaccioli on her groin." He made the sign of the cross in the air, and continued, "She doesn't have any of the black circles, anywhere that I saw, on her body, but sometimes it's like that."

"How much longer do you think she has?" I asked.

"God only knows," said Fra Domenico. "She should have been dead already, once you get the gavaccioli it usually isn't very long after that, but she refuses to let go. She is so weak. I think she has been struggling to hang on until you got back, so she could say goodbye, but the struggle has been so hard on her. She has suffered so much. I tried to give her permission to die. I told her that God was waiting for her, and he would not blame her if she let go of this life, and the pain. I told her that you wouldn't blame her either, that you wouldn't want her to suffer so." Fra Domenico fought back tears and shook his round face, and then added, "Too many good people have died. I fear that we are being punished by God for embracing Savonarola, or maybe it is for forsaking him. It is hard to know the mind of God."

"God," I snapped. I think I was too shocked to feel the pain just yet. My first response was bitterness. I said, "Why did God do this to my mama. You tell me Fra Domenico. You know him best, obviously better than me. Look at all that Mama did for him, for people who were in need, without compensation, because she thought it was the right thing to do, what God wanted her to do. So she believed that he would protect her. I never knew anyone more pious, more worthy of God's protection and love. She doesn't deserve this." I was getting a little angry. I said, "There are so many horrible people, people who hate, lie, steal, even kill. Why don't they just get this? Why does God punish the good with the bad?"

"We can't blame God for our personal pain," Fra Domenico pleaded. "He has a greater plan for all of us, and we don't always see, or understand what, or why he does what he does. You should be praying to Saint Sabastine to ward off ..."

"Ward off!" I barked. "I think it's a little to late to ward off the plague. It's too," then I whispered, "It's too late."

"Lorenzo," Papa said softly, "you must be strong... strong for me, and for Mama. You are like her, your passions run a little colder than mine, but when you feel, you seem to feel anger instead of pain. But you must control your anger, and I must control my pain. She mustn't see us like this. We both must be strong for her."

I saw how hurt Papa was and I was ashamed of my anger. I didn't totally understand it – not then or ever in my life – but Papa was right, I tend to feel anger instead of pain. I think I knew that if I had ever let my anger go, the pain would fill the void and it would be unbearable. But if I couldn't control it, at least I could hide it, for Mama.

I nodded to Papa that I understood and he said, "Well then, we should go in and see her." Then Papa's voice cracked with emotion, he said, "We have to give your mama permission to die."

The light from a single candle next to the bed shined a flickering, yellow glow over Mama. She was lying so still and quiet, at first I thought that we were too late, but slowly her eyes opened. Perhaps my memory is playing benevolent tricks on me, but I swear she looked beautiful. She was a little paler and gaunter than normal, but somehow, the fairer skin just made her look more angelic, and the gauntness just brought out her check bones and thin lovely features. When she saw us, she smiled slightly, and her beautiful gray-blue eyes squinted, and then she raised her hand slowly. We rushed to her side; I went to the far side, and Papa fell to his knees next to Mama on the near side. Fra Domenico went to the x-chair – he must have brought it in some time earlier – picked up his Bible off the seat, sat down, and began praying; he made the sign of the cross in the air. Mama looked at me, and made me promise to take care of Papa.

"Promise me that you will take care of your papa," Mama said in a weak voice.

"Yes, Mama, I promise," I said quietly.

"Now I don't want you to feel bad," she said. "It's just my turn to die, but we will all be together soon." She struggled to swallow, and then said, "This really isn't so bad. There is no pain."

Papa struggled to hold it in, but began to weep softly; Mama was so far gone, I don't think she noticed.

"Now give me a kiss," Mama said.

I leaned down and kissed her; her breath was shallow and her lips were cold. She was so weak, that I barely felt any pressure from her lips. I could tell that Papa wanted to say something to her, but every time he tried, he had to choke down tears. Finally, he buried his head in Mama's chest to hide his pain. She managed to put her hand on the back of Papa's head, and gently stroked his hair.

I remember the last thing I said to her. It seemed very important at the time that I say something. I knew it had to be short and simple; Mama was too far-gone to understand anything else. Maybe I forced the words. Maybe I should have just let it end, but I said, "Thank you for giving me my life. Goodbye, Mama." Just after I spoke, she died; her hand fell from off of Papa's head. Fra Domenico made the sign of the cross in the air and whispered a prayer, then it was quiet. Quiet until Papa looked up to confirm the reason Mama had stopped stroking his hair.

Seeing that she was gone – the light was out of her beautiful gray-blue eyes – Papa murmured, "God, no, please, God, no. You can't take her from me. Katarina, you can't leave me." The pain in his voice, I will never forget. He gently kissed Mama's lips, and closed her eyes, and then the overwhelming pain from the realization that he would never see her smile again, never be with her again, never hold her again, never kiss her again, and never grow old with her, suddenly exploded from him like a cannon blast. He screamed at the top of his voice, "God, No!"

Fra Domenico jumped from the chair. I jumped too, and felt chills throughout my body; the sound of his pain echoed in my head. I can still hear it. Then Papa fell on Mama's lifeless body, crying – uncontrollably sobbing. I saw his heart break right there in that room, when Mama died. He sat Mama's body up, and tried to will her, through his pain, to come back to life. He shook her and begged her to wake up, like she was just in some deep sleep. "Katarina," he called out through his tears. He implored her, he begged her, "Katarina, come back to me. What am I to do without you?" Finally, Fra Domenico put his hands on Papa's shoulders. Thankfully, this simple gesture brought him back. Papa, ever so gently, lowered Mama's body back down on the bed, and somehow managed to pull his insufferable pain back inside himself. He stopped crying, wiped his face and whispered softly, "Goodbye my love, goodbye Katarina."

Surprisingly, my tears stayed inside. As Papa said, I took after Mama; I kept my pain to myself. Somehow, at that moment, it would have seemed selfish to let out my pain, when it was Papa who was struck with the deeper wound. Looking back, maybe I just knew that if I started to cry, I might never have been able to stop.

Chapter IV

It was a typically beautiful day in my city; the sun was shining, it was warm, but not hot – at least not to a native Florentine – a light breeze blew down through the valley, and people were going about their business as usual, except for us – we buried Mama. The sextons had little compassion, and even less scruples, so not only did Papa have to pay a ridiculous amount for their services, but we also – at least one of us at all times – had to watch over Mama's body until it was finally laid to rest. If we hadn't kept watch, the sextons had a tendency to drop the bodies of plague victims in the nearest grave whether it was meant for a rich man or a pauper, one person or many, and they didn't care if the ground was sanctified or unconsecrated soil. When the plague was really bad, the sextons would just stack bodies and burn them. It was at this time that I learned that Bramante's suspicions were truly correct; Papa was very wealthy. Papa told me that he had more money than he knew what to do with.

"I have more money than I know what to do with, Lorenzo," Papa said. "There is a lot in the bank. A lot even though I, like many others, lost money when the Medici Bank closed. That certainly made me less trusting of the bankers in this city, so I spread the money out to several banks, so if one closes I'll still have money in the others. But despite all my doubts in the system, I was still putting it away regularly until I realized that I had put in so much that if I continued, I would soon be mistaken for a wealthy man."

"But apparently, you are a wealthy man, Papa," I said.

"Apparently, yes," Papa said, "but actually I'm just a common man, who happens to have accumulated a lot of money. The difference is that I don't want it and I don't know how to spend it. Unfortunately, there are plenty or people out there who are willing to help me out with this little problem. So I had to stop putting money in the bank, because there are certain people out there, despite claims of privacy by the bankers, who find out who has money and who doesn't even if you don't spend a lot or live extravagantly..."

"Bramante," I interrupted. "That's why he has..."

"Yes, Lorenzo," it was Papa's turn to interrupt. "I think he knows about the ten thousand ducats I have spread around Florence, but as long as I don't admit that I have it, he won't admit he knows about it. That would prove that he has spies in the banks. So we play little games where he tries to get me to admit that I have money, and I try to get him to admit that he already knows I have money. I'm not really sure how he intends to get his hands on it, even if I should admit it. I'm sure he knows nothing of the few thousand I have in the cellar."

"A few thousand!" I exclaimed.

You have to remember that this was when a single ducat or gold florin would be a week's wages for most skilled craftsmen, or a month's wages for an unskilled worker. Before all that Spanish gold came in and devaluated coins across the continent. But still, thirteen thousand ducats is a lot of money – enough to make a man rich.

"Yes," Papa said, a little embarrassed. "There is almost a thousand gold florin, and about another three thousand ducats down there."

"That's almost four thousand," I said, still in shock.

"Well, it's more like five thousand," Papa interrupted. "I only count the big coins. There are several bags of small silver coins, mainly grossi and denari. I haven't even counted the big coins lately, not since before our first trip to Milan when the Duke paid me an advance of a hundred ducats."

"A hundred!" I exclaimed.

"Yes," Papa said. "Ridiculous isn't it, and that was just the advance, of course I didn't get the full amount. The invasion cut off the Duke's funds and I'm sure many were never paid anything. That's why so many deserted him in the end. But I knew from experience that kings or dukes at war can lose and if you don't get paid up front, there may be nobody there to pay you when it's over. Well, at least I got half."

"But, Papa," I asked, "If you didn't need the money, why did you insist on getting half up front?"

"Actually, I insisted on getting paid up front, but only got half," Papa said. Then he explained, "This is something your Grandfather Melchoir taught me. When dealing with the aristocracy or kings, or even with the church, you have to demand payment up front and always overcharge. You must overcharge them because they are superior in attitude, and while they are concerned with budgets, taxes and state expenses, they don't care, or aren't supposed to care about wages or any earned money. So if you ask for a ridiculous amount of money, they pay it because they assume that you do care about making money, and therefore you would only ask what you think that you could get compared to others of your skill level. To their way of thinking, the more you get for a job, the better you must be. For only a fool would ask more than their worth and risk not getting anything."

"And since they want the best," I said, "They seek out the ones who charge the most."

"Right," Papa said. "And now for the other half. You have to demand payment up front. The reason for this is to show that, or make the appearance that, you need money and care about getting paid because you need it, and therefore you are, no matter how much you make, just another common laborer. This puts you in your place as one of the ordinary folk who needs to work to live."

"That's crazy," I said with a slight laugh.

Papa smiled, it was the first time he had smiled since Mama died, and one of the last times I remember ever seeing him smile – which is saying a lot for a man who used to smile with such ease. He said, "Sometimes, when I really didn't want to leave Mama, I would ask for four times the going rate, thinking surely that this king wouldn't pay such an outrageous amount and find an equally competent gunmaker at a reasonable cost, but every time I tried this it backfired. They came up with the money and I would simply have to turn them down." I laughed, and he added, still smiling, "Then sometimes they would offer me more."

We both laughed hard and Papa lifted me up, hugged me, kissed me on both cheeks, and reminded me of how big I was getting. Actually I was full-grown at that time. Then, the moment passed and we remembered what we had done that morning, and what was left to do; Papa used his wealth to pay for two special masses for Mama, and we were to attend one of them. The mass was important to the fate of Mama's soul, at least that's what we believed at the time; I'm not so sure I believe it now. It was presumed, and perpetuated by the church, that a special service preformed by the clergy, for a large sum of course, on behalf of the deceased would assure the departed would have a place in heaven. If this were true, I guess heaven is filled with mostly rich people, because the poor could not afford the service. Even if we hadn't believed in the need for the mass, we would have probably done it anyway, because it was just the way things were done. If you had the money you didn't take chances with the eternal fate of your loved one; you assumed that the church might be right. It certainly was a profitable notion for the church.

We attended the second mass, the one held at San Marco, and officiated by Fra Domenico; the first mass was held at our church, San Spirito. This was uncommon, at least for a man who was supposed to be of moderate means, and there was talk. One of the people listening to this talk was Tommaso Bramante; Bramante attended the service at San Marco. He told Papa that it was a beautiful service for a beautiful lady.

"It was a beautiful service for a beautiful lady, huh?" said Bramante, as we walked out of the church; we stopped on the steps to receive the respects of those who attended the service. Once outside, he added, "I think it was even better than the one at San Spirito."

Papa didn't have the patience he normally did to be patronized by Bramante, or to play any of his clever games intended to get Papa to admit to his wealth. So Papa was curt in his response, "So that's your way of telling me that you attended both services. Why doesn't that surprise me? Is this where I'm supposed to be touched, or impressed with the apparent respect you have shown Katarina?"

Bramante just laughed. "Well I can't resist a free meal," he said. "And I must say the food at San Spirito was delicious and it was quite generous of you, but we both know that a good mass needs parishioners and there is no better way to attract the local rabble than to offer a free meal, huh?"

"Yes," Papa said. "So you have just attested to."

Bramante – a man so low that he was incapable of being offended – just laughed again, and said, "Well, at least I knew the great lady, that's more than I can say for most of these bums." He looked around as if to see if anyone had heard what he had said, and then he added, "Speaking of food, I am sure this banquet will be even grander than the one at San Spirito. After all, grander venue, grander amenities, huh?"

"I'm sure you will let me know," Papa said, and then he began to shake hands and thank the people as they came out of San Marco.

Bramante gave Papa a puzzled look, and said, "So, you are not attending?" Then he smiled and added, "Such generosity from a poor gunmaker, or perhaps not so poor? Huh?" He started to walk away, and then he paused to say to me, "Lorenzo, we must continue your lessons, after a respectable time of mourning, of course. But not too long, I'm sure your mama wouldn't want you to pine your life away. And remember, adversity makes for good muse. I'll be calling on you."

Bramante was true to his word – where profit was to be found, I'm sure he always was – but I limited the amount of time I spent with him despite his protests. Looking back, I'm not sure why I didn't just stop seeing him altogether. I guess, despite Leonardo's opinion, I still wanted to believe that I had a chance as an artist. I completely abandoned my mama's wish for me to join the monastery at San Marco; I only saw Fra Domenico as a friend, and never again as a teacher. Funny, but he never said a word about me leaving my studies until some years later. So after I gave up my spiritual training, and reduced the amount of hours I put into my art, I suddenly had a void of time in my life. This void would be filled by the most unlikely of choices offered by a most unlikely source.

In the months that followed Mama's death, Papa went from working – at nothing – in his shop for days without rest, to sleeping in – not getting up at all even to eat – for days, and then he would repeat the cycle. Then one day, after a three-day nap, Papa got up came up to me, lifted me up, hugged me, kissed me on both cheeks, reminded me of how big I was, and then announced that I was to learn from him the art of war. This was a complete surprise because I still believed that he wanted me to be an artist; I never expected him to want me to be a soldier. I would find that I was much better at the latter than I was at the former.

We began training in the shop; we cleared enough space to move about freely and practiced day and night at trying to kill each other. There I learned to use the pike and sword. I found that I was a natural with a light, double-edged broadsword and a dagger. I was best when I could use my quickness and move around to attack and avoid strikes. The heavy, two-handed broadsword was a little much for me to handle, but to my amazement papa handled it with ease, showing incredible strength and agility, but he seemed to be good handling every weapon. He told me that it only seemed that he was good at everything because he only taught me with the weapons in which he was most proficient. This was partly true; we never trained with common weapons such as the mace, the battleaxe, the long bow, nor the sling. I rarely used a shield; I felt that it slowed me down. Trading defense for offensive agility would become my style of fighting. Sometimes we would go to the field were the militia, when called upon, would practice. This was where I learned the crossbow, arquebus, and the musket. I was a pretty good shot with the arquebus. The musket was a little heavy for me, and I thought the crossbow was difficult to load and even more time consuming to load than the gun. Of course, Papa was a master at all three. I really liked the matchlock guns, but there was a problem; they were unreliable when the weather was damp or wet because it would be difficult or impossible to light the match. Papa told me that improvements were being made regularly, and soon, he believed, firearms would be the primary weapon for the infantry because they were easy to use, relatively inexpensive to make, and could be manufactured in mass quantities. He told me about the wheellock and about barrel riffling far before they became a common reality.

We also practiced artillery. We talked strategy like we did on the road to Milan, and I learned to calculate range; I did the numbers at home instead of my old Biblical translations, and on the field where I practiced firing a small falcon. Papa would give the commands and I would perform all of the firing procedures.

"Brush your vent!" Papa barked, and I cleaned off the hole where the charge was lit.

"Worm your bore!" he said, and I cleaned the bore of debris.

That was followed by the command, "Wet sponge your bore!" where I further clean the shaft with a wet sponge.

"Stop the vent!" meant to seal the vent as I cleaned the bore again; this was done to prevent any air from getting down in the breach that might keep an old spark of powder burning or hot.

Again he commanded, "Wet sponge your bore!" This time followed by, "Dry sponge the bore!"

"Load powder!" was the next command. I gently pushed in the pre-measured charge with the ramrod.

He followed with, "Load projectile!" and set the shot with the ramrod.

"Pick charge!" meant to pick the powder charge wrapper through the vent to make it easier to light.

When I was set, I answered, "Charge is picked!"

"Prime!" was the next order. I poured priming powder into the vent, then answered, "Gun is primed and ready!"

"Ready to fire!" he barked, followed by the command, "Fire!"

Right after I fired, a neat, well dressed man rode up on a well groomed horse, dismounted several yards behind us, and walked over to us. He was in his early thirties, thin, and had gaunt features. What was most prominent was his bony forehead, which stood out because he combed his thin, jet black hair straight back over his head. The shot we fired was right on target, and this impressed the stranger. He was very cordial and complimented Papa on his gunnery skills and wondered how such a proficient and obviously experienced artilleryman could have escaped his notice.

"How could such a proficient and obviously experienced artilleryman as you have escaped my notice?" he asked without asking. He smiled and continued, "In my service with the Signora, it has been my duty to organize and prepare our defensive capabilities. A man such as yourself could be of great service to Florence."

Papa explained that, "I have never really been a soldier. I am a gunmaker and have worked mainly abroad. But since I make cannons, it is only reasonable that I know how to operate them in order to better understand and improve my craft."

"Yes, that's very practical, I like that," he said. Then he added, "Well I guess we just missed out on your services, but what of this young man you are training, he seems to be of a good age. How old are you, young man?"

"I am eighteen," I replied.

"Eighteen is a good age indeed," he said. "We may need you if I am not successful. You see I'm going to Paris to talk with the French and try to convince them to stay out of Florence this time. I plan to make it clear that we will not be as easy a target as Milan, or as we were when Savonarola was in control of the city."

I could tell that with his last words, he was subtly searching for our loyalties – how did we feel about the late Savonarola. We never said a word, but he was very perceptive and knew at once by our expressions and posturing that we were not unhappy with the change in power in my city. Pleased by what he saw, he offered a smile and a hand to Papa and said, "My name is Niccolò and I am Secretary to the Magistracy, and I am currently acting as an ambassador to France. I will be crossing the Alps in two weeks."

"I am Sabastiano Demarco," Papa said. "And this is my son, Lorenzo."

I too was offered a smile and a firm handshake. He said, "I will be certainly looking for you when I get back, especially if I can't convince the French to stay away from Florence." Then he went back for his horse, climbed on, and as if in an after thought, just before he rode off, he said, "If I don't come looking for you, Lorenzo, come look for me. Just contact any city official, everybody in government knows me, and tell them you are looking for Niccolò Machiavelli and they will tell you where you can find me. Farewell." Then he rode off.

I don't know if it was something Machiavelli did in Paris or some other reason, but Louis XII never attacked my city. Perhaps it would have been better for Papa and me, if Louis had invaded because the training that had kept our minds off of Mama was beginning to lose its' effectiveness as a distraction. Papa started getting depressed and once again he slept away days at a time. When he awoke he began looking for a new diversion; the Pope would provide just what he needed. Again, Pope Alexander VI actions would directly affect my life. At the end of the fifteenth century, the Pope called for a year of jubilee in 1500, and asked all good men to go and fight the infidel. Papa saw this as his chance to escape his pain, and as an opportunity to fulfill one of his personal ambitions – to fight the Turks. I told myself that I would go along to look after Papa, but looking back, I too needed another distraction – an outlet for the bitterness I felt and anger at God for taking my mama. I also think I felt some anxious anticipation to put to use some of the training in which I had worked at so hard; I wanted to see what I could do.

I knew little about the Turks, mostly I believed what Papa told me – they were infidels, they were spreading into Christian lands, and they even invaded Italy at Ottoranto just two years before I was born. Looking back, I guess I never really hated the Turks like Papa, but it was enough that Papa did; the enemy of the father is the enemy of the son. We had the motivation, justification, and the training to fight, so we only needed two more things – battle armor and a war. Of course, Papa took care of the armor. For me, he made only the minimal amount of protection to utilize my fighting strengths – speed and agility. The light, perfect fitting armor, allowed me to move freely – almost as good as if I were wearing none – but still protected my sensitive areas like my chest, head, and groin. His armor was a little heavier than mine; he was still quick and agile, but he knew his age would not allow him to survive a sustained fight, so he opted for more protection. He also assumed that he would not be in the front lines, but back firing cannon, therefore more likely to need heavier armor for protection from opposing cannon shot and exploding shells. He was also bulkier and stronger than me, making him more able to carry the heavier armor. We also had matching shields, they were round, not too large or heavy, with a simple raised cross and a lily on the front side – the emblem of Florence – but they would be mainly for show; I rarely used my shield and Papa never had the chance to use his.

When it came to our weapons, Papa could have made them too, but he wanted us to have the best, so he had them custom made by the best sword maker in Florence. We didn't bother with fancy ornaments like expensive jewels or custom engravings, we just got the best functional weapons available; Papa supervised the process. Like my armor, my light, double-edged broadsword was custom made for my fighting style, made from the finest materials; it was strong, razor sharp, and balanced perfectly. The only ornamentation on the weapon was a raised cross and a small lily on the handgrip that matched the cross and lily on my shield. Papa also made me a dagger that was engraved with my initials. It had a large red ruby mounted on the handle near the blade, and four rhinestones – one for each finger – strategically placed not for show but to enhance the grip of the weapon.

We trained together for weeks with our new armor and weapons, and I found that I was getting to be quite good, when we got the last thing we needed to fight – a war. The Venetians were desperately seeking men to outfit their ships for an on-going clash with the Turks in the Southern Adriatic and Ionian Seas, where Venice still maintained several outposts on various islands, once controlled by the Greeks. The fighting had been going on so long that it was getting hard for the Venetians to find good fighting men from their city and territory; mercenaries were welcome.

Papa signed us up as marines, and since we had our own armor and weapons, and Papa had vast experience with artillery, it was easy to get us on board a ship as officers; Papa was a captain of artillery and I was a lieutenant. Papa said that if he had just signed us on as ordinary sailors, then we would probably have been assigned as oarsmen, and he didn't want to row up and down the Adriatic chasing the Turks, he wanted a chance to do some real fighting. Be careful what you wish for.

There was one thing we needed to do before we could go, and that was to make arrangements to have the shop looked after. So Papa invited Fra Domenico over for dinner, told him that we were leaving to fight the Turks, and then after we ate he asked Fra Domenico to look after things while we were gone.

"Will you look after things while we are gone?" asked Papa.

Fra Domenico sat in the x-chair, and as always, it creaked from his weight. He said, "Of course I will, Sabastiano, but I will need some help. I can't be here night and day. The other times, Katarina was always… the place will be empty…"

Papa put a small pouch on the table with the top open so it was clear what was inside – coins, lots of coins. Fra Domenico's eyes widened, and Papa explained, "Here is a hundred gold Florin, fifty to cover your expenses in hiring anyone you need to help in your absence, and another fifty for you and San Marco. Of course that is just a suggestion; you can use the money how you see fit and necessary."

Fra Domenico was shocked. "Where did you…" he began. Then he tried again, "I always thought… or I heard… but this must be most of your…"

"Don't concern yourself with my expenses," Papa interrupted. "Can you do it? Can you keep this place unmolested until I or Lorenzo get back?"

"Of course," Fra Domenico stammered. "I would have done as you asked without payment, we are friends. But obviously you are worried about something or someone to have offered me so much, for so little a task."

Papa looked at me, and I understood his meaning when he said, "Let's just say that I consider it possible that someone may, thinking there is something of value here, and knowing I am gone, come looking around here. That is why I am trying to leave as quietly as possible. Maybe it will be a few weeks before anyone even knows I am gone. It's not like someone should be looking for us, or that we will be missed."

Fra Domenico nodded that he understood, then slowly picked up the bag of coins and stared inside. While he was distracted by the glow of gold, I whispered to Papa, "If you suspect that Bramante knows of your wealth, don't you think it would be better to just put all of your money in a bank?"

"I have thought of that," Papa whispered, "and have reluctantly invested most of what I had been hiding here. As you have noted, it hardly makes sense to hide it from Bramante now, but I still don't totally trust the banks. If something happens to me, seek out the old Jew, Abraham. He is the only banker I trust. He has control over most of my funds and knows where I have invested the rest. But just in case, I left about two hundred ducats down there for you, where I showed you." Papa motioned toward the cellar.

"Then why the protection?" I asked quietly. "If the money isn't here?"

"Bramante doesn't know nothing's here," Papa whispered. "And I don't want him tearing up the place if he gets in and finds only the hundred and believes that there has to be more.

"I can't say that I approve of your fighting with the Venetians," Fra Domenico said, shaking off his brief spout with gold fever. "You know those people fight and kill just for trade rights and territory, not for our God. They only use God to justify their actions when it's necessary and to gain recruits, fools who…"

Fra Domenico stopped short, but Papa finished his thought. "Fools who think they are doing God's work, when they are actually just protecting Venetian interests," Papa said. "Fools like me? Well I know why they fight, and I don't care. Any chance, no matter why it's done, to push back the infidel, is a victory for us – a victory for God."

Fra Domenico nodded, and said, "Yes, with that I must agree." Then he stood up and started for the door. "I must go now and make preparations, for you haven't given me much time." Then he smiled, and shaking the bag of coins he added, "But you've certainly given me enough reasons to try. I will put this to good use. God bless you."

"I know you will," Papa said. Then he added, "And I hope he will."

"Am I going to be seeing you again before you go?" asked Fra Domenico.

"Probably not," Papa answered. "Like I said, I want to sneak away quietly, without incident or long goodbyes."

A sudden deep sadness came over the big man's, round face – a look of pain that told me that he was worried that he may never see us again. "We'll be back," I said with deliberate certainty. "You can count on it."

"God bless you, Lorenzo," Fra Domenico said as tears formed in his eyes. Then he buried me in his chest with a big hug, and then kissed me on both cheeks. Then he turned to Papa and said, "You too, Sabastiano, God bless you." He continued to fight back tears, cleared his throat, and said, "I will pray for you that God will protect you and bless you both, who go to do his work." He made the sign of the cross in the air.

"Thank you," Papa and I both said together. I could tell that Papa was also becoming emotional – his voice cracked. I guess despite their arguments, Papa loved Fra Domenico just about as much as I did. It would be more than two years, before I would see my Dominican friend again.

Chapter V

W e were off of the coast near the Venetian stronghold at Modon, the winds were up, and Captain Grimani had the fire of battle in his eyes; we spotted the enemy fleet. For hours we paralleled their course, keeping our distance – just out of gunnery range – maintaining their speed, heading north by northwest away from Modon, and keeping them pinned against the coast. Then suddenly Grimani gave the order and we turned into them. We bore down on them, oars flying and sails up. Outnumbered in ships, but not in guile and courage, we came at them hard and fast, and being the cowardly infidels they are, they turned and ran – they ran for the safety of the port at Porto Longo," said Johann Holper.

Johann was a big, burly, exceptionally strong man, with blonde wavy hair and a full beard to match. He smiled and laughed easy, even when he was in a fight for his life, and as a German mercenary, he was often in deadly combat; I think he enjoyed it, more than me, and in those early days he was certainly without the guilt. He was only a couple of years older than me, but his experience as a soldier made him seem much older. He was on board as a marine, like Papa and I, and he held the rank of Sergeant. He was telling the story of events that led to our current situation with the Turks. As he spoke, I could tell that many of the young Venetian sailors were having trouble understanding his Italian, so I began to translate for him. He continued, "After days of waiting for them to come out of the harbor, Grimani decided to move north, up the coast and away from Porto Longo, in an effort to lure the rats out of their hole – it worked. We had a hundred and twenty some ships against their more than two hundred, but like now, ours were bigger and better manned." A few cheers and exclamations of affirmation came from his audience, as he continued, "Again, with the wind at our backs, we began to bear down on the enemy fleet. Just as the Trumpets sounded for battle, the great Commander Andrea Loredan sailed up from Corfu to join the fight. A great cheer went up from the fleet of 'Loredan, Loredan!' Of course, Grimani offered the great man his choice of ships to lead the attack. The Commander picked the big round ship, the Pandora as his flagship and chose one of the largest galleys, the Po, to sail at his side. The two great ships, with the legendary Andrea Loredan at the helm of the Pandora headed out in front of the fleet toward the enemy.

"The Commander's seaman ship was so superior that soon the Pandora and the Po were way out front and bearing down hard on the Turks. The Pandora fired first, a deafening blast – terrifying the enemy – destroying a small Turkish Dhow with a shell that exploded on her deck. Another roar went up from the fleet for, 'Loredan, Loredan!' The Turks, forced to fight or die, with their backs to the coast and nowhere to run reluctantly engaged the Pandora and the Po. They unleashed the fury of a thousand guns on the two ships. The smoke from the blasts filled the skies, and for a moment, we could not see the two Venetian ships. Then the Pandora burst through the smoke, her guns firing. Another roar went up from the fleet for, 'Loredan, Loredan!' The cheers spurred on the Commander; he could be seen waving his hat to the fleet as he sailed into hell.

"Then Loredan picked out the largest of the Turkish ships, two great Turkish galleys, and turned his two great vessels dead reckoning on the enemy. He pounded their best into submission and when the battle was nearly won, he ordered grappling hooks and prepared to board the enemy's ships to finish them off. Suddenly, with grappling hooks in place, the Turkish galley burst into flames, obviously a desperate attempt to bring down the Pandora with her own self-destruction. Unbelievably, the cowardly ploy was successful.

"Realizing what was happening, Loredan ordered a retreat. The crews of the great ships struggled, in vain, to free themselves from the enemy vessels. We watched in horror as first the Pandora, and then the Po, each tangled up in grappling chains with a flaming Turkish galley, caught fire. The Turkish cowards sent ships to rescue their men, but only taunted our brave men, as each man made the mortal choice to burn to death or drown in the merciless sea. The wind had died down and there was no time to set oars, so the fleet watched in dismay, helpless to come to their aid. We saw the brave Commander Loredan standing on the bow of his ship, fighting until the end, loading and firing a cannon all by himself, still defiant, determined to take as many of them with him as he could. Finally, the Turks swarmed his flaming vessel like bees around a hive. Loredan was hit by a blast that knocked him off his feet; miraculously he managed to get up, load and fire yet again. Then, with no place to hide, the flames finally did what the Turkish guns could not – the great Commander was consumed in fire and then fell in the sea. The Turks turned their taunts on us as they rescued their men from the water and killed ours, and then they mutilated the bodies of our brave Christian brothers and hung them from their masts."

Johann went on to describe further atrocities involving more mutilation and other Turkish tortures that he said were created just for Christian captives. His morbid descriptions were so colorful, graphic, and explicit that I had to rely on the vocabulary I learned from the Swiss Guardsmen to translate many of the words. I could tell that Johann was deliberately trying to scare the younger, inexperienced recruits, with his vivid tales of torture, and it worked on many of the men – some turned pale, while others fought back sickness. I wondered how much of his story was accurate, and what was just for effect. Papa just shook his head and walked back to his post on the bow.

In truth, the great battle Johann described was hardly a battle at all. Actually, the two fleets never engaged in an all out conflict. There were only a few skirmishes including the one Johann described involving Commander Loredan. More Turkish vessels were lost than Venetian, but Grimani failed to destroy the Turkish fleet as he had promised. The goal of the Turks was never to destroy the Venetian fleet, but to reinforce the besiegers at Lepanto – a Venetian stronghold – with artillery. This, the Turks were able to do; by alluding the Venetian fleet and keeping losses to a minimum, they were able to get to Lepanto with their load of weapons. Seeing there was no hope for reinforcement and knowing that the besiegers now had cannon, the Lepanto garrison surrendered. Captain General Grimani was called back to Venice in disgrace; he was arrested and put in chains. Girolamo Contarini took over command of the fleet as interim commander – and was in charge when Papa and I joined the flotilla – until a new captain general could be chosen back in Venice.

Our ship was commanded by Captain Donato, and she was called the *Shivare*. The *Shivare* was a light galley with about one hundred oarsmen; she was actually a few men short of a full crew, there should be three men to an oar, but several oars were manned by only two. Manpower shortages had left us light, so when speed was important some of the marines joined in the rowing. The rest of the ships company consisted of about fifty men – mostly marines, with a handful of sailors including the captain. The *Shivare* had only ten guns – six mounted aft, and four astern. Papa was in charge of them all, but when he was manning the bow guns, I was in command of the stern guns.

When Johann finally finished telling his tales, he disbanded his audience, and then motioned for me to join him. We walked along the deck – from the stern to the bow – and the big man thanked me for helping him with the translation. He said he was learning Italian, but admitted that he still needed a few lessons, in which I offered my services. We spoke in German, and he told me that I sounded like a German monk.

"You sound like a German monk," Johann said. "From your vocabulary, it sounds like you just walked out of a German monastery."

"That's because I learned German from my mama," I said. I felt a little melancholy, being reminded of Mama, but I shook it off and continued, "My mama was German, so she taught me her native tongue. We often practiced vocabulary by translating the Bible, from Latin, to Italian, and then to German – I was a monastic student for many years."

Johann laughed – a big burly roar – and then he slapped me on the back, almost knocking me over. He said, "All right, Maus, I guess I will have to teach you how the real people talk, and you can teach me how real Italians talk."

"It's a deal, Orso," I said.

"Orso?" Johann asked.

"It means bear," I said and he laughed – another big burly roar. We reached the bow, stopped, and I said, "I've been told that I have a gift for learning languages. It ought to be interesting trying to teach language to someone." I paused a moment, and then I added, "By the way, my actual name is Lorenzo, Lorenzo Demarco from Florence."

"Lorenzo the Maus from Florence," he said with a broad smile. "And I am Johann Holper the Orso from some place in Germany."

The wind was light, but steady, blowing in the direction of the coast, which was a sign that it was afternoon. The air was warm and thick and smelled like boiled eggs; I could feel the dampness on my skin and taste the salt on my tongue. With the wind behind us, it was our chance to attack; the Turkish fleet was once again hugging the coast, and hiding in bays and inlets. As we walked up, Papa was looking out in the direction of the Bay of Navarino where several Turkish galleys were anchored.

"They're not coming out," Johann said. "They would be fools to try. And with these winds, they won't be getting any reinforcements from their big ships to the south. We should take advantage of the situation, don't you think Captain Demarco?"

"I think we would be fools to go in there," Papa answered. "But if they wanted to come out, why couldn't they just row out?"

Johann laughed and said, "I guess you're not a sailing man. With the winds in our favor we could run circles around them." Papa nodded that he understood, then Johann added, "Say, I hope your artillery experience is not as limited."

It was Papa's turn to laugh. He answered, "I've been making cannon since before you were born. I've seen them in action and have fired them in battle, and I have trained hundreds of others to be artillerymen."

"Well, that's good enough for me," Johann said. Then he added, "But have you ever fired a cannon shipboard?"

I think Papa was tempted to save his honor, lie, and say he had, but he didn't. He looked around to avoid anyone else from hearing his admission, and then said, "Yes, but never in battle."

Johann nodded, and said, "Just remember to time your fire at the crest of a wave. It will maximize your distance, and if you always fire at a crest, you will be able to trust your range. You can reasonably trust that the pitch of the ship will be consistent."

"That sounds logical, thanks," Papa said. Then he said to me, "Did you get that Lorenzo?" I nodded I did. Papa remembered that he had not actually been introduced, so he said, "By the way, I'm Sabastiano Demarco, the boy's papa."

"Yes," said Johann. "So der Maus has told me, but even if he had not, I can see the resemblance."

"Der Maus?" Papa questioned.

"The mouse," I answered. Papa laughed.

Then suddenly, from Girolamo Contarini's light galley came the sound of trumpets signaling attack. "I thought you said they weren't coming out," Papa said straining his eyes toward the bay to see what, if anything, was happening.

"They're, not," Johann answered, looking in the same direction. "It is we who are going in."

Captain Donato came rushing toward us shouting, "Captain Demarco. Captain Demarco, the fleet is about to go into battle and there has been an accident on the *Lombardi*. The gunnery captain was killed by a breech explosion." The *Lombardi* was one of the largest great galleys in the fleet and carried the most guns. "They need a good, experienced man to handle all of those guns, and I recommended you. You must go over there at once." Then he turned to me and said, "Lieutenant Demarco, you are now my gunnery captain. Prepare your artillery for battle."

"Aye captain," Papa and I both said. Then Captain Donato was off ordering his crew to battle positions. On the *Shivare*, the marines like Johann had nothing to do at this point but help out the shorthanded crew, some went to row; Johann volunteered to help me. Ultimately, the marines were used to board enemy ships, or lead the fighting when attacking a land position.

I walked Papa to where a small boat awaited him below; Johann followed. We didn't have a long time to say goodbye. I remember I said, "Good luck, Papa." Then he wished me luck in return. He hesitated, but despite Johann looking on, Papa picked me up, kissed me on both cheeks, and said, "You are still my little boy, so take care of yourself."

"I'll look after der Maus for you until you get back," Johann said with a laugh. "That is, as long as I don't have to kiss him."

It was Papa's turn to laugh. "I appreciate it," he said. Then Papa turned to me and said, "Lorenzo, if things get bad, just get down behind him."

I smiled and Johann laughed – a big burly roar – as Papa climbed overboard and into the small craft that would take him to the *Lombardi*. Once they were on their way, he turned back toward us and waved. I stood there and watched Papa, until Johann reminded me of my duty, and asked me where did I want him.

"Hey, Gunnery Captain Maus, where do you want me?" Johann said.

I looked up at him, and he was smiling down at me. "I don't know yet," I said, "but you're with me." Then we headed to the bow guns.

As we started to bare down on the Turks, they chose to come out of the bay and engage us. We picked up speed, and I felt the stinging spray of ocean mist on my face. The *Shivare* was on the end, with the larger ships in the center. The *Lombardi* and another great galley, the *Padua*, pulled way out in front to spearhead the assault. They pulled so far out in front that images of the battle that Johann had described at Lepanto came to mind; I shook them off. By the time we just got in gunnery range, the *Lombardi* and the *Padua* were already blasting through the smaller Turkish ships.

I had the six guns timed so two were firing every minute or less. Johann was incredible; he was experienced enough to do every job I asked. Strong as an ox, yet as nimble as a fox, he easily did the work of several men; he cleaned, loaded, packed, aimed, fired, and took up the slack when any of the lesser men would fall behind. We had success right off – splitting the mast off of a small Turkish galley rendering her helpless. Then having the range on her, we fired again ripping open her deck and setting her munitions on fire. Seeing our success, a roar went up from the crew from bow to stern, including the oarsmen. But just then, the winds died; so we lost speed to maneuver, and to catch up with the engaged lead ships – the *Lombardi* and the *Padua*. From my position, I could see the two great Venetian galleys being surrounded by a multitude of light galleys and other small, fast ships. The sight was not lost on the fleet commander, Contarini; he ordered his, the *Shivare* and the other light galleys to move in for support. But without the wind we were losing speed.

"Damn you! God!" I cried, cursing both the wind and God. I had watched my mama die not more than a year ago, and I wasn't going to lose my papa too – not if I could help it. "Take the command Sergeant!" I shouted at Johann, and then I ran down to the lower deck and shouted at the oarsmen. "Man your oars men and put your backs into it!" When they didn't seem to respond, I shouted again, "Damn you bastards! I said row! Row! Row!" Slowly they acted, but not fast enough for me. I threw myself down in a vacant spot and began to row with such vigor and intensity, that the men around me began to pick up the pace. "That's it," I shouted, "Row! Row!"

The Sergeant in charge was also affected. He said, "You heard the lieutenant, row! Bastards, row!"

I kept shouting, "Row! Row!"

Then the men began to shout in rhythm with each stroke, "Row! Row!" With ever increasing speed, I felt the *Shivare* serge forward.

"Gunnery Captain Demarco!" the Captain shouted. "I need you at your guns!"

I obeyed, but continued to shout back at the men as I ran for my post, "Row! Row! That's it men!" Back on the bow deck, I could see that we were way out in front, bearing down on the swarming Turks. Then a cannon blast from a Turkish galley flashed across the sky, over our heads, and pierced through the hull of the commander's ship, a few lengths to our stern – the vessel began to list. The commander was rescued, but the word was signaled to us that the attack was called off. "No!" I shouted. "We can't turn back, damn it!" The captain ordered the retreat. Again I shouted, "No!" I shouted again and lunged toward the Captain; Johann grabbed me by the arm and despite the added strength of rage, he pulled me back with ease.

"Easy, Maus," he said. "No use losing your head, now. It's too late. Look." Johann pointed in the direction of the bay.

As the *Shivare* began to bank into a turn, I watched in horror as the Turks moved in for the kill on the two large galleys. The *Padua* was set on fire, but the *Lombardi* was still fighting as the Turks began to board her. A parting shot split the mast of a light Turkish galley, and then the *Lombardi's* guns were silent. I could see the Turks overtaking the valiant defenders and celebrating on the great galley's deck. The *Padua* listed to port and began to go down. I remember thinking that they were the lucky ones. Johann had assured me that he had greatly exaggerated the atrocities of the Turks just to scare the young recruits, but it was of little comfort to me. I prayed that Papa died quickly, but I had little faith that God was listening; I didn't believe he heard me anymore, and I wondered if he ever had.

Days had passed since we lost the *Padua*, the *Lombardi*, and Papa. Word came from the besieged garrison at Modon that the Turks were displaying the banners of the *Lombardi* to taunt the men inside. There were other less reliable rumors that the ship was taken in tact and was being brought back to Constantinople, but the survivors were being held nearby as hostages, perhaps right outside Modon itself. It just happened that the *Shivare*, along with several other ships, was ordered to try and get into Modon to bring badly needed supplies to the garrison. So I knew that I was going to be there anyway. What if I could get some men and organize a search for the captives; perhaps even a rescue would be possible. I went to the captain, but he was way ahead of me.

"I'm way ahead of you, Lorenzo," said Captain Donato. It was the first time that he had called me by my first name. Perhaps it was because we were alone on deck – it was the early morning hours – or maybe because the military discipline was almost non-existent throughout the Venetian, thrown-together fleet, but I think it was because the captain was a compassionate man and didn't like losing one of his crew, so he sympathized with my loss. After all, he was the one who sent Papa to the *Lombardi*. "Before we dock at Modon, I thought I should try and find out if the rumors are true about survivors of the *Lombardi* being held in the area. So I sent out a pre-dawn party to try and capture, then interrogate a couple of the infidels." He looked out in the direction of the predawn light, glowing a pinkish red over the coastline. He said, "I believe if you look out toward Modon you will see a small vessel. That would be Sergeant Holper and company. If your father is alive and nearby, we may soon know."

"Thank you, Captain," I said. I tried to say more, but he held up his hand in a gesture that I understood to mean that he wanted me not to continue. We waited in silence, as the small craft grew larger and larger, as the sky slowly lightened. I could make out Johann, standing with one foot up on the bow, as four other men, two on each side of the boat, rowed

– there were two Turks lying prostrate between them. The boat pulled up next to the bow deck – the captain and I threw down the line – and Johann climbed aboard with an unconscious Turk flung over each shoulder; he tossed their bodies on deck. Both prisoners looked badly beaten and were bound – wrists and ankles – in chains. The captain complained to Johann about their condition.

"Sergeant, these men look badly beaten, I hope it was worth it and that you at least got something out of them," he said. Then he squatted down for a closer look. He stood back up, pointed to one of the Turks, and said, "In fact this one's dead."

Johann, kicked the man, then rolled him over with his foot, and finally confirmed the captain's diagnosis, "So he is," he said. "Sorry Sir, I guess we got a bit carried away." Then he picked up the body and unceremoniously tossed him overboard. "At least we still have this one."

The captain looked disgusted, but in this undisciplined, thrown-together fleet, there would be no repercussions for a minor infraction of an order. "Did you at least get something out of them, before you beat them?" the captain asked with disgust.

Johann was a professional soldier and was used to a certain amount of military discipline. He sympathized with the captain's inability to enforce authority. He apologized again, more sincerely, "I'm really sorry, Captain. The men got carried away, but there is no excuse. I think the men were just exacting a little revenge for the *Padua* and the *Lombardi*. I didn't realize that this one was dead until we got here."

"Yes, of course not," the captain said impatiently. "If you had, you wouldn't have bothered to bring back the body, I'm sure. In any case, did he say anything before he died?"

"Yes sir, Captain," Johann said respectfully. "They told us that the *Lombardi* is on its way to Constantinople. About half of the crew survived their attack, but Captain Marco was killed. Most of our men were taken away with the ship, their fates were unknown by these two. But this one," Johann kicked the remaining prisoner, "he speaks a little Italian. He told us that if any of the *Lombardi*'s officers survived, then they would have been taken to a Turkish camp, perhaps to be used as hostages – possibly to be used in a prisoner exchange."

"Is that it?" I interrupted. "Was he more specific? Did he know the rank of the men? Or where this Turkish camp was?" The captain shot me a hard look. I apologized. "I'm sorry, Captain."

He nodded that he understood, and then asked, "Well, Sergeant?"

"No Sir, they didn't know exactly where any of the prisoners had been taken," said Johann. Then he repeated what he had said before, "Just that the officers would have been taken to their camp, somewhere near Modon, in case they can be used in bargaining."

"All right, then. Thank you. You get some rest now," the captain said. Then he looked at me, and in anticipation of my question he added, "I will question him myself. Then, if you want to, you can talk to him." I nodded my gratitude. Then he called out to the sailor on watch, "Get a couple of men up here and take this Turkish prisoner below. Clean him up, but don't damage him anymore than he already is. Feed him, and then chain him to an oar." The captain turned to me and added, "If he's going to be with us, he can work for his keep."

We got into Modon with surprising ease; getting out would not be so easy. A dozen light galleys, including the *Shivare*, got into the Modon docks relatively unopposed. Our plan was to go in, help unload the needed supplies and munitions. At dusk, Johann a few others and I, would go out and capture a few more prisoners in an attempt to find out about any possible survivors of the *Lombardi*. If all went well, we would then plan a limited assault to free the captives with our five hundred marines – the number of marines on board all the light galleys docked at Modon. As I have said, that was the plan. What happened was a little different. We began to unload the supplies from the ships; the garrison was so relieved to see us that they swarmed the ships to greet us, and helped with the provisions. This left the walls lightly guarded. While we were unloading, the Turks attacked and easily breeched the walls, and I got my first taste of the hell on earth that is battle.

I must admit that when I saw those thousands of turbans coming at us, wielding those menacing crescent blades, of which many were already dripping in blood – Christian blood – I was afraid, but I wasn't afraid of dying. I was afraid of failing, looking bad, acting cowardly, performing poorly, letting the other men down, and – even though he would have never know it – disappointing Papa.

On they came, shrieking an ear-piercing battle cry, cutting through our confused, disarrayed defenders with such ease that I thought that they would pass right through us and over us like a giant wave crashing over the surf. Reflexively, I drew my sword, turned into the wave and began to rush forward to meet them head-on; luckily and thankfully, Johann and the rest of the marines were right behind me. We cut into them hard; it was their turn to fall back. I wielded my sword so effortlessly, just like in practice with Papa, but now it was real. The weapon was like an extension of my arm, cutting through limbs and impaling flesh. As one fell, I moved forward to the next, dancing and dodging, and pushing onward. Soon I was covered with the warm, thick, red fluid of life, but very little of the blood was my own, and still I cut and slashed; there were so many of them that wherever I slung my blade a body fell. I hesitated for a moment, just long enough to realize that the ocean of Turks I had plunged into was not ending, and I was alone; I was the only Christian in a sea of infidels. I continued to fight, slash, and kill. I knew I couldn't go on forever, but what choice did I have. Two of those hideous crescent blades came down on me at once; with lightning speed, I met them with holy steel, inches above my head. Without hesitation, with my free hand, I grabbed my dagger and thrust it in the heart of one of my attackers – he fell dead – then I turned on the other. I saw the fear in his eyes, then I closed them forever. But alas, I was tiring, so my deadly blade was becoming an ever-weakening defensive tool – ten pounds of steel between me and eternity. Just when I believed that the end was near, and began to make peace with God, the sea of infidels opened up; it wasn't Moses, but the mighty Johann that parted this sea, but it too was red.

Amidst the chaos he smiled at me and spoke; his voice was calm as if we were shipboard, talking about the weather. He said, "I think you better come with me, Maus."

I gave the big man a nod of gratitude and we began to fight our way back to the docks. I don't want to make it sound too easy, by downplaying the ferocity of the enemy, or by playing up our abilities, but in no time we were back on the dock, fighting shoulder to shoulder with our Christian brothers, with our backs to the real sea – the Ionian. There were still two ships docked at the port, but they were going nowhere; the crews had abandoned them or were dead. Another ship was on fire, and drifting out to sea. The rest of the light galleys had been able to escape to the open waters, while we contained the Turks. There seemed to be no escape when one, then another, and another, and another, cannon blasts came from over our shoulders; the explosions opened up a hole in the Turks ranks and caused much confusion – some of the Infidels were dead and some were running, but many others still held their ground. Fortuitously their ground was one of the other wooden docks, the one across from our precarious position. I turned to see from where the shots had come just in time to see the *Shivare* with Captain Donato shouting from the bow deck. "Reverse oars!!" Then the galley slammed into the dock knocking the enemy into the water and crushing others, and giving us a chance to escape. The last two of the *Shivare*'s bow cannons fired, point blank, killing and scattering more of our would-be assailants, but there were plenty more behind them to take their place, if we were willing to wait; we weren't. With the enemy retreating to regroup, I could see that our numbers were down to about a hundred, mostly marines; we quickly jumped on board.

"Get to the oars, men!" the captain shouted. "We're not out of this yet!" We ran to fill in; it was the first time the whole voyage that the *Shivare* had a full company – three men to each oar. The *Shivare* creaked, but slowly began to back away from the remaining dock – what might have very well have been our final stand if not for the heroic efforts of our brave captain. The enemy surged forward in an attempt to thwart our escape, but Captain Donato had already reloaded the cannons, and fired to cover our retreat; this gave us several more seconds to clear the dock. The Turks had no artillery at the ready, so they were forced to stand and watch as we slowly floated away.

We had cleared the harbor and were on our way to rejoin the fleet when I noticed that the oar I had chosen to help row was the one with the chained, Turkish prisoner. I looked at him and our eyes met; he looked a little sick and pale. At first I assumed that it was probably just a condition of his treatment on board. Then he spoke, in my native tongue, "Are you all right?"

"What?" I asked, wondering why he would question my condition or even care.

He stopped rowing for a moment and slowly reached out and gently touched the side of my cheek. He pulled back his hand and showed it to me; his fingertips were smeared with blood.

I rubbed my hand across my face and looked at it – more blood and lots of it. "I don't think it's mine," I said. "I'm not sure if that makes you feel any better."

He nodded that he understood and went back to rowing. I looked down at myself; it appeared as if I had taken a blood bath. Looking up, I caught a glimpse of myself reflecting in the back of the breastplate of the marine rowing in front of me. With the exception of where I had wiped my head, and where the Turk had touched me, my face was evenly covered in red; my thick curly brown hair had absorbed so much of the life fluid that it was clumping and made the top of my head appear black. Suddenly, I felt ill. I got up and ran to the bow deck – it was the closest – hung my head overboard and threw up until my throat was raw.

In the days and weeks that followed the fall of Modon, I began to lose all hope of seeing Papa again. I interrogated the prisoner, but found that Johann had gotten it all; he knew nothing substantial about Papa or any of the *Lombardi* survivors. He spoke pretty good Italian, but it was his native tongue that interested me; I asked and he agreed to teach me some Arabic. It was my first infidel language, but it would not be my last. His said his name was Aashiq, and I told him I was, "Lorenzo Demarco from Florence." In the few weeks that we had, we spent many hours together. At first it was just curiosity than drew me to him, but after talking to him I found him more compatible than most of my shipmates. He was certainly easily accessible; he was always chained to the same spot – second oar row from the bow, on the port side. For one hour a day, he was allowed to move about, always under guard, though I didn't think he was much of a threat to anyone on board, and I don't think he thought much about escape. I often volunteered to be his guard on these walks. He told me how the Turks treated prisoners of war, and thought he had heard that Christians were cruel to captives, but he was certain that this was just misinformation. He had read our Bible and understood all about Jesus, and even knew Christians, so he believed, that we believed in mercy and forgiveness; I was too ashamed to tell him that our virtues only applied to fellow Christians, and sometimes not even them. He didn't see me as much of a threat either, but he was confused by my growing reputation as a "ruthless warrior." A bored crew, hungry for some action, something positive, or just someone to look up to, began to tell stories of my "heroic fight" and "murderous fury" at Modon. Aashiq saw the contrast between these stories and the person he talked to every day; he didn't understand how the man he talked philosophy with and exchanged language could also be this invincible warrior.

"I don't understand how the man I talk philosophy with and exchange language could also be this invincible warrior I have been hearing about," said Aashiq, shaking his head. "Though I have known a few Christians, you're the first I have really talked to."

"Then how is it that you speak our language so well?" I asked. I picked up on the last bit of his thought to avoid having to talk about the first part.

"I was taught by an Arab trader," he said. "I heard that multilingual soldiers got the best duty – translating prisoner interrogations, treaty negotiations and surrenders – but back to my original thought." My evasive maneuver had failed. He continued, "Is there something in you, or is it in all of your people, that allows you to have these two sides, one side that is kind and charitable – you bring me extra rations, keep me company and treat me as an equal, when no one else will even talk to me, except to throw insults at me – and that other side, that fierce warrior? That man who sat down next to me covered in Turkish blood."

This apparent contradiction had been playing in my own mind since

Modon; how could I, Lorenzo Demarco, have killed so many, so quickly, with such ease, and it was my first real fight. I felt kind of proud of the way the crew was beginning to treat me, with respect, admiration, and a touch of fear. I think Papa would have been proud of me. Then I thought of Mama; I don't think that she would have been impressed with my newfound abilities. Was I really a killer? Should I feel guilty? Maybe it's ok to kill the infidel; after all, this is what the Pope asked for. If this is what the Pope wants, then isn't it what God wants? But if God really wants someone dead, did he really need me, or anyone, to do it for him? I couldn't downplay my actions to my conscious, but I could to Aashiq. "I think that you have been listening to exaggerated half truths, Aashiq," I said. "We haven't seen much action, so the crew is desperate for heroes or entertainment of any kind and I guess I'm it."

"They say you killed twenty Turks in less than twenty minutes," said Aashiq. "Are you saying that this is an exaggeration?"

"I didn't count," I said coldly. The subject was beginning to irritate me.

"You must really hate us," said Aashiq. "Tell me, what is it about Turks or Islam that you hate so much? After all we do pray to the same God."

"I don't know," I said flatly. "I really don't know that much about you. I just know that my papa hated you because you control our holy lands, you took Constantinople, and then you continued to push your way through Greece and are now threatening the continent. You even attacked our homeland at Ottoranto."

"I see," said Aashiq, stroking his thick beard. "So you hate us because your papa..."

"Let's not talk about this anymore," I said, and suggested that we just exchange vocabulary instead. He agreed, but he had one more thing to say, and it kind of surprised me.

"I'm sorry about your papa," he said.

"Sorry?" I questioned. "You're sorry? But I just told you that he hated you."

Again, Aashiq stroked his thick beard and said, "I don't believe your papa hated us as much as you say. Oh I believe he told you he did, he might have even thought he hated us, but I don't think it was sincere."

"Now why would you say that?" I asked. "You didn't know him."

He hesitated, and then answered, "No, I didn't know him, but I know his son. And despite your actions at Modon, I don't believe that you hate us. Therefore, I don't think your papa really hated us because he couldn't even convince his own son to hate us." Aashiq was a bit of a philosopher. When I think back, I wonder if maybe he was right about Papa.

I came to terms with the consequences of my newfound skills as a warrior.   The logic went like this: war is often a necessity, so killing is also a necessity, if you are going to avoid being killed you must be good at killing, therefore being good at killing is just survival. It's ok to be a good killer as long as you don't begin to enjoy it.

Aashiq was a master of languages, like myself, and he was also a student of astrology. We continued to talk and share vocabulary almost everyday; he was becoming my new best friend. Papa was gone. Johann was often busy with the baser things in life – fighting, drinking, sex, and gaming. So it was logical that Aashiq would become my most reliable confidant. After all, he couldn't go anywhere so I always knew where to find him.

Months passed with no change, or action with the fleet. We finally got a new Captain General, Benedetto Pesaro. Unfortunately for Pesaro – a commander seeking glory in battle – the Turks took our inaction as a chance to retreat to Constantinople. We got a late start, and our slower ships bogged down the whole fleet, but we did chase them up the Aegean Sea; we didn't come close to catching them before they reached the protection of the great batteries at the Dardanelles.   Captain General Pesaro was quite a change for the fleet. He had a reputation of being ruthless, but fair; I would learn that the first part was true, but I saw no evidence to confirm the latter. Even though he was over seventy years of age, he had a passion for young women and liked to keep one on board. He did manage to bring some discipline to the fleet, and not being used to it, it came to me as quite a shock. He had men executed for not following his orders. But he also believed in the importance of spoils to supplement the wages of the average soldier. He allowed and encouraged the men to go out in raiding parties, not just to retrieve information, but to steal valuables, and rape or kidnap women. I never went on any of these raids, they disgusted me – money and women were not the reasons I came to fight – but Johann went every chance he got.

Returning from a raid on the island of Mytilene, sixty miles south of the Dardanelles, Johann and a company of five brought back a beautiful young Turkish girl. They took her below the bow deck; the captain agreed to let them use his quarters because they were the most clean and private, as long as they cleaned up after themselves. I tried to ignore their deeds by seeking out Aashiq, but being that close to the captain's quarters I could easily hear the girl's screams of pain and cries for mercy. I did manage to forget about her for a moment; I was distracted by Aashiq and his knowledge of astrology. He knew more about the stars than anyone I had ever met before. He said that his people had known that the world was round for centuries. He also told me a theory that explained the epicycles, and why Venus and Mercury only rise and set in the east or west, and never cross the sky. He told me that many Turks were well versed in the sciences, and had gotten much of their ideas from the Greeks.

"We actually got many of our ideas from the Greeks," said Aashiq. "Centuries ago, volumes of ancient Greek writings were found and studied. Then when Constantinople was taken, even more books, thousands of volumes on art and science, were recovered. Our people are curious and can boast many scholars."

"Christians also study and admire the Greeks," I said. "The writings of Plato and Aristotle are some of the most popular books available."

"Yes, but isn't it true that many Christians, perhaps most still reject science and scholarly studies?" asked Aashiq.

I frowned knowing that he was right, but still I defended my people. I said, "Some of us still reject ideas offered by sources that do not represent God, but we are changing, and the passion for learning new ideas is spreading."

"But what of this thing called the Inquisition?" asked Aashiq. "Isn't it their job to condemn anyone who has any original idea, or learns or teaches anything that did not come from the church?"

I felt cornered and a bit ashamed for my people, so I countered with my own condemnation of Islam. "What about your faith?" I began. "Don't you fight and kill those who are not of your belief, or force others to convert to your faith? Isn't that why you are attacking us now?"

He thought for a moment, stroked his thick beard, and said, "We are spreading Islam and we offer conversions, but we fight mainly for conquest and territory just like all empires." He took a deep breath, then continued, "But we don't usually force people to convert to Islam, we don't need to, most accept our faith once they understand it. But we have many in the empire who have not converted, many Christians and Jews, and they are allowed to practice their faiths. We do make slaves out of our war captives, but they are allowed many freedoms including marriage and children, and the freedom to choose their own faith." He paused again, realizing what he had said, he looked me right in the eye and said, "I truly am sorry about your papa, but if he is alive, he survived the battle, then he is probably still alive. We generally don't kill our captives."

I smiled and said, "Thank you, Aashiq." It would have been an awkward silence except we were immediately reminded of what my people were doing to one of our captives. Again, I felt ashamed of my people, and I was struggling to find the words to explain or at least express my remorse, but nothing came to me.

He spoke first. He said, "Your Arabic is coming along quite nicely. Your gift for language was not exaggerated." He stroked his thick beard, and continued, "One of them must have bothered to get her name. I heard him calling it out – Hana. Here is a little test for you. What does Hana mean in Arabic?"

I shrugged and said, "I don't know."

"Mercy," he said. "I guess that word is not yet in your vocabulary."

I don't know if it was Aashiq's words, or my own conscious, but infidel or not, Hana was a woman, and I had heard enough of her cries for help; I decided to confront the attackers knowing that it would be like asking a hungry wolf to give up a fresh kill. As I approached, the assumption was that I was going to ask for a turn at their prize. The rule was that only those who take the risk can reap the rewards, but my actions at Modon had made me a hero aboard the *Shivare* – and throughout the fleet – and probably because of this they unanimously voted me a turn. When I explained that I didn't want a turn, but wanted them to stop violating the poor women, they just laughed.

"I don't want a turn," I said. "I want you to stop violating that poor woman."

They all laughed, but Johann laughed the loudest. Then he slapped me on the back and said, "Relax, Maus, we are almost through with her. Giulio is the last one." Then he turned to the other men and asked, "Unless any of you want another turn?" They all nodded, groaned, or laughed, indicating that they had enough. Then Johann said to me, "I guess we are through with her. Happy Maus?"

"No, Johann," I said with contempt. "I'm not. We are Christians, we are not savages, and we are not like the infidels. We should be showing them how merciful God can be, and how merciful his Christian children can be."

Two of the men were affected by my words and showed signs of shame, but the others showed no reaction. Johann just looked puzzled. He said, "Maus, we are being merciful." It was my turn to look puzzled. He continued, "As an infidel, and a follower of the false prophet Mohammad, the poor girl would have been condemned to an eternity in hell." He paused for effect, to allow me to reflect, then finished, "We have allowed her to suffer for those sins here on earth, and have punished her for her ignorance. Now God will smile on her, for she has paid for her sins. She can look forward to an eternity in purgatory. It isn't heaven, but it is certainly preferable to hell. Wouldn't you agree, Maus?"

The other men seemed to enjoy Johann's explanation; it made their vicious sexual act seem almost noble. I shook my head and said, "That's the same argument used by the Inquisition – it doesn't make sense when they say it, and it doesn't make sense when you say it. It's just an excuse used to justify torture and terror." Just then I noticed that Hana had stopped screaming; she wasn't crying, begging, or making any sound I could hear.

"Well, Maus, I guess you got your wish," said Johann. "Giulio must be finished."

I went to the cabin door; Giulio was on his way out. He paused to say to me, "I'm sorry, Lieutenant, I didn't know you wanted a turn."

I pushed past him and looked in the open door. Poor Hana was lying naked on the captain's bed; she was on her stomach. Besides my mother, this was the first time I saw a woman naked; even in death Hana was lovely, although her face was badly bruised, a light blue in color, and her eyes were open. She had been strangled with a piece of her own clothes. There were traces of blood coming out of every orifice of her body, but otherwise, they had not beaten her too badly; her light brown skin was still beautiful.

Johann came up behind me, looked over my shoulder and said, "Well, it's all over for her. Was that merciful enough for you, Maus?"

"You're nothing but a bunch of pathetic killers," I said. "Like a pack of wolves slaughtering innocent prey, but at least they only kill to survive."

"Perhaps we are killers, Maus," said Johann. "But, must I remind you of your performance at Modon?" Then he quipped, "Perhaps I should have named you der Toedlich Maus."

Angrily, I pushed past the big man, anxious to get away from that horrible scene and my own guilt; Toedlich means killer.

We had wasted several weeks patrolling the northern Aegean; the Turks were too smart to come out of the Dardanelles and fight, and we were too smart to go in after them. In that time I had continued to learn from my Turkish friend about the Arabic language, the stars, and humanity. I was beginning to wonder which of our peoples was truly in God's favor. Our supplies were getting low, and it was getting unsafe to raid the islands because they were watching for us and had increased their patrols. Besides, we had raided the islands dry of all the easy targets. It was time to head back to friendly waters, but the captain general couldn't leave without making some sort of gesture. About the same time I heard that we were leaving, Aashiq was taken off of the *Shivare*; I would never have the chance to talk with him again.

Pesaro ordered the *Shivare* and several other light galleys to move in close to Mytilene. Captain Donato ordered me and Johann, and the bow's artillery crews, to man our stations. He told us that we were to fire our guns to get the attention of the islanders, and then we were to provide cover for a landing party. I asked the captain, if they needed artillery support, why not send in the big galleys; they had more guns.

"Captain, if they need artillery support, why not send in the big galleys?" I asked. "They have more guns than all of these light galleys put together."

"The captain general wants us in real close, less than a hundred yards," said Captain Donato. "Those big galleys can't get in that close to those shallows during this low tide."

We moved into position with the other galleys. As we did, about a dozen small boats landed on a tiny, sandy island about a hundred yards from the main island, and about that same distance from us. I looked at Captain Donato and I could tell he wanted to tell me something – what was going on – but he didn't say a word, and I didn't ask. Finally, Johann asked the captain what was happening.

"What's happening, Captain?" he asked.

"The captain general's going-away present to the Turks," said Captain Donato. He sounded relieved to finally be asked. "I guess he wants to make a statement. Something to say that he is a man to be feared, or simply ruthless and cruel." He paused, took a deep breath, and then continued, "Our captives, five women and three men, are to be staked out on that little island to be executed. To be executed in a slow burn. He wants us here to make sure that the Turks on the main island see what we are doing, and then make sure that they are not able to stop it. You see, if you are not familiar with a slow burn, it takes time, so if we just left them there they could be rescued. The heat is prepared to a level just hot enough so that the victims are cooked like a roast pig, slowly, so it takes several, up to three, hours for the person to die. Then as a bonus, he is impaling the remaining dead prisoners, and having their bodies displayed, strategically, around the executions."

"That explains why they want our dead prisoners," said Johann.

"And why they wanted Aashiq," I added quietly.

Once the dead bodies were impaled and up in the air, and the poor living victims were securely bound and the low fires burning below them, we were ordered to fire our guns, but I don't think that it was really necessary; we could see a gathering of people near the shore watching. A couple of galleys fired several rounds that landed between the islands to warn off would be rescuers. The victims could be seen squirming as they slowly cooked.

The fires had been burning for almost an hour when the executioners, believing that the hot coals, brimstones, and rocks would be sufficient to finish the job unattended, boarded the small boats and headed back to the fleet. There were several attempts from the islanders to rescues Aashiq and the others, but they were forced back by murderous fire from the light galleys including the *Shivare*; so I had the range. I sighted along my quadrant and ordered an adjustment in the elevation of the barrel of one the cannons, then had it loaded with an exploding shell. Johann noticed the changes I made and asked me if I knew what I was doing.

"Do you know what you are doing?" Johann asked.

I'm sure that Captain Donato knew what I was doing, also, but he said nothing. "Yes," I said. "I'm adding a new word to my vocabulary." Of course he didn't understand what I was talking about. I gave the order, "Fire!" Then I whispered, "Hana." The shot couldn't have been more perfect; it exploded right in the middle of the poor victims and cleared the island. It even knocked down most of the impaled. Then all of the guns on all of the light galleys went silent.

Captain Donato dismissed the artillery crew, except Johann and me. There was a long silence, then the captain said, "That was a one in a million shot, nobody will believe that it could have been anything but an accident."

"I can't let you cover for me," I said. "The captain general has beheaded others who have disobeyed his orders."

"That is why the three of us have to agree," said Captain Donato. "That was a one in a million shot and could have only been an accident." Johann smiled and nodded his head. The captain continued, "Well that's it then. Now, let's go home." Johann and I began to walk away when I heard the captain say, "Damn good shot."

Surprisingly, there was no backlash from my – errant shot. It seems that the captain general was half convinced that most of his fleet was incompetent, and half convinced that nobody in his fleet would want to speed up the results of a slow burn.

The fleet sailed back to the Adriatic, and the *Shivare* went back to Venice; she was one of several ships sent back to pick up supplies. I decided not to go back to sea; I left Captain Donato with my respect and gratitude. It was a good time for me to get out of the action; I had developed a taste for war, but I had no appetite for the enemy. I decided to go home to my city.

When it came time for me to say goodbye to Johann, I was surprised to find that he too had enough of this fight. He said it was the navy that bothered him; he preferred to fight his battles on land.

"I prefer to fight my battles on land," said Johann.

"Well then, Orso, I guess that you will be looking for another conflict to join," I said. Then I added flippantly, "You could stay in Italy where there's always somebody at war. Or you could join the condottiere who always convince somebody to go to war."

"Condottiere?" he asked.

"That's our word for mercenaries like you," I explained.

"I see," he said. "Then you are a condottiere?"

"No," I answered. "I got in this fight because of Papa - it's a long story."

We stood there on the docks for several long seconds - seemed like minutes - silently looking around awkwardly, each of us trying to think of something to say. He spoke first. He said, "Do you think that you will be looking for one of those Italian wars you mentioned?"

"Perhaps," I answered. "I was told by a good friend that if you have a gift for something, then it is your duty to God to exploit that gift, less you waste it. Though I'm not sure my friend would approve of this gift - he's a Dominican monk." I paused, and then continued, "I probably will look for some cause worth fighting for, but I thought that I would go home for a while. I miss my city, my Florence."

"So this Florence is really a nice place?" Johann asked awkwardly. I nodded that it was and he added, "A lot of fine looking women I suppose?"

"Yes, of course," I said. "The finest. Though I must admit that when I left, I was hardly in a position to be looking. I was still a little young, and training for the order, and a life of celibacy."

"You know, I don't have a home or a family, or a city like Florence to return to," said Johann, as we began to walk along the docks, away from the ships.

"That's too bad," I said with false sympathy. "But I doubt that even if you did have a home, it wouldn't compare to my city."

"Though I've never been there, somehow I thing you're right," he said. We cleared the docks and started down the road. He added, "Is there a lot to do in Florence, I mean are there a lot of jobs, work, business?"

"Oh it is a major city, and a center of banking," I said. "We also have over two hundred wool merchants, eighty some silk merchants, and dozens of guilds including metal workers, cabinet-makers, stonecutters, jewelers, and well, just more than I can name. The very heart of Florence comes from her merchants and guilds."

We walked along the canals, and on my lead, we headed west, still talking in the same backhanded way. He said, "What are you going to do with your papa's shop?"

"I don't know," I said. "I haven't had that much time to think about it."

"Are you going to go into his business?" he asked. "You know I have some skill…"

"No," I deliberately cut him off. "Papa never wanted me to go into his business and I was never that interested in making cannons, armor, or weapons of any type. I'll probably give painting another try, and I will go back to training, just in case I find that good fight."

Now he sensed an opening and leaped in, he said, "You know, with your papa gone, God rest his soul, you don't have anyone to train with."

But I was ready for him, I said, "I probably could find someone to train with me, but I don't know if I will bother. I will probably just train alone."

"Oh you can't just train alone," he said with deliberate thoughtfulness.

"Why not?" I asked, with exaggerated surprise.

"Because, there is nobody for you to get better than," he said.

"Well Orso, there's always myself," I said. "I can get better than myself."

"No, you see, that's the thing, Maus," he said with a smile. "People say that but it doesn't really make sense, because if you get better than yourself, then there's always you who have also been bested."

I don't think I ever formally invited him, or that he ever asked me, but there we were, talking and walking our way right out of Venice and on the road to Florence. We hadn't gotten too far out of the city when it was agreed that we should stop at an inn and get a fresh start in the morning. I hadn't slept on a bed in two years, so being reacquainted with a warm quilt and a pillow put me right to sleep – to sleep, perchance to dream.

I should have known something was wrong right away. I was home – at the shop – and Mama and Papa were there, and so was this little boy; the boy was me when I was only three or four. A fire was blazing, because it was cold outside. I was running around the big wooden table, chasing Papa, and I was laughing; Mama was sitting in the x-chair, smiling and watching us. Papa let me catch him, and I shouted, "Again, again, run Papa," and around the table we went. This time Papa caught me and picked me up, kissed me on both cheeks, and said, "My you are getting big."

A strong wind blew open the door, and put the fire out. I went to shut the door, but when I got there I stepped outside and the wind turned warm; it filled the sails of the *Shivare*. "Man the oars!" shouted Captain Donato. I ran down to the oars. Aashiq was in his usual spot – second oar row from the bow on the port side. I said, "Hello, Aashiq."

And he smiled, stroked his thick beard, and said, "It seems unusually hot today, or is it just me?"

On the oar across from Aashiq sat Mama and Papa; Papa was rowing,

Mama was just sitting and smiling at me with her squinting gray-blue eyes and thin lips. I asked her, "What are you doing on the *Shivare*, Mama?"

She said, "I'm not on the *Shivare*, I am at home." And we were. Mama was sitting in the x-chair, but now Papa was sitting at the table counting coins.

"It's good to be home," Papa said.

"Why don't you sit down, Lorenzo?" Mama chimed in. Then she asked, "Can I get you something to eat?"

"No, Mama," I said. "It's really good to see you.

"It's good to see you too," Mama said. "Now come over here and give me a kiss." I obeyed.

"I love you, Mama," I said. Then I got a horrible, awful feeling inside. "Something isn't right," I said.

"What's wrong, Lorenzo?" Mama asked.

"The boy knows," Papa said.

"He knows what?" Mama asked.

Papa looked at me, but he stared right through me; there was sadness in his big, brown eyes. He said, "The boy just realized that he is dreaming. We aren't really here."

"It's all right, Lorenzo," Mama said. "We're ok, everything is fine. We'll be together again."

I felt a deep, horrible ache way down in my chest, as I looked at them, and I realized just how much I missed them both. I could see them, they were so real, saying doing everything that I expected them to, just like always, like before, like never again, and then I started to wake up. "No, not yet," I said. "Mama, Papa, I miss you, I miss you both and I..." And they faded away as I slowly opened my moist eyes. I buried my face in my pillow to stifle the sorrow, and the cry of pain that I didn't dare let out, as Johann snored in the bed next to me.

Chapter VI

The trip to Florence was relatively uneventful, with the exception of our second night out of Venice. I had purchased some horses outside of the city, and we rode through *Padua*, on our way to Ferrara, when we decided to stop at another inn. This time we stopped not just to rest, but to indulge; we made sure there was a tavern nearby with good food and plenty of wine. We were told by the innkeeper that there would be tough men and prostitutes at the tavern. Being still a little naive in the ways of women, I was not interested in prostitutes; surprisingly neither was Johann. It certainly gave us an idea of the kind of atmosphere we could expect; perfect for two soldiers home after a long fight.

The dinner was the first good meal we had in months, and we ate like we were starving. We had bread porridge, which Johann drank from his bowel; a small stream formed at the side of his mouth and ran down his thick beard. Then we had some brown bread, grilled steaks, and beans; Johann hung over his plate like a pig over a trough. Food fell from his gaping mouth back onto his plate only to be eaten on the second, or sometimes, third try; I found it repulsive. On the *Shivare*, I could always go off and eat at my post, or at least somewhere alone, so I could stay away from the crass manners of my shipmates. Ironically, it was back in civilization where I was forced to sit and eat, and watch others consume. It wasn't just Johann; the tavern was filled with other equally loud, vulgar, belching men. Though I could avoid watching most of them, it was hard not to see Johann for he was sitting just across the table from me.

Then, of course, we had wine – lots and lots of wine. Johann drank it by the decanter. Then he would belch real loud, laugh – a big burly roar – and cry out, "More wine, wench, bring me more wine." The wench he referred to was the tavern owner's daughter – a rather large woman obviously used to the attentions of loud, obnoxious, dirty, grabbing men.

We finished eating, but it would be a while before we were done drinking. The wine kept coming and I quietly paid the woman – with a generous gratuity – to make sure that the wine didn't stop flowing until my big friend had enough. Being a fairly inexperienced drinker – I had gotten drunk a few times shipboard – I stopped drinking, or at least slowed down, unnoticed by Johann, to avoid getting too inebriated. Now I had also paid for the dinner, the rooms at both inns, and our horses. I thought I had been discrete, but these facts had not gone unnoticed by Johann. He picked an inopportune time to declare his observation – surrounded by a variety of unsavory, hard-looking men, of which many were armed, and most looked to be veterans of a number of fights. It was certain that there were highwaymen and bandits in the crowd. The only women in the tavern besides the tavern owner's daughter were professionals, who were also interested in alcohol-blinded characters with money. It was not the time to shout out, are you rich or something.

"Are you rich or something?!" Johann bellowed. I noticed several heads turn our way. "You must have already spent most of the money you made for a years service on the *Shivare*."

"No, Orso," I said, "I am not rich." Then I tried to pretend that I was broke. Despite my attempt to slow down my consumption, the wine was having a strong effect on me; I found myself wanting to laugh at this most inappropriate moment. I started to snicker, and then I pretended to look in my money pouch. I knew how many coins I had left, and it was most of what I had earned on the *Shivare*; Johann had exaggerated how much I had spent. I also had – and Johann didn't know this – Papa's earnings from the *Shivare*; Captain Donato insisted on giving me Papa's share. Of course I couldn't say any of this at the time. Instead, I said, "I guess I blew it all, I'm down to my last denari." I tried to whisper to Johann between my giggles, "This is not the best time to talk about our funds."

Apparently, Johann didn't hear me, or didn't understand why I was saying it. He said, "What happened to all those coins I saw you counting? You couldn't have spent them all already. I mean I'm drinking a lot of wine, that was a fine meal, and those horses are pretty nice, but with what I saw you with, you could have …" I kicked the big man under the table, and then buried my face in my arms on the top of the table to conceal my laughter. "Hey, Maus, why did you kick me for?" Johann bellowed. His reaction made me laugh harder. Then even harder still when Johann said, "Uh-oh." He had just realized what I had already – we had an audience, one that was quite interested in how much money we really had and how drunk we really were.

Now it was his turn to pretend. "Well, I guess we're broke then," he said in an exaggerated tone and in a loud voice. "Down to our last denari, eh Maus? Me, too. Don't know what we're gonna do now, being broke and all." He paused to take a big swig of wine, then he added, "But I think we can scrape up just enough to get some more of this miserable wine. Ale, that's a man's drink, all we drink up north."

I sat up and wiped tears of laugher from my eyes. Nobody was looking at us, and between the wine and the amusement, I was able to convince myself that maybe nobody was listening either, or they just didn't care. Johann was convinced that we were safe also, but he believed that it was because of his performance. "It's all right, Maus," he whispered. "I threw 'em off the trail." Then he gulped down the rest of the wine, belched loudly and deeply, and bellowed, "Now, how about some more wine?" I was still a bit amused. I sniggered, and signaled with a finger to my lips for him to not be so loud. So he repeated in an exaggerated whisper, "How about some more wine?"

I said, "All right, but let's pour it in your water pouch and take it with us so we can get out of here."

"Good idea," he said. Then he added a bewildered, "Why?"

He seemed to have forgotten our whole pretense and I didn't want to start it up again, so I just said, "It's a nice night, Orso, and I could use some air and a little walk before I can sleep."

"I see," said Johann. He thought for a moment, and then smiled and added, "Too much wine for the little maus." Then he laughed and said, "All right, let's get out of here."

We got the wine and filled Johann's water pouch and then quietly stepped outside, just as discreetly as you would expect two drunken men to be – stumbling and clanging our swords.

It was a beautiful night, comfortably warm and dry, with all the stars in heaven shining above us, along with a bright waning, half moon. We didn't head straight for the inn; thinking back, we probably should have. Instead we staggered along the road, in the dark, in the opposite direction as the inn. Johann found a convenient tree, and then he not so conveniently passed out under it – slumped over on his side. I tried to wake him by gently, well not so gently, kicking him on his backside, when I heard footsteps coming toward us. I strained to hear or see whom, or how many were approaching, but the wine had deadened my hearing and dimmed my vision. The sound suddenly stopped. It was quiet again. I put my hand on the handle of my sword and prepared for a fight. The excitement helped to counter the effects of the wine; my senses rapidly came back to me. I heard a twig snap. I had just honed in on where the sound had come from when Johann let out a loud belch; I jumped. If they didn't know exactly where we were before, they certainly did now. I wasn't going to wait to be attacked; the situation called for decisive, aggressive action. I drew my sword and got down into a crouch, and then moved along slowly and quietly through the brush toward the last foreign sound I had heard. As I approached a large shrub, I saw a shadow on the other side; I leapt into action. I jumped out, saw a man, thrust my sword in his face, and demanded to know what he was doing out here at this time of night.

"What are you doing out here at this time of night?" I demanded to know. Before he could answer, I added, "Are you alone? Were you following us?" The man was visibly shaking. I could see he wasn't a threat; he wasn't even armed. I tried to calm the fear that I had instilled in him; I lowered my sword and said, "It's all right, I'm not going to hurt you. I thought maybe you were... I mean I heard someone and thought... I guess I'm just a little jumpy. Are you all right?"

It took him a moment to recover, but he finally spoke; he had a thick accent that sounded almost German. He said, "I'm fine. I apologize if I startled you. It's just that I was walking along, looking at the sky when I heard this intense sound, like a low growl. It was frightening, but curiosity got the better of me and I came to investigate."

"Oh," I remarked with a smile. "I think I know what that sound was." I pointed back at the tree where Johann was passed out and said, "That was just my friend. I'm afraid he had a little too much to drink, perhaps a lot too much to drink." Then I added, "He is German," looking for some acknowledgment from the stranger about his origin. When he offered none, I finally asked, "I noticed your accent. Are you German?"

"No," he snapped, with a touch of annoyance in his tone. Then in a more pleasant and proud voice he said, "I am Polish."

"I see," I said. The wine was once again affecting my speech, I babbled, "Being an Italian, I guess, and German and Polish being both foreign to me, yet they are similar – I mean to me they kind of sound alike, the language not the names – and they are close together in area...up there in the middle of the continent. I'm sorry I am babbling on. My name is Lorenzo Demarco, and I am from Florence."

"I am Nicolaus," he said.

"Well Nicolaus," I said. "Let's move away from my friend, so as not to disturb him. Not that we could, I tried very hard to disturb him just a while ago with little success." We slowly walked away from Johann, and I asked, "What brings you out here this time of night, alone, and so far from home?"

"The stars, the view," he said. I could tell that he felt that he needed to explain, so I let him, or let him try. "I am a student from the University of *Padua*. I am studying medicine and astrology, and that's why I'm out here tonight – to study astrology, or the stars, that is. And by learning about the stars, of course, then you are learning about medicine, for the heavens govern our lives and our well-being. All that is up there is in here, in our bodies and souls." It was his turn to babble; he babbled on, "The sky, you see, on a night like this when it is cool, and not very humid, is so clear. Yet it is not cold, so it is comfortable to be out in the night air. So I wanted to make some observations on the movements of Mars and Jupiter. Jupiter in particular because it is in retrograde."

He pointed toward a bright light, I nodded and he went on, and on. It's not that I wasn't interested in the stars – I found astrology fascinating and had learned much from Aashiq – but my head was beginning to ache and I was just too tired to care much about anything. I certainly wasn't in the mood for any scientific study, or for that matter, any conversation that involved thought. But as he was rambling about retrograde motion and epicycles, something Aashiq had told me suddenly came to mind.

"Something Aashiq told me just came to mind," I said. We stopped walking and he stopped talking. I realized I needed to explain. I said, "I had an Arab friend named Aashiq, he had studied astrology. He told me that Arabs are quite fascinated by the stars and the sciences." He nodded that he understood, or at least that he was interested in what I was talking about, so I continued. "Aashiq taught me a little about retrograde motion and epicycles," I said. "He said there was a theory that not only explained epicycles but also the strange rising and setting motions of Mercury and Venus." He was listening intently, so much so that his interest made me self-conscious about what I was saying – I really didn't understand the words I was repeating, I only hoped I was repeating them accurately. "Aashiq said that the mathematics of the orbits all work out, if you just change the focal point of the orbits of..."

"Change the focal point? You can't just change the focal point," he interrupted.

"Well I really don't understand mathematics," I said. Then I qualified what I was saying – almost making an excuse – I added, "I'm just trying to repeat, that is what I remembered I was told. Aashiq said that all the planets have circular orbits of different lengths or diameters, and if you assume this then the numbers all work out if you just change the focal points."

He gave me a puzzled look, but seemed to be at least considering what I was trying to tell him. He asked, "Circular orbits for all of the planets, even Mercury and Venus?"

"Yes, I guess," I said. "It was explained to me like this. If we do a thought experiment it helps because we can visualize what is going on. Picture a model where all the planets are orbiting a single focal point. All the planets have orbits of different lengths, and the Earth is just one of these planets with an orbit between Venus and Mars. Assuming that Mercury and Venus are closer to the focal point than the Earth, from the Earth they would always rise and set in the east or west, appear relatively low in the sky, and never cross the zenith – just what we see. The rest of the planets are further away from the focal point than the Earth, so they can be seen moving completely across the sky. The apparent retrograde motion occurs because the Earth's shorter orbit means that our planet is moving faster than those farther from the focal point. When the Earth catches Mars or Jupiter in the race around the focal point they appear to us to be moving backward for a while. Then once we are sufficiently past them, they begin to move forward again. I don't know, maybe I'm not saying it right, but Aashiq insisted that the numbers all work out perfectly if you just change the focal point away from the Earth ..."

"And make it the Sun," he interrupted. "You change the focal point from the Earth to the Sun, yes, that just might work."

That was his reaction and the last sentence he made that actually made sense to me; he began to mumble about equations and numbers. I smiled and nodded for a few minutes then I remembered Johann. I tired to interrupt to tell him I was leaving, but he didn't hear me; he was lost in his thoughts. Finally I just started to leave. I got several paces away when he called out to me.

"Hey, it was nice talking to you, and thanks for the ... Arabic astrology lesson," he said. "Lorenzo...?"

"Demarco, Lorenzo Demarco from Florence," I said. "And you're welcome. I hope I got it right. Enjoy, or good luck with your observations, Nicolaus...?"

"Copernicus, Nicolaus Copernicus," he said.

Now I don't know how common that name is up there in Poland, but just a few years back, decades after our chance encounter, somebody by that name published a book about the revolutions of the planets, where the sun is the focal point for the orbits of the planets; I never read it. It was far too complicated for me to understand.

When I got back to Johann, he was still unconscious. I tried to wake him again and had the same lack of success; the best I could do was make contact with a half-asleep, groggy shadow of him. It was just enough to get him to help me, help him to his feet. I ended up standing under him with his arms draped over my shoulders, so we moved forward by me pulling him along, allowing him to use my back and legs for support – with his size it was very painful for me. We continued on, in this comic manner, down the road, and almost made it to the inn, when we were set upon by bandits – four ruffians or would-be highwaymen. They appeared from nowhere – not that I was in any condition or position to have noticed their approach anyway – presumably from somewhere behind the trees on the side of the road; they blocked our path and ordered us to stand and deliver.

"Stand and deliver all of your coins," one of them demanded.

I remember I snickered; the lingering effect of the wine prevented me from perceiving any real danger. I said, "It seems that you have us at a bit of a disadvantage. As for your requests, standing seems to be all that we can do. As for delivering, you may have to help yourself to my money pouch – I don't believe that I can get to it from my current position. But I am sure that helping yourself suits you fine."

The one who spoke, sneered, and then motioned for the villain on the end, to his right, to take my pouch; the scoundrel moved forward and reached out his arm. Then with lightning speed, my sword was unsheathed and wielded, with surgical precision, lopping off two fingers on the hand of the would- be thief; he jumped back, clasped his wounded, bloody hand in his good hand, and howled in pain. But it was not me who inflicted the damage, but Johann, and my light sword was like a dagger in the hand of the big man. The other three attackers brandished their weapons. The one on the opposite end of the wounded man leapt forward but was sent reeling by yet another lightning blow from Johann; the blow clipped the man's beard and cut his face deeply releasing a thick flow of blood. In one smooth move, Johann pushed off of my back, tossed me my sword, and then drew his own.

"Not bad work for a drunken Orso," I quipped.

"Indeed," said Johann. "But I keep aiming for the middle one."

"Which middle one?" I asked.

"There's more than one in the middle?" Johann retorted.

It was apparent even to them that, despite our being a little drunk, they were still no match for us. Johann swung his heavy blade up and over their heads and roared; this was more for effect than to inflict deadly force. It worked. The four would-be highwaymen turned to run, but before they could get away, I leapt forward – it was my turn to show off – and clopped the ear off the leader and stole his money pouch with my free hand. They ran; three out of the four were now marked in blood. I looked in the money pouch and found only three denari, so I wadded up the pouch and threw it after them. I shouted, "Here you forgot something! You obviously need this more than we do." The leader stopped to pick up his meager wealth, and then ran after the others. Johann and I just watched and laughed, and continued laughing long after they had disappeared into the darkness.

We continued on to the inn without another incident. The sudden jolt of excitement had sobered us, somewhat – a problem we remedied by drinking the wine in Johann's water pouch.

Of course, I was happy to be back in Florence again, but going home was not so pleasant; home was now an empty shop full of memories. It would have been a lot worse if Johann hadn't been there; his presence prevented me from dwelling on my loss or drifting into melancholia. I even gave Johann my parent's room – it was give him their old room or let him sleep in the shop or on the floor by the fireplace. The latter was a suggestion he had made in respect to the memory of my parents.

"In respect to the memory of your parents, I can sleep on the floor by the fireplace," Johann suggested, as we stood in the doorway of my parent's old room.

"No, Orso," I said, "You take ..." I almost said Mama and Papa's room, but I caught myself. "...this room. There's a nice bed in there, why waste it. Besides, you might be here for a while and a man needs his space, and can often use some privacy. Let this be your space until you decide on another."

On my insistence, Johann walked into the room and looked around. He said, "I never had a room of my own."

"Well this one is yours, as long as you want it," I said.

He made a quick assessment of his surroundings, and then continued. "Nice, not too cluttered. Simple, I like it." Besides the bed, there was: a small table with a candle on it; a shelf, on the same wall as the door, with an oil lamp; a plain tapestry on the north wall designed for warmth, a small rug to cover most of the wooden floor from the door to the bed; and a cassone pressed up against the wall beyond the foot of the bed. "Is this all of your parent's belongings?" He asked.

"Mama and Papa were never much on possessions," I said. Actually,

Papa and I had cleaned out a few of the little things not long after Mama died; there were too many little things with big memories attached to them. "The cassone has a few of Papa's and Mama's things still in it, I'm certain, but we can move those out if you need a place to store your gear."

"You don't have to do that, you know I don't have much," Johann said. Then the big man smiled at me, and said, "All right, Maus, I'll take the room, but I don't know ..." A sudden, loud knock at the door cut him off. I went to see who it was; Johann lagged back to explore the limited provisions of his new room.

I opened the door and there stood Fra Domenico, and a rather formidable looking man behind him; he was as big as Johann, and he had a hard looking face with a nasty scar on his cheek. The good Father looked surprised, and then happy. It took him a long moment, but he finally spoke, "Lorenzo, it is very good to see you again." He gave me a big, long hug, swallowing my frame in his robes. When he released me, he had yet another expression on his round face – confusion. Of course, I invited him in. Fra Domenico motioned for his companion to wait outside; the big man grunted and obeyed. Once inside, Fra Domenico looked around the room, towards the bedrooms, and the shop.

"He's not here," I said, believing I knew for whom he was searching. "Papa was lost in battle."

A deep sadness came over Fra Domenico's face. He said, "I'm so sorry, Lorenzo." Then he whispered a small prayer and made the sign of the cross in the air and with tears in his eyes, he asked, "How did it happen?"

I didn't feel like going into all the details just then, so I said, "I don't feel like going into all the details just now, there will be time for that later. So let it suffice to say that it was during a sea battle. We were separated, and the ship he was on was captured."

"Then you didn't see him die," said Fra Domenico, with exaggerated optimism. "He could have been captured alive? He could still be alive?"

"Yes, I guess he could be," I said. "I did what I could to find out if he had survived. I had a good captain and he allowed me every opportunity to investigate Papa's capture. All I know is that there were survivors from Papa's ship – perhaps as much as half of the crew was taken alive – but I don't know if Papa was one of them. I was told by someone very reliable that the Turks did not kill their prisoners. Most of the time, prisoners are forced into slavery. And that same person told me that Turkish slaves often lived well."

Fra Domenico looked hopeful, and wiped an errant tear from his cheek. "At least he may still be alive," he said with confidence. "And if he is alive, there's a good chance he could come back to us someday. I will pray for his safety and his return."

"Thank you, Fra Domenico," I said. Once again, Fra Domenico began looking around the room with curious eyes. "What is it you are looking for?" I asked.

He took one last glance over my shoulder, toward the shop, and then he said, "You remember that your papa asked me to keep a watch on the shop. Well, I was told just a little while ago that two men had gotten in here - that's why I came, and that's why I brought that big soldier with me. From the description, I thought one of the two men seen coming in here could be you - I guess it was - but the other man. He was described as a strong looking, large bulking..."

From behind Fra Domenico, Johann came out of, what was now, his room, and interrupted. He said, "That would be me, strong looking, large bulky, eh Maus?" Fra Domenico turned, and came face to face with the big man - or should I say face to chest; the good Father took a step back. "Sorry if I startled you, Father," said Johann.

I stepped in and introduced my oldest friend to my newest. I said, "Fra Domenico, this is Johann Holper. He will be staying here with me for... I don't know how long. Johann, this is the Dominican monk I told you about."

"Good to meet you, Father," Johann chimed, with a broad smile.

"Good to meet you too, Son. Good to meet you," said Fra Domenico.

After the two men got past the introductions and some friendly banter, Fra Domenico sat down in the x-chair, Johann and I sat at the big wooden table, and we reminisced about the old times; Fra Domenico and I reminisced, while Johann listened and let out several laughs - when the stories involved my abasement - a fact not lost on Fra Domenico who began to tell only stories that invoked laughs at my expense. But I didn't mind being the source of their amusement; it was just good to see Fra Domenico again and even better to see him getting along so well with Johann. It was also good to see that he was not dwelling on losing papa, and had faith that he may, somehow still be alive. This seemed to make me feel a little better too; his faith was bolstering mine. When the well of stories of my embarrassing youth ran dry, Fra Domenico turned to me to tell me that he was wondering about my future, and wanted to know what my plans were now that I was back in Florence.

"I was wondering about your future, Lorenzo," said Fra Domenico. "What are your plans now that you are home again?"

I knew he wouldn't approve of the tentative plans I had made, so I tried to defer my answer to a later date. I said, "I just got home, I don't know what I am going to do for sure."

"Of course, Lorenzo, of course," said Fra Domenico. "I was just thinking, or hoping, that you would consider, or might be considering, resuming your training." He hesitated, and then he added, "You know, it's what your mama wanted, and with her gone, I thought maybe..."

"Papa's gone too," I interrupted.

"Yes, I'm sorry, Lorenzo," Fra Domenico said solemnly. "I didn't mean to dismiss his wishes."

Feeling I might have hurt my old friend's feelings, I quickly added, "It's all right, Fra Domenico, you always agreed with mama when it came to my future. But, that being said, perhaps I should try and fulfill Papa's wishes for me to be an artist. I was getting pretty good at it before I left."

"You are an artist, Maus?" Johann said. "I didn't know that. You think maybe you could paint me, not as I really am, of course, but looking proud, strong and invincible." He struck a pose, and then added, "All right so that would be how I really am, but maybe you could make me look even better."

I ignored Johann's silliness and continued my thought. I said, "I could be an artist and a Dominican like Fra Bartolommeo."

As I have suggested, I had no intension of telling the good Father that I was considering training to become a professional soldier – I knew he wouldn't approve, I didn't totally approve – but regrettably, or perhaps just awkwardly, Fra Domenico found out.

"He's going to train to be a condottieri like me," Johann blurted out proudly. Fra Domenico looked horrified, but Johann didn't seem to notice, even when the good Father made the sign of the cross in the air and whispered a prayer. Johann continued – unfortunately, "Maus, that is, Lorenzo, despite his slight build is quite a capable soldier. You might even say gifted, and I believe it was you that advised our friend that if you have a God-given talent you should use it." Fra Domenico gasped, and Johann added, "I intend to put a little meat on his bones, which should make him extremely formidable."

Then, just when I thought the worst was over, it got worse; to my horror, and Fra Domenico's, Johann told the account of my bloody exploit at Modon. I tried to signal Johann several times to stop, and even interrupted him, but he ignored me and continued not leaving out any gruesome detail. A couple of times, Fra Domenico, with disbelief in his eyes, looked at me for confirmation, and with just a look I would, regrettably, confirm what the big man was saying. Finally and mercifully, the story came to an end. A little pale and bewildered, Fra Domenico got up from the x-chair and indicated it was time for him to leave. He reiterated his gladness at meeting Johann, looked forward to seeing him again, and said his goodbyes. Once again, he offered me his deepest sympathies for the loss of Papa, but even after all that he had heard, Fra Domenico managed a smile for me, and sincerely told me that he was glad that I was home. It was good to see him too, and that was what I told him, but I would wait for another day to try and restore, or at least soften my image in the good Father's eyes.

A rose without its scent would still be beautiful but something would be lacking – that's what Florence was like without Mama and Papa there. Business was doing well in my city, and under the leadership of Piero Soderini – the head of the Signora, with the title of Gonfaloniere, meaning protector of the seal – Florence was prosperous again. The vibrant, colorful festivals went on; music still played in the streets; the church bells rang on Sundays; children laughed, and played; people shopped in the outdoor markets, and criminals were executed in the piazzas; but it just wasn't the same for me. In fact, seeing my city go on, and do so well, without Mama and Papa, depressed me. Fortunately for me, as I have already stated, I had my new friend to keep me from drifting too deeply into melancholia.

That first year Johann and I did everything together. We spent our days sparring and training in the shop, and as Johann promised, I began to finally put some muscle on my bones. If Mama were alive she would have said, "You look just like your papa," except I didn't have his powerful forearms or his powerful nose. When we weren't trying to kill each other, we attended festivals, executions, and preformed the many necessary tasks and functions of daily life. I also helped Johann with his Italian, as I had promised, but he would have gotten better on his own just by living in my city; he was a remarkably quick learner. We spent our nights drinking at the Severed Limb – one of the seedier taverns in the Santo Spirito Quarter – because it was not far from the shop and it attracted soldiers, the condottieri, and other hard-bitten men. They also served beer – Johann's preference – as well as wine, and a new, very potent drink, called whiskey; it tasted awful, but it got you drunk real fast. Johann told me he preferred seedy taverns because he enjoyed the occasional brawl, and the type of woman a seedy tavern attracts. Johann had many of these women; they liked him because he was the type of man a seedy tavern attracts. I, on the other had, had few of these women; I was not the type of man a seedy tavern attracted, but that was all right because I found them equally uninteresting. Fighting in the Severed Limb was not only common, but encouraged, even the tavern owner occasionally got into it; he was a big man – actually he was just fat – who ran the place, and was proud to show off his missing teeth, lost in one such fight. When Fra

Domenico found out how and where we were spending our nights, he, as expected, made the sign of the cross in the air and prayed for our salvation, and then condemned me for patronizing this, "den of inequity."

We did little to earn money and lived off of what we had saved from our service on the *Shivare*. When that ran out, I resisted using Papa's small fortune and earned what we needed painting; Johann didn't look for work that first year because I told him we didn't need it. Reluctantly, he went along, vowing to repay me someday. For the most part, I painted portraits of women. Most of these women came to me for reasons other than artistic ones; it would have been hard for me to believe that they came because of my exceptional talents as an artist. My work was good but I knew my limitations, and fostered no illusions about my abilities to paint. I was aware that there were rumors that I had inherited lots of money, which was certainly true though I never admitted it. At least part of the rumor came from my old art teacher, Bramante, but I think our spending, though it wasn't extravagant, was more than the average citizen would spend. That meant that either we had some source of financial security or that we were just crazy; actually it was both, we had money and we were crazy. But I don't believe that it was just the rumors of wealth that brought those women to me; I looked good, and I was in good physical condition. I resisted most of their advances, but modesty prevents me from writing about any of those I chose not to resist, for I wasn't in love, and therefore I am a little ashamed. As you will see, I openly disclose my indiscretions in my romantic adventures when, I at least believed, I was in love.

There was one night at the Severed Limb that I will never forget. It started out typical enough: it was noisy and crowded; the place stank of stale beer and wine; Johann tried and succeeded to get drunk; I tried and failed to stay sober; and there was sex and violence in the air. Johann was off chasing women and trying to instigate a brawl, and I was standing alone, in a corner with my back to the wall – a prudent defensive position to be in considering the surroundings – when I saw a familiar face coming toward me through the crowd – Bramante. I thought about escape, but while the corner is a good defensive position, it's not so good for retreat; I hadn't considered the need to run until then. My first thought was that I didn't think that his being there was a mere coincidence – Bramante rarely did anything unplanned – but I knew he wouldn't admit to checking-up on me, and he didn't. Instead he told me it was a surprise to see me there and asked me how long I had been back in Florence.

"Lorenzo, what a surprise it is to see you here," said Bramante. "How long have you been back in Florence?"

"For months," I answered, "but I suspect that you knew that."

"Now if I knew that, why would I ask?" he asked with a smirk. "You don't think that I've been spying on you, do you Lorenzo? Huh?"

"Of course not," I answered sarcastically. Then I noticed that he didn't have anything to drink, so I offered. "Could I buy you a glass of wine?"

"Thank you, no, Lorenzo," said Bramante. "I don't drink."

"You don't drink, interesting," I chuckled. "Then why is it you are in a tavern? Particularly in one that specializes in 'drink' and lots of it."

"Why for the atmosphere, of course," said Bramante with a smile, and without hesitation. "And for the people. I run into a lot of old friends in places like this."

"I'm sure you do," I said sardonically.

"Like you, huh?" he quipped, still smiling. Then he asked, "How is Sabastiano?"

I was certain he knew what had happened to Papa, but I played along and told him an abbreviated version of the story of Papa's demise anyway.

He put away his insufferable smirk momentarily, and offered me a surprisingly sincere condolence. "I'm very sorry for your loss, Lorenzo, sincerely," he said. "I really liked Sabastiano. He was a good man, and I am sure that God has saved a special place for him. It must be hard for you, but you can console yourself with the knowledge that your mama and papa have been reunited."

"Thank you, Bramante," I said.

"Well then, I shall be coming by to see you, huh?" he said, with that insufferable smirk back on his face – so much for condolence.

"Actually, I have sold a few paintings on my own," I said, with a bit of pride. "Portraits."

"Really," he said, acting surprised. "Then I must come by and see you work. I can still be of assistance to you. There's much I can teach you, and I know lots of wealthy patrons." He paused, and when I said nothing he added, "No need to thank me. I take care of my friends, particularly in their time of need. Now I will be leaving you to your carousing. See you soon, huh?"

"I am certain of it," I quipped.

He just laughed, and then slithered back through the masses. I didn't see him again that night, and was certain then, and now, that he had only come to the Severed Limb to see me and begin to burrow his way back into my life.

My cup was empty, so I started for the bar for more wine, but on the way I came to my senses – what was left of them – and realized that I had drunk enough wine. I found myself stranded in the middle of the room, surrounded by the crowd. There were no tables in the center of the room

– all the tables were against the side walls – so everyone stood, and pushed and shoved their way around until they reached the back of the room where the bar was. At the bar they refilled their cups or took one of the many decanters of wine or beer, or had one of the small glasses of whiskey that were lined up along the rail. Then they moved back, or were pushed back, from the bar and toward the front door. The masses pushed and revolved around the room, each person made his way back and forth, getting to the bar when he needed to, like pigs at a trough. The side tables were only used by: drunks who had passed out; those who had been knocked unconscious and laid to rest; men fondling women; and others who were involved in dubious dealings. That's why I thought it was unusual when I saw, through a brief opening in the crowd, a small man sitting, apparently sober, and alone; he appeared to be sketching in a notebook. The crowd shifted and he disappeared.

It was a cool night, so I had worn my cape, but it was hot in that crowed room, so I took off my cape and held it over my shoulder with my left hand. Noticing that my cup was empty, several had tried to fill it; something about an empty cup seems to offend the heaviest of drinkers. I figured that it was better to have no cup at all, than to be holding and empty one, so I tried to conceal my glass by palming it in my right hand and hiding it against my right leg. Just then the crowd moved, so I could once again see the man sketching; this time he saw me too. Something struck him, almost like familiarity, but I was certain that we had never met. He began to motion for me to come over. When I appeared confused and puzzled by why he was motioning to me, his look became agitated, and his gesturing more vigorous. Curious, I pushed my way over to the man. I started to speak, to ask him if it was me to whom he had been motioning. Without as much as an introduction, he began to order me about, telling me to stand the way I was before, and to turn my head to the side.

"Stand the way you were before," he said. "And turn your head to the side. Keep your left hand up there." I didn't understand exactly why, but I found myself trying to accommodate him – maybe it was because he had that kind of command in his voice that made you listen, and I had become somewhat used to taking orders from my military service. When I didn't get the position just right – I couldn't remember exactly how I was just standing – he barked at me, "No, no, not like that. Put your hand down on your … your other hand, put it down on your thigh again." Again I obeyed. He added, "Now keep your head turned away like that, don't look at me. Yea, that's it. Now stay like that for a minute."

I tried to glance over to see what he was doing; I knew he was sketching, but what? "Keep your head turned," he insisted, but in a friendlier tone. "All right, almost finished, almost finished, just a little more." And then a few seconds later, he said, "Done, thank you."

Slowly I looked over, and once I was certain that he was in fact finished with me, even though he was still drawing, I relaxed. I stood there for what seemed like several minutes, while he made various changes to his sketch; he never looked up. Just when I was about to walk away – I had made a step back away from the table – he spoke up. "Where are you going?" he asked, as he sketched.

"I just thought that you were ..." I began.

"Stay, sit down," he interrupted and insisted.

Again, I listened to him and sat down. Thinking back, I should have recognized the little man who sat across from me; I had heard about him most of my life, though I had never actually seen him before. He was not an attractive man. He had large features for a thin face, and black curly hair, with a short, black beard. His slight build was contrasted by powerful looking arms – forearms like Papa's – and unusually large hands. Despite his hard look, and his demanding tone, I saw a deep sadness in his brown eyes. And although he appeared not much older than me, it was the kind of sadness you usually see in an older man who had lived a life unfulfilled. I believe that it was this sadness that ultimately had compelled me to obey his words in spite of his curtness, and not just my newfound commitment to following leaders blindly.

He made a few final marks, and then put down his sketch, and got right to the point. Assuming by my mere presence in that tavern, and by my modest dress, that I was a man of little means, he made me what I'm sure he thought was a generous offer of a half a florin, if I would model for a statue that he had been commissioned to do for the city of Florence.

"I will give you a half a florin," he said, "if you would model for a statue that I have been commissioned to do for the city of Florence. You don't have to do anything, but stand still for a few hours a day. Easiest work you probably have ever done or will ever do."

I realized that, at the time, he thought little of me to have made me such a meager offer, but I understood his preconception of me, so I smiled and said, "I don't need a half a florin ..."

"Then I will make it a whole florin," he barked, impatiently.

"No," I said still smiling. "I am not a poor man, who needs work. I am quite ... secure..."

"Oh, I apologize," he interrupted. "I just assumed that since you were in this rat hole, that you must not be a gentle..."

"Must I remind you that you're in this place," it was my turn to interrupt. Then I added, "Should I assume that you are a man..."

"I, Sir," he interrupted yet again, "am Michelangelo Buonarroti. I assure you, that my being here is strictly for muse. And, I believe that I have found it. Provided you agree to model for me, I will be out of the rat hole before you can bat your eyes." He paused, and when I said nothing, he added, "I assume that you have heard of me, unless, of course you are from somewhere on the other side of the world, or have been locked away in the Alberghettino in the tower of the Palazzo della Signoria for most of your life."

I was stunned, nervous, and excited all at the same time, but I fought to hide my emotions. 'Michelangelo!' I was screaming inside. I wanted to blurt out that I knew all about him, that I knew that he was a great artist and how much I admired him, and that I too was an artist, but instead I said in a calm controlled voice, "I know of your work, and would be honored to model for you."

"Good," quipped Michelangelo. "Now you see, just bat your eyes and I will be out of here." He stood up, and then added, almost as an afterthought, "Your name, I will need to know your name. So when you come calling, I will know it is you, and not have you turned away as some sycophant."

"Lorenzo, Lorenzo Demarco from Florence," I said proudly.

"Lorenzo Demarco," he repeated. "But your nose is too slight, and your eyes are blue, rare for an Italian in these parts, and not what you would expect from a Lorenzo Demarco from Florence."

"My mama was German," I explained. "Papa, now he was from Florence."

"I see," said Michelangelo. "That explains that. The combination works well for you, Lorenzo. You are a fine looking man. Will you come to see me tomorrow?"

"Yes," I answered without hesitation.

"Good," said Michelangelo. "You can find me working in a shack near the Duomo. If you have been near there lately, then you must have seen a temporary wooden structure. You can't miss it, it's right off of the Piazza della Signoria. You've probably seen it. It's ugly, but it wasn't built to look at. It serves its purpose, and will be torn down as soon as I have finished The Giant. More the reason for me to finish soon." Then he managed a friendly smile, and said, "With your help, maybe that won't be too long."

I smiled back and mumbled something like, "I'm honored to work for you."

"Of course you are," quipped Michelangelo, and he headed for the door.

Michelangelo had just left, when a decanter came flying, just over the top of my head, and smashed against the wall. The decanter was followed by a body that landed on the table in front of me; I stood up. The body was followed by Johann, who ran up to me and said, "Come on, Maus, join in. The fun is just beginning." Then someone smashed

Johann over the head with a cup of beer; beer and a little blood ran down the big man's cheeks and into his thick, curly, blonde beard and mustache. He licked the beer and blood from around his lips, smiled, turned, and then threw himself into the agitated crowd, shouting over his shoulder, "Come, on, Maus!"

Chapter VII

The first couple of years of the new century, and the new republic, in my city went well, or at least they appeared to me to be going well, but by 1503 even appearances were beginning to look strained, and whispers of dissention could be heard directed toward the council and Soderini – the Gonfaloniere was being blamed for a number of growing problems. First of all, Soderini had promised, when he first took office, to bring Pisa back under Florentine control, but he had yet to succeed and so Pisa was openly courting anyone who would protect them and be an enemy of my city. Desperate for some action toward the former protectorate, Soderini entertained a plan proposed by Leonardo da Vinci; Leonardo, back in Florence, was acting as advisor to the Signory. Between Florence and on its way to the sea, the Arno runs through Pisa. Leonardo's bold plan called for a series of cannels to be dug to reroute the river around Pisa. The plan never came about. Another problem for Soderini and my city was the threat of invasion, and the threat came from a number of sources. Italy was now being partitioned in the north by the French and in the south by the Spanish. It was just a matter of time before one of them, or both, tried for the middle. A more pressing threat came from Cesare Borgia who sat on our border in southern Tuscany. Borgia had been expanding his sphere of influence for some time and was openly threatening Florence.

Because of the threats, military expenditures for paying the condottiere were draining my city's wealth. Soderini tried to get the Signory to raise taxes to cover the cost, but they refused; the Signory didn't want to anger the people with more taxes. Soderini had the power to impose a tax, but he feared personal reprisal – loss of his office or worse. Looking back, Soderini probably should have gone ahead with the tax because he was going to be blamed for Florence's problems anyway. With the money, he might have been able to pay an army to take back Pisa earlier in his reign, and bring confidence back with a strong Florence. Niccolò Machiavelli, Soderini's most trusted advisor, came up with an alternative that bought him a little time and saved money – he suggested that the city raise a militia. Florence would fight Pisa and defend herself with her own army, but once again I am getting ahead of my story. First I have to tell about my time working with Michelangelo, as a model for "the giant."

By the time I began working for Michelangelo he had much of the colossal statue completed. We never agreed on payment for my time. I insisted that he not, but he always said he was going to pay me – he never did. I think he thought he needed the pretense of an employee/employer relationship so he could order me about, and make demands on my time. There would be times when weeks would pass and I would not hear from him, and then he would send for me, with perhaps a days notice, and I would be there, posing, fifteen hours a day for a month.

I had heard, and continued to hear all my life, that Michelangelo was "quick tempered," "hard to get along with," "cold," and "moody." I suppose that he was all of those things, but he was also, shy and thoughtful, and to his few friends, generous and loving. While he didn't have time for students, Michelangelo did have a few devoted followers, including a biographer. Though I wasn't one of the devoted followers, I knew that he liked me, and I believe I know why. I was enough of an artist to truly appreciate his brilliance, but he knew I wasn't good enough to become a competitor or steal any of his technique; I had shown him some of my sketches. Michelangelo was very paranoid about his work, and rarely shared his gifts or techniques with others; he didn't like anyone to see his work until it was finished, which was unfortunate because he left so many unfinished pieces that few people saw until after his death. A lot of these unfinished projects were sculptures, and because they are unfinished they appear as struggling figures, trapped in stone fighting to free themselves. Michelangelo saw himself as a sculptor first, and believed that all other forms of visual art – particularly painting – were inferior in expression. He once told me that he believed that his skill at working in marble and stone came from being weaned by a wet nurse who was part of a family of stone cutters; Michelangelo's mother, Francesca, was too ill to nurse him. He said, "I sucked in the craft of hammer and chisel with my foster mother's milk." Of course, I don't believe that is possible, and I don't think he really did either, but it was a good line for his biography.

His perception of what he was doing, as a sculptor, was unique and equally good for a line in his biography – whether he believed it or not. He said he would look at a block of marble and see the finished statue inside. What he did was to release this image, as if it had been there for all time, trapped in the stone, just waiting for someone to set it free.

The great statue that I was modeling for, "the giant," or "David," had been conceived and commissioned in the days of the gifted artist Donatello – the stone had been picked and the image had started to be released – but money and politics got in the way and the huge slab of marble, with David trapped inside, sat in the workshop of the Duomo for forty years. The statue had been intended for placement on the great Cathedral of Florence, but the new Republic of Florence wanted the statue to be placed in front of the Palazzo della Signoria. This location was agreed upon by the Signory, and confirmed by Leonardo da Vinci, just one of his many duties as adviser to the counsel. Michelangelo also liked the decision of placement because he saw his masterpiece as, "a symbol of our republic." David replaced another symbol of the republic, the Judith and Holofernes that had stood in front of the Palazzo since the exile of the Medici. At David's unveiling ceremony, I was amused and a little disgusted to see that the counsel had prudently covered the statue's naked loins with a brass garland of leaves. There had been some objection to having an openly nude male statue displayed in the square, and the Signory caved under the pressure. If anyone should have objected to the naked loins it should have been me; after all, they were mine. But again, I am getting ahead of myself.

I guess I was one of the first to see the finished colossal statue and it truly is a giant standing almost seventeen feet high. It combines classical themes in the Greek and Roman traditions, with modern ideas of emotion and motion in art. Modesty aside, David, like me, is athletic and manly in character with a very muscular, well-proportioned body – well at least it was like me as I was in the early part of the sixteenth century. The face came from another model, not I. Unlike me, the statue has very Roman features – although I would say the hair is similar to mine.

I don't recall him asking my opinion, but I remember giving one. He was up on a ladder making some adjustments, hammering and chiseling away and covered in marble dust from head to foot as usual; at the end of a day's work he had so much marble dust on him that he looked like a statue. Of course, I said it was magnificent, brilliant, and made several other accolades that were both expected by him and earned by his work.

Then I got a little critical; a few things about the statue had been bothering me. Despite its excellence, I saw a few things that didn't seem right. Why were the hands and head so large? And it appeared to me that one leg was slightly longer than the other one.

"Why are the hands and head so large?" I asked. "And it appears to me that one leg is slightly longer than..."

"That wasn't my fault," he interrupted. "It was the damn piece of marble, it was flawed. I did what I could to make it work, and thought I succeeded, and it was hardly noticeable."

"No, no," I interjected, but he kept talking right over me.

"See, this is why I go out to the quarries and pick out the stones myself, and supervise their excavation," he said as he quickly slid down the ladder so he could get up to me and bark right in my face. "What else did you say? His hands and head are too large."

"It's just that I used to paint a lot of hands..." I tried to say, but he would not let me.

"If you knew anything about sculpture," he growled, "you'd know that sometimes it looks best if you slightly exaggerate certain features if the work is going to be seem from a distance. This statue will be seen high upon a pedestal and it was originally intended, even after I started work on it, to be placed up on one of the Duomo's high buttresses. The head and hands are intentionally made large so from a distance the features will be easily seen, and they will not appear too large, but correct and proportional. Now do you see anything else wrong with my work? Perhaps you think it best if I postpone the September unveiling ceremony?"

"Of course not," I said flatly. I was used to Michelangelo's temperament, and unaffected by his curtness and sarcasm. I knew that all I had to do to change his mood was to wax his ego, but I also knew that I must be sincere; he hated phoniness and hypocrisy. I looked past him, actually over him, at the great statute and said, "The emotion in his posture, the intensity in his watchful eyes, the strength in his body – emphasized by his big, strong hands, his beauty, his massive size, all this shows that you have surpassed all who have come before you, even the Greeks and Romans, for their work, while similar to yours in style, lacked the expressiveness that is abundant in this masterpiece."

I looked back down at the Maestro, who looked into my eyes for truth. When he saw what he believed to be sincerity, he smiled and gave me a friendly jolt on the arm, and then went back to his work. "I'd think that you were just patronizing me," he said over his shoulder as he climbed the ladder, "but everything you said is true."

Michelangelo made a few light taps and bits of dust and stone fell to the ground, while I watched. The silence began to irritate me so I searched my thoughts for something to say. I remembered that I had heard that Michelangelo had been asked by the Signory to paint a mural for the Hall of the Council – an appealing and important enough commission on its own, but even more so because Leonardo had just begun work on his own fresco in the very same hall. The talk in my city was that this could be a great contest to see who was truly the most talented artist of the pair. I puzzled for a way to broach the topic, and then decided to bait Michelangelo by asking him, in regards to his commission for a mural for the Hall of the Council, did he feel that he was at a disadvantage having to work in the inferior medium of paint and brush, side-by-side with Leonardo.

"In regards to your commission for a mural for the Hall of the Council, do you feel that you are at a disadvantage," I said, "having to work in the inferior medium of paint and brush, after all, your work will be side-by-side with ..."

"I am at a disadvantage with no artist living or dead," said Michelangelo as he paused in his work to smirk down at me. "By the way, the finished paintings will be on opposing walls, not side-by-side." He went back to chiseling, as he spoke, "Though it is true that painting is a bastard form of art, and better suited for someone like Leonardo, or perhaps that young Raphael I've been hearing so much about. Artists with simple two dimensional abilities." I started to say that Leonardo was also an excellent sculptor, but Michelangelo cut me off. He said, "I am to paint a scene of a moment just before the battle of Cascina where the men are bathing and then are suddenly called to arms."

"It will give you the chance to show off your perfection of depicting the nude male in dramatic action," I quipped.

Michelangelo paused, and again, stopped chiseling and looked down at me. With a curious frown he barked, "What the hell was that? You sound like one of those dammed art critics. Is that what you do? I always wondered how you made a living, if those rumors about you being rich aren't true. Writing a book? Do you advise patrons? Not good enough yourself, so you go around and analyze others work for those with the means but not the brains to judge for themselves?"

"No," I said curtly. I think when I was with Michelangelo some of his rudeness and ill temper rubbed off on me, or more simply, I just learned to respond to him in kind. I continued, "I was just making, what I thought, was a fairly simple and obvious observation."

He looked at me a long time, again seeking out sincerity in my eyes. Satisfied, he went back to his work, and said in a pleasant tone, "Yes, it is obvious, to me and you, and perhaps a few others." He paused, and then added, "Perhaps you could be my biographer. You are quite good with words. I have been considering having someone put my genius into words, if that is possible." Of course, I didn't become Michelangelo's biographer – that job would be left to Giorgio Vasari and Ascanio Condivi – but looking back such encouragement, or perhaps acknowledgement is a better word, from a man like Michelangelo, began my thoughts of becoming a writer, or at least gave me pause to consider it.

For a long time, Michelangelo hadn't really needed me to pose, yet he was still insisting on my presence – another sign that he was actually fond of me. With little or nothing for me to do I was beginning to feel like I was wasting my time; I knew there was something else I should be doing, even if I wasn't exactly sure of what that something was. We had spent so much time together in a relatively short period of time that we had exhausted most of the more interesting topics of conversation. We were forced to chat about the mundane, like he asked me if I still go to that rat hole where we first met.

"Do you still go to that rat hole where we first me?" asked Michelangelo.

I smirked and said, "When would I have the time, I'm always here." My sarcasm brought out a shrug in him, and I continued. I said, with a little more sincerity, "I used to go there with Johann because it was where he liked to go. Now that he has been spending so much of his time courting Maria Velata, he has lost interest in going to the Severed Limb. I don't believe that she would approve of him going even if he wanted to."

"I'm not surprised. I don't know of many women who would approve of their men going out drinking, fighting, and whoring," smirked Michelangelo. Then he said, "He's German isn't he?" I nodded an affirmation and he continued, "Well he's probably having to work extra hard to impress the girl's family. It usually takes a while for the Florentine ego to accept an outsider as being good enough for one of their own." He took a long pause, and then he asked, "How about you? Are you courting any young Florentine maiden?"

Again I smirked and said, "When would I have the time? I'm..."

"Some things you just make time for," interrupted Michelangelo.

"Funny you should say that," I said. "Tell me, do you take your own advice?"

He glared down at me with a look to let me know my question wasn't worthy of answering, but he answered it anyway. "I have different priorities than the average man," said Michelangelo, as he went back to work – scraping and chiseling. "I assure you, I have an outlet for my passions. Besides, abstinence creates a void to be filled by creative energy."

"I got used to the idea of a life of celibacy when I was studying for the monastery," I said. "I don't think it did anything for my creative energy. My old art teacher, Bramante used to say ..."

"Bramante!" Michelangelo barked, and once again he glared down at me. "Which Bramante?"

I paused – surprised by his reaction to the name – and then said, "Tommaso Bramante."

Slowly and deliberately, Michelangelo came down the ladder; he had a serious look in his eyes. He came up real close to me as if he thought someone in that big empty room could hear what he was about to say. He said, "When I was young and working at the school in the Medici gardens, there was this older boy, a young man compared to me, with some small talent for painting and even less for sculpture, and some big talent for conniving and even bigger for unscrupulousness. He had been at the school longer than me, but he had yet to prove himself to the Maestros. I was just completing my first small relief, *The Madonna of the Stairs*. And this older boy, he knew how good my work was, how good I was already, better than he could have ever dreamed of. So he tries to talk me into letting him finish my work. He said it was good, my work, but it needed something. Something he could give it, like his name at the bottom of the canvas. He tells me that it would not be good for me to present it the way it was. That I might be dismissed, sent away, because it would be discovered that I had no talent, but he was going to help me. He would fix my work and I could stay. He just wanted to share the credit, the credit he claims he would be earning by fixing my work. Of course, I knew better, I was young but I knew how good I was, and how good he wasn't. I refused. He insisted. Still I refused, and then he insisted with his fists. We fought. He was bigger than me then, and more experienced at fighting. He gave me a black eye, a bloodied nose, and a bruised ego, but I did not yield. When word got back to Lorenzo de' Medici he was angry. He would have no fighting in his house. One of us had to go, and Lorenzo knew talent, so the choice was easy."

He looked around, still concerned about someone overhearing him, and then Michelangelo said in a surprisingly sincere and concerned voice, the kind of voice you might expect to hear being used by an older brother speaking to a younger brother, "Lorenzo, you must not trust this man."

"Oh, I know ..." I began, but he cut me off.

"He, this Bramante, is no good," Michelangelo continued in his sincere tone. "He has become a most successful thief and confidence man. He never gets caught because he is too smart to do the dirty work himself, so nobody actually sees him do anything criminal. He is sneaky, cold-blooded, and dangerous. They say he has had people killed. It's true. They say you cross him and you might just disappear." He hesitated and then added, "I believe it. He scares me. I think he still holds a grudge against me and is out to get me."

"After all this time? I don't ..." I started.

"Yes," Michelangelo interrupted, with earnest. "Part of being cold-blooded allows him to be patient for revenge. If he wants you, he will get you on his own time, and in his own way. You haven't done anything to cross him, have you, Lorenzo?"

"No," I said, but Michelangelo's paranoia was effecting me. I added, "That is, I don't think so. I was kind of rude to him the last time I saw him, but I don't think ... no. Hey, it was the night I met you at the ... that rat hole ..."

"Bramante was there?" Michelangelo interrupted again. "What did he want?" Did he say anything about me?"

"No," I said. "Again, I mean I don't think so. I'm pretty sure that he was there just to see me." I paused. There was concern and a lot of fear in his paranoid eyes. I knew Michelangelo needed reassurance to ease his anxiety so I said, "Bramante's been nosing around me and my papa's shop for years. He thought my papa had money, so now he thinks I have it, and he's trying to get his hands on it. He's been having me followed and watched." Michelangelo wasn't convinced so I offered a little more. "Johann and I have been living off of our earnings from our service with the Venetians, and it's about gone. He's waiting and watching to see how two men can get along so well without any means. I've been getting some money from painting, but Bramante knows I'm not getting that much, and Johann has yet to find employment."

After a long look, the corner of Michelangelo's mouth began to rise slightly. He said, "He's right isn't he? You've got money, and ... you're playing with him, huh?" It was my turn to smile. Then he added, "You be careful, Lorenzo."

Flattered and touched by his concern, I assured him that I would.

It was getting late, about time for me to be getting home, but every time I started to leave Michelangelo would ask me something trivial about what I was doing, or my plans, which was odd because he never asked about my life. What was even more rare was that he was talking to me and not working. Then it occurred to me – we both knew that he didn't need me anymore, and with the unveiling date fast approaching, there was no need for me to come back. Finally we ran out of small conversation and there was no reason for me to stay. I was touched by Michelangelo's insistence that I come back and see him from time to time; I agreed. I was honored to.

"I'd be honored to," I said.

He smiled and said, "Of course you would."

With the threat of war, and little support for raising a tax to pay for the condottiere, it was decided – on the recommendation of Soderini's most trusted advisor, Machiavelli – that Florence would raise a militia and train them for defense. More than just a man of words and politics, Machiavelli took charge of recruiting, outfitting, and training the militia. He went to the countryside to enlist all males over fifteen and capable of fighting. Those eligible in the city were not called upon for fear that they would all expect to be in the more prestigious cavalry or be given command.

It just so happened that Johann and I were on the same field outside of Florence, where Papa and I had practiced, firing cannon, when along came Niccolò Machiavelli returning from a recruitment expedition; he must have seen us first because he was riding hard in our direction. I recognized him even from a distance. Once again he looked neat, nicely dressed in black, with a black cape that rippled behind him as he rode on his well-groomed horse. His thin gaunt features, bony forehead, and lean form were unmistakable. He had changed little in the few years since we met, but now there was a hint of gray in his jet-black hair – not surprising for someone working for the Signory.

Machiavelli pulled up his horse and dismounted. He called me by name, and reminded me that he would come looking for me, if I didn't come looking for him.

"Lorenzo Demarco, I told you that I would come looking for you, if you didn't come looking for me," he said. "It's good to see you again. You may recall that it was on this very field that we met and I made that promise. Well here I am."

"Yes, I remember," I said. I was impressed the he remembered me, but I didn't say anything. Instead, I turned to Johann and said, "Johann, this is Niccolò Machiavelli."

"Good to meet you," said Johann. "Maus has told me much about you and your work for the Signory. And I have heard people speak of you many times in the streets and in the taverns of Florence."

"Well I hope we can be friends anyway," joked Niccolò. Johann laughed – a big burly roar – and I smiled. Then he added, "Your Italian is good, but your accent is unmistakable. I've been up north many times, beautiful country."

"And I will say the same for your country," said Johann. Then with a smile, he added, "And your women."

"On behalf of the women of Florence, I thank you," said Niccolò.

"As for my Italian, I owe it all to my language teacher, Maus," said Johann. "He's quite the linguist, you know."

"No I didn't," said Machiavelli.

"Oh Maus speaks several languages fluently including German," said Johann.

"Indeed," remarked Machiavelli. Then he took a more serious tone, and said to me, "You may have heard that I have been in charge of raising a militia. I have enlisted more than four hundred men, a dozen just today. They are all young and, or inexperienced, and are to be molded into an effective, well-disciplined fighting force. I am finding enough recruits and unfortunately have too many unqualified volunteer officers. What I really need are experienced men, like your father, to help me train them."

He paused for a response, and I told him, "Papa was lost in a naval engagement in the Adriatic Sea."

"Oh, I am sorry to hear it," Machiavelli said sincerely.

"Thank you, Niccolò," I said. "But if it's an experienced artilleryman you need, I would like to volunteer my services. I gave Niccolò a brief version of my experiences on the *Shivare*, and he appeared genuinely impressed enough to invite me to come down to the Piazza the next day and review his new recruits. I accepted. He also noted that my language skills might be of an even bigger service to him in his diplomatic duties. Again I accepted.

With me volunteering, Johann was quick to offer his abilities. He told Niccolò that he was a mercenary or a condottiere, and could fight with a variety of weapons – a fact I confirmed – and he had years of combat experience.

"I was a mercenary or what you call a condottiere," said Johann. "I can fight with a variety of weapons."

"That's true," I confirmed.

"And I have years of combat experience," added Johann.

"That's also true," I said.

"Well then, I will expect to see you at the Piazza tomorrow also," said Niccolò as he turned and then mounted his horse. "We'll talk more later and work out the details – your pay and things like that. Until then, Florence and I thank you for your service."

As agreed, the next day Johann and I met Machiavelli and his recruits in the Piazza. Four hundred men turned out to join, what would be called, the Bandiere. Each man was given a white waistcoat, red and white stockings, shoes, white cap, iron breastplate, and a lance or a musket. Having our own superior armor and weapons, Johann and I only accepted the clothing – so we would blend in with the ranks. Since most of the men were so young, they would need extensive training to become an effective fighting force, but the advantage of recruiting the young is that they are not set in their ways, and more susceptible to discipline and orders. They also haven't had the time to pick up many bad habits, as have the older more experienced men, making them easier to train; it's easier to train a young soldier in the style and form you need, than to try and retrain an old one.

As predicted by Machiavelli, many young noblemen showed up to volunteer to lead – most of them were turned away. Of course, Johann and I were invited. I agreed to work part-time and train an artillery battery. Johann had a more ambitious proposal. He hadn't a regular income and since he was courting a young woman, he knew he would need steady employment. He presented to Niccolò, with my support, a brief description of his exploits and experience – surprisingly he was modest and concise. The modest version was enough to impress Machiavelli; Niccolò was a man-of-action and therefore more impressed by a man's deeds than his words. Johann was made a captain in charge of training for the entire regiment; Machiavelli would be too busy to oversee all the actual day-to-day activities. We decided that we would meet later that evening at the Severed Limb to celebrate our new relationship. Niccolò had never been there so we told him what to expect – about the kind of men and women who went there. When hearing that many experienced soldiers and condottiere would be present, Machiavelli proposed to address the men to seek experienced men for a special elite platoon; Johann and I advised him against it, but Niccolò insisted, and even asked us to help.

I must admit Niccolò Machiavelli had a certain undeniable ability to gain respect with his charisma and words. I think it might have had something to do with the fact that he was more than a man of words and that fact came through in his presence. Even in a rat hole like the Severed Limb, when Machiavelli talked, men listened.

He stood up on a table – his thin frame cloaked in his black cape. He wisely kept words simple and his message brief. Everyone stopped talking to hear what he had to say – they continued to drink, of course – but their attention could not be counted on for long. Niccolò got right to the point; he appealed to their patriotism and played up the fear of foreign invasion. Everyone remembered how the French came marching into the city and forced Florentines to pay a tribute.

"Everyone remembers how the French came marching into our city and forced Florentines to pay a tribute," said Machiavelli, "or more like a ransom." The crowd let out a unanimous growl, moan, and cheer of agreement. "Once again we have the French in Milan and threatening to come down the peninsula. The Spanish have taken Naples and are now threatening to come up the peninsula. So you know where that leaves us." He paused for effect, and then continued, "Right in the middle. Are we to be pawns in their fight to partition our Italy? I say, No!"

The crowd echoed him with a hardy, "No!"

"But what can we do!" I shouted, holding back the urge to smile; Johann didn't hold back, he laughed.

"I'm glad you asked, my friend," said Machiavelli in earnest, showing his experience and composure when playing a crowd. "We can defend ourselves."

Then Johann said, holding back his amusement, and in an over-rehearsed voice, "But we are few and they are many."

"That's true, my friend," snapped back Machiavelli in perfectly rehearsed timing. He paused to build suspense and interest as he looked over the crowd. Then he continued, "We have powerful friends who share our concerns and fear of invasion."

"Who?" I baited.

"Rome for one," hooked Machiavelli. "They have the wealth to raise a mighty army of men like you – strong experienced warriors – and it just so happens that I, Niccolò Machiavelli, am the official representative to the new Pope, Julius II."

"But how does that help us?" I questioned, begging the answer.

"It means I can personally assure all of you that Rome will support you, will support us, will support Florence in any fight," answered Machiavelli.

"What about Florence?" asked an unrehearsed voice from the crowd. "Does Florence have the wealth to raise a mighty army of men like us?"

There was a brief pause; this was a question that Machiavelli didn't want to have to answer, because he knew it wouldn't be what they wanted to hear, and he – to his credit – didn't want to lie to them. He said, "You are all good, strong men, many of you are professional soldiers. In her hour of need your city, the cross and the lily, calls upon you to volunteer."

"Volunteer!" the crowd moaned.

"You mean we wouldn't get paid!" shouted a voice.

"That's generally what volunteer means," quipped Johann.

"We don't have the funds, that's why we need you," Niccolò pleaded, but he had lost them – no coins no condottiere. The crowd began to turn away. Machiavelli tried to rally them back. "Perhaps just once in your lifetime you will be called upon to serve and defend a cause as just as the defense of our homes and families." As the men began to drift back into their normal behavior – drinking, whoring, talking, laughing, shouting, belching, and fighting – Machiavelli tried to compensate by raising his voice. He bellowed, "Men, join me today, and then when you are old and gray, when most of your life is behind you and there is very little living ahead, with nothing left but your memories, you can look back to this day and say, I was there …" But they weren't, so Niccolò gave up, and climbed down from the table; I lent him a hand.

"I think that went well," I said with a broad smile. Johann laughed.

Niccolò frowned and said, "How do mean? They completely rejected my proposal, not one volunteer."

"Yea, but they didn't try and kill you," I quipped.

We pushed our way to the bar, where Johann grabbed a decanter of beer; I got a bottle of wine for Niccolò and me. After a few quick drinks, even Machiavelli was laughing at himself. I couldn't resist from making light of his zealousness and patriotic nature.

"I liked 'the cross and the lily calls upon you to volunteer,' " I said in a mock serious voice. "Oh, and who could forget, 'once in your lifetime you will be called upon to serve and defend a cause as just as the defense of our homes and families.'" Johann was laughing again, and Machiavelli was trying hard not to, when I added, " 'When you are old and gray, when most of your life is behind you and there is very little living ahead, with nothing left but your memories, you can look back to this day and say, I was there' when Niccolò Machiavelli stood up on a table at the Severed Limb and tried to get a bunch of drunken oafs to volunteer for the militia." Johann let out a big burly roar, and slapped Niccolò on the back; now Machiavelli had to laugh.

"I guess I can come across a little heavy on the patriotism," said Niccolò, smiling, but in a serious tone. "I believe in public service. To serve is an honor. I don't understand why everyone doesn't see how important it is to be involved, stand up and be counted when your city needs you. That's what a republic is all about. If the people don't care, then they will get what they deserve – a self-serving dictator. Didn't Savonarola teach them anything? He put us right in the hands of the French."

"I understand what you are trying to say," said Johann. "But these guys don't care. They can't feel anything like patriotism or loyalty to a place. I know because I'm one of them. To them it's all about collecting the spoils."

"If you are one of them, then why did you volunteer?" asked Niccolò. "I guess you are getting paid, but you are not collecting any 'spoils.' "

"That's true," said Johann, "but they say women will change you, and if I want to keep Maria..." He paused, downed a whole glass of beer, belched loudly, and then added, "I'm going for respectability. I need steady work in one place, here, and not unreliable opportunities even if they may offer spoils elsewhere. Besides, I never had a place, a homeland, to defend, and Maus here has convinced me to adopt Florence. If she'll adopt me back, I will defend her."

We talked about nothing – at least nothing I can remember these many years later – for the rest of the evening, but I remember we remained in good spirits. Niccolò stayed just long enough to appear as a respectable drinker, but left before things got too wild. Johann and I stayed too long as usual, or at least what used to be usual. We didn't know it then – there's no way we could have – but we wouldn't be back there for a long time.

Ever since I had got back to Florence, I had heard about a young painter, who it was being said, might surpass all that had come before him. I can't say I disliked him, because I didn't know him, but I did find that the mentioning of his name brought about a certain negative feeling inside me. It wasn't just because he was being praised for something I wish I could do; it was because he was younger than me and being praised for something I wish I could do. Raphael Sanzio had been in Florence for some time when, on a sunny afternoon on my way to the Palazzo della Signoria, I met him on the street. Another thing that should have put me off about him was that he came up to me and said that Bramante had pointed me out to him, saying I was acquainted with both Leonardo and Michelangelo; a referral from Bramante had to be questioned. So I should not have thought much of him, but some people are just born to be liked.

Raphael had been studying the two great artists work and wanted to know what they were like as people. I told him what I knew, and about my experiences with each man, and he listened intently. He then asked about me. After giving him a brief account of myself – very brief – I asked about him. I must admit, I found him friendly, personable, and quite generous with his ideas and talents; he offered to help me with technique and anything else to improve my skills. He then asked my opinion on what I thought were the strengths of the two great artists that he had come to Florence to see work. I told him that Leonardo is a master at depth perception.

"Leonardo is a master at depth perception and at the use of soft shading to delineate features," I said. "He also loves to contrast light and dark images."

"Yes, that's called chiaroscuro," said Raphael. "I have picked these very same qualities of the great Maestro to emulate."

"And Michelangelo is really exploring emotional themes using expressive detailed anatomy," I said.

"Yes, I have seen that too," said Raphael. "Lorenzo, my you have a keen eye. Are you sure that your skills are not just a little better than you make out?"

"I wish they were," I smiled and said. "I guess my eyes can see in the work of others, what my hands cannot do in my own."

We were just approaching the Palazzo Spini when I spotted Leonardo talking to a group of men seated on some benches; we walked toward them. When we got close enough, I could hear them arguing about a passage in Dante. Then from out of nowhere, Michelangelo came scurrying by; he passed us heading in the direction of Leonardo and the group of men. I called out to him and he stopped. I said, "Michelangelo this is Raphael ..."

"Yes, I know who he is," interrupted Michelangelo. "Another painter, just what the world needs. Take my advice, young man, throw away your brushes. If you're really interested in art, pick up a hammer and a chisel and look into a piece of marble. Though I doubt that you will see anything."

Then Michelangelo walked away on his original heading with a visibly disappointed Raphael and me close behind. I began to console Raphael and made excuses for Michelangelo's behavior when I heard Leonardo say, "Michelangelo will explain it to you." Again, Michelangelo stopped. He then turned toward Leonardo and the group of men. "These men were wondering ..." Leonardo began.

"You designed a horse to be cast in bronze," snapped Michelangelo. Thinking Leonardo was somehow setting him up for ridicule, he chose to attack first. "You realized that you could not cast it, so you abandoned it from shame. You seem to have a habit of running away and not finishing what you start. Afraid that people will find out that you are a fraud?" Leonardo looked stunned and a little embarrassed. Michelangelo added, "And those stupid Milanese believed in you." Then he was off, not waiting for a response.

"See," I said to Raphael with a smile. "It wasn't you. He treats everybody like that." Then watching Michelangelo walking quickly and receding in the distance, I added, still making excuses for the great artist,

"He's not really so hard, he's just temperamental. He has a lot on his mind and can't talk with others when he's thinking." Then I said, "Come on. I'll introduce you to Maestro Leonardo. I think you will find him more congenial."

We walked up to the group of men and I introduced Raphael to Leonardo da Vinci, and then, being in a hurry to get to the Palazzo, I made my exit. I left Raphael looking the way you would expect a young artist to look in the presence of an older maestro and mentor. Though we never had the time to become good friends – Raphael was soon off to Rome to work for the Pope – I liked him and we would meet again.

I hadn't gone very far when I saw Bramante coming toward me; it had been so soon after leaving Raphael, I assumed that he had seen us together – he had. The first thing he said to me was that I see you've met Raphael.

"I see you've met Raphael," said Bramante.

"And I see you've been following me again," I sneered.

"Oh Lorenzo, you know I love you, but you overvalue yourself," said Bramante with a grin. "I have more important things to do than follow you. I was just on my way to the Piazza when I saw you talking to the young Raphael, and I believe I saw Leonardo too, huh?"

"Yes, I introduced Raphael to his idolized inspiration," I said. "He seemed quite pleased."

"Of course, who wouldn't," said Bramante. "Speaking of which, when are you going to introduce me to Leonardo? Huh?"

I knew Bramante wanted an introduction, but I had been avoiding it; I didn't want Leonardo to remember me as the one who put Bramante on him. So I avoided a direct answer. I said, "I didn't know you hadn't met him yet. You seem to know everyone in Florence." Then before he could answer I tried to quickly change the subject. "I'm kind of in a hurry. I have to meet someone at the Palazzo della Signoria. So if you don't mind, I have to get on my way." I started to walk away, but Bramante followed.

"Well I am also heading that way, the Piazza remember," said Bramante. "I'll walk with you." He quickly scurried to my side. "I've always felt that a walk passes more pleasantly when you are accompanied by a friend, huh?"

"Yes, I agree," I said. "In fact, I am expecting a friend to join me, and I think I see him, there up ahead, waiting for me."

It was Johann; he was coming from seeing Maria Velata. Now that Johann was working, he was spending fewer days with Maria, so he was making it up with more evenings. We were both working for Machiavelli that day; Johann was working with the militia, and I was to translate a few letters from, and craft a few letters to, the German Emperor Maximilian.

The first thing I had to do, after saying hello to my old friend was to introduce him to Bramante – a prospect I had successfully avoided until now. I had told Johann a bit about the suspicions I had concerning my old art teacher, but I wasn't too anxious for him to find out for himself. I guess I was afraid that Bramante would take advantage of my not so sophisticated friend – I need not to have worried. After several minutes of Bramante's boasting of how good a friend he was to me and to my family, Johann bluntly cut him off to ask him if he was so close to me, then how come in the four years he had been in Florence they have never met.

"If you are so close to Lorenzo, then how come in the four years I have been in Florence we have never met?" Johann asked, curtly. "I've been living with the Maus all this time and have never seen you before."

Bramante just laughed and said, "Perhaps Lorenzo has been hiding you from me, huh?"

"I don't know, I'm pretty hard to hide," said Johann. "I'm loud and I take up a lot of space."

"Didn't you know he was staying with me at the shop?" I asked, certain that he did.

"Now how would I know?" asked Bramante with his insufferable smirk.

"I thought you were having the Maus watched, or followed," Johann blurted out with his usual tact.

Bramante laughed and said, "Oh Lorenzo, have you been telling this man stories about me? It doesn't matter. It is true that I hear things. Can I help it if I have lots of friends that tell me things? That doesn't mean that I am spying, you understand. I just listen. For instance, I hear that you Johann are going to marry one of our own fair maids, Maria Velata."

Bramante had just slipped, he admitted that he at least heard of, or knew of Johann, but I was too surprised by the idea of Johann getting married that I didn't even notice his mistake until later.

"That's ridiculous," I said. "Sure they have been dating and things are getting serious, but I would know if that were true." Johann said nothing, I continued, "So you can just go back to whoever told you that rumor and tell him that they were wrong."

"Perhaps," said Bramante with an insufferable smile. He had noticed and interpreted Johann's silence more accurately than I, but he felt no need to confirm his suspicions; he knew that I would find out he was right soon enough. Instead he asked me, "What about you, Lorenzo? Is there a woman in your life? Huh?"

"You tell me," I quipped. "Haven't your many friends had anything to say about my affairs?"

"No, I haven't heard a thing," said Bramante. "But sometimes there are things that just haven't gotten to me yet. And as I always tell you, I do have other interests besides you, though you are often in my thoughts." He paused and then added, "You know, you could use the companionship, as well as the other assets that a good woman brings to a man."

I think my mistake was that I hesitated, or maybe something in my face revealed that I thought he might be right – Bramante was not a man easily fooled – though I proclaimed the opposite. "I'm not interested in romance, I've got too many other things on my mind," I said. "Besides, I don't even have any prospects and I don't see that changing anytime soon." Saying that was probably my next mistake, though I didn't know it at the time, I would soon find out.

"Well that could change at anytime," said Bramante. "The secret is to keep an open mind and an open heart and anything can happen, huh?"

"I suppose," was all I remember saying. Then mercifully, Bramante bid us a good day and was off leaving Johann and I alone to cross the Piazza to the Palazzo della Signoria. On the way I asked him about the progress of the militia; he kept his answer short and followed it by asking me about my artillery battery. Sensing that there was something else on his mind, I also kept my answer brief. We stopped outside the Palazzo where I tried to pry out what I was certain he wanted to tell me. I pointed out that I hadn't seen a lot of him lately, and was curious as to what he had been up to; he answered that I would be seeing even less of him.

"You will be seeing even less of me, Maus," said Johann. "Damn that Bramante. He was right though. I wanted to tell you later tonight. Maria and I are getting married. Her family finally approved. I hope God approves, and that you will approve."

"Of course, of course, I do, congratulations, Orso!" I said, and slapped the big man on the back and gave him a manly embrace. "Though, I guess I'm not that surprised. I've noticed you haven't been around the shop, especially at night."

"Well that's part of the reason we decided to go ahead and get married," said Johann with a grin.

"Oh Orso," I said shaking my head, and also grinning. "What does her family say about it?"

"At first they weren't so sure," said Johann. "You know they were worried because I am not from Florence or even Italian. I didn't have an income until recently, but now with Maria's condition, they say, how soon can you get married?"

"And so what is your answer? How soon?" I asked.

"I told them that I wanted to talk to you first," said Johann. "You are the closest I have to a family – a brother. I wanted to ask you to stand with me. It will be almost all her people, I need somebody on my side."

"Of course, Orso, of course," I exclaimed. "I am so happy for you. This is what you want isn't it?"

"Yes, I think so," said Johann in a rare serious tone. "She is good for me, and I would like a son. I'm earning enough with the militia for now to get by, and there is a modest dowry. Her family is in the wool trade. Did I tell you that? They are going to give us a place to live in the Santo Spirito Quarter, not too far from your shop. Maria will also be working, after the baby of course. All the women in her family work as weavers." I wasn't totally convinced that Johann really wanted a wedding, but if it did work out, it would probably be a good thing for him. He then turned the question of marriage on me. He asked, "Now that I am taking the fall, we have to see about finding someone for you."

I laughed, "I haven't given it much thought, Orso. I mean, I have to have a woman first."

"Yes, Maus," said Johann. "I believe it's an absolute must. Perhaps I can help. Maria has a sister, and there are a few other single women in the weaver's guild. They will all be at the wedding. You can have your pick or I could pick someone out for you."

"Thank you, but no," I said. "I prefer to let fate take care of any romantic possibilities."

"Then let it be in God's hands, but you should consider that my taste in women may be a little better than his," said Johann with a laugh.

I chose his moment of self-amusement to change the subject. "Where and when is the blessed event to take place?" I asked.

"Her family will be working out the details," said Johann. "But it will have to be sometime soon, and it will be on the steps of San Spirito. Fra Domenico, we agreed, will do the ceremony."

"What about the reception?" I asked.

"They can't really afford much," said Johann. "And considering my station, and my not having any family, they ..."

"Nonsense," I interrupted. "Leave it to me, Orso. I will handle the reception."

"No, I couldn't let you do that," said Johann.

"I insist," I said. "We'll call it a wedding present. I'll keep it simple. I'll talk to Fra Domenico about using the courtyard at the cathedral, and I will have it catered."

"Are you sure?" asked Johann.

"Of course," I said. "And you know I can afford it."

Johann laughed. "Well then it's settled!" he exclaimed. "I can't wait to tell Maria, she will be so pleased. Maus you are a true friend."

With that settled, we went inside the Palazzo della Signoria.

Johann's wedding was nice, simple, and typically Florentine, and I will tell you all about it, but first I have to write a few words about the contest between Leonardo and Michelangelo. As it turned out, it really wasn't much of a contest – I mean it didn't come off as planned. Again, I'm getting ahead of the story. It was Machiavelli who brought Leonardo to work for the Signory in Florence; the two had become friends when they both were staying with Cesare Borgia, the Duke of Valentinois. Leonardo was given a contract from the Signory to create a wall painting depicting the battle of Anghiari in the Hall of the Great Council in the Palazzo Vecchio. It was to be on the right side of the Hall, as you walk in – a twenty-three foot high by fifty-seven foot wide mural. Leonardo had finished the massive cartoon for the fresco and had begun putting paint on the wall, when his counterpart was brought in to paint the other wall. Michelangelo was also to do a war scene – the battle of Cascina. He finished part of his cartoon and prepared to start work on the left side of the Hall. The two cartoons were put on display together to give the public an idea of what the finished room would look like. Leonardo created a ballet of violence and horror with swirling masses of men and horses engaged in mortal combat. Hatred could be seen in the warriors screaming faces, and strength in their bulging muscles. Like Leonardo's, Michelangelo's drawing showed energy of bodies in action. His men are called to arms as they are bathing in the river; each soldier shows swift reaction to the danger in various states of dressing or bounding from the water.

Imagine the two great artists working back-to-back, each with their assistants – paints, brushes, wet plaster, scaffolding everywhere – pushing each other, not to be outdone, with pride and reputations at stake. But alas, it wasn't meant to be. For whatever reason, neither man seemed to want to commit themselves wholeheartedly to their projects; Leonardo was working slowly as usual, but it was Michelangelo who was first to completely pull out of the competition. The Pope called Michelangelo to Rome to work on an ambitious project – forty large statues for a tomb. Leonardo feigned an attempt to continue his part until he too was called away; he went back to Milan after being summoned by the French governor, Charles d'Amboise. Neither paintings were ever continued or completed. So ended the great competition between the two premier artists of their time.

Johann and Maria's wedding was, as I have said, simple and typically Florentine. They had the perfect day; it rained in the morning – a sign of good luck – but then it stopped allowing the proceedings at the church and the courtyard to go on as planned.

A procession of about fifty people – the Velata family and friends mostly from the weavers guild – walked through the damp streets to San Spirito. As the sun burned off the moisture, a fine mist of steamy fog rose from the flagstones. When we reached the church, as we climbed the steps, I caught a glimpse of Machiavelli observing the proceedings; he smiled at me. I didn't see him again that day and I am not surprised; it was more unexpected that he showed up at all, because he was always so busy – on the go.

Johann and Maria stood hand-in-hand at the door of San Spirito. Fra Domenico officiated – he led prayers for the couple, blessed them, and prompted Johann and Maria to recite vows of love and commitment to each other. Johann wore his best breeches and a plain white doublet and a red vest. His hair appeared to have been recently combed, and over it he wore a small red cap – in the Italian style – to match his vest; it was the only time I ever saw Johann wear a cap. He looked uncommonly stiff – more uncomfortable than what I would call nervous. Maria looked sweet and lovely. She wore yellow flowers in her black hair that complimented her smooth olive-colored skin. Her skirt was simple, yellow and white, made of fine wool with a matching, square-necked, loose fitting sleeveless bodice. Despite the warmth of the morning, Maria wore a green shawl around her shoulders and body that partly concealed her condition. Maria's father gave her away freely – with his blessing – the couple exchanged rings, and completed their vows with a kiss. As the modest crowd applauded the new couple, a notary asked me to spell Johann's last name for the official record.

Everyone agreed, the reception was quite impressive, but it probably wouldn't have taken that much to impress the modest Velata family and their weaver friends. In the air, there was a steady flow of joyful music – flutes, mandolins, harmonic voices and solos – that prompted much dancing. The caterers provided more food than could be possibly eaten by a group five times as large as the one that had gathered in the courtyard at San Spirito. Fra Domenico assured me that he would see to it that nothing would go to waste; even in good times there were always those who went hungry in Florence.

The food was spread out and served on several large wooden tables, each covered with fine embroidered table cloths, silver settings, decorative majolica plates, glasses, and sculptures made of flowers and sugar treats.

Some of the guests sat at the tables and ate, while others chose to carry their food about and eat as they danced or socialized. Cold dishes included breads, olives, raw vegetables, fruits, mushrooms, pecorino cheese, and finocchiona – a salami flavored with fennel seeds. Hot dishes included: split chicken; skewed broiled sausages; Florentine grilled flat steaks, served rare; small boar hams; soups, such as ribollita, bean, vegetable, and bread porridge; beans, broad beans, and peas; and a variety of vegetables like spinach, asparagus, and artichokes. There were also a variety of cakes and pastries, and of course, lots of wine and beer. I ate too much but drank little. It was early in the afternoon when I noticed that Johann was already drunk, in fact, more inebriated than I had ever seen him before. I was used to seeing him drunk, but usually I was looking at him through unclear eyes of my own, so perhaps it was my perception that was off.

I was a good distance away, but I could still hear Johann's voice and roaring laughter over the music and other voices; he was talking with his new wife and Fra Domenico and I could make out his words. When the good Father saw me standing alone, he left the newlyweds and came over to talk with me. He told me that Johann and Maria had been coming to hear his sermons on Sundays. Fra Domenico wondered where I had been, and when I reminded him of my loss of faith he quickly moved on; ordinarily he would have pushed me more about my absence and diminished belief but it was a festive occasion, and I guess he didn't want to spoil the mood with threats of hell and the supposed eternal damnation of my immortal soul. Instead he went on to tell me that he had been spending a lot of time with my big friend – counseling him and Maria and dining at the Velata home. He believed that the match was a good one.

"I believe that the match is a good one," said Fra Domenico. "Speaking of matches, when will I get the honor of officiating your nuptials?"

"You know I have been hearing of that a lot lately," I said. "Why is it that everyone seems to be so concerned with my affairs?"

"Because you are not having one," said Fra Domenico with a smile. "And it is not natural for a young man to be alone, so naturally your friends wonder."

"It is natural if you are preparing for a life in the monastery," I said. I knew it was a mistake the moment the words came out of my mouth. I knew I unintentionally implied that I might be considering a recommitment to the order – and the good Father responded.

With wide-eyes Fra Domenico said, "Does this mean that…?"

"No," I interrupted, putting a quick end to the misunderstanding. "I was just making a point."

"Well then, we are back to where we were. You should be pursuing the company of a young woman, unless..." said Fra Domenico leaving his thought unfinished.

"No," I answered completing his thought for him, and answering it.

"Well I just thought, or it just occurred to me that... well there were all those artistic types at the Medici Palace," Fra Domenico said awkwardly. "You know what they were saying about them, all those young boys and older men together. And then there's that Leonardo da Vinci, and you spent a lot of time ... and you're an artist ..."

"That's true, but I never got into the palace," I said. "And Leonardo is just a friend, and though I'm not sure the two are connected, I'm really not a very good artist." I paused. He still looked unconvinced so I said bluntly, "I like women."

Relieved, Fra Domenico made the sign of the cross in the air and whispered a brief prayer. "Then get yourself one," he said, the smile returning to his round face. Finally letting the subject go, he said, "Now I must complement you on your generosity. The music is wonderful, the food is delicious, and so much of it. As promised, I will take care of the cleaning and I will find mouths for every crumb, every morsel of leftover food. It will be much appreciated, Lorenzo."

"Thank you, Fra Domenico," I said. "But it is you that deserves the high praise. All I did was donate money, money I didn't even earn. You did all of the preparations and most of the arrangements, and you are handling the clean up. And as far as the surplus of food goes, I figured it better that we have too much, so everyone gets as much of their favorite as they please, than run out of anything. Besides, on this happy day, no one in the Quarter should go hungry."

"Yes," agreed Fra Domenico. "God bless you, Lorenzo." Then still smiling, and patting his ample frame, he added, "Now speaking of hungry, I believe I will see to my own needs. God forgive me, food is my one weakness."

"You could never tell it by looking at you," I joked. Then I added, "Enjoy," and he was off.

I hadn't been alone for more than a few seconds when the bride and groom came to me to offer their appreciation. Maria spoke first, she said, "Lorenzo, how can we thank you for this wonderful reception. The music, the dancing, oh and the food, so much food..."

"And the beer and the wine, so much wine," Johann interrupted with a loud laugh.

Maria just smiled, but I laughed too. Then I said, "It was nothing, believe me. Just enjoy the day ... the night ...well do the best you can."

Again Johann laughed, but Maria blushed. I apologized. "I'm sorry," I said. "That was a bit crude of me."

"Don't apologize, Lorenzo," said Maria. "You are right, we will do the best we can." Then she giggled.

"We've been doing it so long we should be good at it," Johann roared, slurring his words. "Speaking of which, have you looked around? Did I not tell you that there would be lots of beautiful available women here? Well, there are at least a few." He looked around in vain, and then added, "A couple. I know there are..."

"Don't worry about it, Orso," I said smiling. "I can take care of myself. Just have a good time. Eat, but don't drink too much..."

"Too late," Johann interrupted with a laugh.

"Then eat some more," I suggested.

"Yes, dear," said Maria to Johann. "You should eat some more. It will clear your head. It's still early and you need to keep on your feet for a while longer."

"Nonsense," bellowed Johann. "My head is clear. So clear you can see right through it... nothing in between. And I can always keep on my feet, except when I'm sleeping, of course. What I really need is more beer."

"Oh no," both Maria and I said, almost at the same time.

"Eh tu, Maus?" barked Johann. "What kind of town is this that doesn't approve a man getting drunk on his wedding day?"

"We approve of a man getting drunk on his wedding day," I said. "We just don't like to see him spoil his wedding night, if you get my meaning."

"Oh, oh," Johann slurred, and attempted to wink. "I get ya, Maus. I get ya." Again, Maria blushed, but she was smiling. "Woman, lets go get something to eat. Then more beer, more beer."

"Anything you wish, my husband," said Maria as she looked into Johann's face with shining eyes. She seemed to really be in love with him.

"Did you hear that Maus," Johann roared. "Anything you wish, my husband. That's me you know. Well let me think about that." Then he let out another big burly roar.

Johann and I shared a manly embrace – he nearly broke my ribs – and then I gave Maria a kiss on the cheek. "What are you doing, Maus," barked Johann. "Give her a kiss on the mouth, come on. We're family now."

It was my turn to blush, but I obeyed just to avoid an extension to the embarrassing scene. Then they said that they would see me later and went to search for something else to consume – a task easily fulfilled. I watched them for a few minutes, and then I decided that I should go on home. As I walked out of the courtyard at San Spirito and clicked my heels on the flagstone street, a wave of melancholia swept over me. I was going home to an empty shop; for the first time in my life I was going to be truly alone.

"You think you can handle the militia for that long?" asked Machiavelli. "It may be months before I return."

"Of course," said Johann. "But I know you can't stand to let anyone else be in charge."

"I have confidence in you," said Machiavelli. "It's just that I have put so much time, money, and energy into raising and training the men, it's hard to walk away even for just a short time." He paused, and then added, "I guess I don't really have a choice. Duty calls. I am the ambassador to the Emperor. If the Signory needs me to meet with Maximilian it is my duty, and privilege, I might add, to go."

"Someone has to go and convince the old Emperor not to invade the Peninsula," said Johann. The Emperor was considering joining the French and the Spanish in the conquest of Italy.

"I know," said Machiavelli. "It just goes against my nature to push off my responsibilities on others."

"It's called delegating authority," I quipped from the small desk in the corner of Machiavelli's office.

"I know, it's just not easy for me," said Machiavelli, as he paced across the room.

"Perhaps you've taken on too many responsibilities," I said.

"Nonsense," barked Machiavelli amusingly. "In fact, I could do more. I'm just having a little trouble being in more than one place at one time."

"And doing more than one thing at the same time," I added, waving the letter from the Emperor I had been translating. Machiavelli was quite capable of doing the work himself, but asked me to translate several official documents from the Emperor from German to Italian for the members of the Signory, to save time – his time, of course. He continued pacing as he reviewed papers for his trip, checked my translation, wrote a letter, and gave last minute advice to Johann concerning the militia; Johann was casually leaning against Machiavelli's desk in the center of the room – a rather large office in the Palazzo della Signoria.

After several seconds of contemplation, Machiavelli responded to my last comment. He smiled and said, "Perhaps you are right. And by the way, have I told you how much I've appreciated your help these past few days?"

"Only about five times a day," I quipped, "but not in the past hour."

"Well, I really am grateful for all your help," said Machiavelli as he walked over to me and patted my shoulder. "You know, if you came with me, it could be a very valuable experience for you. This could be your chance to show the Signory your value to the city."

"Yea, Maus, and it's not like you've got so much to do here," added Johann. "Go. Though, it is a little cold this time of year, but the women are warm. And the mountains will be difficult to cross, but the views are tremendous..."

"Orso, you make it sound so tempting," I said, cutting him off. "I think I'll stay here and let Niccolò have the glory of keeping the peace with the Germans."

"I guess it's just as well that you stay," said Machiavelli, as once again he began to pace and look through his papers.

"Yea, I guess he can help me keep the men in line," Johann chimed in.

I could tell that Machiavelli had something else on his mind. I knew he wanted to ask me something; he just hadn't found the words yet. Instead, he turned to Johann and asked him about his newborn son, Hans. I went back to my translating but listened to the proud papa talk of his boy like he would be the next gonfalonier, or at least a captain in the militia. After a few jokes about Hans leading the militia as soon as he learned to walk, Machiavelli asked Johann if it was true that Maria was pregnant again.

"Is it true that Maria is pregnant again?" asked Machiavelli.

I put down my pen and turned to see Johann smiling proudly. I said, "You devil, Orso. You've got to give that poor woman a rest."

"No," said Johann, still smiling and leaning on Machiavelli's desk. "I'm just doing my duty to God and my adopted city – being fruitful and multiplying for his glory and the preservation of Florence."

"That's if it's another boy," I quipped.

"Nonsense, Maus," said Johann. "We need women too. At least most of us Florentine men do."

Before I had a chance to respond to yet another jibe on my celibacy, Machiavelli rescued me; he finally found the words to ask me what was on his mind. He told me, or asked me, if I knew that Michelangelo was back in Florence.

"Did you know that Michelangelo was back in Florence?" he asked.

"Yes, Niccolò, I saw him briefly right after he got back from Rome," I said, knowing that there was more he wanted to say.

"Did he tell you why he's back home?" asked Machiavelli.

"Something about the Pope and his funds being cut off," I answered. "But I think that there was more to it, he just wasn't in the mood to tell me."

Machiavelli came over and sat on the corner of the little desk where I was sitting, and looked me in the eyes. "Do you think that he would go back if the Pope resumed payment for his services?" Machiavelli asked in a serious and sincere tone.

"I don't know," I said. There was a pause; Machiavelli was still looking down at me. I sensed he wanted more, so I added, "I could talk to him, but as I said, there seemed to be more to it than just money."

Machiavelli crossed his arms as he nodded his head in understanding, and said, "Well this is the thing. The Signory, and Soderini himself, is getting pressured from Pope Julius to get Michelangelo to return to Rome. He wants Michelangelo to work on a colossal bronze statue of himself to give to the people of Bologna, and to do some cathedral project. So Soderini came to me wondering if I had any influence over Michelangelo."

"I don't know of anyone who has influence over Michelangelo," I interrupted. "I doubt if anyone can make him do anything he doesn't want to do." There was yet another awkward pause, so I added, "Of course, I will talk to him and try and find out what he wants. If he will go back, can I tell him that the Pope intends to give him his money?"

"Yes, Julius has assured us that he will be paid what he is owed," answered Machiavelli, obviously pleased that I was going to help. He uncrossed his arms and once again patted my shoulder, and said, "I appreciate the effort no matter what the results, and I assure you that the council and Soderini do also."

"I can't promise anything," I hedged, feeling the pressure.

"I know," said Machiavelli. "Just let him know that he will get his money, that the Pope really wants him back, and how much it would mean to Florence to have Julius' favor again."

I didn't know for sure yet, but I didn't believe that just money or civic pride would have much of an effect on Michelangelo, but I agreed to try and do my best.

"I will try, and do my best," I said.

"That's all I, or anyone can ask for," said Machiavelli bounding off the desk to resume his pacing. He then added, "I have every confidence in you."

I went to see Michelangelo at his villa, and after some wine and the appropriate amount of conversation expected between two old friends that hadn't seen each other in a while, I got to the point and asked him if he planned on returning to Rome anytime soon.

"Do you plan on returning to Rome anytime soon?" I asked. "It seems that Pope Julius…"

"Julius is a fool," interrupted Michelangelo, nearly spilling his wine as he leapt from his chair; I remained calmly seated. "He's been listening to that bastard architect, Donato d'Agnolo Bramante. I know it was Bramante who talked him into canceling my commission and cutting off my money. All Bramante cares about is his cathedral, this new monster St. Peter's. He sees it as a symbol of his immortality, and it probably will be. It was his idea to have me paint that dammed fresco and cheat me out of my statues, my immortality. Now Julius wants a giant statue of himself to impress the people of Bologna and show off his newly acquired power over them." Bologna had recently come under the authority of Rome; it would only be temporary.

"What is it you want? What would make you happy?" I asked casually as I sipped my wine. I hoped to get Michelangelo to blow off a little of his anger, so he might calm down and be more willing to listen to reason. After a few minutes of listening to him go on, I could tell that he wanted to work in Rome. Just as much as Pope Julius II wanted his help in creating a new glorious city. As he put it, it would be his chance for immortality. I had no doubt, that with the right words or perhaps the right situation, that Michelangelo would go back to Rome. It was just a matter of when and on what terms.

"I want to get paid!" barked Michelangelo. "I want to do the forty statues for the tomb. A work like that would be noticed, remembered. Imagine forty magnificent statues. But now with that Bramante whispering in his ear, the Pope backs down, he gets cheap, says he spent too much on the new cathedral. He can't afford all those statues. He didn't care about the money until Bramante told him to care about the money. So he expects me to be satisfied with one big statue and painting this damn fresco for him. I tried to tell him that if he wanted real art, something that will last, forget the painting and let me do the statues."

"You always said that painting was a bastard art form," I interjected just to encourage him.

"So he says he wants a statue, but just the one of him," Michelangelo continued. "A giant bronze statue to impress the people... I told you that already. I'm so mad I'm repeating myself."

"So you think this is all about vanity and m..." I began.

"It's about money, vanity, ego, ambition, immortality, jealousy," interrupted Michelangelo. "But I guess it is cheaper to commission one statue and a fresco than to commission forty statues."

"If you don't want to do the fresco, why don't you suggest that they get Raphael?" I asked.

Michelangelo, now standing almost over the top of me, rolled his eyes and said bitterly, "They really want Raphael, Bramante and the others, that's the thing. They hate me. It's Pope Julius that wants me. So they talk the Pope into insulting me with these puny commissions and take away my big one hoping that I will quit."

"And you did," I said. "They got their way. It seems that…"

"Now they can get Raphael, who the Pope's parasites wanted all along to do the painting. But that's not all," interrupted Michelangelo. "If I go back and do this little fresco, knowing I don't want to do it, and because it is a nothing project, they will expect me to fail, fall out of favor with the Julius, and then I will be out. Then they can call in Raphael to fix it. Which is what they wanted all along."

"It seems to me that you are already out," I said. "If you stay here, they will win."

"I know," said Michelangelo slowly going back and sitting in his chair. "But what can I do? Forty statues for a tomb, for the Pope, would be remembered. This ceiling fresco will be nothing to speak of, just twelve figures, the apostles and some other minor decorations." He went on to describe in detail the chapel and the fresco that Pope Julius II wanted him to do, and it really did sound like a minor commission particularly compared to the forty statues for the tomb, and extremely minor for a great talent like Michelangelo.

"So you make it memorable," I said. "Put everything you have into this project. Does it really have to be just the twelve apostles? Make it your own creation."

Suddenly his eyes lit up, Michelangelo said, "Creation, that's an idea, the beginning, the beginning of an idea. Yes, the beginning and…" He had that look on his face, the same one he had that night we first met at the Severed Limb, and I had seen it again on nights when he was deep in his work on the David. I knew it was time for me to leave. There was nothing more for me to say, and once he was in one of his thinking moods he wouldn't be listening to me anyway. I drank down what little was left of my wine and got up to go, but before I left I asked him what he was going to do."

"What are you going to do?" I asked.

He looked flustered by my question or more by my interruption of his thought. "About what," he grumbled.

"About Rome, the Pope, the fresco?" I clarified.

"What about them?" Michelangelo snapped back, fighting to get back to his thought.

"Are you going back to Rome to work on Pope Julius' fresco for the Sistine Chapel?" I further clarified.

He hesitated, then looked at me briefly and said, "Yes, yes of course."

Michelangelo went back to Rome. Machiavelli was in Germany. Johann was busy by day with the militia, and by night with his growing family. I was alone, perhaps even lonely, and I had too much time on my hands and money in my pockets; a very dangerous combination of circumstances for a young man who's never been in love. My friends finally got what they all had been asking for – unfortunately for me. But I won't say anymore now, that would be getting ahead of my story.

Chapter VIII

The summer of 1508, June 24 to be precise – easy to remember because it was during the Feast of Saint John the Baptist – was when, once again, my life would take a drastic turn. I remember the morning streets were packed with colorful banners and processions, and smiling happy people moving about. It was sunny and warm, but by late afternoon the clouds had rolled in and there was a chilling breeze; my over indulgence in wine might have contributed to my perception of coolness in the air. I watched a few of the comedies, but the humor seemed old and tired; I even saw the old castration routine again. Alone and feeling a little self-pity, I began to think that it might just be me who was getting old and tired. Little did I realize that I was just entering the second quarter of my life; I would get much older and a lot more tired. Youth is inherently naive to the deep experiences and the true passionate emotions of life.

I had just watched the prisoner release out front of the Palazzo Vecchio and was walking around the Piazza, when I decided to head back to the shop. It was still early, but my mood and my city's wasn't in synch; I was down and Florence was up. That's when I spotted Bramante; as usual, I got the feeling that he had been following me for some time, but when our eyes met, he was compelled to come forward. He spoke first; he called me his friend and asked how I was.

"Lorenzo my friend, how are you?" Bramante said.

"Fine," I responded. "How are you?" I guess I was awfully lonely because I stopped to talk with Bramante, and didn't mind. "Enjoying the festival?" I added.

"I am well, and yes, yes the festival is grand as usual," he said with a smile. "I'm looking forward to the horse races tonight. A chance to make a little money or lose some, huh?"

"I suppose," I said. "I've never bet, or even watched the horse races, or any of the festival races."

"Never?" said Bramante with exaggerated surprise. "You should go, they're great fun."

"I'm sure they are," I said. "They're just a bit late for me tonight. I don't think I want to stick around until then."

"Then go home," said Bramante enthusiastically. "Get a nap. With a little rest you will be as good as new, huh?" He continued for a while to try and get me to go to the races, but I resisted and he finally gave up. Then he suggested, "Hey, how about we have dinner together. I know a great little inn, it's new. The food is exquisite. You go home and rest for a while and I will come by and pick you up. I'll hire an expensive carriage, not that one I have, and we will go in style."

Another sign that I was tired and bored with myself – I considered his offer, but finally I said no.

"No, thank you," I said. "I'm just going to go home. Perhaps another time."

"All right then," he said. "But let me walk with you. I've always felt that a walk passes more pleasantly when you are accompanied by a friend, huh?"

I agreed and we began to walk and talk our way out of the Palazzo and toward the Arno. It was subtle, but I got the impression that he was leading me; we took roads that I would not ordinarily have taken. It wasn't out of the way, just different; so it didn't really seem to bother me at the time. Finally we came to a crossroads next to the Arno and Bramante said that I was on my own and that he was going back to the Palazzo.

"You're on your own, Lorenzo," he said with his insufferable smile. "I am going back to the Palazzo and wait around for the races."

"Good luck then," I said. And still feeling surprisingly jovial toward Bramante, I added, "Thanks for the company, it did make the walk more pleasant."

I turned and started to walk away from him when Bramante called out, "Hey where are you going?" I turned back and gave him a puzzled look. "The Ponte Trinità is right here," he said.

Understanding, or what I thought was understanding his apparent confusion, I said, "Yes, but earlier I saw a nice little food stand here on the right back next to the Ponte Carraia. So I thought I would stop and get something to take home to eat."

"Nonsense," said Bramante, again with his insufferable smile. "On the day of the festival you can get great food anywhere. Besides, about right now the Ponte Carraia is crowded with floats and people from the parade. It will take you forever to get across. Take the Ponte Trinità. It will be faster. See, it's clear, hardly anyone around at all."

There were people on the bridge, but it was relatively peaceful looking, and since it sounded harmless enough, and I really didn't want to get caught in the parade, I agreed, waved goodbye to Bramante, and started across the Arno on the Ponte Trinità. It was late afternoon, the sky was cloudy, and I felt a chill as I walked along next to the railing. Looking downstream, I could see the Ponte Carraia – no floats, no parade. I remember thinking that they must have already past. Then suddenly, there she was, standing facing the rail right in front of me – beautiful long, curly, black hair gently blowing back away from her ivory skin. I stopped; I couldn't help but stare. She stood out from the crowd in loveliness, her round soft curves gently veiled in a pink skirt, with a white, laced bodice clinging to her ample bosom, and she stood out in temperament; as the world was moving around her – people in motion, talking laughing, celebrating – she was alone, staring out over the river. There was a deep sadness in her pretty face; a tear tracked down from one of her big brown eyes, and rolled down her delicate cheek past her deep red lips. From that moment on, I was hers. Now I don't believe in love at first sight; I suppose I must have then, because seeing her standing there I felt something I never felt before. Though I was twenty-five, I was young at love, or what I thought was love; it was actually a different sort of passion coming from a place a bit south of the heart.

I would have stood there all day, frozen in time by her lovely aspect, but suddenly she lunged for the rail. I couldn't believe it. I threw myself toward her; thankful for my agility, I caught her just in time before she went over the side. And there she was in my arms, face-to-face. The first words she ever said to me were, let me go.

"Let me go," she said. "Please, let me go, for your own good."

Even her voice was beautiful, soft and melodic like a morning dove. I said, "I can't," and I meant it in more ways than one. Then she fainted. I looked around, wondering what I should do, and then I swooped her up – though she was my height, she didn't weigh much – and carried her to the left bank of the Arno. I still wasn't sure what I was supposed to do – she was still unconscious – so I took her home. Surprisingly, or not surprisingly, nobody paid us much attention. It seemed that on the day of the Feast of Saint John nobody thought it was that unusual to see a man carrying a lifeless woman through the streets in the late afternoon. I took her in the front of the shop, past my unfinished paintings and dust covered art supplies, through the empty warehouse into the living area, and finally gently laid her body to rest on Mama and Papa's – and Johann's – old bed. I pulled a quilt up over her, lit the lamp next to the bed, went out and started a fire, and then brought back some water and a damp cloth; I put the cloth on her forehead and the water on the table next to the lamp.

It appeared that the damp cloth revived her; after just a few seconds, she moaned softly, and then opened her eyes. Again I heard that sweet melodic voice. "Where am I?" she softly spoke.

"You're safe," was all I could manage. Then I gently lifted her head and offered her a drink. I said, "Here, drink a little water." She took a sip. I was distracted by her red, full lips on the rim of the cup and accidentally over poured; I quickly grabbed the rag from her forehead and dabbed her chin. "Sorry," I whispered.

"Do you have something a little stronger?" she asked.

"I have wine," I said awkwardly, and she nodded her approval. "I'll get you some wine. I'll be right back."

I went down to the cellar to get a bottle; it gave me time to compose myself. I remember thinking, 'Relax, you're acting like a foolish boy,' and I was. 'What was the last thing I said to her, I'll be right back. Where else would I go? I've got a mysterious, beautiful woman in bed, in my house, what was I going to do, go for a walk.' I needed to calm down, so after I picked out the wine I quickly opened it and took several long, deep swigs right from the bottle. Then I went back up in the living room, covered the cellar opening with the big wooden table, found two glasses and hurried back to the bedroom; she was sitting up with her back on the headboard. That's when I saw her smile for the first time; perfect ivory teeth framed by those soft, red, sensual lips. The flickering candle loved her – the yellow light danced off of her ivory skin and beautiful long, curly, black hair, and glowed in her big brown eyes – and I too loved her, so I believed at the time. Never fall for someone you are first drawn to by their physical beauty – they will own you; she owned me. Then she asked me again, where am I.

"Where am I?" she asked.

I suddenly became aware that I was staring at her and that she had asked me that question at least two times while I was standing there. I concentrated on deliberately pouring the wine to regain my focus. "You are in my home," I finally said. Then I handed her a glass; our fingertips touched briefly. I sat down next to her on the bed.

"Is this your bed?" she asked. Her head dipped slightly giving her a coy look.

The question or the look, or both, embarrassed me, and once again I was off balance. "No," I said awkwardly. "It's my... It was my... It's nobody's anymore. This is a spare room. It used to be my parents, but they are both gone now."

"Oh, I'm sorry," she said. "Then you live here alone?"

"Yes," I said. "I live here alone."

"Where exactly is here?" she asked.

"We're in the Santa Spirito Quarter," I said. "On the southeast side. Not far from the Ponta a San Pier Gatolini, on Via dei Serragli."

"Now the big question," she said with another coy look and a smile. "Who are you?"

I smiled back at her and said, "I am Lorenzo Demarco from Florence... from here." I let out a nervous little laugh.

"Hello, Lorenzo," she said. I had never heard my name sound so soothing as it did rolling from her lips. "I am Giovanna Vasari." What a lovely name, I thought. At least I thought I was just thinking it; I must have whispered it out loud because she said, "Thank you."

I tried to hide my embarrassment by turning the attention back on her. I asked, "Why were you on that bridge?"

Giovanna took a sip of wine; she was in no hurry to answer. Finally, with a far away look in her eyes, she spoke, "Have you ever felt that everyone, even God had abandoned you, that you were truly alone. People who you loved and trusted had turned against you. Trying to make you..." She censored herself, took another sip of wine, then added, "Sometimes when you run out of choices, you consider doing things that you would not ordinarily do," then she looked at me and added, "even if it means hurting other people. You might do things that you know are wrong, but you feel that you have no other option."

I nodded I understood, but I didn't. How could I, she was talking about more than just the bridge, as I would find out later. Giovanna went on describing her melancholia and predicament in this same peculiar, indirect way, and I listened. When she finally paused, I asked, "Were you really going to jump?"

She didn't answer right away. Giovanna drank some more wine, and then she said, "I don't know. Maybe not, I can't say for sure, all I know is that you were there. You were my savior."

I smiled sheepishly. It never occurred to me at the time, but if she were really on that bridge to jump, then nothing would stop her from going back to the Ponte Trinità and plunging into the Arno.

We talked for two, maybe three hours, getting to know each other.

Maybe it was the wine, but I loosened up a bit; I became a little less awkward and a little more like myself. Giovanna asked a lot of questions about me, and I tried to answer everything modestly, and briefly; I wanted to be open with her, but I didn't want to appear too boastful. Whenever I asked about her she was always evasive. She had a family – I got that much out of her – parents, two older brothers, and a younger sister, but there was something wrong between them. I found out that Giovanna was several years younger than me, but as I would learn, in love and romance she was much older than me. I got her to tell me that the Vasari family lived somewhere on the east side of Florence in the Santa Croce Quarter, but when I tried to get more specifics out of her, like exactly where and what business they were in, she was evasive. Giovanna was not only beautiful, but she was mysterious, a lure that was too irresistible to ignore; I had to know more about her.

Throughout our conversation Giovanna became less depressed and more light, and charming – smiling freely and often. I thought that it was probably the wine, but hoped that it might have been me that had sweetened her mood. What did I know, I didn't care; I was just happy that she was smiling, and talking to me, and me alone, alone in my house, in bed – in an innocent way, of course.

It was getting pretty late when my practical instincts suddenly came back to me; what was I going to do with her tonight? I had to take her home.

"I have to take you home," I said.

"No, I can't go home," insisted Giovanna, almost pleading.

"Why not?" I asked.

She paused, but came up with nothing to add, Giovanna said, "I just can't go home."

"Then where can I take you?" I asked.

"I don't know," Giovanna said, sounding a little worried.

"You could stay here, but what would people say?" I said, more out of respect for her than a real possibility. I didn't talk to many people around the shop anymore, so if I were to become the topic of scandalous gossip, I would probably never even know it. So I wasn't really worried about what people might say but, my sensibilities still ran to the pious and conservative; men and women just didn't stay alone together under one roof unless they were married or related, and I just assumed that she felt the same way. My assumption was incorrect, and my own sensibilities were about to undergo a dramatic change. "What would your family say if they found out?" I added.

"I don't care what they think," Giovanna insisted with slight anger in her tone. "I don't care what anyone thinks about me." She paused, and then in a lighter voice, and with sincerity, Giovanna added, "I'm sorry, Lorenzo. I was thinking only of myself, and not your reputation as a gentleman. What would your neighbors think if they saw me leaving here, unescorted, in the morning. I'm sorry, I wasn't..."

"No, it's all right, I don't care what the neighbors think," I said. "It was only you that I was concerned about." Then Giovanna started to get up, insisting that she must leave, and I reflexively – at least I think it was just a reflex – put out my free hand to her chest and eased her back down; she laid back down with gentle resistance. It was then when I realized exactly where my hand was. I started to pull it back, but the look in her eyes told me that it was all right; I think that made it worse, that is, it made me feel even more uncomfortable. I quickly released her. In one big gulp, I drank the rest of my wine – about a half of a glass – and then said, "You can stay here tonight. We'll figure out what to do in the morning."

She seemed relieved and immediately relaxed after my decision. Giovanna said, "Maybe it's the wine, but I suddenly feel really tired." Her big brown eyes batted up and down slowly in a testament to her words.

I wished her a goodnight and started to leave. I reached for the remainder of the wine, but she asked me to leave it; I did and left her alone.

I remember thinking that perhaps I'd been wrong about God. After all, here I'd been feeling lonely and now here she was. So perfect, like an answer to a prayer.

The next morning I got up early – as I almost always did – and looked in on Giovanna; she was still asleep. I kept little food in the house – I ate out most of the time – so I decided to go to the market and get some fresh bread, jam, and some fruit. I left a note for Giovanna, but I need not have bothered; when I got back she was still asleep. I peeked in on her, again, to make sure. She looked like an angel lying there with one arm above her head and the other across her stomach – her chest slowly rising and falling. The morning light loved her as much as the candlelight had the night before. Suddenly she loudly sucked in air through her nose – it made me jump; Giovanna was snoring. So she was human, but that made me want her all the more. I smiled and closed the door.

She finally got up, not long after I had looked in on her. I had just finished putting out the food on the big wooden table when she walked out. I told Giovanna that I got a little bit of everything because I didn't know what she liked.

"I got a little bit of everything because I didn't know what you liked," I said.

Giovanna smiled at me, and then looked at what I had put out and said, "I see, and then some." She was right; the table was filled with more food than I could have eaten in a week. I was beginning to feel a little embarrassed again – I had overdone it – when Giovanna said, "How thoughtful of you, Lorenzo. You are so sweet to have gone to so much trouble for me."

I smiled sheepishly as we sat down to eat. Giovanna barely touched anything, but it didn't matter; I already had been rewarded for the effort. She didn't seem completely awake – perhaps she had been used to sleeping until midday – and I could tell that she was a little uncomfortable. I didn't want to be indelicate to her needs, so I suggested that I go out and run a few errands and let her have a little privacy; Giovanna seemed pleased and quite grateful for my suggestion. Before I left I started to remind her to keep out of sight, but decided that she probably knew that already. Instead I just told her that we would figure out the best way to get her home when I got back.

"We can figure out the best way to get you home when I get back," I said.

"Lorenzo, are you in a hurry to get rid of me?" Giovanna quipped.

"No, Giovanna, no…" I stumbled over my words. "I was just thinking about how to get you out so… I just meant that…"

"I know what you meant," Giovanna said with that lovely smile. "And while you're gone, I will clear the table."

"That's all right," I said. "I'll take care of it later, when I get back. Don't worry about it."

"No, I insist," said Giovanna. "It's the least I can do, for all that you have done for me."

I spent the rest of the morning walking the streets of the Quarter; it's funny how slowly time passes when you're trying to waste it. I did make a dinner reservation at the Arno Inn, just outside of the Porta San Freliano. The Arno Inn was a very expensive, nice place, with a great view – looking upriver – of my city. Many visiting dignitaries ate and stayed at the Inn; I had never had cause to go there until now. Finally it was early afternoon and I decided that I could slowly head back to the shop.

When I walked in, the big wooden table was cleared and cleaned, with a bowl of various fruits left over from the morning meal, in the center. There was a small fire still burning in the fireplace drying out the big iron pot that we used for making soup and heating water. Giovanna must have heard me, and came in from the warehouse area; she was smiling and looking radiant. She was wearing one of Mama's old bodices; it clung to Giovanna a little tighter across the chest than it had Mama, but it looked wonderful. She told me that she had found it in the cassone in the bedroom and put it on while she washed out her own bodice.

"I found this bodice in the cassone in the bedroom," said Giovanna. "I hope you don't mind me wearing it while mine is drying. I washed my bodice out along with a few other things and hung them back in there, in the shop. I would have just put them outside but then I remembered, I wasn't supposed to be here. The fire got everything pretty dry, but it was starting to get a little warm in here, so I let the fire die down and moved everything in the other room. I thought that the sight of my underskirt and other things might have made you feel uncomfortable."

It was then I noticed that, without the benefit of her underskirt to force it out, Giovanna's skirt clung to her round hips, accenting her feminine form. I tried not to stare, but it was difficult, particularly when she crossed between me and the fading glow from the dying embers and I could see a silhouette of her natural shape through her skirt; mercifully the fire went out.

"Not at all," I said with awkward delay, referring to her concern for my comfort over the possibility of seeing her underthings. "My mama wasn't an overly modest woman when it came to such things, so I've seen it all." It was a pretty good bluff, I had no idea at the time what "all" was, but at least the subject was dropped.

We spent the afternoon hiding out in the shop and getting to know each other. I showed her around: my room; the warehouse, where I learned a few new things about what "all" was; the front of the shop, my studio, where I told her briefly about my painting; and then the cellar. We talked and laughed; up until that time in my life, it was one of my most wonderful days. I almost forgot how just yesterday I was lonely, and Giovanna had been on the verge of killing herself, but even when I did remember it didn't change my perception of how right things were; I allowed myself to believe that it was our being together that had changed her feelings about ending her life, and was the reason Giovanna was happy now.

We shared stories and experiences about growing up in Florence. Giovanna didn't remember much about the Medici, but of course she had heard all about them. She did remember Savonarola; her family had gone to see the aborted trial by fire. She was quite impressed when I told her that I knew both Michelangelo and Leonardo da Vinci and insisted that I tell her all about them – what they were like, and about the time I had spent with each artist. Whenever I tried to steer the conversation onto questions about her immediate past, or her family, Giovanna would resist, and I didn't force it; I didn't want to push her away.

As the afternoon waned into evening, I told Giovanna about the dinner reservations; she had heard of the Arno Inn too and knew of its reputation, and was quite impressed and anxious to go there. She only expressed regret over not having something more elegant to wear. I offered her anything of Mama's that she wanted, but Giovanna's clothes were already of a higher quality than anything Mama had. We did find a hat and a small pouch that matched her skirt and bodice quite nicely.

Once again I left to give Giovanna privacy to prepare herself for dinner, but this time the time went by quicker because I had things to do. I went down the street and bought some flowers. Then I stopped at a jeweler's and bought a modest gold necklace – modest because I didn't want to appear overanxious. Finally I hired a carriage to come by the shop in an hour and pick us up and take us to the Arno Inn. When I got back to the shop Giovanna was ready and I presented her with the flowers, and then gave her the necklace; her reaction was much stronger than I expected. Giovanna looked shocked, and then almost in tears told me that it was a lovely gift and that she would treasure it.

"Oh Lorenzo, this is such a lovely gift," Giovanna said with moist eyes. "And I will treasure it." Then she gave me a warm embrace that caught me off guard; I was barely able to react to hug her back, or appreciate the feeling of holding her next to me.

"I know it's really not that much," I said. "But you were worried about the way you would look going to the Arno Inn."

"That's so sweet," Giovanna said with a soft smile. "So you got me flowers and a necklace to add a little elegance."

She put one of the flowers in her borrowed hat, and then asked me to fasten the necklace in back of her neck. Giovanna pulled back her long, black, curly hair exposing the white nape of her neck; my hands shook as I clasped the hook. Then she casually dropped her hair with a flip of her wrist and spun around and said with a smile, "How do I look?"

I didn't hesitate, happy to be asked I said, "Beautiful, but I believe that it's you that is making the necklace and everything else look good." I really said that.

"Oh Lorenzo, are you flirting with me?" Giovanna said coyly, burying her chin in her chest. I could feel my face turning red; I couldn't recall that ever happening before. It must have made Giovanna feel a little uncomfortable also, for she quickly changed the subject. "Now, how are we going to get out of here without anyone seeing us?" she asked. We both still pretended that it mattered what other people thought.

"I don't think that will be a problem anymore," I said. "I have a carriage coming by to take us to the Arno Inn. As far as the neighbors know, or anyone who sees us coming out, you might have just come by a few minutes ago, and they just didn't see you come in, and we were waiting inside for the carriage. It's not the morning or late at night, everything will appear innocent enough. I mean... it is innocent enough..."

"What about when the carriage brings us back?" Giovanna asked.

"I don't think that will be a problem either," I said. Giovanna gave me another coy look. With the implication being that she expected to be coming home with me and didn't object to the idea or being seen doing it, I naturally blushed once again.

Soft music played as dish after dish was put on our table – melons, raisins, nuts, ham, trout, and gamebirds, just to name a few. Again, Giovanna ate little. I don't think I ate much either; I was feeling too good to eat. The evening was clear and comfortable, so we ate out on the patio, surrounded by a dozen other occupied tables, and under a crescent moon; looking upstream you could see my city lit up for the night. I drank a lot of wine, and Giovanna drank even more. There were quite a few people dining at the Inn, and Giovanna was by far the most beautiful woman there.

"Giovanna, you are by far the most beautiful woman here," I said. "But I suspect that's true wherever you go." I really said that too.

"That's so sweet," Giovanna said as she smiled and buried her chin in her chest. "But I bet you say that to all the girls you take here."

"No, I've never been..." I said awkwardly. "I mean, I never said that, to anyone before."

"I'm sorry, I didn't mean to spoil your compliment," said Giovanna. "And thank you."

"No, it's all right," I said. "It's me who should apologize. I mean it was very forward of me to get so familiar. After all we just met."

"Yes," agreed Giovanna, but then she said. "Well then let's pretend that we are old friends, so we can exchange such kind words and compliments and not feel awkward about it." I agreed.

The dessert plates were put out, jellies, fruits in syrup, cakes, and more; we chose to have another bottle of wine for dessert instead. As the wine built up the nerve in both of us the conversation became a little more blunt, and made it easier, as alcohol often does, for us to talk in a more familiar tone. Despite that, I still didn't find out much more about her situation. After I asked, Giovanna told me that she still didn't want to go home.

"I still don't want to go home," said Giovanna. "But I don't expect you to put me up for the night again. I know I've been an imposition."

"That's not true," I said. "It's just I wonder what..."

"I know you don't want your neighbors to…" Giovanna began.

"I don't care what they think, I don't know many people around there anymore, and I generally keep to myself," I interrupted, trying to finally put to rest that tired excuse. I paused, and then babbled, "You're very beautiful, and a… something just isn't right… I know you can't or won't tell me. But staying with me, well… there are, or will be, temptations, though you can trust me… It's just men and women don't… Well of course they do, but not…"

Again, Giovanna buried her chin in her chest and said coyly, "You're very sweet, Lorenzo. I know I can trust you. And you need not worry about me. I'm harmless, really."

"Thank you…and, I know," I said. "But, I would feel better if you stayed somewhere else." Her expression suddenly changed to fear, or worry, or something, it wasn't good, so I quickly reassured her, "It's all right, though, I wasn't talking about just dumping you in the street. I've made arrangements for you to stay here at the Arno Inn. I've got a nice room upstairs, for you. It's a corner room and they say it has the best view. It's yours, if you want it, and for as long as you need it."

There was a long, or what I perceived as a long pause, and then that beautiful smile came back to her face. "You got me a room here?" Giovanna said. "That's got to be very expensive…"

"Don't worry about that," I said.

"But, you've given me so much already," said Giovanna. "I have to worry about it. It has to be a lot of money. I can't let you…"

"It has already been arranged," I said. "And don't worry about the expense. I know I may not look it, because you've seen how I dress, where I live, and you know I don't have a lot of material possessions, but I can afford it."

Giovanna stared at me for a moment, and then she said, "I don't know what to say. Will you promise to visit me?"

"Every day, Giovanna, if you'll have me," I said. "So then it's settled."

We passed a fine tapestry on the wall, as we walked on a plush, Persian rug in the hall that led to Giovanna's room. We passed several doors before we got to the end of the hall; it was the last door on the left. I opened the door and the light from a burning oil lamp illuminated the room. The first thing that caught Giovanna's eye was the balcony – the curtains were open – and she ran to it exclaiming her excitement about what a beautiful room it was and that she just had to see the view.

"What a beautiful room," exclaimed Giovanna. "I've just got to see the view." I followed her out on the balcony. Below was the restaurant patio where we had just eaten; we could hear the music. There was a half-wall providing some privacy from those below, but it didn't take away from the view. Being higher up, our perspective was even better than at the restaurant; I could see the towers and spires of Florence including the Palazzo Vecchio tower and the magnificent Duomo. The crescent moon was now low on the horizon – back and to the left, away from Florence. None of this escaped Giovanna. "And what a beautiful view," she added to her earlier exclamation. I agreed.

For a moment, I too was caught up in the splendid beauty of my city at night. When the spell was broken and I looked at Giovanna she was already looking at me – we were so close, almost touching. She spoke first.

"Have you ever been out there in the countryside and seen the wolves?" asked Giovanna pointing away from the city, but not looking away from me; I nodded I had without looking away either. I could feel her warm breath on my face. She continued, "They have such beautiful gray-blue eyes, just like yours, Lorenzo, wolf eyes."

We stood there for a moment just staring at each other. I'm sure I didn't move, but suddenly she was in my arms, our lips pressing hard together. It was a long slow kiss and I could feel her body quiver as I held her tight against me. Then she gently pushed me away, turned and looked back over the skyline.

"Will you promise to come see me tomorrow?" she asked

I stood behind her, not knowing what I should do next – but of course I agreed to come see her. "Yes, Giovanna, of course I'll come see you," I said.

Giovanna turned back to me for one last time, put her hand on my cheek and softly pressed her red, full lips against my other cheek and whispered to me, "Goodnight, Wolf Eyes, until tomorrow." And then she turned away.

I left her on the balcony. Once on the street and nearly back to the Porta Santo Freliano, I looked back to see if she was still there; she wasn't. I continued on home, walking three feet off of the flagstones. One sensible thing did come to me on the walk – at least I thought it was sensible at the time – I decided to ask Fra Domenico to look into Giovanna and the Vasari family's situation. Maybe I could help them, or help her. I don't know if I realized it at the time, but I spent more money that day than I had in the past year. Luckily I could afford it, because it was only the beginning.

The next day I took Giovanna shopping; if she wasn't going home, she would need clothes and some other necessities. We went to all the best shops and bought everything she needed and even more of what she didn't need. I had everything delivered to her room at the inn. She thanked me every time we bought something, but didn't seem concerned about the cost, or surprised that I spent so much on her, like a woman that was used to being lavished with expensive gifts. After what I thought seemed to be a wonderful afternoon, Giovanna suddenly became distant and evasive; the same way she acted whenever I asked her about her family. She told me that she wanted to be alone that evening. I reluctantly agreed, but what choice did I have? It did give me time to go see Fra Domenico.

The good Father was happy that I had apparently found someone and agreed to find out what he could about the Vasari family and Giovanna. In fact, he said that he was happy to do it, as he put it, "Until you are married, who else is there but me to look after you?"

That night at the shop was one of the longest I could remember – alone wondering what she was doing, where she was, why she didn't want to see me – and then it got worse. I saw Giovanna the next day – she met me at the Porta Santo Freliano and we took a stroll along the Arno. It was there she told me that she couldn't see me for another four days. When I protested Giovanna said that she would need time to herself now and then, and if we were to continue seeing each other, I would have to accept this; again, what choice did I have. To make it up to me, Giovanna invited me to dinner on Friday, this time her treat. I was to pick her up at her room at dusk; where we were to go next, she left as a mystery. It would be another night that I would never forget.

I knocked on the door and I heard Giovanna's lovely voice telling me to come in. Once inside, Giovanna was nowhere in sight, but I could hear her moving about; she told me that she was almost ready. It gave me a chance to admire the quality of the accommodations. The room was actually two rooms, a living room, and a bedroom, separated by a short hallway just to the right of the entrance. I was in the living room, but I could see into the bedroom, though only a small part of it; Giovanna was around the corner in the part I could not see. I saw two brass bedposts that stretched to the ceiling, and a thin, transparent, vale curtain that hung down and around the bed. I had already seen the balcony, but it was now hidden by a heavy, maroon curtain, made of fine wool. There was a high-backed couch against the wall to the bedroom, an x-chair on the wall opposite the couch, and a finely ornamented oak table between them, and in between me and the balcony. A silver chandelier hung over the table from the ceiling and lighted the room. Every inch of the wall was painted with flowers and intricate repetitive patterns of lines and shapes in a variety of colors; on close inspection I noticed that the patterns were not painted directly to the wall, but part of a new wall covering technique called wallpaper. There was a large mirror on the wall above the x-chair that reflected the light and made the room appear larger than it was. Next to the chair there was a small fireplace coming out of the wall, for cold winter nights.

Giovanna came around the corner and I remember my first thought was that, 'she's not ready yet,' because she wasn't wearing any stockings – her feet and ankles were bare. Then I noticed, like that first day at the shop, that Giovanna was not wearing an underskirt, just a nice, red dress, and boned on the seams to pull the material tight around her thin waste. Her long, black, curly hair was perfect and was down on her shoulders, her lips were a deep red, and there was a hint of pink on Giovanna's cheeks. She was carrying a bottle of wine, a half-filled glass and an empty one. Her big, brown eyes sparked as Giovanna smiled at me and asked me if I would like some wine.

"Would you like some wine?" Giovanna asked. I didn't have to answer – maybe I nodded – she just handed me a glass, filled it, and then motioned for me to follow her. We went toward the balcony and Giovanna said, "Would you get the curtain for me? Please." I obeyed.

On the balcony there was a small table and two more x-chairs. On the table was a small, lit oil lamp, another bottle of wine, and a modest variety of bread, fruit, pecorino cheese, and some finocchiona. "I thought we'd eat in tonight," said Giovanna. She sat in one of the x-chairs and said, "Have a seat." Again I obeyed. Then Giovanna drank down her wine and refilled her glass; she put the bottle down on the table. It was then I noticed that the bottle was already half empty.

"This looks wonderful," I said awkwardly. I then forced myself to eat a little to not make it appear that her efforts had been in vain, but I really wasn't hungry for food. I did drink plenty of wine; I needed it to calm the burning in my loins. How naive I was, I didn't need to calm the burning; I just needed to be patient.

Giovanna talked little, so we talked little; we just looked out over the river and enjoyed the wine. There was no moon out that night; clouds covered my city. I thought maybe her melancholia had come back. Then when the wine was almost gone, Giovanna rose and took me by the hand; she smiled at me, but there was sadness in her pretty face. I stood up and she led me through the living room and into the bedroom, and there she kissed me; I could taste the wine on her lips. Sometime, even now, I can still taste it. Then she lit a candle next to the bed; it gave off a low, yellow glow. Giovanna went behind the thin veil onto the bed. On her knees, she slowly raised her dress up and over her head. Of course I couldn't take my eyes off of her, and I would tell you exactly what she looked like and how it felt to see her naked body for the first time, but I honestly don't remember. Oh I remember what her body looked like – I saw her many times over several months and got quite familiar with her every curve – but on that first night, I was under some kind of spell. All I remember thinking was that she was glorious, but perhaps a little too thin – undoubtedly a product of her sparse eating habits. The last thing I remember her saying to me before we made love was, "Are you just going to stand there and stare at me with those wolf eyes, or are you coming to bed?"

A lot of important things happened that summer of 1508: Johann and Maria had another baby, a girl, Costanza; Machiavelli successfully warded off imperial invasion; Michelangelo began work on the Sistine Chapel; Raphael also began work for the Pope; when Julius II wasn't rebuilding Rome he was starting wars – Julius invited the French into Italy to help fight the Venetians, once again the rats were invited into our house; and Lodovico Sforza, the former Duke of Milan, passed away. None of this mattered to me; I had Giovanna. Until I met her, I didn't know that I had such lust inside of me; if I had been with her every night, it still wouldn't have been enough. Most of the evenings that we were together were spent in her room at the inn where nobody seemed to care what we were doing; after all, everyone there was either getting paid well, just passing through, or doing the same we thing were doing – having a discrete liaison. Occasionally Giovanna stayed with me at the shop. By day we shopped, ate at restaurants, attended festivals, took long walks in the countryside, and carried on as if we were a married couple.

More than a month had passed since that first night of passion at the Arno Inn; it was early August. We were taking one of our walks in the county – just west of my city – when the first sign of my inevitable fall from paradise came about; of course I didn't recognize it as such at the time. It would be a slow, but hard fall. Giovanna had been quiet all morning. I was afraid that her melancholia had returned, but it wasn't sadness that was muting her, it was anger. I had tried a few times to start a conversation – get her to talk. When she finally spoke, her words were cold, harsh, and accusing, but not without some merit. She wanted to know why I was spying on her.

"Why are you spying on me?" Giovanna said coldly.

"What?" I exclaimed, off guard and a little confused. "What are you talking about?"

She stopped walking – so I stopped – and then Giovanna turned to me and said, "Your friend Father Domenico came to see me at the Arno Inn. Lorenzo, you should never use a priest to spy on someone, they just don't know how to lie. All I had to do was ask and he told me that you had sent him."

I still don't know what she meant by spying, but I felt guilty just by the tone of her accusation. "You met Father Domenico?" I asked awkwardly.

Giovanna glared at me and said, "You're not going to pretend that you didn't know that he was coming to see me, that you didn't send him to check up on me."

"I didn't... I... I," I stuttered.

"You didn't what?" Giovanna snapped. "You didn't know he was coming to see me, or you didn't send him to spy on me? Are you calling your priest friend a liar? You do know him don't you? He sure knows all about you."

"Of course he knows about me," I said. My defensive instinct took over and cleared my head. I calmly added, "Father Domenico and I go way back. And yes, I did ask him to stop in at the Inn and see you. He's a very wise man, and a good friend, and anyone suffering from bouts of melancholia and has considered taking their own life, could use the consultation of a good priest. I was just concerned about you."

"Well you needn't be," Giovanna scoffed. "And anyway, I don't believe you. He knew too much about me, and asked too many rude questions to have been just there to look into my welfare. I tell you I don't want to talk about my family, so you send a priest to ask prying questions about them, and to spy on me."

"Giovanna, I didn't ask him to spy," I said. Which was truthful, though I knew he was planning on looking into her family's business because he said he was going to. I knew I never asked him to spy. I added, "He did that on his own. If he went too far, or put his nose in where he shouldn't have, I apologize. He just cares about me, so he wanted to know more about you, the woman I..."

"Well he doesn't need to be coming around and asking a lot of personal questions about my family," Giovanna barked. "We agreed that I would tell you about them in time. When I felt it was right."

"I know," I said. "But it's only natural that, with the way that we have been carrying on, for me to know, or want to know about the woman that's become such an important part of my life. We should know all about each other and our families. You know all about mine."

"What's to know, Lorenzo?" Giovanna quipped. "You have no brothers or sisters, never had. You had a mama and a papa, like most of us, but now they are..." She stopped short of saying they were dead. Then she added, "I don't want to talk about this anymore. Just tell that priest to keep away from me and my family."

"I'll tell him," I said solemnly.

"Good," Giovanna said flatly. "Now leave me. I have a terrible headache." Without a word, I started to leave, but then I turned back. Giovanna anticipated my question correctly and answered it. She said, "Give me a couple of days, and then come see me. It will be all right then."

On my request, Fra Domenico came to see me at the shop; I wanted to know what had happened when he went to meet Giovanna that had made her so angry, and since he had taken the initiative, what had he learned about the Vasari family. When I told him what Giovanna had said to me about spying on her and the rest, Fra Domenico said he was sorry to have caused a problem for me, but insisted that it was necessary to find out what little he had about Giovanna.

"I'm sorry to have caused a problem for you, Lorenzo," Fra Domenico said sincerely, "but it was necessary to find out what little I did about Giovanna." He then shook his head, flapping his flabby jowls, and then added, "I don't know, Lorenzo. Maybe it would be best if you just didn't see this woman anymore."

"Why, Father," I quipped with a smile. "How can you say that? I thought this is what you wanted for me – to meet a nice girl."

"Yes, of course Lorenzo, I want you to meet a nice girl," said Fra Domenico gravely. "But this girl, this woman, she's not nice, she's not for you."

I stared at my old friend across the big wooden table. I know he was in earnest and only thinking of my welfare, but what does a priest know about romantic love. Finally I said, "Father, what is it you think you know about Giovanna that makes you say she's not for me?"

He looked at me very seriously and said, "Not much, Lorenzo, but..."

I laughed and inadvertently cut off his words. I said, "Not much? I'm sorry, go ahead, Fra Domenico."

"I was going to say, not much but what I do know is very curious," said Fra Domenico, still very serious.

"All right, I'm listening," I said.

"The Vasari family lost a lot of money recently," said Fra Domenico. "Giovanna's papa, Mario, is a banker, or was a banker. He made a lot of bad investments. I heard he lost money in the wool trade, when the price fell last year after Florence lost all those export markets up north. Mario was forced to sell his partnership in the bank to pay his debts, but it wasn't enough, and so he was in jeopardy of losing his huge family estate, and their farm here in Tuscany, near Urbino." Then Fra Domenico got real quiet and very serious. He said, "They say someone bought Mario's bank notes erasing his debt, but the word is that someone is very powerful and is holding it over him."

"But they don't say who this mysterious benefactor is?" I asked.

"No, just that he is a powerful and dangerous man," said Fra Domenico in the same whispery voice as if he were afraid of being overheard.

"So what does all of his have to do with Giovanna?" I asked, in a deliberately loud and full voice just to counter his timid tone. "I know it's her family, but what does this have to do with her not wanting to see them and what does it have to do with her melancholia?"

"That's the thing," said Fra Domenico, like he was revealing the key to a rare lock. "Giovanna does see her family. When I went to see her, one of her brothers was there, and I heard them talking, when they didn't know who I was, and it didn't sound like there was any problem between them at all. When I introduced myself and told them that I was a friend of yours they suddenly got quiet. Then Giovanna got angry and accused me of spying on her for you – she was very rude."

"Well, Giovanna is a very private person," I explained. "You just caught her off guard and so she was a little defensive."

"Private!" exclaimed Fra Domenico. "I don't think so. It was easy finding out about her family, and I'm sure if I stuck my nose in a little deeper I could find out a lot more about this Giovanna. I think she's just keeping things from you, and you are not finding them on your own because you are not looking."

"I sent you to see her, didn't I?" I said.

"Yes, but you didn't, and don't, want me to actually find out anything about her, but I did, so I'm telling you, as a friend, what I found out," said Fra Domenico. "But I don't think that you really want to hear me."

"I hear you," I said. "I just think you are making too much of this. The family was in debt, but now they are out of debt. That sounds like a good thing, but you see something suspicious in it. Giovanna talks to one of her brothers, I'm glad she does. I'm sure I will meet them all soon enough. Maybe she is just ashamed about the debt and afraid of what I would say knowing that her papa can't afford a dowry…"

"Lorenzo, you are thinking of marrying this woman?!" Fra Domenico exclaimed.

I smiled and said, "The idea has crossed my mind. I paused and added, "Yes, I am thinking of asking her soon."

"Oh Lorenzo," said Fra Domenico, and then he made the sign of the cross in the air and whispered a prayer. He said, "Did you know that she was engaged to be married before?" The revelation did set me back some. He continued, "It's true, Giovanna, was engaged to a young notary, but the engagement was broken off."

"That's understandable," I tried to explain, without really knowing. "Giovanna is a beautiful woman, but maybe the family debt was too much for this other man and his family. He might have been counting on a dowry."

"It's true, that he was not a wealthy man," said Fra Domenico, "but the engagement was called off after her family's debt was paid."

"Do you know this man Giovanna was engaged to?" I asked, feeling a little concerned, but not too worried.

"No," said Fra Domenico. "But I will continue to look into it, if you wish. I'm sure I can find out a lot more."

"No, no you've done enough for me already," I said. Then I added sincerely, "Thank you, Fra Domenico."

"Are you sure?" he asked

"Yes," I answered.

Fra Domenico looked away for a moment, and then turned back to me and said, "Will you promise me that you will not hurry into a wedding or even an engagement with this woman? Will you wait at least until you have met her family, and looked further into these things I have told you?"

I couldn't promise him what he asked, so he said that he would not promise to stop looking into Giovanna's background. After all, "Who else is there to look after you?" he said. It was obvious, though not at the time, that Fra Domenico was seeing Giovanna with clearer eyes than my own.

Weeks passed and summer turned to fall; it was an unusually chilly autumn, that year in my city. Fra Domenico continued to look into Giovanna's affairs – without talking to her again, and with a little more discretion – but he didn't find out anything else of interest, at least nothing I wanted to hear. I never talked to Giovanna about Fra Domenico, and she never brought him up again. I still knew little about the Vasari family, and learned almost nothing more from Giovanna, but I didn't care because everything seemed to be going so well between us – that is me and my love fantasy. Giovanna and I saw each other three to four times a week – that is the way she wanted it – and we made love one or two times a week – this is also the way she wanted it; I would have liked to have been with her every day.

There was one two-week period in October where we were together almost every day, she came to the shop where I painted her picture; it was her idea. She knew I painted from that very first day we spent together – I showed her my studio – so now she wanted me to immortalize her on canvas; Giovanna must not have been much of a judge of artistic talent to trust me to paint her after seeing my work. Of course I was happy to do it, particularly because it was a nude portrait – that was also her idea – and I did a pretty good job; her hands were perfect. I suggested that we title the painting, "The Reclining Venus," to give it respectability; nude portraits, particularly of women, just were not done unless the theme was a historic event – real or mythological. I purchased several nice, soft, large pillows just for the project. Then for two glorious weeks, for several hours a day, Giovanna removed all her clothes and lay down on the pillows in my studio.

From a strictly artistic point of view, Giovanna was an excellent subject for painting; she was very well proportioned – her legs were the right length for her body size, and her upper feminine curves were a perfect match for her round hips. From a man's point of view, Giovanna was an excellent subject to look at; her body was delightfully exquisite. Supported by red and white pillows, Giovanna reclined on her side with her weight resting on her bent right arm – her left shoulder was turned slightly away. Giovanna's legs were crossed just below the knees – left over right – and her left hand, ever so casually, covered nearly all of her most feminine area with just a hint of tiny black hair revealed. Her ivory skin was even in tone, smooth, and hardly had an unwanted dimple or blemish on it from head to toe. Giovanna's long, curly, black hair hung down over her right shoulder and slightly covered one of her perfect breasts; her left breast proudly pyramided upwards in an idealized form. Her head was tilted slightly downwards as she stared up with a proud look of sublime confidence that transcended all modesty – a look befitting the model, Giovanna, and the subject, Venus, the Goddess of love. With such beauty and perfection of form, she almost made me believe in my God again. I put in a nice background of still water, a shoreline, a few shells, and a few fig trees to give the painting an antiquity look, and reinforce the mythological theme.

With the speed that I work, I could have finished the painting in about half of the time it actually took, but I ask you men, if you had a beautiful curvaceous woman volunteering to lie naked in your studio day after day, would you be in any hurry to finish? After asking that question, you may be surprised to know that we didn't make love while she was posing – well there was the first day. There is a certain amount of objectivity for the model by the artist who is seeking the perfect recreation of the subject on the canvas. And though I can relate to the experience – after modeling for Michelangelo – it still seemed odd to watch Giovanna moving about and carrying on a casual conversation while she was completely naked.

It was one of the last of her modeling days, I had just finished painting and was cleaning up the brushes; Giovanna had not yet gotten dressed and was calmly walking around and looking around my studio. Of course I had one eye on her the whole time. It was a chilly afternoon and I had a fire going, but the flames were dying down, so Giovanna shivered. With her arms crossed and her back toward me, I was admiring her slim rounded form – quivering ever so slightly – when she discovered my portrait of Mama on an easel near the fireplace. It had gone by unnoticed before because I always kept a piece of cloth draped over it to protect it from dust. I suppose that curiosity got the better of Giovanna because she lifted up the cloth. She was standing there holding up the corner of the material, when Giovanna playfully accused me of hiding the portrait from her to keep her from getting jealous.

"Lorenzo, you devil," said Giovanna. "You have been hiding this portrait from me to keep me from getting jealous." I walked up beside her and slipped my arm around her bare waist; Giovanna put her left arm up and around my neck and rested it on my left shoulder; she still held the cloth up with her right hand.

"Your mama was beautiful," said Giovanna sincerely.

"I didn't tell you who it was, how did you know it was my mama?" I asked.

"You didn't have to tell me," said Giovanna. "I know you are too clever to leave a portrait of one of your girlfriends just lying around with nothing but a simple cloth to hide it from me. Besides you have her nose, her mouth, and you both have those wolf eyes." She paused, and then added, "I bet you really miss her."

"Yes, everyday," I said. "Especially now that I have met someone as wonderful as you. I would have been proud to have introduced you to Mama and Papa of course."

Giovanna dropped the cloth back down over the portrait. There was a brief silence between us. I believe my words, though unintentionally brought up the mystery of her family; why wasn't she proud to introduce me to her mama and papa? But I didn't ask; I didn't want to spoil the moment. We stood there in silence staring at the covered portrait, and then I swooped Giovanna up in my arms; all right, so there was one other time that we made love on a day that she had been modeling for me.

On one of the days that I wasn't supposed to see Giovanna, I decided to pay her a visit anyway; I don't know why except maybe that I felt that we were getting so completely involved with each other that such a surprise would only be pleasant, and welcomed. I was wrong.

It was a bitterly cold late November afternoon – I had to wear my heavy wool stockings, cap and cape. When I got close enough to the Arno

Inn, I saw Giovanna on her balcony talking to, whom I presumed by his dress, a man – that's all I could tell for sure from where I was. I waved, I didn't think that she saw me, and they disappeared inside. I didn't think much of it at the time – so confident I was in our relationship; I presumed that it was probably one of her brothers, and perhaps, if I walked fast enough, I might finally meet a member of her family. I picked up the pace. Away from the protection of the city walls and buildings, I was out in the open air and a bitter wind blew across the Arno; I held my cape tightly around my neck with one hand and blew on the other and switched hands periodically as needed. On such a cold day, there weren't many people on the streets walking, particularly outside the city where I was. Almost at the inn, I passed the stables where I had hired a carriage for that first night Giovanna and I went out together; it was there I spotted a familiar form – Bramante. For once, I saw him first. I wasn't sure if he was going in, or coming out; he just seemed to be huddling near the entrance. I believe it was because of the cold and not just my normal aversion for the man that made me decide to just continue on to the inn, but unfortunately, Bramante just happened to look over my way – with so few people on the street it was nearly impossible not to be seen and recognized by anyone who knew me even wrapped in a cape. Just for a second, our eyes met, but I knew it was long enough, so I looked back his way and waved; he waved back. I hesitated for a second, and since he was nearest to shelter, I decided to go to him, but I took solace in knowing that I could use the weather as an excuse to keep our conversation brief. I wondered why he was huddled outside in the cold instead of going inside and getting warm.

"Why are you huddled outside in the cold instead of going inside and getting warm?" I asked

"The door is locked," said Bramante, shivering. He also looked to be out of breath; his breathing was heavy and labored. "Can you believe it, Lorenzo, huh? The middle of the afternoon, on such a bitter day, and the stables are closed."

"Looking to hire a carriage for a cold ride in the country?" I asked.

He didn't answer me right away, but then Bramante said, "For a ride into town."

"Where is your carriage?" I asked. "It's odd for you to be walking on such a day as this."

He didn't even try to answer me this time; instead he quickly put the question on me. "What brings you outside the city on such a lovely day?" Bramante asked. "They say that water may freeze tonight."

I smiled and proudly answered, "A young woman."

"Ah, of course," said Bramante with his own, insufferable, smile. "So Lorenzo's finally found love. And just see what love does for you, dragging you out in this weather."

"I thought you were one of the people anxious for me to find someone," I said jokingly."

"Oh yes, I am glad for you," said Bramante. "Love is good for you, you look very happy despite these conditions. I bet she is beautiful, huh? Of course she is, to have lured you out of your shell. So how did you meet her?"

I didn't want to go into all the details, or have to explain her melancholia so I kept it simple. I said, "As a matter of fact, it was that day we met during the Feast of Saint John. You know I never thought of it before, but I have you to thank for meeting her that day."

"Oh really," Bramante said with exaggerated surprise.

"Yes," I said, beginning to really feel the cold. I shivered and said, "You insisted that I take the Ponte Trinità and I met her on the bridge."

"Well isn't that something," said Bramante. "I guess this means you owe me, huh?"

"Yes, I guess it does," I said. I didn't really mean it. At the time I thought I met her despite his attempts to keep me out at the festival. I just said it to use my false gratitude as an excuse to get out of the cold. I asked, "Would you like to meet her? She has a room right over at the Arno Inn. I could pay you back by bringing you inside out of the weather where you could sit by the fire, warm up and catch your breath."

"Catch my breath?" Bramante questioned. "No, I am all right. It's just this cold makes me breathe a little heavy."

"Then come with me," I said again, feeling confident that he would say no. "Not only can I pay you back by warming you up, but also by showing you one of the most beautiful women you have ever seen. You can come back to the stables later when someone is here. You can see this place from her balcony, so you can watch and see when they open."

"No, no," said Bramante. "You go ahead. You are just trying to make me jealous with this beauty of yours. Besides, I don't want to get in the way of young love. You can pay me back another time. It might get below freezing today, so get out of here before you freeze off anything that you might need later, now that you've found another use for it, huh?"

I bid Bramante goodbye, and hurried on next door to the inn – grateful that he hadn't taken me up on my offer. Once inside, I found it as cold there as it was outside, Giovanna was in a foul mood, presumably because of my uninvited visit, but she quickly warmed up.

When she answered the door, Giovanna didn't give me the usual greeting – a smile, a kiss and a few kind words – instead she gave me a sour look, and demanded to know what I was doing there.

"What are you doing here," demanded Giovanna. I walked past her, and after she closed the door, I tried to kiss her, but she turned away at the last moment and I had to settle for a soft cheek. "I know I'm not mistaken," Giovanna growled. "This is not a day that we were supposed to be together. So don't try and tell me that we had a date."

"I know," I said. "I just thought I would surprise you … surprise." Giovanna turned away from me but I playfully snuck up behind her and put my arms around her waist; she stiffened up. "I saw you on the balcony," I said.

Giovanna broke free of my grip, turned and said, "You saw me on the balcony? When?"

"Just a few minutes ago," I said. I paused just to tease her, and then asked, "Was that one of your other lovers, or just one of your brothers? I waved, but you didn't wave back. So I guess you didn't see me."

"No, I didn't," Giovanna quickly agreed.

"So, was that your brother with you?" I asked again.

"My brother?" Giovanna said looking a little confused and a little like she was trying to figure something out.

"Yes, with you on the balcony," I said again. "It was just a few minutes ago. I saw the two of you. A bit cold to be standing out there, I should think. I thought he would still be here. I was hoping to finally meet someone from your family."

"Sorry, but we didn't know you were coming," said Giovanna turning away from me again. "You weren't supposed to be here, remember. He had to leave. I'm surprised you didn't run into him on the way out. He left just a few minutes before you came knocking."

"But if even I had run into him, I wouldn't have known who it was," I said. "Because I have never been introduced."

Giovanna turned back to me, back in control and recovered from my surprise visit and revelations. She said, "Maybe it's about time you met Marco, my oldest brother. He comes here and visits me often. We'll see all right? Now tell me, was the walk terribly cold?"

"Yes, but it was worth it to see you," I said. "I would have gotten out of the cold a little sooner, maybe in time to have met your brother up here, but I ran into an old acquaintance of mine on the street."

"An old acquaintance," Giovanna said inquisitively. "Now that doesn't sound too friendly."

"Yes, I know," I said. "It was my old art teacher. I think I told you a little about him – a bit unscrupulous, a bit mysterious, and always in control of every situation, and at the same time, trying to be charming. That was what was so odd about seeing him out this way on such a cold afternoon. He was acting strange, for him. I think it was the first time I ever caught him off his guard. He said he was waiting for a carriage, you know next door at the stables, but they were closed. It was odd that he didn't know that, and then chose to just wait when he has no idea when they will be coming back. Then something, maybe that, set his whole demeanor off. He was acting very suspicious, which is unusual for such a successful ..."

"You know, it's been my experience that when people like that are caught off guard they lie, and lie badly," Giovanna interrupted.

"I'm sure that's probably true," I said. "I've always believed that Bramante was being less than honest even when he was in control of the situation."

"Maybe you should think about it some more, but later," said Giovanna. "Now since you are here, make yourself comfortable. I will be right back."

Giovanna disappeared into the bedroom. The fire was warming the room, but there was a draft coming from the balcony, so I went to close the heavy curtains. I remembered Bramante and looked down toward the stables; he was no longer there. I looked up the street and saw his receding figure in the distance; I remember thinking that he must have changed his mind about the carriage. After I closed the curtains, I saw Giovanna's reflection in the mirror above the x-chair; she was standing in the doorway between the two rooms. I turned to confirm the lovely imagine I thought I saw in the looking glass – it was true. Giovanna was wearing nothing but a look of pure mischief and primal attraction. She walked toward me slowly, like a wild cat, slipped her arms up and around my neck, and then kissed me hard on the mouth. We never made it into the bedroom, it was warmer in front of the fire, but I don't believe I would have noticed the cold anytime in the next hour or so.

It was Christmastime in my city and I hardly even noticed. There were the usual festive decorations and shop window displays – a nativity in every window – but I paid them little attention. I didn't go to see any of the dramas, participate or listen to any of the caroling, and didn't attend Christmas mass; Giovanna accounted for all of my time. Even when I wasn't with her, I thought of her, and planned and anticipated our next date. I rarely saw anyone else during those days, but I still kept in touch with Fra Domenico and Johann. In fact, Johann used the Christmas celebrations as a reason to invite me over to dinner at his new home; I agreed provided Giovanna was also invited – she was. Johann had only met Giovanna once in passing, and I had yet to see Johann's newborn daughter, Costanza.

When I told Giovanna of the invitation, she insisted on going over early and helping Maria prepare the feast. She said that it was the only way that she would feel comfortable accepting their gracious invitation, and not feel like she was intruding on their family's holiday. I agreed and made the arrangements with Johann and Maria.

On the day of the Christmas feast, I had a carriage deliver Giovanna to their home several hours before I arrived. When I got there, Maria and Giovanna were laughing and talking like old friends, and I assumed that this was why Giovanna really wanted to get there before me – so she could make friends with Maria by spending a little time alone with her. The newborn, Costanza was asleep; unfortunately for her, she looked just like her father. The older boy, Hans, was sitting up and watching his mama. Johann and I sat by the fire, drank and talked of old times – our days in the Venetian navy. I could tell he missed the adventure, fighting, the excitement of battle, the victories, and the spoils. Talking about it made me miss those days too. The house was small but nice. I remember thinking that in a few more years, with a few more children, they would have to get a bigger house or they would have no privacy – with one bedroom and one average-sized living room it was even smaller than the living area at the shop.

Maria seemed the perfect matron – with two young children and ready for more, she had grown a little plump. It was odd seeing Johann in that little house playing the papa, especially after seeing the big man in action – fighting, killing, raping, and pillaging. Thinking back, Johann didn't really fit in well – he was very restless playing the family patriarch – but I was too busy with my own infatuation to have really noticed.

We sat down to eat – with Giovanna and I on one side, and Johann and Maria on the other. The table was a little smaller than mine, and it was completely covered with food including, goose, vegetables, bread, pie and much more. As usual, Giovanna ate little, but the rest of us more than made up for her petite appetite. I ate too much and couldn't eat another bite.

"I ate too much," I said. Then as Maria offered me more, I added, "I couldn't eat another bite. It was delicious."

"Yes, Maria," echoed Giovanna with a smile. "Everything was just wonderful."

Maria smiled back, and said, "Thank you both. And thank you,

Giovanna, for all your help." Then she turned to Johann and said, "How about you, my husband? Haven't you any kind words for our efforts?"

"Eating speaks louder than words," Johann said boldly. "And I've eaten more than all of you put together." Then he motioned toward his infant son and newborn daughter – wrapped in blankets by the roaring fire – and added, "And that includes what those two little mouths will suckle from their mama's breast."

"Johann!" Maria exclaimed. She was a little embarrassed.

Johann laughed – a big, burly roar. "Oh don't worry, Maria," joked Johann. "I'm sure Maus knows how babies are fed. I even bet he knows where they come from. And if he doesn't, Giovanna here can explain them both to him."

"Why, Johann, you are just terrible," Giovanna said coyly. "But let me assure you, Lorenzo needs no explanation. In fact, I bet he could teach you a few things."

Maria blushed and Johann's eyes widened, and I quickly interrupted to direct the attention back to Johann. "Now, nobody can doubt that Orso must know what he is doing." I said. "Two babies in two years, shall we expect another in the up and coming year?"

"God willing, Maus," Johann boasted with jocular pride. "I'll certainly do my part." Then he paused for effect and then added, "Just as often as I can."

"Oh Johann, stop it," said Maria with playful anger in her voice and a false frown. She got up, and from behind, kissed Johann on the cheek, hugged his broad shoulders, and then began to clear the table.

"Let me help you with that," said Giovanna as she too got up, kissed me on the cheek and hugged my shoulders.

"Oh that's all right," said Maria. "You're our guest and you have done enough to help. But if you would, could you check on the babies for me?"

"Certainly, I would be happy to," said Giovanna cheerfully. Then she went by the fire, picked up little Costanza and held her to her breast – the baby smiled and laughed playfully.

I was smiling and watching Giovanna holding the baby and seeming to enjoy the experience, when Johann said, "Giovanna seems to be good with children."

"Yes," I agreed, still smiling. "But I knew that she would be, and that she will make a perfect mother."

Giovanna shot me a quick glance, and then quickly put Costanza back down. She looked over at a sleeping Hans, and chose not to disturb him. "They both seem to be just fine, Maria," said Giovanna in a deliberately cold voice that I don't think anybody else noticed but myself.

"Thank you Giovanna," said Maria, still clearing the table. Then she added, "When are you going to start a family of your own?"

Giovanna looked uncomfortable by the question. She seemed to deliberately avoiding looking at me, and then she said, "I haven't thought much about it. I mean not until ...Maria please let me help you with those."

Maria didn't press the question, and let Giovanna help her clear the table. I still had a silly placid smile on my face, as I tried to make eye contact with Giovanna, who was still avoiding looking at me. I remember thinking that her discomfort was probably because she hadn't been formally proposed to, so the subject of marriage and family was not to be discussed, for she might appear to be anxious or desperate; of course, I was wrong.

"Maus, are you feeling as full as me?" asked Johann.

"Yes," I said. Then to be sarcastic, I said, "And I can only assume I do know how full you feel, considering you ate more than all of us put together."

Johann ignored my bad humor and said, "Why don't we go for a little walk to get over this stuffed feeling." I agreed and got up and got my cape and cap. Johann grabbed his also, and then picked up a flask and filled it with wine. "This will help keep us warm," he chuckled.

We left the little house and walked through the wool district. It was almost dark and the lamps were being lit – it was misting a chilly rain. Several blocks had passed without a word between us – we just shared the wine. Then I finally asked, "Well Orso, what do you think of Giovanna?"

He paused, and then Johann said, "She's beautiful, Maus, that's for sure."

"Yes, she is," I said, agreeing to the obvious, but I could tell Johann wanted to say more; he was still searching for the right words, and that can be difficult for a man not used to relying on them.

"Have the two of you talked about marriage yet?" asked Johann.

"Actually I was just thinking about that," I said. "I may bring it up tonight."

"Do you think that she will agree to marry you?" asked Johann.

"I can't say for sure," I said with false modesty. "But by the way we've been, I can only assume that she will agree."

Johann stopped and turned to me, and said, "Look Maus, I don't like to get in between a man and his woman, but we are friends, and there's just something not right about this woman. I've been talking to Father Domenico..."

"Oh, I see," I said taking the flask from his hands. I took a long drink and said, "The good Father is set against Giovanna. He has heard some rumors, and, I know he means well, but what does a priest know about women."

"Agreed, but apparently, you know little of this woman yourself," said Johann. "Father Domenico says that she hasn't been telling you much about her family or her past."

"She's just going through a hard time with them," I excused.

"Then he told me that she kept her engagement a secret from you," said Johann.

"Oh that," I said casually. "She is just embarrassed that's all. She was rejected because of her family's financial problems and she doesn't like people to know, so she doesn't talk about it."

"Then how come I know about it?" asked Johann.

"What?" I said, a little confused. "Didn't Father Domenico tell..."

"I overheard her talking to Maria," said Johann. "And I am almost sure that she knows that I heard her talking. She was going on about this Donato fellow that she was engaged to and she didn't sound too embarrassed talking about him."

I started to walk again – Johann followed at my side and more than a foot above me – as I searched for another good excuse. I couldn't think of one, so all I said was, "I didn't know that his name was Donato, but it doesn't change a thing. He was her past, and I am her future."

"Maybe," said Johann. "But will you do me one favor before you run off and marry this woman? Come see me and Machiavelli at his office."

"So now the good Father has got Niccolò in on this too," I said a little surprised and irritated.

"When Father Domenico came to me, he was very upset," said Johann. "You know that Machiavelli can find out anything about anyone in this town. So I asked him to look into this."

"What did he find out?" I asked.

"I don't know yet," said Johann. "Or I would tell you now. That's why I'm asking you to come to the Palazzo Vecchio and we'll find out together."

"I wish you would have come to me first," I said. "Instead of dragging Niccolò into this, he has enough things on his mind, and shouldn't be expected to have to deal with a bunch of silly rumors. I could have explained the good Father's foolish concerns to you."

"Maybe, Maus, or maybe not. I think that this woman has blinded you from the truth," said Johann, sincerely. He finished off the last of the wine, and said, "I can't say that I blame you. She is quite beautiful and could blind any man."

"I can't believe that she would do anything deliberately to deceive me," I said. "And I'm not blind."

"Then it won't hurt you to come down and see what Machiavelli has found out," said Johann.

I hesitated, but I couldn't argue with his logic. I said, "No, I don't suppose it would hurt, and I don't think it will change anything no matter what he thinks he has found out. But if it will make you feel better about Giovanna, I'll be there. I had hoped that the four of us could become friends and spend a lot of time together."

"We still may," said Johann. "God willing. But no matter what, we will always be friends. No woman can come between us. Who knows, maybe Machiavelli will have nothing but good news about this woman."

"Nothing but good news," I echoed. "I am certain of it."

With the real purpose for Johann wanting to take a walk completed, we turned and quickly headed back to his house for more wine, and the warmth of the fire.

The first half of the carriage ride was quiet. I remember admiring the fine nativity scene outside of San Marco. I can't say what was silencing her tongue, but I was searching my mind for the right words, and how to create the right situation to bring up the idea of marriage. As I've said, I wasn't really worried about being rejected – at the time I thought that marriage between us was just inevitable – but I wanted it to be right for Giovanna, a moment that she would always remember. I couldn't think of anything clever or romantic. So I just ended up blurting it out, when do you want to get married?

"When do you want to get married?" I blurted out.

Giovanna looked at me rather calmly, like she expected the question – as I had believed she did – but then she said nothing for several long seconds; it seemed like minutes. I began to hear my own heart pounding over the horses clicking hooves on the street below. Finally she said quietly, "The spring is always nice, with the lilies in bloom. I've always wanted a spring wedding. If you can wait that long."

I was stunned. It took me several seconds to respond. I said, "Yes, the spring would be perfect." Then there was a long silence between us. Finally, looking into her beautiful, brown eyes, I leaned over and kissed her ever so tenderly – her lips were soft and warm, but lacked all passion. It certainly wasn't what I expected. Maybe she was just overwhelmed.

"Would you mind if I went home alone tonight?" Giovanna asked. "I have such a headache."

I agreed, I said, "We can talk about the wedding plans another time."

I can't really explain how I felt, but I'll try. I was happy, of course, that Giovanna accepted my proposal, but I wasn't so blinded that I couldn't see that she was less than enthusiastic about the idea. Though I guess I was just visually impaired enough to accept that the wine, the weather, her melancholia, or her headache was keeping Giovanna from expressing the joy of becoming my wife.

Back from his trip to Germany and dealing with yet another uprising in Pisa – amongst other crisis of state – Machiavelli found the time to investigate Giovanna and the Vasari family. Looking back, Niccolò, Johann and Fra Domenico did me a great service, but I didn't see it that way at the time. As I sat in his office at the Palazzo Vecchio and listened to Niccolò tell me what his investigation had uncovered, with Johann eagerly looking on, the first thing that came to my mind was, why were all of my friends against Giovanna?

"Why are all of my friends against Giovanna," I said. "Everybody was telling me, Lorenzo, you need a woman. I find a woman, and a beautiful one at that, and everybody, those same friends, are against her."

"She's not what she appears to be, Maus," said Johann. "You would see it too, if you were not so close to her. What is it they say, you can't see the forest for the trees."

"But I can see the trees," I said. "And the trees are the forest, aren't they? So I guess I can see the forest."

"You are debating metaphors," said Niccolò. "The reality is that you are not seeing her true nature, what she really is, or seeing what she is really doing."

"And you and your spies," I said, "they can see Giovanna's true nature?"

"Not exactly," said Niccolò. "But they do know the facts. It will still be up to you to determine her true nature."

"So what is it you think you know?" I asked, confident that I had heard it all before and that I could explain everything.

"You knew that Giovanna was engaged to Donato Carracci, a nobleman who was forced to take on a position as a notary in the Santo Croce district when his family's fortune ran dry?" asked Niccolò.

"I didn't know his full name, until now, or that he was a nobleman," I said. "But, yes, I knew of the engagement."

"Did you know that she was forced to call off the engagement after the family debt was paid?" asked Niccolò.

"Yes," I said self-assuredly. "Giovanna was embarrassed to tell me because this Donato wasn't man enough to keep his word after learning that the family was no longer wealthy he left her."

"Neither of them wanted to call off the engagement," said Niccolò, ignoring my explanation. "They were forced to call off the engagement by her family at the insistence of their benefactor. Then Giovanna was offered to this benefactor, the man who bought their bank note, with the condition that he call off the debt, but he refused. Instead he proposed that they find her a rich husband who would be willing or pay their debt, and the interest that was mounting."

"That's a lie," is all I could say.

"They say she is still seeing this Donato," said Johann.

"That is impossible," I defended. "I would know."

"Didn't you say that you see her about two to three times a week?" asked Niccolò.

"Three to four times a week," I corrected.

"All right, three to four times a week," repeated Niccolò. "That leaves about half of her time spent away from you. If you don't know what she is doing in that time, then how do you know that she is not seeing this man?"

I shook my head in disgust. I was beginning to get angry – angry because the logic of his words was threatening my fantasy. Niccolò hadn't said anything important that I hadn't heard before, not yet, but he was saying it better than Fra Domenico or Johann had. I was starting to consider the possible truth that I might have been wrong about Giovanna. But I wasn't ready to give up my fantasy just yet. I said, "Just because I don't know where she is every hour of every day doesn't mean that she is sleeping with another man."

"Not just another man," said Johann. "But a man that she was, until recently, engaged to be married. Why would anyone lie to us about finding out such a thing?"

"And the strange thing is," added Niccolò. "Giovanna and Donato are not particularly secretive about their affair. You can find out for yourself. It's almost like she doesn't care, or wants you to find out. I can give you the…"

"I don't want to hear this," I said irritably. "Giovanna is going to be my wife. She has agreed, and I will not listen to such fabrication about her."

"Then she has agreed to marry you?" asked Johann.

"Yes," I said. "I asked her on the way home from your house, while riding in the carriage home. We are to be married this spring."

"Did you know that the man who bought Mario Vasari's debt is actually an old friend of yours?" asked Niccolò. And that was all the preparation I had before he blurted out the name, "Tommaso Bramante." My heart stopped and I couldn't speak. Suddenly I remembered that cold November day when I saw Bramante, so out of place and out of character, at the stables next to the Arno Inn. Now I know why Bramante was out in the cold. He had seen me from the balcony, and tried to make his escape but his carriage wasn't there. Of course it wasn't there, because he had sent it away thinking that he was going to be with Giovanna for a while. I was beginning to believe with my head, what my heart would not consider. Machiavelli continued, "Now that little bit of information, unlike most of what else I have told you was not so easy to come by. It seems that not many people knew who this man was, and those who did wanted his name kept a secret, at least most of those who knew didn't want his identity known. But Donato will tell anyone who will listen, and he says that Giovanna was the one who told him that Bramante had bought Mario's debt."

Machiavelli kept talking, but I was no longer listening. For all their efforts, they were successful, the damage was done; I doubted the woman I loved. Then I remembered what Giovanna said to me after I surprised her that day. I remembered it because it stood out as not making sense to me at the time, but it did now, in this new horrible light. "You know, it's been my experience that when people like that are caught off guard they lie, and lie badly," she had said. Giovanna wanted me to be suspicious about Bramante being there and hoped that I would look into it. Maybe she even wanted me to be suspicious about her – her words applied to her attitude that day also. But why tell me in riddles? Why not just say it right out if she wanted me to know? I could no longer think; my head was spinning. I remember getting up and leaving Machiavelli's office, but I don't think I said a word, not even goodbye. I knew what I had to do; I had to hear the truth from Giovanna's own lips.

Chapter IX

It was a new year, and two days after Twelfth Night, when I finally got up the nerve to go and see Giovanna. We had made plans for the last day of the Christmas holiday, but I canceled them. As I approached the Arno Inn, I knew that Giovanna would know that something was wrong; I had never canceled a date with her in the six months that we were together, plus the date I canceled was a special day, a holiday, and it had been over a week since I had seen her – the night I proposed. I needed the time to myself to prepare and rehearse the conversation over in my head. What would Giovanna say? I played out dozens of scenarios in my head that included possible explanations, hostile or guilty reactions, excuses, and confessions, with each case conveniently worked out in my mind to a positive ending, but it was impossible for me to know what Giovanna would actually say. Even after all that time, I realized that I hardly knew her; it's difficult to know someone who doesn't want to be known. I guess the only genuine reasons for delaying the inevitable was to hold on a little longer to my fantasy – as long as I didn't confront her we were still engaged – and to prepare myself, the best that I could for the worst, which I learned wasn't really possible. I even contemplated going back to that day just before I walked into Niccolò's office at the Palazzo Vecchio, and erasing my mind of everything I heard from Machiavelli about Giovanna. Of course, that too was impossible. I did manage to reduce all the questions and thoughts down to two names – Bramante and Donato.

I anxiously knocked on the door, and Giovanna let me in and greeted me with her usual smile, a kiss and a few kind words. I didn't delay – I couldn't, after all that rehearsing the words just burst out of me – I immediately told her that I knew about Donato.

"I know about Donato," I said.

Giovanna was surprisingly unaffected. She said, "Yes, I know you do, I told you that I was engaged."

I know Giovanna was looking at me – I could feel her eyes – but I didn't dare look back, not yet; I was afraid that seeing that beautiful face would weaken my resolve for the truth and strengthen my desire to remain in my fantasy. We stood there in silence for a long moment, and then I said, "No, I mean I know that you were forced to call off your engagement to this Donato and that it wasn't something that you really wanted to do…"

"Yes," interrupted Giovanna, in a casual tone. "We've been over this before." She went and sat down on the couch.

I had gotten off to a bad start; I was having trouble and losing my nerve. What if they had been wrong about Giovanna, I suddenly thought. I could lose her with a demonstration of my lack of trust, but if I kept quiet, I would always wonder if I could trust her. I had no choice; I had to continue.

"What I meant when I said, I know about Donato, was that I know that you are still seeing him," I said flatly.

Giovanna jumped up on her feet, surprised, but she quickly recovered and went on the attack. "So, you've been spying on me again," said Giovanna. "Or shall I say still? What does that priest friend of yours think he has found out about me know?"

"I'm not talking about Father Domenico," I said.

"No? Then who?" Asked Giovanna. "Or have you taken up your own spying."

"It's not important how I know," I said, as I finally looked her in the eye. I was hoping to see truth in her lovely face; I did not. I added, "I just know that you've been seeing him. Do you deny it?"

Giovanna sighed deeply, not yet taking my questioning seriously. She said rather flippantly, "So I still see him. I don't see what business it is of yours. We were together for more than two years when we were forced to call off our engagement. It was devastating for him and for me at the time. Of course I still care for him, so he comes to see me from time to time."

"Is that all there is to it?" I asked. I was beginning to get irritated with her lack of remorse and flippant attitude. So I shot back, "Just affection between two old friends? So when you say you see him you only mean above the waistline?"

"How dare you!" Giovanna snapped bitterly. "I told you that we were just good, old friends now."

"Then why is it that you see him almost as often as you see me?" I asked coldly. My natural aggression was beginning to take over; I could sense that she was lying and on the defensive, so I pushed hard. "Is spending the night with you something you usually do with old friends."

"Where did you hear that from?" Giovanna asked. She was beginning to look uncomfortable – nervous and agitated.

"I said it wasn't important how I know," I said. "What's important is that it is true."

"Well it's important to me," said Giovanna, obviously trying to avoid my question, by pressing her own queries.

"It seems that Donato Carracci has been saying, or bragging about being with you, quite openly," I said. "And it also seems that the two of you have been seen by just about anyone who cared to look."

"Are you trying to tell me that you have been talking to Donato?" asked Giovanna, still trying to avoid dealing with me directly.

"Are you trying to tell me that the two of you are not still lovers?" I bluntly countered. Her beautiful face went from ivory to snow white, and I knew my answer; she couldn't even attempt a lie. Before she had the chance to recover, I went in for the kill and hit her with the other name. I said, "I know who bought your papa's debt. You pretended not to know who Tommaso Bramante was when I told you I saw him at the stables next door." Giovanna's eyes widened, and then she quickly turned away. I continued, "As a matter of fact, Bramante was coming from here when I ran into him that day. He was the man with you on the balcony, not your brother Marco. You must have seen me, so he hurried out, but then I saw him outside, by the stables. That's why he was acting so strangely. He thought maybe he had been caught, that I would put it all together, but of course, I was too stupid."

I was beginning to get angry and it must have showed in my voice. Giovanna was getting frightened, frustrated, or something, because tears began to swell in her eyes as she fell back onto the couch. Her reaction, like that of a child caught in a lie, removed all doubt in my mind and confirmed that all that I had heard from my friends was, unfortunately, true. The truth was painful, and only intensified my anger. I said, "Bramante's the one that paid your papa's debt. How much is it now? But why all the deception? Why not just ask me for the money? You know that I would do anything for you."

I took two long strides and reached out and grabbed Giovanna by the arm. I pulled her up off of the couch and held her by the shoulders, and then I kissed her hard – deliberately too hard, cutting her lip. She tried to pull away, but I didn't let her go until I was ready to; I gently pushed her away and back onto the couch. A spot of blood formed on her lower lip; the color blended well with her natural crimson hue. I stood above, looking down on her, but she averted her face from me. Giovanna said, "You knew I had the money, Bramante told you, I'm sure. Why not just ask for it? After all that's why you picked me, wasn't it? Or Bramante must have picked me. He was..."

"Stop it, please, stop Lorenzo," Giovanna pleaded with tears running down her ivory cheeks. She sobbed uncontrollably for about a minute. It was foolish of me, but I took pity on her, or maybe I was still just blind enough – my friends were obviously right about me, I was blinded by Giovanna – to hope for some magical explanation that would redeem our love. So I listened to her.

Despite her apparent loss of control, Giovanna still knew what she had to do to assure my cooperation. She was quite conveniently able to regain her composure and give her explanation; perhaps that was the true purpose of her tears – to buy time to think, that and to gain pity. First she had to downplay her relationship with Donato. Giovanna still claimed that Donato was now just a good, old friend and relied on my desire to believe this and the sincerity of her emotion to convince me. She said that Donato and her brother Marco were her only contacts to her old life and family.

"Donato and my brother Marco are my only contacts to my old life and family," said Giovanna wiping her eyes. "Donato is just a good, old friend. Papa doesn't know I see him or my brother. He won't allow anyone in the family to see me until the debt is cleared. He is angry with me for not doing my part to clear the family debt and restore our, his financial security. You know he offered me to Bramante as a wife, or a mistress, to call off the debt. When that didn't work out, Papa was really mad at me."

The thought of Giovanna being offered to someone like a piece of property, particularly to someone as repulsive as Bramante, redirected my anger away from her. I even felt sympathy for her and was now more willing to listen to her explanation. Undoubtedly this was her intention. How could Giovanna know me so well, while I hardly knew her at all? This too was undoubtedly her intention, and had been all along.

"Papa finally broke down and sold the farm near Urbino," said Giovanna. "That nearly killed him. He thought that would be enough, but it didn't cover the interest. It seems the buyer found out about Papa's financial problems and used that to force Papa to sell the property for much less than it was worth. Bramante's been pressuring Papa, reminding him that the original agreement was for a year or he took everything, the farm, the house, everything. Papa has until May to pay Bramante the interest or he takes the villa, and my family will be out on the streets. Papa was desperate. That's when he offered me... When that was turned down, they came up with a plan for me to meet and marry a rich man – you. Papa would borrow the money from you and then pay you back, or make you his business partner. Papa thinks he can get back into the business once this debt is cleared. I only wanted you to..."

"How much is the debt, now?" I asked. The sincerity in her tone had gotten to me.

Giovanna looked up at me. Once again tears formed in her eyes. "It's just the interest, the principal's been paid," she said with a look of hope in her eyes, and got up from the couch. We were very close to each other, almost touching, but we both avoided looking at one another for more than a second at a time. "I can't ask you to do this now," she added.

"How much is the debt?" I repeated.

"Well, it was about two thousand florin," said Giovanna. "But the interest on the interest has been growing, I'm not sure of the exact amount."

"I'll pay it," I said, still avoiding prolonged eye contact with Giovanna.

"Oh Lorenzo, I can't..." Giovanna started to say, but I cut her off.

"Of course you can, and you will," I said. "Just look at all the trouble you went to, to get me to agree to pay it, you can't back down now."

"I know," said Giovanna as she tried to get me to look at her. "I thought I could before, but not now. Not after..."

She didn't finish her thought – our eyes finally met and stuck, it was my turn to be hopeful. "I will need a couple of days," I said. "To get the money."

"I won't forget this," said Giovanna. "I don't know what to say. This will mean so much to my family."

"Tell Bramante to come and see me the day after tomorrow, Thursday," I said. "Make it in the evening. I will come here Friday night and let you know how things went."

Then Giovanna kissed me tenderly, sweetly, and for the last time.

I had spent everything that I had earned working for Niccolò, and even the two hundred ducats Papa had left me in the cellar, so I would have had to become more sparing or go and see Abraham, the old Jew, about acquiring some of Papa's money anyway. I had told myself that I would never touch Papa's money, and had even thought of donating it all to the church, but love makes you do strange things, and even change the way you think. I told myself that the money wasn't for me, and it was to be used to help others – Giovanna and her family.

I went to see Abraham. The Jews were periodically persecuted in Florence, throughout Italy and elsewhere. I was never quite sure why, except that they rejected Christ as our savior. I know they were often moneylenders, because the Church did not like usury, but my enlightened city had many Christian bankers, and they were not persecuted. I'm sure there was some good excuse why the Jews were persecuted and even occasionally expelled from my city, but I never knew the reason. If all Jews were like Abraham I would never understand why; Abraham was the trustworthiest man I would ever meet. He was responsible for other people's money, made them profits, took only his agreed percentage, and accounted for every denari. Papa had entrusted Abraham with almost fifteen thousand ducats. When I went to see him, just nine years later, Abraham had increased the total worth of Papa's account to over twenty thousand ducats. I told him what had happened to Papa, and he was very sympathetic and genuinely sorry for my loss. He then told me that the last time he saw Papa, Papa had anticipated the possibility that he would not return.

"Your papa anticipated the possibility that he would not return," said Abraham. "I anticipated the worse because it has been so long since I heard from him. It was not like him to go so long without any contact. Then, I expected to hear from you because you are the only heir he named."

"I didn't want to use Papa's money unless it became absolutely necessary," I said.

"Then I take it that it has become absolutely necessary?" asked Abraham.

"Yes, I'm afraid it has," I said.

"I sympathize and respect your convictions to remain financially independent," said Abraham. "But now, this money is yours, and only yours. This is what your papa wanted. You are not borrowing or stealing from someone. You are just collecting your own funds. Now, how much do you need?"

His words made me feel less guilty. "Two thousand," I said. "Maybe a little more, I'm not sure of the exactly how much I'll need. It's to pay a debt."

"That's all I need to know, for now," said Abraham. "I just wanted to make sure that I can cover the amount at a moments notice, and I can. Now if you wanted to clear the account, I would need a few days. I will give you a note for payment in gold florin. You just fill in the amount and the name of the one to receive payment and send him to me."

It was that simple. I took a few extra gold florins, in coins, for my expenses. I still felt a little bad that I had been manipulated into using Papa's hard earned money this way, but I took solace in knowing that I was just spending the interest. I was surprised that Abraham never asked me what the money was for – it seemed like a large amount to me, and enough to spark some curiosity in any man – but I guess in his business, he was used to handling much larger transactions, and I guess that discretion probably just goes with the job.

I told Abraham that I would keep in touch, just like Papa had, but if anything happened to me, that I wished the money would go to the church. He should seek out Fra Domenico at San Marco. He said that I was a young man and shouldn't speak of death, but since he was an old man, he could, and should talk of death all the time. I don't know exactly how old he was, but he looked ancient; I didn't know anyone could look as old as Abraham and still be alive. I guess that's why Papa always referred to him as the old Jew. Bringing up his inevitable demise was his way of leading up to telling me that his son, Abraham, was his apprentice, and now his partner, and he would honor all agreements and investments. I told him to keep doing whatever it was that he was doing, and that I would honor any agreement Papa had with him regarding his profits.

So I had the paper I needed, and now all that was left to do was to go home and wait for Bramante. In anticipation of seeing him, I felt angry, bitter, and surprisingly curious for what my old art teacher would say; it was the only time I was ever anxious to see him.

I sat facing the door, with a bottle of wine and the bank note on the big wooden table in front of me. It was another cold winter's evening; it might even have reached the freezing point that night. I could hear the wind howling outside, and I felt a draft. I sat in the half-light with only the glow of the fire to illuminate the room. Finally, I heard a carriage pull up outside, and a few moments later, there was the knock at the door. I didn't get up, I just yelled, come in, in a loud voice.

"Come in," I said in a loud voice.

The door opened and Bramante came in; one of his men closed the door behind him – a move I suspected designed to let me know that he was not alone. He looked surprisingly subdued, as he sat down across from me; I assumed that he would have been in a gloating mood, or at least his usual arrogant one. I slid the bottle on the table toward him. He picked it up and then glanced around. He spotted a cup drying on the mantel above the fireplace; he retrieved it, sat back down and then commented that there was no reason that we shouldn't be civilized.

"There's no reason we shouldn't be civilized," said Bramante. He poured, drank from the cup, and then slid the bottle back to me.

"Why me?" I said, not yet wanting to look directly at him; I was afraid he would smirk and I would lose control of my temper.

He hesitated before he answered, and then he said quietly, "I knew you had the money, and I knew that you would come to her rescue and bail out that pathetic father of hers if she asked you to. A man like that Mario doesn't deserve to own land, or have wealth. Given the chance, and it now seems that he is going to have another one, he'll probably just lose it all again. But, I also thought that I was doing you a favor." Now I had to look at him, to see if he was making a bad joke; he looked surprisingly sincere. He continued, "You needed a women and this girl is beautiful, huh?"

"Is this where I'm supposed to thank you?" I said sarcastically.

"No, I will tell you when it's time," he said. "You know, they offered her to me first. Can you imagine that lovely body in the arms of this bony old crow? With this face and this hawk of a nose? What kind of man offers his daughter to cover his debts? I will say that Giovanna is loyal to her family, she did her best to try and seduce me, but some things are more valuable than sex, and business is business. I guess she must agree with that on some level because Giovanna broke off her engagement to that notary that she was so in love with, just so she could act as her papa's commodity. Well since they were willing to give Giovanna to me, I suggested that they marry her off to a rich man and have him pay their debt. After all I just wanted the money, I didn't want their farm, their, villa or any of their other junk, I would just have to sell it and I don't want to have to deal with that."

"Why not?" I asked. "It would have been worth a lot more than the debt."

"True," said Bramante. "But this wasn't really about the money. You see, men like Mario Vasari have always looked down on me because I earned my money. They think they are somehow superior because they were born with wealth and rank. But all that's changing. His class is going to have to get used to men like me, like us, yes, you may not like it, but you are a first generation wealthy man, not unlike me in that way. You will establish a Demarco family dynasty. But people like the Vasari's will still treat you like you are something unpleasant that they stepped on in the street. I just wanted to teach him a little lesson, and show him and his aristocratic friends a glimpse of the future. And it was then I thought of you. I could force him to marry his daughter into a class lower than her own, and I just thought it would be a good match."

"You thought it would be a good match?" I repeated, as I began to feel the much anticipated anger building. "So you were acting as an unscrupulous marriage broker, and the debt was to be your fee?"

"Actually, that sounds pretty good, I wish I would have put it to him that way," said Bramante. "It sounds almost noble, except that unscrupulous part, though I can't deny its accuracy. But you know that

Giovanna has even less scruples than I do. She played all of us. She cleared the debt without having to marry anyone. I suppose that she will now go back to that notary, if you let her."

"What do you mean, she played us all?" I asked, and then drank deeply from the bottle.

"Then you still don't know it all," said Bramante and for the first time he released that insufferable smile on me. I wanted to reach across the table and tear that smirk from his face. "You know that day that you saw me, of course I was coming from checking up on Giovanna's progress. She saw you from the balcony, but pretended she didn't, and then she tried to get me to come inside before I saw you too – but I saw you."

I guess he read my confused expression, or muteness correctly because he added, "Don't you get it? She wanted you to find me there, knowing that once you knew about me, it would all be over. Then she correctly assumed that you would pay the debt for her without her having to marry you."

"So why didn't she just tell me it was you that her papa owed money to?" I asked, as I felt the tensing in my muscles; my throat even tightened up making it difficult to speak clearly.

"I never wanted you to know it was me," said Bramante, still smiling. "I made it part of the deal that they couldn't tell you, or the deal was off, but that whore found a way for you to find out, without breaking our agreement."

That was it, I shot up and lunged across the table and grabbed Bramante by the cape around his neck, knocking the wine off of the table; the bottle shattered on the hard wood floor alerting the century outside. He burst in as I shouted, "You didn't want me to know because you were afraid if I found out, that I would kill you, and I will if you call Giovanna a whore again."

Bramante was surprisingly calm, considering I could have killed him with one quick blow to his bony neck, long before his man could come to his aid. Bramante raised a hand to signal the man to stop. "Lorenzo," said Bramante in an even tone. "After all that we have been to each other, you would kill me? No, you are not that kind of man, huh?"

He was right, I wasn't that kind of killer, but when he flashed me that insufferable smile, it was almost possible. I released him and sat back down.

Bramante motioned for his man to leave us again, and then as the smile left his face, in a very serious, cold tone, he said, "You have no idea who you are dealing with do you? Why I could make the Gonfaloniere disappear if I so desired." Then he flashed that insufferable smile once again and added, "But I'll let you get away with your insolence this time, for old times sake. I guess Giovanna must have really gotten to you, huh?"

When I didn't answer, he continued, "Now the real reason why I didn't want you to know it was me was because I knew that I would probably lose you as a friend, and I do enjoy seeing you from time to time. And, I knew as long as you didn't know it was me, and about my little deal with Mario, you could go through with it and marry the girl. But now, how can you be with her knowing what you know about Giovanna, and that it was just a set up all along. They were supposed to have borrowed the money from you after the wedding. Now to show you that I have no animosity toward you..."

"No animosity toward me?" I interrupted, not believing what I was hearing.

"Well, you did threaten to kill me," said Bramante. Then he finished this original thought. He said, "I can still arrange it so Giovanna marries you and not that notary. I can refuse the money. Force them to honor our original agreement. After all, how can I collect a marriage broker's fee, if there is no wedding, huh?"

Not taking my eyes away from his ugly face, and not blinking, I picked up my pen dipped it in the ink, and said, "How much should I make this out for?"

Bramante just stared back at me for a moment like he was still expecting an answer to his offer. Then he said, "Twenty-two hundred gold florin. Actually they owe me another hundred for this month, but in honor of our friendship."

I filled out the note – for the full twenty-three hundred – and slid it across the table.

Bramante looked at the note and said sarcastically, "Oh Lorenzo, you hurt me." He paused, smiled that insufferable smile, and added, "But I'll take it." Then he stood up, and pulled his cape around his long skinny frame, and said, "If you are thinking of seeing this woman again and that maybe somehow, she will marry you without my help, you will be very disappointed. She will not even be grateful to you for doing this. We tend to hate our benefactors more than we love them – I should know. If you do not believe me, and are planning on seeing her, check up on her tomorrow at the Arno Inn. I will tell Mario tonight that the debt has been paid. But get there early, because once she knows, my guess is that she will not wait around to face you again, and will run back to her papa's villa."

I didn't say another word, and neither did Bramante; he just picked up the note, smiled, and left. I never made it to my bed that night; I just sat there at the table staring into the fire until it burnt out, and fell asleep sometime later.

The next morning I reluctantly took Bramante's advice and went to the Arno Inn, early. I hadn't slept well, so I was tired, and I hadn't eaten in more than a day, so I was hungry and weak, but either in spite of this or because of this, I felt more alive and awake than ever; I guess this is the way a condemned man must feel on the way to the gallows.

When I got to Giovanna's room, I knocked on the door. Of course I wasn't expected – not yet, at least, I was supposed to come and see her much later that evening – but Giovanna was expecting someone because she said come in Don.

"Come in, Don," said Giovanna, in that pleasant sweet tone that I had been foolish enough to believe was reserved only for me.

Once inside, I noticed a collection of personal items on the table, including the necklace I gave her and a small pile of clothing; Giovanna was around the corner in the bedroom and hadn't seen me come in.

"You can see, as I promised, I'm not taking much," said Giovanna. "I will be glad to leave most of this junk behind along with the memories of this place. We should be able to bring it all down to the carriage in one trip on the way out, don't you think?"

She was still talking when she came out from the bedroom and realized that it was me who she had just been talking to. Of course she looked surprised, at first, but that expression was soon replaced by something colder and ugly – colder than anything I felt that winter, and uglier than anything I thought I would ever see on her beautiful face. She turned up the corner of her upper lip and flippantly said, "So what brings you here?" Then she went back to gathering her things. Bramante was right about Giovanna, she certainly wasn't grateful, and if I hadn't gotten there early I would have missed her. "Did you come back for your thank you?" she sneered, not looking at me. "Well, thank you. Don't worry about the money; Papa will pay you back as soon as he gets his business going again. Now if you don't mind, you can see that I am busy, and that I am expecting someone else."

"So I heard, Don," I said flatly. "I guess that would be Donato Carracci. I guess everything I heard about the two of you is true."

Giovanna didn't stop what she was doing and still didn't look at me. She sniped, "It's about time you figured that one out. I tried telling your priest friend, but I guess I didn't make it clear enough for him – that day, he was here, that wasn't my brother, Marco, that was Donato that he met. But I guess either he isn't a very good spy, or priests just don't understand real feelings between a man and woman, how could they. He was supposed to tell you about Don, but when he didn't figure it out..."

"You told Maria and Johann about your engagement to this man, knowing that Johann would tell me," I said. Her words and attitude began to seed an even deeper pain of betrayal and filled my heart with anger.

"Finally he gets it," snapped Giovanna sarcastically. "Why else do you think I wanted to get to their little shack early, to practice being the good cook and good wife?"

"So I guess you had this thing all planned out, all right," I said flatly. "You figured that I would be curious about an old lover, especially one that you were going to marry, but mysteriously had called it off. You wanted me to find out about your affair knowing that it would end our relationship, and free you from your deal with Bramante."

Giovanna stopped to correct me – she finally looked at me – and said, "Close. Actually I wanted you to find out about my relationship, knowing it would end our affair, and it was Papa's deal with Bramante, not mine." She looked away again, and continued to gather her belongings, and then added, "It sure took you long enough. You know it's amazing how blind you were. All you had to do was look, and this thing would have been over a long time ago."

"I didn't look because I thought I was respecting your wishes for privacy," I said, fighting back the growing rage. "I had promised not to look into your affairs, or spy on your family or friends."

"I think you confused respect for foolishness," said Giovanna.

That sweat melodic voice had turned into something sour, and dissonant; she was cold, condescending, and sniping. That lovely face, which now wouldn't, or maybe couldn't, even look at me, was now twisted into something distant, hateful and conniving. This fueled my rage like too many logs on a fire. My heart was now a flame that I could barely contain, and with every sniping word from her twisted lips the heat grew more intense; yet I pressed on to hear it all. My muscles were tensing, and even my throat was tightening, so I had to force out the words, I asked, "How could you be sure that I would pay the debt for you after I found out about Donato, and heard that you two were still lovers?"

"That was the easy part, given the choice, I knew you would believe me if I said that we were just good, old friends," smirked Giovanna.

"Then why did you want me to know about Donato at all?" I asked bitterly.

"That turned out to be the hard part," said Giovanna flippantly, and still not facing me. "He was supposed to be the one to tell you about Bramante. I wasn't supposed to tell you, or wasn't allowed to tell you, that was Bramante's idea. So I thought that once you heard about Donato, you would be so curious that you would look into it, seek him out even. But my gentleman, Lorenzo, was respecting my wishes, so I had to find another way for you to find out."

I had about enough of her flippant attitude, and was tired of talking to her back, so I reached out and grabbed her by the arm, turned her toward me, and didn't let go. "What if I insisted on you still marrying me," I said bitterly. "I am told that you cannot refuse, that it is part of the deal."

Giovanna stared at me defiantly, and snapped confidently, "You won't. And even if you did, I would have to allow myself to be forced to be your wife, and then cheat on you with Don. I guess I could even be forced to give you children. Of course, you could never be sure that they were yours."

I pulled back my free hand and, I swear, I almost hit her. I saw fear in Giovanna's brown eyes, but when she realized that I couldn't do it, her contemptuous smirk reappeared. "Are you going to hit me, Wolf Eyes?" she sneered. "I know you can't do it. It's not in you."

For the first time, she was wrong about me; she had read my hesitation incorrectly, and I told her so. "You're wrong, Giovanna, it's in me," I said, barely able to force the words through my clenched jaw. I pulled her closer; Giovanna swallowed, but was able to maintain her defiant grin. I added, "The reason why I'm not going to hit you, and the only reason, is because I don't believe that I could stop with hitting you just once." I saw another flash of weakness behind her impudence, but I chose not to exploit it, and just let her go; I could see the mark on her arm where my fingers had torn into her ivory flesh. I began to back away, slowly.

As a final insult, Giovanna picked up the necklace that I had given her, off of the table and threw it at me – it hit my chest and fell to the floor. I turned and walked out; that is I lifted my legs the best that I could and walked out the door, down the hall on the plush Persian rug and past the fine tapestry, and into the street. I felt like there was a tremendous weight upon my shoulders, making each step a labor, and forcing my heavy feet through the ground; I walked three feet below the flagstones.

Then it hit me: I would never be with her; I would never touch that beautiful ivory skin again; I would never make love with her again; she never really wanted me; she never really cared for me; and she never really loved me. It had all been a set up from the start. Then the pain, oh God the pain; it was like when Papa died, when Mama died. No, it was different; it was really worse, much worse – deeper. Like the sun was never going to shine again; it would always be night, and always be cold. How was I going to get past this? I lived most of my life without her, why did it now seem, after only six months, like I couldn't go on unless she was there beside me? It was then I realized that I was running as fast and as hard as I could. The weight was still pressing on my shoulders, so with each stride my feet would slam hard upon the ground; my ankles ached. My heart was pounding, and I was gasping for air, but I pushed on. I remember hearing this horrible sound, like a wounded, howling wolf crying out in agony; I was barely aware that the sound had come from me as I cried out a distorted version of her name – Giovanna.

I remember bursting into the shop going into the cellar and opening the first bottle of wine; after that, I only have a partial memory of the next two days. I remember on Saturday, sometime in the afternoon, waking up on the floor of the studio covered in my own vomit. There was a gash across the painting I did of Giovanna; I didn't remember, and still don't remember doing it. I took the time to clean myself up, and then started in on the wine again. Later I remember a cut lip and a fair amount of blood on my clothes, acquired sometime between Saturday afternoon and Monday afternoon; perhaps I had been brawling, but I suspect that I just fell down. I have some other vague thoughts of walking the streets of my city late at night, looking for the Vasari's villa, and being very cold; I'm sure I didn't bother myself with proper winter attire.

When I didn't show up to work for Niccolò on Monday, they became concerned, and Johann came to the shop looking for me. He found me, so I was told, on the floor of the cellar; apparently I had left the door wide open and Johann came in, saw that the cellar was also wide open, came down, found me, picked me up and carried me upstairs, wrapped a blanket around me, put me in front of the fireplace, and started a fire. After some time, I awoke to the smell of bread porridge, and a pounding in my head. At first I thought I must be dreaming, or perhaps still intoxicated; I understood why my head was pounding, but I wondered if that was really bread porridge I smelt.

"Is that really bread porridge I smell?" I asked myself, and apparently out loud.

"Yes, it is," said Johann. His booming voice came from somewhere above, and behind me. "It's the only thing Florentine I really know how to make. Hell, it's one of the only things I know how to make."

I sat up and looked around, a little too fast – my head was spinning – and saw Johann at the big wooden table. "I thought you could use something to eat," said Johann. "You said you hadn't eaten since Wednesday." He read my look correctly; I was confused. He added, "You told me earlier this afternoon. I guess you don't remember. You were still pretty out of it."

"What else did I say?" I asked as I rubbed my eyes and massaged the sides of my head.

"First drink this," said Johann as he handed me a flask. "It's mostly water, with just a touch of wine. It will help your head and make you feel better."

I drank and didn't stop until the flask was empty, and said, "There, I drank it, but it didn't help my head, and it didn't make me feel better."

"Give it time, Maus," said Johann with a smile, and then he answered my question. "You told me what happened with Giovanna, and that old bag of bones, Bramante. You babbled a lot, but I think I got the story pretty straight."

"That must have been some conversation," I said. "Too bad I wasn't there to hear it."

Johann laughed, a big, burly roar, and I cringed. He said, "Oh Maus, it's good to hear that you haven't lost your sense of humor."

"Oh, oh, not so loud, Orso," I said holding my head, and covering my ears.

"Sorry, Maus," said Johann in a slightly softer tone.

We both sat quiet for a moment and then Johann said, "Well I guess it just wasn't to be, but I think you did what you had to do, and God willing, you will find yourself a good woman someday." Then he added something that wasn't quite right, he said, "I know this woman really got to you, but you couldn't go through with it knowing what she pulled on you, you had to call off the wedding."

"Did I really say that?" I said, almost laughing. "I must have really been delusional."

"No, you didn't tell me," said Johann. "Bramante told me. I nearly killed that old cloak and bones. When you didn't show up this morning, Niccolò and I agreed that I should go looking for you. You weren't here when I first checked so I went to the Arno Inn, and found out that your Giovanna had left there days ago. Then I thought that you might go after that Bramante, so if you hadn't already killed him, then he might know where you were. He didn't know. He doesn't scare easily, I'll say that much for him. Well he told me that after he had seen you here that you had gone to have it out with Giovanna the next morning. He hadn't seen you since, but had heard from her family that the wedding was off. You had rejected their lovely Giovanna, but I guess she doesn't blame you because you were tricked into paying her father's debt. Then I guess that she was so distraught, she even turned down that Donato character's proposal, but I guess you probably wouldn't know about that, it happened after you left her. So now she's considering going to a nunnery."

I jumped up, momentarily forgetting my condition, but my body soon reminded me – I staggered, but steadied myself. "I've got to talk to her," I said and started for the door.

"Hold on, Maus," said Johann. "What are you talking about? I know it seems like a waste, a woman who looks like that joining the order, but she's got a lot to answer for. Maybe this is the only way for her to make her peace with God."

"Maybe," I said, not wanting or feeling the need to explain the real reason I felt I had to go to her. "But I have to see her." I made another weak step toward the door.

"Wait, do you even know where you are going?" asked Johann. "I thought you said you didn't know where the Vasari family villa was."

"You're right," I said turning back toward Johann. "But Niccolò, he knows, doesn't he. He'd have to have gotten that bit of information when he was spying on them."

"Now Maus..." Johann began.

"Don't try to talk me out of it, Orso," I said. "Do you know where I can find Niccolò? Is he even in Florence, right now?"

"Yes, he's down at the Palazzo Vecchio," said Johann reluctantly. "He finally got the go ahead to make a move on Pisa, so he's been down there planning it for days, hardly sleeps and never leaves the office." I turned to go, but Johann stopped me. He said, "Don't you think you better eat something first? As I said, Niccolò will be there all night. The porridge is almost done."

I wanted to go, I didn't want to wait, but my body knew that he was right. We ate and then we both headed out into the night to the Palazzo Vecchio.

Johann was right; Machiavelli was hard at work in his office planning a siege of Pisa. After years of promise, it was finally happening; Florence was going to take back what was rightfully hers. Reluctantly, Niccolò gave me directions to the Vasari's villa, knowing that I could easily find out elsewhere; with a little investigation I could find it myself, I just never tried before. But I was grateful for his help; if I did have to go elsewhere, it would take longer, and I couldn't wait.

When I got to the Vasari home, it was late, but I was immediately let in by a servant when I told him who I was; apparently I was known even to the servants. The servant went to announce my arrival, to his maestro – Mario Vasari. Standing in the entranceway to the grand, but modest-sized home, I tried to calm myself by admiring the numerous paintings and sculptures, the fine rug and other furnishings that I could see. I couldn't help thinking that it was odd that a man who had just been in debt should still have so many expensive possessions. I estimated, from what I could see that the value of his belongings could have probably paid about half of his debt. What kind of a man would sell his daughter before selling his belongings? I would never find out, because while I was waiting, Giovanna came down the grand staircase. She didn't see me at first, but when she did, the expression on her face was one I had never seen her use in the six months that we were together – fear. Despite her trepidation, Giovanna completed the descent and slowly walked toward me. She didn't expect to see me again, at least not so soon.

"I didn't expect to see you again," said Giovanna. "At least not so soon." When I didn't respond right away, she added, "Have you come here to kill me? I don't believe anyone could blame you if you did."

For some reason, this amused me. I smiled and said, "Assassins rarely come knocking at your front door and then wait to be announced." It was her turn not to respond right away, so I continued, "I was let in by one of your servants." She nodded that she understood, and then I said, "I hear you are thinking of going to a nunnery."

Giovanna paused, and then said, "Yes, that was one of my first thoughts, but I don't think that the Lord would have me."

"Not if you plan on going back to Donato," I said a little sarcastically. "The Lord wouldn't like you having an affair with him and a relationship with Donato." This was my backhanded way of finding out if she had really rejected Donato; she had.

"Oh I sent him away, on that same day..." Giovanna cut herself off, not liking where her words were taking her. She restarted, "After you left, he took me home, and then I told him that I could never see him again."

"How did he take it?" I said, and then I added sardonically, "Better than I did, I have no doubt."

"I don't know," said Giovanna solemnly.

"I guess that was a busy day for you," I said, again in a sardonic tone. Then I noticed that distance in her eyes, like that first day that we met on the bridge, and there was that same sad, calmness in her tone. I softened my tone and said, "I also heard that your version of what happened that day between us has me rejecting you, and withdrawing my proposal of marriage."

"Well, who could blame you," said Giovanna. "After the way I disgraced you, and deceived you."

"But that's not what happened," I said. "Why would..."

"That's what should have happened," said Giovanna. She thought for a moment, and then said, "I thought if I could make you hate me, that it would be easier on you. It wouldn't hurt you so much." Then there was a slight break in her even tone, a crack in her voice as she said, "But there was such pain in your wolf eyes. Such sadness, and anger." She regained her calm demeanor and finished, "I didn't realize how much it would really hurt you. If I would have known, if I would have realized, I would have..."

"It really wasn't that bad," I said. I lied, of course, but I found her pitying me worse that her hating me. "Sure it was a shock, at first, but I have adjusted. We all have to do what we think is right for ourselves." I went on like this, babbling rhetorical nonsense; I can't remember all that I said. I was just trying to keep her from feeling sorry for me.

Actually, there really wasn't much more of substance for me to say. I had found out what I had come to hear. Now she stood there, just a few feet away from me, but we were miles apart, like two strangers, almost as if the last six months that we were together had never happened – almost.

Finally, when I was done rambling, Giovanna said, "You know, I would do anything for my family."

Like that was an explanation for it all, so I couldn't help but be sarcastic again. I said, "I guess that includes selling yourself, so your papa doesn't have to sell all of his nice things."

"If we were forced to sell all of our possessions, then we would be no better than the common people on the streets," said Giovanna like she was reciting someone else's words – Mario's, no doubt. She continued, "The Vasari family name has been respected in Florence for generations and to soil it with poverty would be a disgrace to my ancestors, and a crime against my brother's heritage."

I knew better than to try and respond to, or argue with the arrogance of nobility, but it was making me sick and angry – angry at the father who would use his daughter in such a way to save his name and status, after he was the one who had put it in jeopardy. I knew I had to leave before Mario finally came down. Even with my low status background I knew that it was considered impolite to kill a man in his own home.

I had heard enough and had turned to leave, without saying goodbye, but one last question came to mind. I would have thought the answer obvious, if I hadn't come back and seen her this way again, distant and melancholy. I turned back and asked, "On the bridge that day, were you really going to jump?"

Without hesitation, like she had already thought this question out, she said, "No, but I wish I had."

I left feeling even worse than I had before; Giovanna was right, it would have been easier to get over it, if I hated her. Now we just both pitied each other: she pitied me for being a lovesick fool; I pitied her for being compelled to prostitute herself for her papa. Looking back, I believe that she had the worst of it, but at the time I was too full of my own pain to see just how deeply she had been affected by being used this way by her family.

Chapter X

Time passed, slowly at first, with each day me reliving, rethinking, reworking, and rewriting the pages of my romance with Giovanna, but little good it did knowing that I couldn't rewrite the ending. I continued to try and drown her memory in wine and whiskey, but this just made me sick. I tried sleeping her away by staying in bed for days at a time, only to have her invade my dreams. Weeks passed – seemed like years. My friends helped me as best that their time and abilities would allow. Johann occasionally drank with me and carried me home when necessary; it was often necessary in those weeks, but unfortunately for me he was not always there. Fra Domenico woke me if I slept away too many days, checked up on me if I stayed in the shadows too long, and prayed for me. Niccolò provided me with work by allowing me to aid him in his siege plans, and I know he really didn't need my help. Even my city helped me by allowing me to serve against her enemies in Pisa. When it was time to go into the field, Johann and I accompanied Machiavelli and the militia; we surrounded Pisa and dug in. I was later involved in a deadly skirmish that rekindled my warrior instinct, but alas, I am getting ahead of myself.

At the end of January, we – Niccolò, Johann and I – found ourselves patrolling around the besieged city, looking for any weakness in the lines. There was little fighting to do, just a few skirmishes breaking out here and there, but the exercise of just walking or riding, even in my light armor, exhausted me. There was little else to do but wait, as it is with most sieges, so Johann and I resumed some training exercises together. But just being there with the militia, with my friends, and with the everyday anxiety of a possible fight helped me begin to think less and less of Giovanna, yet she still dominated much of my thought.

Evenings offered the usual distractions a siege army is privy too – wine and women. I gladly participated in the drinking for I had gotten quite used to waking up with an aching head. Chasing the peasant girls, or paying the professional camp followers did not interest me, though I believe they were the main reason Johann was so eager to come along; he certainly knew that a siege would provide little fighting. I think that he was restless for his old life and already tiring of marriage. He complained that Maria was growing even too plump for his liking, and he was concerned that with the inevitable next child, Maria would no longer have the strength or desire to fulfill his abundant needs.

In February, we took a thousand men and dug in a line north of the city to prevent any outside help from rescuing Pisa. We were particularly weary of the French; while they had been traditional allies of Florence, they were also sympathetic to the Pisans. No help would come, but that didn't stop the Pisans from trying to breakout. Machiavelli, who wielded the most authority as the sole representative of the Signory in the field, took on the responsibility of the whole campaign, and being a man of action, he insisted on overseeing everything from entrenchments to capitulation negotiations with the Pisans. When Niccolò went off to Lucca – a nearby village – to insure that they did not try and assist the besieged, he left Captain Johann Holper in charge of maintaining our position; I acted as his aid. Together we rode out every afternoon, the length of the line, to look for weakness; it usually took until dusk to complete the inspection. On one occasion, as the shadows were growing long and we were just about to head back to camp for the night, I thought I saw some movement in the brush.

"I thought I saw some movement in the brush," I said. Then I pointed and added, "Over there, Orso, on the other side of that creek."

We pulled up our horses, and sat there and watched – nothing.

"Maybe it was some animal, Maus," said Johann.

"Maybe," I said, but not too convincingly.

He hesitated, and then Johann said, "Let's look it over anyway."

We rode down a small valley, across a dirt road to the creek. We entered the water – it was shallow – and followed the stream toward the brush where I had seen the movement. When we got to the spot there was nothing there, but it was clear by the trampled ground and broken tree limbs that someone had been there quite recently, and they had horses. We found their tracks. They led east, so we followed; knowing that they couldn't have gone far, we drew our swords. We heard them before we saw them. They were paralleling our line probably looking for an opening, or a weakness. They wisely walked their horses, but their armor was far too heavy for sneaking about; they were clanging as they moved. We dismounted, left our horses and approached. We moved in right behind them and could have easily attacked them without warning, but Johann was feeling a little Christian charity; after all, they were Christians too. He called them good men of valor and implored them to head back to their lines and save this fight for another day.

"Good men of valor," said Johann in a booming, but sincere voice. "I implore you to head back to your lines and save this fight for another day."

Of course they were startled and turned abruptly – so much so that two of their horses ran off, back toward Pisa. Seeing this, Johann added, "Follow those steeds, good men, and, God willing, you will all live long and prosperous lives."

The sergeant in charge, seeing that there were only two of us, smirked and snapped back, "There are only two of you. You are outnumbered three-to-one. It is you who should make a run for your lines, that is, if we choose to let you."

Johann laughed and said, "Boys, I've been in more fights than you've all had haircuts."

One of the young Pisans defiantly quipped, "That only proves that you are an old man." The rest of them supported his jest by laughing.

Then in a most menacing tone, Johann stared down the young man and said, "It also proves that I have survived many days and through many battles. It appears that perhaps you will not live to see another sunset." The young man swallowed deeply and struggled not to flinch.

It was my turn to try and save their lives. "Now men, this fight is not really necessary, nothing can be gained for either side. I know right now that I would like to be back at camp having that first drink. Just think, tonight when you're drinking that first glass, you can tell your friends of how you stared down the enemy. You can even tell them that we ran from you like cowards, after you challenged us to battle."

But alas, they were young, brash, bold and full of valor; they would never grow old. They drew their swords and came at us. The one who had spoken so daringly was the first to fall, for he, to his credit, was the first to reach us; Johann dispatched him by blocking his thrust and then slit his throat, nearly decapitating him. I struck down the next one by ducking under a head thrash and then thrusting my jeweled dagger under the poor fool's breastplate; he fell dead at my feet. At the same time, with my sword in my other hand, I fought off the sergeant. Now with my full attention on him, he had only seconds to live. He wielded his sword with wild, untrained fury, and I easily danced around his crashing blows. The end came when, after one of these blows; I ended up behind him, and when he turned with his sword raised up over his head, he exposed the opening in the armor under his left arm. I dug my sword into him just long enough to pierce his heart; withdrawing my blade quickly, I was dowsed with a warm, crimson shower. I spun around, preparing for the next attack, but there was none. Johann was standing over the last of them, twisting his big, broadsword into his victim's bowels; the young man sat up and raised his feet momentarily, and then collapsed dead to the ground.

Johann removed his sword, turned to me and said, "Senseless waste of life."

"Yes," I agree. "But you did try to warn them."

"And I knew that they wouldn't listen," said Johann, as we both wiped their blood from our blades, and returned them to their sheaths. "We could have just followed them and waited to see if they were really going to try and make a break through our lines."

"Why, Orso!" I said. "Are you developing a soft side?"

"No, Maus," said Johann. "I just long for a real fight, a fair one between men." We mounted our horses and he added, "It's one thing to engage the enemy in a great battle in a combat to the death, and quite another to engage him in a skirmish. An engagement that could have been avoided if we had been patient, and just followed him to see if he was really a threat, but we didn't because I wanted to get back to camp for the whoring and the wine."

"You are getting soft," I said again. As we rode along I looked at my bodice and said, "Now I know why these uniforms are white. With all this blood, we look quite terrifying. Too bad there isn't a real fight around, we would scare the hell out of them." The taste of blood had gotten me hungry for a real battle too. Then I added, "But let us choose our next fight against a foreign enemy. It felt strange killing men that could have been my brothers."

"You have no brothers, Maus," said Johann. "And if you are going to be a mercenary, it would be good to remember that." Then Johann looked at his blood soaked clothes and said, "Since we have no enemy to terrify with our savage look, let's go and scare us some whores." Then he laughed – a big, burly roar.

There would be no great battles for the militia in the campaign to recapture Pisa, but the Pisans would still be compelled to capitulate by the end of the spring. I dare say that it was a triumph for Florence, the militia, and Machiavelli, though Niccolò got very little of his well-deserved credit. It was also the high water mark for the militia and Machiavelli; my city would go on, but the militia would soon show its frailty and be disbanded, and Machiavelli would soon be an outcast. But I am again, getting ahead of my story.

As the weeks passed into months, I was able to begin to distance myself from the memory of Giovanna and time resumed its normal pace; it even seemed to go fast for me. It took about a year for the pain to subside to a tolerable level. I drank less – not as often and not too much at one time. I began to sleep better – I went to bed in the evening and got up in the morning. You know, I never met Mario Vasari and he never paid me back. Perhaps it was because I never got anything in writing saying he owed me; unlike Bramante I didn't get a note of payment. Perhaps Mario had every intention of paying me back but he just waited to see if I would ask for the money. I decided to let it go; letting go of the debt meant letting go of Giovanna, forgiving the debt meant forgiving her, and finally, forgetting the debt meant forgetting her – or something like that. It all made sense to me at the time.

Once I was conscious and sober most of the time, I needed things to do. I worked for Niccolò and visited Fra Domenico regularly. I even saw Michelangelo over the Christmas holiday of 1510. He was back in Florence because, once again, he was fighting with Pope Julius II over money; the ceiling fresco wasn't finished, but Michelangelo refused to do any more work until he got another 500 ducats that was owed him. Things got worked out and Michelangelo went back to Rome some time after the holiday. In confidence, Michelangelo told me that he was just using the money as an excuse to take a break and come back to Florence for the holidays.

I spent a lot of time with Johann – in Niccolò's office, drilling the militia in the field, and training together in the warehouse. Though I enjoyed his company, it was a little sad to see Johann spending so much time with me and struggling to find excuses to avoid going home to Maria and his children. There were now three of them, Hans, Costanza and Johann, or little Jon, as his papa referred to him. As predicted, Maria had gotten even plumper, and had little time or energy to perform her marital duties. Johann was anxious for another fight both as another test for our militia, and as an escape from marital bliss; he got his wish.

Once again the rats were invited into our house. Pope Julius II formed a new Holy League to ward off the threat of French invasion; he called upon the Spanish to join the Holy League, and therefore invited them in to do his fighting. Florence, who had been a friend of the French so many times, refused to join the League and this infuriated the Pope, but first he had to deal with the French.

On Easter Saturday 1512, the forces of the Holy League, led by the Spanish, were stopped on their way to relieve the besieged city of Ravenna. In the savage battle that ensued, both sides were devastated with each taking heavy casualties. Never in recent history had so many men fallen – almost twenty thousand men were killed. The losses were equal on each side, but it was the Spanish and the Holy League that was forced to relinquish the field. The French celebrated a victory, and after hearing the news, Florence did too; huge bonfires were lit all around the city to rejoice in the Pope's defeat. When Johann heard of this fight, he was so disappointed not to have been there. When I asked him on which side would he have fought, he responded like a true mercenary, "The one with the best offer." As it turned out, the victory celebration was premature. The French, short on supply, were not able to exploit their victory and were forced to retreat north to Milan. This left Florence exposed to the revenge of the League. But the League was weak from their defeat at Ravenna and they were unsure about Florentine defenses. They hesitated to attack, but through the insistence of Cardinal Giovanni de' Medici, the League pushed on to our borders.

After Piero de' Medici died in exile, it was Giovanni, another son of Lorenzo the Great, who became head of the Medici family. He used his rank, name, and even his own money when necessary, to ensure the resolve of the army. When reasonable terms for surrender were asked for by the Florentines, it was Giovanni who rejected them stating that the only terms acceptable would have to include the resignation of the Gonfaloniere and the restoration of the Medici to power in my city.

Battle lines were drawn twenty miles northwest of Florence at the city of Prato. Machiavelli's militia dug in at the city's strong points; Niccolò was there to set up the defenses with the Gonfaloniere hiding in a safe place in the city. Johann and I were on the front wall. The Spanish troops that approached the city's defenses were seasoned men, still bearing the fresh wounds of their defeat at Ravenna. Their first attack was repelled, but Johann and I knew that it was too easy; their attack had just been a preliminary assault designed to look for weakness, but our inexperienced militiamen let out a great roar of victory. We knew that the enemy lacked supplies and, above all else, they were hungry. I suggested that maybe we should offer them some bread, and just maybe there wouldn't be another attack.

"Maybe we should offer them some bread," I said to Niccolò. "Then just maybe there won't be another attack."

"Yes," agreed Johann. "As much as I would like a good fight, I don't believe our white shirted boys know what they're in for if those Spaniards breach these walls."

Niccolò nodded that he agreed, and said to a messenger, "Get word to the Gonfaloniere that we suggest that he make an offer to the Spaniards of a hundred bushels of bread for peace." Then he turned to me and Johann and said, "Good thought, but even if Soderini goes for it, I doubt if Giovanni will, but maybe the hunger of the men will overrule him."

As we watched the Spanish in the distance, maneuvering into position to attack, I asked Niccolò, "Do you really think that we can stand an all out assault?"

He hesitated, and then answered. "The walls will hold, and we have enough men," said Niccolò. We were three thousand strong. "But it will depend on the resolve and the courage of the men."

Several minutes passed until the messenger returned with a flat, "No," from the Gonfaloniere. To which, Niccolò shook his head and said, "Soderini is not a brave man, but that first assault must have fooled him too, and given him confidence in our chances."

All we could do was watch as the Spanish put their cannon in position and lined their men up for the next charge. Then the sound of cannon, culverins, and falcons split the air; the smoke from their barrels could be seen rising in the distance. The men were startled and restless, but when the balls fell harmlessly short another cry of victory went up the line.

Niccolò shook his head again, and said, "Fools, I thought we trained them better than that."

"God help us," added Johann.

The three of us seemed to be the only ones who realized that the Spanish were just getting their range. When the next volley came they landed just yards from our walls, a few even passed overhead, whistling and sizzling, and hitting somewhere in the city. No cries of victory went up this time, just moans and gasps. The next round of fire came crashing down on the walls and our men, and another great moan went up from the ranks, followed by cries of agony from the wounded. The Spanish continued to fire, causing only a few more casualties, we were well dug-in and protected, but soon they had blasted a hole through a place in the wall. From my vantage point it looked like nothing more than the size of a door or a window, but the men began to cry out, "We have been breached!" and "We can't stop them!" and the Spanish had only begun their charge across the open plain; a bad time for a breakdown in courage. There were plenty of pikemen and bowmen to fill the tiny breach, but as the Spanish came closer, and began to run toward our walls and the hole, the men closest to the breach suddenly threw down their arms and ran.

Niccolò leaped into action, he threw himself in front of where the men were retreating and tried desperately to rally the troops. "Where is your courage, men?" Machiavelli shouted. "It's only a small breach, we can defend it, if we stand together. Remember your families, your wives, children and mother's back in Florence."

A voice shouted back, "Yes, we remember and we are trying to get back to them as fast as we can."

Johann and I went to the breach to face the enemy, but soon we were overwhelmed; the Spanish poured in that small opening in the wall like water through a hole in a levy. Back-to-back, Johann and I fought the enemy, but we were soon surrounded; we slashed and blocked blow after crashing blow. It was the first fight I was in that I was grateful to have my light, round shield to protect me; the cross and the lily on the front side were soon covered in blood, and some of it mine. We fought well, but for every one of them we wounded or fought off, another would rise in his place. At the most dire point in the conflict, I couldn't help but remind Johann of what he had said after our last skirmish, that he wanted to engage the enemy in a great battle in a combat to the death, and that he longed for a real fight, a fair one between men.

"Well, you wanted to engage the enemy in a great battle in a combat to the death," I barked over my shoulder. "You said you longed for a real fight, a fair one between men."

"Yes, I did," Johann shouted back. "Glorious isn't it. This is the way real men fight, and real men die."

"Unfortunately we are practically alone in the desire for a real fight," I yelled. Hundreds of our skillfully trained, hand picked militiamen were now laying down their arms and surrendering. I continued to block with my shield and slash with my blade. Then I added, "Considering that we are almost alone in this fight, as far as that dying part goes, I don't believe it would really be that glorious, Orso."

"Agreed," shouted Johann. Even over the noise – his voice yelling – I could detect the disappointment in his voice; this wasn't the fight he was wishing for. "God willing, we will survive this fight yet. Look, Maus, the enemy is thinning out."

I dispatched the young Spaniard in front of me by removing his left arm, and stole a moment to look at what Johann was referring to; the attacking army was being overwhelmed not by defenders but by those surrendering, and their own passions. With the city undefended, the angry and hungry Spaniards began running after the good citizens – particularly the women – and attacking their homes and shops searching for spoils.

Soon we were only fighting a few reluctant men-at-arms; surely they would have preferred to join their comrades in the rewards of conquests and not be one of the few still risking death fighting with us. Without saying a word, we agreed to disengage on mutual terms; we just stopped trying to kill each other so they could join in the looting, and we could escape. We left six men dead on the ground, we wounded several others, and were cut up ourselves, but lucky to have survived. We ran for the stables. We could have walked; so many of our comrades had surrendered, or run away, that men in uniform were being ignored, or at least considered harmless and of no value. We were able to mount our horses and ride out of the city unopposed. The road back to Florence was littered with retreating militiamen and a few of the lucky citizens who managed to escape.

The rest of the unfortunate citizens of Prato would suffer for our militia's cowardice. For two days, the Spaniards ran through the city stealing food and valuables, raping women and young girls, killing priests and ransacking churches, burning monasteries and breaking into convents – modesty prevents me from saying what they did once they got inside. Hundreds of people were stripped naked, tortured for pleasure and for information on where to find more valuables, and then they were brutally killed. Over two thousand people died – practically none of them in battle.

When we rode into Florence through the Porta a San Gallo, the city was in chaos; the word of the sack of Prato had already reached my city and the people feared that they would be next. Medici supporters marched to the Palazzo della Signoria and demanded that Soderini resign; the Gonfaloniere had escaped Prato ahead of us with the help of Machiavelli, and was in hiding. Unnerved and afraid for his life, Soderini gladly gave up his office.

In the days that followed, Niccolò arranged for Soderini's safe passage to the Dalmation coast. Florence agreed to allow the Medici to return, join the Holy League, elect a new Gonfaloniere, and dissolve the militia. Machiavelli would have gladly worked for the Medici – after all, he lived only to serve – but he too was replaced. His position in the republic and his attitude toward the Medici when they were in exile – when acting as an ambassador, he paid them little respect when he met them as guests in the courts of foreign governments – left Niccolò on bad terms with Florence's first family.

It was the end of the republic. Florence was restored to the conditions under which Lorenzo the Great had ruled, but now it was Cardinal de' Medici who was in charge. He rode into the city with fifteen hundred troops and entered his former palace under the atmosphere of one who plans to rule. But fate and his ambition would lead the Cardinal to a greater destiny than just governing my city. In less than a year after his triumphant return, Pope Julius II died. It was Cardinal de' Medici who would become the new pope, Pope Leo X, leaving his younger brother, Giuliano as the new power in Florence.

In November of 1512, the new Signoria formally dismissed Machiavelli of his duties, and then to add insult to his disgrace, they sentenced him to be restricted to Florentine territory and ordered him to pay a fine of one thousand gold florins – a huge sum for a man who earned relatively little for all of his efforts for the city. I, along with others paid this fine for him, but the dishonor hurt him deeply. Depressed and distraught, Niccolò went into exile to his country house at nearby Saint Andrea in Percussina. The last time I saw Niccolò at that time was at Saint Andrea, but he would not stay in exile for too long; he would be back to serve Florence again, but I am getting ahead of myself. I will get to that story in my next volume.

Johann was only briefly out of a job; the new government wanted some experienced fighting men, and with the militia disbanded, they turned, once again to the condottieri. He actually came out better because the new government kept fewer men and paid them a lot more than the republic had been able to afford; they got the standard mercenary fees. As a captain, Johann made twenty-five gold florins a month, when he was called into active duty, but even if he only worked two months out of the year, he stood to make a lot more than he had before. So much more that Johann could easily afford to move into one of Florence's finer districts, but he didn't. Johann was a common man with common values, and always would be. Besides, Maria didn't want to leave the weaver's district. Johann would manage to waste most of his newfound wealth on women, wine and other frivolous indulgences.

I was also out of work, but, of course, I didn't need it – at least not the money. I don't know, maybe it was the fall of the republic, the tragic memories of Mama's and Papa's early departures from this world, or the failure of my romance with Giovanna, but I got the sudden, overpowering urge to leave my city. I decided I wanted to go to Rome. I had never been there, and I never really thought about going there before, but now the sense of adventure and exploration – or maybe just escape – came over me. Besides, Michelangelo, Raphael, and Leonardo were all in Rome at the same time; it was a chance to see their work again. But I had an even more ambitious venture than Rome; I planned to go north to Germany. I spoke the language pretty well, so it wouldn't be too difficult to get by. Then if I went to Wittenberg, maybe I could find some of Mama's relatives. Mama told me that there were probably still Melchoirs living there; Mama's brothers and their families, if they were alive and married, they might still be in Wittenberg.

First I made my financial arrangements with Abraham. I only took a modest number of coins for travel, but Abraham gave me a bill of exchange in case I needed a large sum, though I didn't think it likely, he insisted. The bill had a limit of a thousand florins, and Abraham told me to take it to the city of Hamburg where a partner of his would honor the note; if I needed more, I could write him. Next I packed. I planned to travel light so I picked only what I was sure I needed like an extra set of clothes, my sword and shield, a rolled blanket and pillow for sleeping outdoors, my jeweled dagger, and my money pouch. I bought a horse to carry me for the first leg of the trip. Whatever else I needed I would purchase on the way, or after I got where I was going. Finally I said goodbye to my two best friends. I invited Johann and Fra Domenico over to the shop the night before I left Florence to tell them my plans; Fra Domenico arrived first, and Johann soon followed. Once they were both seated – Johann at the big wooden table and Fra Domenico in the x-chair – and drinking wine, I told them I was leaving in the morning.

"I'm leaving in the morning," I said.

"Leaving?" they both said at once.

"Leaving where?" asked Fra Domenico.

"I'm leaving Florence," I said.

Then they both bombarded me with more questions, "Where are you going?" "Why are you going?" and "When did you decide this?" and more, but these are the only ones I remember answering.

"I'm going to Rome, because I have never been there," I said. "Then I thought I would go to Germany, and look for Mama's brothers. I never have been there either. But I guess the main reason I am going is because I can. This is my chance to see a little more of the world. There is nothing or no one keeping me here. I just decided, in these last few days, that it was a good time for me to get away for a while."

"Now Lorenzo, if you are running away because of that wo..." Fra Domenico began.

"I'm not running away from anyone, or anything, Fra Domenico," I interrupted. I felt I needed to explain myself to Fra Domenico, probably because I always thought of him as family. "I just thought I needed a change, and experience a little more of life. You should understand that, Orso. You've been a lot more places and lived a lot more lives than I have." I was looking to Johann for support and I got it, sort of.

"Yes, a man without roots needs to move," said Johann. Then he smiled and added, "Maybe I should go with you. I've never been to Rome either. Of course, I have spent some time in Germany, but that only means that I could be useful to you."

"You can't be serious, Johann," protested Fra Domenico. "What of Maria and your children?"

"How long will you be gone?" Johann asked me.

"I can't say for sure," I said. "But probably for a couple of years, at least."

"I'm serious, Father," quipped Johann.

Fra Domenico mumbled a prayer for Johann and made the sign of the cross in the air.

"No, Orso," I said, smiling. "I can't let you do that. I would appreciate the company, but Maria and the children need you far more than I do."

"Are you sure, Maus?" asked Johann with exaggerated disappointment in his voice.

Fra Domenico shook his head in contempt, but that soon passed. As we talked, the realization that we wouldn't be seeing each other for a while, at least, began to sink in, and Fra Domenico became melancholy. Johann and I avoided any uncomfortable emotions by continuing to make light of my departure; like Johann warning me to be careful because I was a small man and Germans tended to be rather large.

"You have to be careful, Maus," said Johann. "You are a small man and Germans tend to be rather large. The men, even larger." Then he let out a laugh – a big, burly roar.

"I'll keep that in mind," I said, smiling again.

"Now seriously, Maus," said Johann. "Is there anything you need? Do you have enough warm clothes?"

"No, but I thought rather than carrying a lot of things, I would buy what I needed on the way, as the need arises," I said.

"But you will need a good wool cap, stockings, and a heavy cape to cross the mountains," said Johann. "It gets cold up there even in early fall. And you might consider growing a beard. It's not fashionable here, but it is up north and will keep your face warm in the winter."

I hadn't thought too much about the conditions crossing the Alps – just goes to show how sudden my decision to leave really was – and I thanked Johann, and then assured him that I would take his advice. Though I wasn't too sure about growing a beard; it just didn't seem right for me.

We talked a lot about nothing, and reminisced about old times. I brought up more wine and we drank several toasts. The last bit of real business was the shop. I told Fra Domenico that I would appreciate it if he looked after the shop again.

"Father Domenico, I would appreciate it if you looked after the shop again," I said.

"Of course, Lorenzo," said Fra Domenico.

"But this time it could be for a long while," I said. "A lot longer than any of the other times. So if you like, I mean, I would like it if you rented out the place and collected the money for the church. Or maybe just use the building as a shelter from which to feed the poor, or something. Whatever you think is best, or needed."

"But Lorenzo, you will be back?" asked Fra Domenico with confusion in his voice.

"Of course," I said.

"Well you talk like you may not be coming back," said Fra Domenico with concern. "You want me to use the shop? How can I use it if you are coming back?"

"If I, or when I come back, if you are using the shop, I can just stay somewhere else for a while," I said. "Believe me, I can afford to stay anywhere I want. So please, promise me to make use of the place if you possibly can. It would make me feel so much better than to think that it was just sitting here, empty and decaying. I could just sell the place, but well…no, I really couldn't, not just yet."

Fra Domenico finally agreed to see what he could do to put the shop to good use, and Johann said that he would help.

We stayed up late and drank wine, not wanting to say goodbye. When it came time for them to leave, we still never said goodbye, instead we wished each other well and talked about the day that we would see each other again. When they finally got up to leave, I could scarcely look at the good father's big round face; his eyes were red and swollen with tears. When he hugged me, I could hardly breath, smothered in his mass and robes. I fought off the thought that I may never see him again for fear that I too would succumb to emotion. I did have a little of my papa's warm blooded emotions, but I had more of my mama's cold, quiet, reserved passion. It made me wonder what kind of people I would find north of the Alps. Perhaps it was the cold climate that bred people to be strong, stoic, and in control of their emotions. Johann and I shared a manly embrace, slapped each other's backs and wished each other well. I walked them out, waved to them as they receded into the darkness, and closed the door – then I was alone.

The fire was still burning, and I was not quite ready for bed, so I lit a lamp and walked to the front of the shop – to my old studio. I looked at the picture of my beloved Giovanna with the slash in the canvas. I saw Giovanna standing there completely naked and relaxed – glorious.

"Lorenzo, you devil," said Giovanna. "You have been hiding this portrait from me to keep me from getting jealous." I walked up beside her and slipped my arm around her bare waist; Giovanna put her left arm up and around my neck and rested it on my left shoulder; she still held the cloth up with her right hand.

"Your mama was beautiful," said Giovanna sincerely.

"I didn't tell you who it was, how did you know it was my mama?" I asked.

"You didn't have to tell me," said Giovanna. "I know you are too clever to leave a portrait of one of your girlfriends just lying around with nothing but a simple cloth to hide it from me. Besides you have her nose, her mouth, and you both have those wolf eyes." She paused, and then added, "I bet you really miss her."

"Yes, everyday," I said. "Especially now that I have met someone as wonderful as you. I would have been proud to have introduced you to Mama, and Papa of course."

Then I went over and lifted the cloth that protected Mama's portrait and remembered.

"Jesus, Mary, and Joseph, it's beautiful," said Papa. He stared at the painting a little longer then he looked at me and said, "Come here boy." I obeyed, and he lifted me up with his big hands, hugged me, and then kissed both cheeks. Then he put me down and went back to staring at the painting. Several more seconds passed, then he abruptly said, "I have to get your mama. When she sees this she will know, as I do, what God has put you in this world to do."

Papa disappeared into the shop, but he quickly returned leading Mama by the hand. To my surprise, even Mama seemed to be impressed by my effort – perhaps moved or touched would be a more accurate description of her reaction.

Her eyes squinted; she smiled and said, "Lorenzo, it's wonderful." Then Mama kissed me.

I dropped the cloth and walked into the warehouse where I saw two men engaged in mock battle.

Papa and I cleared enough space to move about freely and practiced day and night at trying to kill each other. There I learned to use the pike and sword. I found that I was a natural with a light, double-edged broadsword and a dagger. I was best when I could use my quickness and move around to attack and avoid strikes. The heavy, two-handed broadsword was a little much for me to handle, but to my amazement Papa handled it with ease, showing incredible strength and agility, but he seemed to be good handling every weapon. He told me that it only seemed that he was good at everything because he only taught me with the weapons in which he was most proficient.

Then I thought I smelt the old kiln and the misty vapors of water on red-hot steel.

I saw Papa slightly bent over his anvil pounding a white-hot piece of metal with a hammer; his powerful arms flexed. He squinted his big brown eyes as a small stream of sweat ran down between them and dripped off of the tip of his big, hawk-like nose. He pounded again, and again, sparks flew, until finally, he was satisfied, stopped pounding and examined his work

I watched for what seemed like a long time, and when Papa finally saw me standing there, he put down his tools, wiped the sweat from his face with the back of his hand, and waved for me to come to him. As always, Papa lifted me up, hugged me, kissed me on both cheeks, and reminded me of how big I was getting.

"Oh Lorenzo, you are getting to be so big," Papa said, as he lowered me down.

"I'll be too big for you to pick up soon," I said proudly.

"Never," Papa playfully barked back at me. "The day you get too big for me to lift in my arms, or I become too weak to pick you up, is the day I die."

From the warehouse, I crossed through the living room and held the lamp in the other bedroom.

"No, Orso," I said, "You take ..." I almost said Mama and Papa's room, but I caught myself. "...this room. There's a nice bed in there, why waste it. Besides, you might be here for a while and a man needs his space, and can often use some privacy. Let this be your space until you decide on another."

On my insistence, Johann walked into the room and looked around. He said, "I never had a room of my own."

"Well this one is yours, as long as you want it," I said.

He made a quick assessment of his surroundings, and then continued. "Nice, not too cluttered. Simple, I like it. Is this all of your parent's belongings?" He asked.

"Mama and Papa were never much on possessions," I said. Actually, Papa and I had cleaned out a few of the little things not long after Mama died; there were too many little things with big memories attached to them. "The cassone has a few of Papa's and Mama's things still in it, I'm certain, but we can move those out if you need a place to store your gear."

"You don't have to do that, you know I don't have much," Johann said. Then the big man smiled at me, and said, "All right, Maus, I'll take the room, but I don't know …"

I started to leave but then I saw Mama lying on the bed, Fra Domenico, Papa and me at her side.

"Thank you for giving me my life. Goodbye, Mama," I said. Just after I spoke, she died; her hand fell from off of Papa's head. Fra Domenico made the sign of the cross in the air and whispered a prayer, and then it was quiet. Quiet until Papa looked up to confirm the reason Mama had stopped stroking his hair. Seeing that she was gone – the light was out of her beautiful gray-blue eyes – Papa murmured, "God, no, please, God, no. You can't take her from me. Katarina, you can't leave me." The pain in his voice, I will never forget. He gently kissed Mama's lips, and closed her eyes, and then the overwhelming pain from the realization that he would never see her smile again, never be with her again, never hold her again, never kiss her again, and never grow old with her, suddenly exploded from him like a cannon blast. He screamed at the top of his voice, "God, No!" Fra Domenico jumped from the chair. I jumped too, and felt chills throughout my body; the sound of his pain echoed in my head. I can still hear it. Then Papa fell on Mama's lifeless body, crying – uncontrollably sobbing. I saw his heart break right there in that room, when Mama died. He sat Mama's body up, and tried to will her, through his pain, to come back to life. He shook her and begged her to wake up, like she was just in some deep sleep. "Katarina," he called out through his tears. He implored her, he begged her, "Katarina, come back to me. What am I to do without you?" Finally, Fra Domenico put his hands on Papa's shoulders. Thankfully, this simple gesture brought him back. Papa, ever so gently, lowered Mama's body back down on the bed, and somehow managed to pull his insufferable pain back inside himself. He stopped crying, wiped his face and whispered softly, "Goodbye my love, goodbye Katarina."

Finally I took the lamp into my room, tired and ready to sleep, but there too I saw something – a young boy at a desk hard at work.

Everyday, after the morning meal, I spent hours studying, on my own, in my room. My most frequent, and favorite activity – because I was so good at it – was translating the Bible from the Latin, to Greek, Italian and German. German was the one I had the most trouble with because I had no other written sources to accumulate diction, so I had to constantly ask Mama for the words. But as my German vocabulary grew, it too became an easy translation. If I had kept my notes, I wonder how my work would have compared to Luther's translation.

On a piece of paper I would write, three columns across, first the Greek, then the Italian and finally the German. I found that through the repetition and the thoughtful study of the words – necessary in translation to not just one, but three languages – I came to know that holy book that had ruled the continent for a thousand years. Though I must admit, I did not always understand its' meaning; I still don't.

Then I saw myself drawing, at my desk – with only a dim candle for light – until I heard a noise out in the living room.

I walked toward it. I thought I heard my name; curious, I opened the door ever so slightly and peered out the crack. I could not see them – they were behind the table on the ground by the fireplace – but I could hear them. To my delight, Papa asked Mama to let me pursue my passion for drawing and she agreed – as long as it didn't get in the way of my studies.

"We will let him do his drawings, as long at it doesn't get in the way of his studies," Mama said.

"Then I think I should look into finding someone to look at his work," Papa said. "To see if he has any real talent. Of course, I think he does, but who am I? Just a poor gunmaker."

Then it got quiet. I waited several minutes and heard nothing but the crackling of the fire and a few soft muffled moans. I was just about to close the door and go to bed, when I saw my mother stand up from behind the table; she was naked. Her ivory skin glowed, yellow, in the firelight.

She stood there alone, not moving, for several seconds, then my father stood up; he was also naked.

I remember thinking that they looked funny at the time, and almost laughed.

I looked at the big wooden table and saw Papa; Fra Domenico was sitting in the x-chair.

"I understand, Fra Domenico," Papa interrupted. "But Lorenzo is just a boy, and he should be allowed some time to pursue childish things. When he is a man, he will ..."

It was Fra Domenico's turn to interrupt. "Ah, but these are not childish things, as you call them," he said sternly. "Lorenzo is being corrupted by the times, this place, this town, and from this house. This art thing, for example, is not a common childish pursuit, and it promotes secular ideas. I have often found him daydreaming and doodling in the margins of his studies."

"What is wrong with that?" Papa asked, with a smile.

"Ah ha, then you are encouraging this art thing," snapped Fra Domenico. "It is as I suspected."

Papa ignored his comments and repeated his question, "What's wrong with a little drawing?"

"It's a waste of good ink and paper," barked Fra Domenico.

"But these doodles, they are good aren't they?" Papa asked, still smiling.

"That's hardly the point," Fra Domenico shrugged.

"Sure it is," Papa said sardonically. "If these doodles are good then you can hardly call it a waste of good ink and paper. Perhaps the boy has talent."

I blew out the lamp and turned to go to bed when the fireplace suddenly flared up with one last flaming fury. I turned to look and saw a small boy playing with his papa.

A fire was blazing, because it was cold outside. I was running around the big wooden table, chasing Papa, and I was laughing; Mama was sitting in the x-chair, smiling and watching us. Papa let me catch him, and I shouted, "Again, again, run Papa," and around the table we went.

This time Papa chased me and when he caught me and picked me up, kissed me on both cheeks, and said, "My, you are getting big."

He put me down and I ran to Mama and I threw myself in her lap; she jumped.

"I came to give you a hug and a kiss too," I said.

"Thank you, Lorenzo," said Mama, as he hugged and kissed me back. "I really love your hugs and kisses."

Then I took off around the table again and said, "Come on, Papa, chase me."

Papa moaned and said to Mama, "You would think that the boy would get tired of the same silly game, night after night."

"That's just the way three-year-olds are, Sabastiano," said Mama.

Around the table I went shouting, "Again, again, run Papa. Again, again."

Then like breath over a candle, the fire went out and it was dark. I was thirty years old with a touch of gray in my black, curly hair, but I felt like that young boy, who slept in this room when another Medici ruled my city – everything was still ahead of me. I climbed into bed and fell right to sleep and dreamed of adventures not yet realized, in places full of images yet unseen. I got up and left for Rome in the morning – just after sunrise.

The End of Book I